THE BAKER'S SECRET

LELITA BALDOCK

Storm
PUBLISHING

Ebook ISBN: 978-1-80508-464-8
Paperback ISBN: 978-1-80508-465-5

Cover design: Eileen Carey
Cover images: Trevillion, Shutterstock

Published by Storm Publishing.
For further information, visit:
www.stormpublishing.co

For my mumma

ONE

ZENTA

South Australia, 2018

The flour slips through my fingers. Soft, silky, familiar. Outside dawn is just peeking her head over the horizon, the orange tendrils of her reach lightly tinting the dark with colour. I crack an egg, collected the morning before, and begin to knead. Years of practice move my hands confidently, rhythmically, despite the new shape of my fingers. Crooked, curled, old.

But still useful.

I dust my work in a light sprinkle of caraway seeds, breathing deeply, thinking of the herby scent that will fill the house as they roast in the oven. I knead some more, working the dough, mixing in the caraway. Soon it is firm, slightly elastic. Ready. I know this without thinking, it just is.

Shaping the loaf into a neat circle I place it next to the two I've already made, ready to rise a while as I prepare the next.

Baking bread is my morning routine. Usually just the one loaf, small and round, to sustain my day. But today is different. Today, my family is coming.

I pour out a measure of rye flour, shape it into a cone, three fingers to make the well at the top, water, an egg, knead.

The scuff of a footstep breaks into my subconscious, but my hands keep working.

"Mamina-Zee?" Crissy's voice is gentle, as always. She uses her special moniker for me, Mamina, from the Latvian for Grandmother, and Zee from my name.

She's called me this since I first opened my door to her. I can see her like it was yesterday, small, frightened, the Marmite of breakfast toast smeared on her cheeks.

"Mamma's gone again," she would say, every time Aina disappeared.

"It's all right, I'm here," I'd reply, readying myself to pick up the broken pieces once more.

I keep kneading, the dough is almost ready for the seeds.

"Mamina-Zee, you are baking? But it's not even light yet."

"Bread won't make itself." I smile a secret smile. A memory comes to me of a home far away, gentle guiding words, a long time ago.

"Mamina, I can get bread from the shops."

"That's not real bread. Why waste money? I make my own bread." I allow a little pride to enter my tone.

"I could have done this for you."

I scoff, flick my eyes up. "You bake like your mother."

A small smile tickles the edges of her mouth, then a full grin breaks over her face.

I've won our little stand-off. I always do.

Sighing, she rounds the table between us, wraps me in a quick hug then fills the iron kettle and places it on the hob to boil.

As the water heats, she takes a seat at the table, currently my kitchen bench, and watches as I finish the fourth loaf. Four should do. Loaf lined up with the others, I rest my flour-coated hands on my hips and try to stretch my back. The tension in the middle of my spine won't ease, but the stretch feels good regardless. My eyes land on Christine. My Crissy. The world calls her the daughter of my niece. What does that make her? My greatniece? I don't know. And I don't care. She is the daughter I never had, my second chance. She is family, that is enough.

Crissy's hair is fair, with a touch of auburn that lights in the sun, sprinkled now with silver that gathers at her temples, her blue eyes rimmed with fine wrinkles that bury her eyes when she smiles. Almost fifty, still my baby.

Still beautiful.

She's come early for the celebrations. I knew she would. She understands what it means to me. Or she tries to. Latvia is my ghost, my burden. I freed her of that. Her husband, Neil, will bring her children, one daughter, one son, tomorrow. She calls him an "ex" but I've seen no divorce papers. Foolish indulgence, to think a love that created life can end. Through our children, we are forever bound.

Her mother, Aina, is due then too, but we will see.

Aina. My heart squeezes tight in my chest. My breath is suddenly shallow. I squeeze my eyes shut, fighting the thought that scratches inside my skull. The memory. The choice. My guilt, which has stayed with me all these years, and only grown.

Bad memories score into the brain. You can't outthink them. You have to physically shift the thought. Move!

"Time to feed the chickens," I announce, throwing myself into action.

Bemused, Crissy rises to join me, turning off the hob as she passes. The tea can wait.

She joins me on the back porch, linking her arm through mine. In affection, but also to steady my step. I swallow my retort. I am old. Perhaps too old. But I can manage in my own home. We walk out onto the garden path. The air smells of earth and gum leaves and morning dew. Concrete slabs, now cracked and uneven, divide the grass in two. On my left the clothesline Neil installed for me last summer when I refused to use the drying machine they tried to foist on me. On the right, my water tank, rusty and weathered, a greying nylon stocking wrapped about its tap to trap the wriggling mosquito larvae that grow in the water, but still standing. Like me.

At the back of the yard, pressed against the ever-encroaching bushland, is my chicken coop. A simple hutch for the chickens to roost and a space to scratch fenced off by wire. Safe from foxes. We pick our way over the uneven path, me sure-footed, Crissy tripping twice. I don't miss the irony.

At the coop, I free myself from Crissy's arm and open the gate. The air is cool outside, but the roosting space is warm. The gentle coo of sleepy chickens fills my ears, and the scent of feathers and poop is oddly comforting. I make my way along the row, gently slipping my hand beneath warm feathers and collecting brown eggs. I leave one; Bessie, my oldest girl, shouldn't lay daily anymore, and these days I have plenty of food. I can indulge her. Running a soft caress down her silken feathers I retreat, locking the coop and returning to the house.

The back door creaks as we go in.

"This place is falling apart," Crissy says.

I ignore her. I know where that line of discussion will lead, and today, as the 18th of November, Latvian Independence Day, approaches, I have no interest in discussing Crissy's thoughts on my home. This year will mark one hundred years since the end of the Great War, and the liberation of Latvia that was won in its wake. A celebration of all my father fought for. A reminder of all that my people lost once more, mere decades later. All I lost in that bloody conflict...

I hear Crissy huff and I shake my head. There is no point discussing things that I won't change. A waste of time and energy. At my age I have to be careful about conserving both.

I know she wants me to move into the city, to be closer to her. So she can monitor me.

It comes from love. From worry. And part of me knows she has a point. It would be nice to have her visit more often, to watch her children grow slowly, rather than in the bounds of elapsed time that have shaped their transitions in my life. But I've lived here since I arrived in Australia. On this remote square of rust-coloured land that borders the bush. I have my chickens and my apricot trees, a small plot of seasonal vegetables.

It's not much, my home. One large central space for living framed by two bedrooms to one side, the main bedroom and bathroom to the other. Tin roof, thin walls. Too hot in summer, too cold in winter. A place of extremes, like the country I once knew, long ago. But this land is mine. I have freedom here. I know what it means to be free. I've lived the alternative, forced from my home, lost and alone. Never again. This is my space. I am not giving it up.

I place the eggs in a bowl by the sink and, taking a box of red-head matches, go to light the oven. It's an old oven, iron, painted pale green, open flame. Another appliance Crissy and Neil have tried to update for me. But bread tastes better when cooked by flame. My fingers fumble with the tiny matchsticks and I drop one to the floor. Lost. These hands will never retrieve that from the sticky linoleum flooring. I go to kick the offending match under the cupboard, to the place of lost matches, vegetable peel and utensils, but Crissy beats me to it. Plucking the match from the floor, she takes the matchbox and lights the oven.

I resent these little things. These moments that prove her right, that show the passage of time. The ache in my back, the fumbling fingers, the slowed walk.

I grunt and set about making tea. I should thank her. I won't thank her.

"Two sugars?" I ask. I know she takes one.

I feel her smile behind my back. "What a treat." She plays

along, lets me spoil her in this little way, as I did when she was a child. She lets me mother her once again, as her own could not, if only for a moment, if only over a cup of tea.

Later, after the bread has baked and the sun has risen, I retire to my front porch to rest. I have a seat here, overlooking the open scrub that stretches from my front door to the dirt road that leads into town. No houses visible in any direction, but I know they are there, tucked behind the gums and native grasses. The silence of the bush envelops me, broken only by the occasional warble of a magpie going about its day, the flutter of my canaries in their cages that line the porch...

...The bell above the bakery door chimes. The sound of heavy footfall. Black boots, polished to a reflective shine. Fear chokes the air from my lungs...

"Mamina-Zee? Telephone."

Her voice calls me back to the present. Crissy is standing at the door to the house, my cordless phone in her hand.

I blink rapidly, momentarily confused before realising that I must have drifted off to sleep. The old nightmare visited. It's been years since it's come into my peace. The past feels close today, its ghosts present and pressing. Feeling an unsteadiness that is nothing to do with age, I rise to my feet and shuffle inside. Concern is etched across Crissy's face. I ignore it. I don't have the strength to pretend.

Not today.

"Hello, Zenta Vanaga, to whom am I speaking?"

I wait. At the other end of the line a person takes a deep breath.

"Hello, Mrs Vanaga. My name is Heather Bradford." The voice is warm, flavoured with an unmistakable Texan accent. I frown.

Heather continues. "Thank you for taking my call. I have been searching for you for so long. I believe you knew my mother."

I sigh. I don't know how, but this poor woman has clearly mistaken me for someone else.

"I am sorry, dear," I explain, "but I don't know anyone from America. Thank you for calling." I go to hang up the phone, I could just press the button, but I like to return it to its cradle. I'm old-fashioned that way. But Heather's urgent voice halts my hand.

"Wait a moment, please." I pause. It's instinctive, isn't it? To follow a polite request. I hear the sound of shuffling paper, the huff of Heather's breath. At length she continues. "Do you mind confirming the details I have?"

She doesn't wait for an answer, rushing on. "You were born Zenta Kalnina, once of Riga. Your parents, Nikolai and Dārta were bakers in the old town? And you have a sister, Estere?"

My mouth goes dry. Who is this woman? How does she know about my family, about me?

"...You fled Danzig on foot with my grandparents, Stefans and Alma... you had a baby..."

Guilt, cold and hard, plummets through my gut. My hands begin to shake. What does she know about that time? About me?

My secret. My choice.

The phone crashes to the floor. My legs give.

The last thing I know is Crissy's panicked cry as she races across the room.

"Mamina!"

But I can't answer. I'm no longer here, not really. I am falling through time and space, age and knowledge. I am back in a small house in central Riga, the scent of bread wafting on warmed summer air.

I am there.

The past is here.

PART ONE

THE FIRST OCCUPATION 1940–1941

TWO

ZENTA

Riga, 1940

The lump on the bed moved. Snug beneath the thin woollen blanket, Zenta pressed her eyes tightly closed, willing herself back to sleep. If she pretended to dream...

It was no use; the soft light of a Riga summer morning filtered through the threadbare curtains and called her from slumber.

"Zee, be still or get up. I am trying to sleep," her sister, Estere, groaned from her bed against the opposite wall.

Suppressing a huff of impatience, Zenta tried to obey. She lay still, counted, one, two, three...

It was no use. She was awake.

Throwing her covers off her, she bounced from the bed and padded across the cool wooden floor, grabbing her nightgown as she left the room, leaving her sister to sleep.

Out on the landing the scent of baking bread was already filling the upstairs rooms, drifting up from the bakery ovens below. Drawn by the smell of rye and caraway, and the company of her parents, Zenta made her way down the stairs.

Their home was part of a traditional Riga terrace, tucked in the middle of a set of houses clustered around a central, shared yard, each one with a shop below and home above. Tall and thin, the top three floors were used for family life. Nestled in the roof, Zenta shared the attic with her sister Estere, below them was her brother Tomass' room. In the middle of the house was the family kitchen and her parents' room.

Under their living space was the shop, her mother and father's bakery, the front windows tall and wide to display their offerings to passing customers. It was one of Zenta's favourite tasks to set up the morning display: pastries, freshly baked rye bread, cakes topped with patterned cream. Stretching out behind the bakery storefront were the ovens that comprised the bakery kitchen. Three in total, large, constructed of metal, painted a pale green to preserve them against rust. Heated by an open flame at their base, they radiated a welcome warmth on chilly mornings.

Both kitchens were plumbed, cold water only. Though electricity had been added before Zenta was born, personal hygiene required a bowl and washcloth, and water heated by a small fire in the back garden, a space shared with the other families that made up their encircled building.

Coming to the door of the bakery kitchen, Zenta paused and watched as her parents, Nikolai and Dārta, went about their work. Her father, a halo of rye flour misting the air around his hand, kneaded the dough. He had broad shoulders, but was short, and appeared rounded, despite his strength and vitality. Her mother, classically beautiful like Estere still sleeping above, had blonde hair drawn back into a bun at her nape. Hands clean, she was piping icing over small cakes. Zenta's stomach grumbled as the scent of baking caraway seeds wafted to her nose, her mouth watering on cue.

Her father looked up, and Zenta grinned, their matching

grey-blue eyes meeting. A moment passed between them, of greeting, of love.

He crossed the room towards his daughter with a heavy limp, an old injury from the War of Independence, barely slowing his pace as he moved and gathered Zenta up into a mighty bear hug, as she squealed in delight. She perched on the edge of childhood. Her body showed the first signs of becoming a woman, small curves, leaner limbs, but only just. She still adored her father, and Nikolai would savour every last moment of this precious time.

"What are you doing up?" her mother, Dārta, chided, the smile playing on her lips softening the sharpness of her tone. She knew her child well. Since her arrival into the world, Zenta had never slept late. Nikolai released Zenta and returned to his kneading, while Zenta joined them in the small workspace before the fire-lit ovens. Her sister should be helping, she knew. But Estere was out late last night, again. Zenta didn't understand why her parents had not admonished her sister. Surely they knew of her late-night escapades. Her thoughts skipped away as her father opened the oven, the full heat of its open flames spilling out into the shop, blasting away the last remnants of the night-time chill that lurked at the edges of the room.

"Come," her father said simply as he placed a fresh ball of dough before her. "As I do."

He began to knead the new dough. His large hands moved deftly as they squeezed and stretched. Rolling up the sleeves of her nightgown, Zenta floured her hands and copied.

"More force," Nikolai instructed. "Yes, like that. Keep the pressure consistent."

Zenta grinned, focusing on the task before her. It was tough kneading the rye, working the starches, bringing the dough to a thick but buoyant consistency. Soon her hands began to ache, her arms tiring. But she did not stop. Only practice would ease these aches, she knew. And if she wanted to take over the bakery one day, she had to be strong. It was her dream, held tightly in her heart. By custom the bakery should go to one of her older siblings, but neither was drawn to the flour like Zenta. For her, working the bread was as natural as breathing.

Time slipped by and Zenta worked, lost in the rhythm of the bakery until her mother's voice called her from her focus. "Time to dress for school. Wake your sister, she can take her place here in the shop."

"I could stay," Zenta ventured, eyes hopeful. "I don't mind."

Nikolai smiled privately, turning back to remove the latest loaves from the oven as his wife replied, "One day, Zenta, when you work all day in this shop, you will long for the hours outside it."

Zenta opened her mouth to protest, unable to imagine ever wanting more than the bakery with its warmth and yummy scents, its purposeful work; unlike the useless letters and numbers of school. But her mother continued. "Upstairs now, child. Or you will be late for Ava."

Recognising that she would not sway her mother's mind – Dārta was not one to be challenged – Zenta nodded, plodding up the stairs to fetch Estere and prepare for the day.

Soon afterwards, she met Ava on the corner of the church square that opened just beyond the bakery, as she did every schoolday. Her oldest and most beloved friend smiled as she approached.

"Late again, I see? Working the bread?" Ava asked, pushing her dark curls behind her ear, her brown eyes twinkling.

Zenta smiled back, looping her arm through her friend's. They had been friends since infancy, their fathers having served in the Great War together, their mothers bonded by pregnancy. Her mother Rosa was a seamstress, and so Ava always dressed in the latest patterns and styles. Zenta dreamed of having a new dress one day, something made just for her.

There had been a short time when the girls feared they

would be sent to different schools; Rosa preferred the Jewish Culture Academy, in a nod to her heritage. But President Ulmanis ensured that could not be when he abolished all but the National Schools just before their studies began. So, the girls were never separated. Nothing, Zenta thought, would ever come between them.

They made their way along the cobbled roads of Riga, heading for Brīvības bulvāris, Freedom Boulevard, the main thoroughfare in and out of the old town. The salt of the Baltic was sharp on the cool summer air. Alongside them men in neat trousers and shirts made their way to offices. Women, with hair bound back by silky scarves, led smaller children towards Riga Central Market, the large domed buildings on the edge of town that had been made from the former zeppelin hanger. The rattle of a tram filled their ears as it passed, its carriage over-flowing with workers on their morning commute. A busy, bustling city.

As they wound their way through the small park that bordered the centre, Aleksandrs joined them. Tall with soft brown hair, a smattering of freckles across his nose and cheeks, he loped with the gait of a boy who had grown too quickly, his newly elongated limbs gangly and uncoordinated. Zenta felt her face flush as her heart thrummed. She met his warm eyes, then they both quickly glanced away, a knowing grin on their lips. It hadn't always been this way when she saw Aleks. The rush of excitement deep in her belly, the tingle of her flesh, were new and exciting sensations. She didn't fully understand why he suddenly had such an effect on her, not yet. But it was the most marvellous feeling.

Without a word, he fell into step with the girls as they crossed past the Freedom Monument, Brīvības piemineklis, the green-tinged statute stretching for the skies above as they headed for school.

. . .

"Come to the river? I've a new line to test."

It was the end of a boring school day and Zenta, Ava and Aleks were strolling through Rathausplatz, the town hall square, the beauty of the red-bricked stepped roof of the House of the Blackheads lost on them as they made their way towards home.

Zenta looked at Aleks. She longed to say yes. One of the best things about summer was the long hours of light that meant more time to enjoy the day before bed. But it was Friday. And Zenta knew tomorrow was their monthly trip to visit her Uncle Artūrs in Jekapils. Her mother would need her home to pack, bathe and prepare food for the train.

"I can't tonight, Aleks, I'm sorry. Mother needs my help."

Aleks nodded, accepting this without argument. They were both still young enough to obey their mothers.

"What about you, Ava?" he asked, voice raised to be heard above the tram that rattled down the centre of the road, now empty, its passengers still at work for the day.

"I don't fish, Aleks, you know that!"

Aleks grinned. He did. River fishing was something he and Zenta did together. But it was only polite to invite Ava too.

"I will catch you a herring," he said by way of goodbye, eyes lingering on her a moment before he headed off towards the Daugava River that ran through the centre of Riga and into the Baltic.

Zenta watched him go, the bounce of his step inviting her to follow. She fought the urge to race after him, to be naughty and disobey her parents' expectations.

She met Ava's deep brown eyes. A grin played about the corners of her friend's lips.

"What?" Zenta demanded.

"Nothing," Ava laughed. "Nothing at all."

They stared at each other a moment, before bursting into peals of laughter.

"I had better be the maid of honour at your wedding," Ava giggled, wiping tears from her eyes.

"He'd better like baking," Zenta retorted.

Ava grinned. "I think Aleks will like anything you like, Zee. Anything at all."

Ahead Aleks stopped suddenly before the Riga Town Hall, its tower reaching to the blue sky, and turned back towards the girls. "Come to the river," he shouted. Even from the distance, Zenta could see his eyes willing her to disobey.

Beside her Ava whispered, "Go on."

Zenta looked at him, and her heart split. She so wanted to be the responsible daughter. She was also still a child, for this summer at least. Her mouth twitched into a smile.

"All right," she called back.

Delight spread across Aleks' face, lighting up his eyes. Zenta's parents wouldn't notice if she was a little late, surely? So long as she was home before dark, would it really matter?

Decision to disobey made, she caught up with him and they set off at pace, still walking, but fast. They bustled past the other students also on their way home, slowing their pace only when an elderly couple, clad in matching tawny cardigans, mouths open wide, panting for air from the exertion of walking, turned onto the street before them. Heads dropping as one, they instinctively moved closer together, their shoulders pressed close enough for Zenta to feel the warmth of Aleks' skin through his shirt, the cotton soft against her bare upper arm.

Breaking from the condensed, winding streets of the old town, the expanse of the Daugava opened before them. Zenta paused. The vast river, its currents powering towards the Bay of Riga, always took her breath away. Quickly they crossed the wide road that lined the riverbank, coming to the built-up riverside. The waters were lined with men, fishing lines already plunged into the deep.

Broad grin on his face, Aleks cried, "Race you to the bridge!"

Zenta looked up at the looming metal arches of the railway bridge, imposing and grand, and a sense of wonder caught the breath in her throat. She opened her mouth to say so to Aleks, to try and find the words for the feeling this view always inspired in her, but before she could speak, Aleks was off.

Laughing, she followed. Their run was fast, spirited. A release of the pent-up joy of childhood repressed by long schooldays, desperate for escape. Zenta pumped her legs hard, but no matter how she tried, Aleks pulled further in front. His longer legs and longer stride allowed him to easily outpace her. But she didn't care, just laughed again and redoubled her efforts.

At the bridge they stopped, bending over their knees to suck in breath, the warmth of the earth radiating up through their limbs, their lungs burning to draw in air. At their feet the expanse of the Daugava flowed. Wide and deeper than expected, its currents bubbled a soothing melody, deceptively calm, belying the great power that lurked beneath its waves. Overhead white fluffy clouds puffed across an achingly blue sky. Insects buzzed along the river surface. With dusk birds would descend from the canopy of trees to feast on their tiny shell-bodies before returning to their preferred branches to sleep.

The two children sat on the bank, feet dangling above the waters. Aleks twined his fingers with Zenta's, his digits sticky with drying sweat. She gripped his hand, palm to palm. They faced each other, meeting one another's eyes, smiles on their lips. A cooling breeze rose from the river, casting a relieving balm over the heated city. Hand still in Aleks', Zenta closed her eyes and relaxed.

Happy and content and free.

THREE

ZENTA

Zenta stood on the train platform, hair freshly washed and plaited, summer dress tufting in the breeze that ran along the train track. Beside her stood Estere, suitcase sitting neatly at her feet.

Behind them their mother, Dārta, waited calmly, while their father, Nikolai, glanced around the station, flustered, sifting through the rows of people waiting to depart for various towns across their small nation.

Her brother was late.

"He does this to vex me," Nikolai said, frown lines cutting deep into his forehead.

"Tomass will be here. There is plenty of time," Dārta replied smoothly.

Her brother had recently started working at the docks, and regularly came home late, or not at all. At almost twenty-one, he was pushing into manhood, but he still made time for this family trip each month, usually. Zenta glanced up at the big clock that hung over the station. Their train was due in the next five minutes, so there wasn't much time left for Tomass to make an appearance.

Soon the white cloud of the steam engine filled the horizon as the large locomotive made its way to the platform.

Her father gave an exasperated huff. The gentle but firm press of her mother's guiding hand moved Zenta forward and they began to board. As Zenta stepped up into the carriage, she turned her head, and finally saw him. Tall for a Latvian, blond and blue-eyed, Tomass came running down the platform, face flushed from exertion.

Smiling broadly, her brother swung up into the carriage behind her, pressed a swift kiss to Dārta's cheek and nodded to Nikolai.

"See?" Dārta said. "Plenty of time."

Tomass settled beside Estere, nudging his sister playfully with an elbow. His younger sister, Zenta, watched from the seat opposite. Her siblings, born a mere year apart, bound together by the shared experience of babyhood, had always been close. Estere reached over, smoothing Tomass' thick pale hair back into place. They were a picture of beauty, the pair of them, fair, tall, delicately featured. A mirror of their mother, where Zenta was her father, shorter, plainer. She dreamed of one day growing her hair to be as long and glowing as her sister's.

Tomass glanced over, winked at Zenta. She smiled shyly, longing to move over and join her brother and sister in their cocoon of friendship. But she didn't move, instead remaining in her seat by her father and turning her head to watch as the city passed from the train window.

The train journey to the station at Krustpils, in the eastern region of Latgale, took around three hours. Dārta had boiled eggs to keep them fed, the job of peeling them a distraction from the hours on the train. Zenta munched dutifully on her egg, its soft flesh melting in her mouth as she gazed out at the country-side of her homeland. Fields of bright grass and crops inter-spersed with large patches of woodland, impossibly green and lush. As much as she loved the neat order of Riga, Zenta always

found the country, with its wild freedom, its open space,
beautiful.

Arriving at Krustpils, situated along one side of the
Daugava River that also ran through her city, they disembarked
and crossed the bridge into neighbouring Jekapils to begin the
hour's walk to her uncle's small plot on the outskirts of the
town. A run-down hut greeted them, gutters rusted and
crooked, wooden doors splintered. In the garden raised beds of
vegetables overflowed with vibrant produce. Zenta spied beets,
cabbage and new potato shoots. A few chickens scratched about
the soil searching for worms and warming themselves in the
summer sun.

It was where her father grew up, with his brother Artūrs
and their parents. Her grandfather, Bogdans, had worked as a
farm hand in Russian-controlled Latvia, setting his sons on a
path for the same. But the Great War had brought change,
sparking the Latvian people to revolution. Her grandparents
did not survive the harsh winter of 1916. So, when the fighting
was done, the brothers returned home to a free Latvia, but an
empty house. Artūrs stayed to work the small farm that was now
his own, and Nikolai ventured to Riga, drawn by the heart to a
small bakery in the old town, run by a widow and her beautiful
daughter, Dārta. Nikolai married her that first year after the war
and moved into the rooms above the bakery, taking on the work
of the shop, allowing Dārta's mother some rest for her ageing
joints. They were quickly blessed with the arrival of Tomass,
one year later came Estere and then a gap before the surprise of
Zenta.

Uncle Artūrs also married, but he and Berta never had children. Since Berta passed the year before, Nikolai insisted they
visit his brother monthly to keep him from feeling lonely.

Zenta suspected there was more to it.

As though her thoughts had conjured him, Artūrs strode
from his home, hands held high and wide in open greeting.

"Brother, sister, children!" he cried, smile splitting his face in two.

He was not much older than her father, but he bore the years more clearly. Deep wrinkles carved through sun-hardened skin, large black pores lining his ample nose. But Zenta didn't care.

His arms were strong, his embrace warm and his laughter rich and full-bodied.

She threw herself into his embrace, burying her face in the earthy scent of him, ignoring the lingering fumes of alcohol. Lately the smell of moonshine hovered around her uncle but she loved him nonetheless.

Pulling back from her, Artūrs scanned her face, his eyes red-rimmed, unfocused.

"Brother," her father said as he stepped beside them. The brothers embraced, holding each other's eyes a moment, as some unknowable understanding flowed between them. Artūrs gave a small nod, then turned back to Zenta and her siblings, and said, "Come in, come in. I have beet stew ready for lunch. I know you will need feeding after your journey. Come."

The rest of the day was passed in quiet company. Artūrs' house may have been falling apart on the outside, but inside it was clean and tidy: an open central space dominated by a hand-crafted wooden table, a stove against the wall and two bedrooms on the side. They shared the stew, Zenta savouring the rich, earthy flavour of freshly picked beets.

After their meal, Artūrs took an axe and selected a chicken. Estere and Dārta boiled water to soak the carcass, softening the flesh to ease the plucking of feathers. As they prepared the chicken, the gummy scent of boiling flesh filled the small hut, and Zenta peeled more beets and carrots, before chopping cabbage.

As they worked, the men sat in the sun, smoking cheap

rolled tobacco, their laughter carrying through the summer air and into the small house.

As the light softened, they gathered again at the table. Nikolai carved the chicken, Dārta served the boiled vegetables and Artūrs placed a glass of homemade rye kvass before each of the men.

"It is good to share this time with you," he said simply. "You always have a home here."

He eyed Nikolai, that secret something again passing between them.

Artūrs continued. "You heard that Paris has fallen?"

Nikolai nodded.

"It did not take long." He paused, taking a swig of his kvass. "Everyone looks West. No one looks East. No one is watching Russia. But I watch them." He leaned forward, tapping his index finger against the side of his nose. "You know they are amassing troops on the border..."

"Enough now, Artūrs. This is not talk for the dinner table," Nikolai said.

"There is no point hiding it. We both know what is coming. We have lived it."

"I said, enough." Nikolai's tone was sharp, pointed. Zenta shrank back in surprise, the force of her father's words unfamiliar.

The brothers stared at each other across the table. A moment. Two. Then Artūrs rose, breaking the tension.

"I almost forgot. I've a fresh batch of šmakovka. Brother, will you take a measure?"

Zenta watched as her father paused, considering. Artūrs' traditional Latgale-style moonshine was strong, she knew.

But Nikolai nodded.

Glasses were fetched and a bottle of clear syrup-like fluid placed on the table before them.

"Tomass?" Artūrs held the bottle above her brother's glass, eyebrow raised.

Tomass flicked his eyes to his mother's, seeking permission. Dārta nodded.

Grinning, Artūrs poured a measure, the liquid so thick it clung to the glass in long, glistening streaks.

"Priekā!"

"Cheers!"

The men held up their glasses in salute and downed the traditional liquor.

Tomass coughed, pressing a hand to his throat, eyes watering.

"What do you think, boy?" Artūrs asked.

"Can I have another?" Tomass replied.

The adults laughed.

That night, as her siblings and mother slept peacefully beside her in the cramped guest room, Zenta snuck from her cot, tiptoeing out into the night. In the moonlight her father and uncle stood, the glow of their cigarettes burning red in the dark. Crouching by the back door, Zenta listened, their soft voices drifting through the starry night.

"War is coming, Nikolai. You know it. Russia is coming. They already press our borders. You have to decide."

"There is nothing to decide, Artūrs. What can we do?"

"We can fight."

Her father's rueful laugh rang out into the night.

"Fight? Artūrs, I can barely walk after... you know."

Artūrs placed a hand on his brother's shoulder. "I got you out. I would do so again."

Nikolai stared at Artūrs. The night was so silent about them it seemed to ring and echo in Zenta's ears.

A small shake of his head. "I have different responsibilities now. You must understand that?"

"But what of their freedom?"

"I would have my children alive."

"You may not be in control of that. They know we fought for Latvia, in the end."

"You assume too much, brother. Latvia is free still!"

"To pretend that it will remain so is to lie to yourself. You have to choose. Keep quiet and pray, or join the resistance."

"There is no choice. I will not leave my family. And you should not speak of resistance! Keep to your farm, be small, cause no fuss. It will pass."

"If you believe that, Nikolai, then you are a fool."

"I would rather be a fool who lives, than one who willingly signs up for death."

Throwing the last of his cigarette to the ground Nikolai turned from his brother, striding for the house.

Zenta melted back into the dark of the house, gliding quickly to the bedroom. Slipping beneath the sheets to lie beside her sleeping sister, she nestled into the warmth of Estere, the weight of her sister's solid body a comfort against a cold fear that had taken root in her belly.

Estere stirred, rolling over to draw Zenta into her arms.

Zenta didn't resist, allowing herself to be enveloped by her sister's sleepy embrace. Slowly her body calmed and her mind slowed. Heavy eyelids shutting, she drifted to sleep, not noticing that her father never joined them to rest.

FOUR

ZENTA

The patter of pebbles against the attic window called Zenta
from half-sleep. Excitement lit a spark in her belly.

Someone was at the window.

Estere beat her to the windowsill; the slump of her sister's
shoulders in the moonlight answered the question of who stood
below before her sister spoke.

"It's your boy."

Aleks.

Zenta felt her breath quicken. Aleks had come, just as he'd
promised. A smile broke across her face.

Estere turned from the window and climbed back into bed,
pulling her covers up to hide her face.

Bouncing from her mattress, Zenta ran to the small window.
Carefully sliding it open, she swung a leg out into the night.

"Be careful," Estere said, voice muffled by her blanket. "You
really shouldn't sneak out at night."

Zenta regarded her sister from the corner of her eye. Rich
coming from her, she snuck out most nights to meet her beau.

"I will," she said simply.

Clutching onto the drainpipe tucked against her neighbours' wall, Zenta shimmied down, storey by storey, to the street side where Aleks waited.

Dropping the last few inches, Zenta landed lightly on the cool pebbles of the night-dark street. Aleks leaned casually against the wall of the bakery, still dressed in his school clothes, though his shirt had come untucked. Zenta smiled. She loved these sneaky nights when Aleks came to visit.

"Did you bring my herring?" she asked. His hands were empty, so she knew full well he'd brought no fish, but it was fun to tease him.

Aleks had invited her to the river that afternoon as they returned from school. This time, she'd held fast to her refusal. Her parents had been more insistent about her movements recently.

Aleks huffed a laugh. "I didn't go in the end. Mother has liked me home earlier lately."

"Mine too."

They fell silent. The two children, on the brink of adulthood, contemplated the subtle shifts in their worlds, without the context to understand.

"Father is worried," Zenta said. "Uncle Artūrs said the Russians are coming..."

That secret knowledge of her parents' fear had dwelt in her chest this past week, swelling daily with the silence. As she spoke it aloud to her friend a strange sense of relief settled over her. She expected, or hoped, Aleks would deny the possibility of this rumour.

He only nodded.

"Father says there was a fight on the border. A civilian was killed. Russia is blaming us."

Aleks' father, Boris, was a teacher at their school, highly educated, intellectual, opinionated. He heard things.

"Will there be an investigation?"

He shrugged. "I guess so..."

They lapsed into silence again. Zenta shuffled closer to Aleks, seeking the warmth of his closeness. Without a word he slung his arm about her shoulders as if it were the most natural thing in the world. She rested her head on his side. They stayed like that, leaning together under Zenta's attic window, as the moon rose and the stars brightened the sky.

That fight on the border turned out to be more than a skirmish; it was the start of Russia's occupation. Zenta and the rest of her classmates learned of the invasion at lunchtime, when their mothers appeared at the school gates to bring them home. Zenta knew something was wrong the moment she saw her mother's face.

Ava's mother Rosa stood beside Dārta. The two friends pressed shoulder to shoulder, standing as one in the middle of the cluster of parents, faces a mirror of each other, blank but twitching.

"Mother?" Zenta asked, confused as she walked to her side.

"Hello, daughter," Dārta said, over-brightly, smoothing sweat-laced hair from her brow. She must have come in a rush. "Come."

With a knowing nod to Rosa, Dārta had turned Zenta towards home. Ava gave Zenta a small wave as she followed Rosa. The gathered women dispersed as their children filed from class.

Zenta searched the bustling crowd for Aleks, but his grinning face did not surface from the moving mass, and Zenta was forced to leave without saying goodbye. Dārta set a clipping pace, her skirts rustling as she urged Zenta through the unusually empty streets.

They gathered in the family kitchen above the bakery: mother, father, Estere and Zenta. Even Tomass had come, his factory closing early with the news. They sat around the dining table, radio placed in the centre of the table and listened.

"Your government has accepted the Soviet Union's terms," came the stern voice from the radio. "There will be no fighting, there is no risk to civilians. Stay in your homes."

Zenta's father stood from the table and gathered his coat, a look passing between him and his wife.

"I'll come with you," Tomass said, standing.

"No, son. I need a man here at the house. You will stay while I am gone and won't venture out?"

"Of course, Father."

Nikolai nodded to himself, kissed his wife and turned for the door, ruffling Zenta's hair as he passed.

She watched as he made his way from the room, fear uncoiling in her gut. Their city had been invaded, the radio warned them to stay at home, yet her father was leaving. He hadn't said where he was going, but Zenta could put the pieces together. There was only one person outside this room her father would risk disobedience for: Uncle Artūrs.

"Right, well, we'd better start on dinner. It will be nice to have the extra hands," Dārta said, her voice too loud, too high-pitched.

"Come," Estere said, rising from the table to join their mother at the sink. "Time to pitch in."

Zenta followed, accepting a carrot and peeler from Dārta and getting to work. But even the steady rhythm of preparing stew with her family could not settle the nerves that now jangled through her body.

That night Estere never went to bed. Cloak pulled tightly about her she pushed open the window to the night.

Zenta sat bolt upright in bed. "Where are you going?" Her

sister often snuck out to meet with her boy, but tonight Zenta didn't want to be alone.

"I have to see Valdis," Estere replied. "He will be in danger."

"In danger from what?"

"The Soviets, other Latvians."

"Why would anyone care about Valdis? He is just a student."

Estere's face softened with sadness as she looked at her sister.

"He believes in an equal Latvia, a country where we all have freedom."

"Isn't that the Latvia we do have?" Zenta asked, hands unconsciously gripping her blankets tighter.

"Not for everyone. Valdis believes in more structured equality." She stopped, shook her head. "Some people think he is a Communist."

Zenta frowned. "What's a Communist?"

"A Soviet."

Glancing over her shoulder and down to the street below, Estere swallowed hard, suppressing some deep emotion. "I will be back before dawn. Stay in bed. If Aleks comes, pretend you do not hear him. Do not leave this room." She fixed her with a piercing stare. "Understand?"

Zenta nodded in silence, watching wide-eyed as her sister lithely descended the drainpipe to the street below before slipping into the shadows.

Securing the window Zenta crawled under her covers, hiding her face beneath the scratchy wool, seeking the dark cocoon of bed. She comforted herself as best she could, reminding herself that Tomass slept in the room below, staying as her father had asked. But the silence of the room was haunting, her blanket her only security. She snuggled down, heart pounding, mind buzzing with fear until, sometime near the first light of the sun, sleep finally claimed her.

The tanks rolled in that morning. Loud, heavy, lumbering they rumbled along the tight cobbled twists of the centre, heading for the town hall. Alongside the tanks marched lines of soldiers, men, tall and bulky in their brown uniforms, guns slung over their shoulders. Zenta watched from the bakery window. The sign on the door was set to closed, unheard of for a weekday.

"Zenta, come away from the window, we have much to do inside today," her mother called from the stairs, gesturing her child back up into the home above the store.

Zenta understood the unspoken message. They were hiding. As her father had said to Uncle Artūrs just weeks before, they were keeping small.

As always, Zenta obeyed.

The house felt cold, smaller somehow without the heat and scent of the bakery operating below. The absence of her father and the silence where a steady flow of noisy customers should be made Zenta's home feel like a new, unfamiliar place. In one night, everything had changed.

Joining her mother and sister in the family dining room she accepted a pile of socks to darn and set about her task without complaint. Estere had returned just in time for breakfast, hair wild from the wind, eyes wide. Brazen in her disobedience, Zenta was amazed at her ability to lie to their mother with such ease. She longed to ask Estere questions, to understand more about what was happening and why Valdis was in trouble. But she understood, without being told, that it was not something to bring up in front of her mother.

At the open window her brother sat silently smoking, eyes on the street, as the rumble of the tanks continued to fill the air. Zenta looked up at her brother, seeking reassurance. But the strain on his face only deepened her fear. She returned her focus to mending the socks and prayed for her father's swift return. He would make everything better.

Nikolai arrived home the next day, face drawn, limp more heavily pronounced. Dārta rushed to her husband's side, helping him up the stairs and to his chair, ordering Zenta to boil water for tea which she instantly busied herself with. Her father leaned heavily on the table, hands shaking slightly.

Zenta kept quiet, making the tea. Silence stretched and Zenta stole a glance at her father now seated at the table. The pain in his eyes tore her heart. She turned back to the tea.

"He would not come?" Dārta finally asked, breaking the silence.

"No. He would not." Nikolai smiled sadly at his wife. "But he promised not to join any local fighters. He promised to stay on the farm and obey."

"That is good, husband. As good as we really could hope for."

"Perhaps. But we know what comes next. They will assign him work. Nationalise his land. What might he do then? At least if he were here..."

"Stop now, husband, shhh. You have done what you can for Artūrs. It is enough."

Nikolai watched his wife's face, mouth turned down, shoulders slumped. Closing his eyes, he rested his forehead against his wife's. Zenta left the tea gently on the table and slipped silently from the room. This was bigger than her understanding, an adult moment that belonged to her parents alone.

The people's vote to join the Soviet Union was held two weeks later. To vote was compulsory for all men, the punishment for noncompliance unnerving in its obscurity. Nikolai accompanied Tomass to the voting booths in Rātslaukums. Before the booths were shut, while rows of men still lined the streets of Riga to have their say, the results were announced in Moscow. With a majority of ninety-seven per cent, Latvia had spoken and asked to join the Soviet Union, to be ruled by Russia once more.

That evening, Nikolai opened a bottle of clear liquid. Zenta knew it was moonshine; she'd seen the alcohol drunk at her uncle's home often enough, but never in her own.

The next day two soldiers arrived. Zenta peeked down from the top of the stairs, watching as the men spoke with her father, handing him papers to sign before leaving, their heavy boots loud against the floor.

"What has happened?" Zenta whispered to Estere. The way Nikolai had allowed the soldiers to loom over him had unsettled her still further. It wasn't like her father to cower.

"The bakery is no longer Father's," she replied, voice cold and bitter. "Now we work for Russia."

It took a few days for Zenta to understand the difference. First their usual flour was taken by a different set of soldiers, then new flour, coarser, arrived. It was harder to work, but Nikolai did his job. Customers came in less frequently, and when they did they were quieter, their movements smaller, their eyes darting furtively. Nikolai still smiled as he served them, but Zenta noticed that the light never reached his eyes.

The rhythm of their days changed. Gone was the easy laughter, the joy of baking. Replaced with an imposed quietness, withdrawal.

Things changed at school too. There was a new uniform, complete with a bright red scarf for each student, red for Reds: Aleks wore his about his neck, Zenta over her hair. Each morning the whole school gathered in the courtyard and recited a motto. It was in Russian, so Zenta had no idea what she was saying, but following Ava's lead, complied. Russian language classes were added to their lessons, so she supposed one day she would know what they were chanting.

Then their teachers disappeared. There one day, gone the next. Replaced by men in smart suits speaking heavily accented Latvian. Russian scholars. The changes were bewildering. Everything Zenta knew and trusted was being taken away, piece by piece, and a new Riga was beginning to form.

One Zenta didn't recognise or understand.

Aleks wasn't at school that day, or the next, so Zenta and Ava went to his home to check on him. They should have realised what had happened; Aleks' father was a teacher after all. Yet the changes were so foreign, so inexplicable that it never occurred to the children their friend would be impacted directly.

It had taken time for them to come, but come they had. They'd arrived at Aleks' house in the dead of night to force his father Boris to pack a single suitcase and climb into a waiting truck. Aleks said he saw other teachers looking out of the truck as his father climbed in, their faces strained with worry. He'd not heard from his father since that night, and his mother had not stopped crying.

Aleks had stopped attending school then. Lauma was too afraid to let him out of her sight, no longer trusting of the schooling system, or the soldiers. After all, they had taken her husband. He wasn't the only student to leave school. Zenta told her mother she no longer wished to attend either. But try as she might, Zenta was not spared her daily classes. Soon more lessons were taught only in Russian and Zenta found she had to apply herself to her language studies or fall behind. She knew her father valued education, so she did what she could to keep up.

Neighbours also disappeared. People Zenta had known her whole life, if only from a distance, to share a nod as they passed on the pavement, were suddenly gone. And new people, Russians, moved in.

As the icy winds of winter strengthened, people withdrew into their homes, no longer visiting friends or even going to worship, the Sunday morning church bells that had rung out across the city, echoing off the cobbles, silenced by invasion and fear. The citizens kept to themselves, only venturing from the safety of locked front doors to gather essentials before locking the city behind them once again.

Soldiers patrolled the streets, watching everyone, guns slung casually over their shoulders, cigarettes burning bright as they dangled from firm mouths, eyes sharp. They stank. Of sweat and grime and unwashed clothes. Zenta knew to keep away. She was happy to obey.

Winter that year was fierce and brutal, the harshest the country had seen in decades. Snowstorms layered the streets in a thick blanket of white, knee-deep and frozen, gusts of wind swirling in spirals off the rooftops, icicles dangling from windowsills, blizzards so heavy they smothered the city in an impenetrable white curtain.

With the blizzards came shortages, of food, of supplies.

The vegetables Zenta's mother brought home from Riga Central Market became older, smaller. The cuts of meat more bone than flesh, their last jar of salted herring not replaced. The scarcity wasn't helped by the change in currency. The Lat changed to rubles, at a ratio of ten to one, leaving most Latvians in poverty. Zenta's skirts grew loose on her hips though she was still growing taller. Her cheeks were narrower, her hair dull.

As the days grew shorter and the nights darker and colder, her mother suggested her daughters share a bed to stay warm as they could not spare the firewood to heat the bedrooms; every available log was needed for the bakery.

When the edges of the Daugava froze over, Nikolai took Zenta out to the icy waters to fish. They weren't alone, it seemed the whole city had come out to try their luck in the slush of ice and sea that mingled in the river. Zenta felt like the old woman from the tale of the Golden Fish, hungry, desperate. Using a mallet, Nikolai smashed out a section of ice that clung to the bank's edge, and Zenta dangled their pole and bait, a small morsel of bacon fat, they didn't have much to spare. Around them the winds off the Baltic whipped across the frozen river surface, the current, visible only at the very centre of the wide waterway, a mush of ice, trying to freeze across the gap, to join both sides of the mighty Daugava.

No fish came.

FIVE

ZENTA

The bell above the bakery door chimed.

Old Mr Bērziņš shuffled into the store, bringing with him a blast of frozen Baltic sea air. His worn boots, crusted with snow, landed heavily as he approached the counter, leaving a melting trail behind him.

Zenta would mop it later, but she didn't mind.

Her father beamed at the old man. "Edgars! Labrīt, good morning!" They'd served together in the Great War and the Latvian War of Independence that followed in its wake – most of the men of Riga aged over forty had. They were the only customers who brought the true warmth and joy of the old Nikolai to her father's smile.

"Yes, yes," Edgars grumbled, placing shaking hands on the countertop. His hunched shoulders swallowed his neck, his eyes peering out from beneath a mountain of scarves. Riga in winter was a bitter mistress.

Smiling to himself, Nikolai collected Edgars' order. Rye bread and fruit pastry – whatever filling was going. This time of year it would be apple jam. It was almost always apple jam in winter. As her father placed the baked goods in a brown paper bag, Zenta rang up the order. Edgars pushed his gnarled fingers into a small purse, fishing for the coin to pay. Once a factory worker, Edgars was well into his retirement, but the cost of war and occupation meant tightened belts for everyone, even the elderly.

Men and women who should be enjoying the comfort of family: meals prepared by daughters-in-law, firewood chopped by sons, the simple joy of holding pudgy grandchildren and singing hymns, were scraping to get by; they all were under the Soviet regime.

No one had anything to spare, not even time for ageing relatives, it seemed.

"Leave the pastry," Edgars said, waving a hand in dismissal.

Gently, Nikolai placed a hand on his fellow veteran's arm.

"No charge," he said simply. Watching on, Zenta smiled at her father's kindness.

"I have always paid my way. I will not take from you."

"Ah, but it isn't me you are paying, or taking from, anymore."

Once again Edgars grumbled, shuffling uncomfortably.

"The soldiers will know... when they come to audit."

"All will be well. Take the bread, and the pastry. Be fed."

Zenta watched in silence as Edgars took her father's hand in his, their eyes meeting across the counter. A pause. The nod of a head. Edgars collected up his parcel, the paper crackling in his unsteady grip. He began to turn for the door.

Zenta felt her heart swell, tears forming in her eyes. Her father was a good man, she knew. It was in his smile, his gentle hands, his love of her mother. And, she realised, his care for the people of Riga.

The bell chimed again.

Looking up, Zenta froze. Motioning subtly, Nikolai gestured for her to move behind him. She did as he asked. Old

Mr Bērziņš shuffled to the side of the store, hunching in on himself, making himself smaller.

Peeking from behind her father, Zenta watched as three tall soldiers entered the bakery, the stench of wet wool and sweat radiating from them. The man at the front was clearly in charge, dark eyes flicking about the store, never resting in one place for long, until they landed on her father and stopped, narrowing as they focused on his face.

Nikolai straightened, squaring his shoulders, and said, "Good morning, comrade."

Zenta started. She knew the words, of course, her Russian classes over the previous months had seen to that, but she'd never heard her father speak Russian so clearly. The words came smoothly to his tongue.

The soldier didn't reply, only strolled casually across the shop, taking his time, eyes never leaving Nikolai. He paused at the counter, then finally, "How much have you baked this morning?"

Not missing a beat, Nikolai answered, "Our flour delivery arrived just days ago, so we anticipate a full shop today. Twenty loaves are complete, our next round of ten are in."

"We will take the twenty complete. And your remaining flour."

Her father paused, blinking rapidly. "Comrade, the flour is for the week..."

"We all give to the cause, do we not?"

"But my customers..."

"You forget yourself, baker. You serve the Soviet Union. We are all in this together. Your customers are no more important than anyone else. Just as I am no more important than you." The soldier smirked, the irony not lost on him. "We all must give."

Zenta swallowed, she could feel the anger that pulsed

through her father's body. She was terrified of what he might do.

Nikolai opened his mouth to speak but he was cut off.

"We know of your brother."

The words seemed to land a physical blow to Nikolai. His mouth snapped shut, his shoulders bunched.

Zenta frowned. Uncle Artūrs? What did he have to do with anything? She didn't understand, but her father's reaction was telling. Subconsciously he stepped back, one arm reaching to press Zenta further behind him. He nodded to the soldier.

Grinning, the soldier flicked his hand at his two comrades who moved forward, pushing past Nikolai and into the bakery kitchen beyond. Zenta remained silent, terrified, tight against her father's side. Aleks had talked about this, soldiers taking what they willed. Food was essential and at the moment, a limited resource.

The scrape of footfall at the front of the shop drew Zenta's attention. Behind the exchange Edgars was moving for the door. She'd forgotten he was still inside. He'd almost made it to the exit, hand reaching for the handle, as the soldiers reappeared from the kitchen, arms laden with flour and bread, steam from the still warm loaves rising into the air.

"Halt!" the first soldier called, voice firm and authoritative, hand raised to the ceiling. Zenta blinked, who was he talking to? Slowly the soldier turned until his eyes bored into Edgars' continued retreat.

"Good morning, comrade," the soldier said, stepping towards the old man, intent ringing from the soles of his boots. "Allow me to get the door for you."

Edgars, eyes down, bobbed a quick nod as the soldier stepped up beside him.

The soldier looked down at Edgars, scanning his body, eyes pinched.

"You fought in the Great War?"

Edgars nodded again.

"And after...?"

Edgars went still. Tension, a physical, palpable thing, filled the room. At her side, her father drew a sharp intake of breath.

The soldier continued to look down on Edgars. Then leaning forward, he swung the door open wide, the cold of the Baltic blasting into the shop once again. "After you."

On feet made even more unsteady from fear, Edgars exited the shop. The soldier and his bread-laden comrades followed close behind.

Her father didn't take his eyes from the door. "Zenta, go to your room."

Zenta looked up at him, eyes wide with confusion. His face was as pale as bleached flour, his upper lip twitching. Something was wrong... something was very wrong. She turned for the stairs, then...

A shout of anger, a cry of fear. The scuffle of men and an enormous bang rang out from the street.

Instinctively Zenta ducked, hiding behind the counter. Nikolai hunched beside her, his body wrapping about hers. They waited. The sound of an engine firing, a vehicle disappearing down the street. Silence.

Breathing fast, Zenta stayed squatting behind the counter, Nikolai clutching her to his chest. The seconds stretched. Still silence. Her mother appeared at the stairs, eyes wild, presence pensive. Slowly Nikolai rose.

He drew Zenta to her feet. She felt as if her knees might buckle. "Go to your mother."

His eyes met his wife's. Dārta silently gathered Zenta into her arms, holding her close in the stairwell as Nikolai crossed to the bakery door.

He disappeared onto the street.

Coming back in moments later, the white of his hands was covered in bright red blood.

Huddled by the stairway with her mother, Zenta sucked in her breath, frozen with horror.

Her father stood in the doorway in silence, the red dripping onto the floor. It mixed with the ice and melting snow, turning pink as it seeped across the wooden boards. Releasing Zenta from her grip, Dārta screamed. Knees weak with fear, Zenta could only stare.

Soldiers came to collect Mr Bērziņš' body at noon. Zenta watched from her bedroom window as they lifted his lifeless form, so small, so insubstantial, into a wheelbarrow. Covered in a simple white sheet, they wheeled him away. There was no investigation. No funeral or wake. Mr Bērziņš was just gone.

Creeping down from her room that evening, Zenta stood in the bakery doorway, her parents framed by the now cooling oven, a tableau of their existence. Her face was red and swollen from her tears, and shock. She had never known such fear before, or seen a dead body.

"They knew," her father whispered into her mother's neck. "He fought for Latvia after the Great War, like me." Zenta watched as they stood in each other's arms, holding on as if their limbs alone could keep them safe.

"Hush," Dārta replied, smoothing a hand through her husband's hair.

"What do I do?"

"Keep going."

Zenta swallowed, her chest tight. She didn't understand what had happened to Mr Bērziņš, not fully. But, listening to her parents, she knew with terrifying certainty that it impacted her father too. Fear, pure and raw, traced her limbs, rendering her still. She longed to step forward, to snuggle between her parents, embraced by their strength and love. To feel the comfort of their warmth surround her.

The tears on her father's cheeks held her back. Usually so strong, so confident, his distress terrified her. She didn't know what to do, how to help. Silent as a field mouse in the snow, she returned to her room, alone.

Dārta washed the bakery floor clean.

The bloodstain on the pavement was soon covered by a fall of snow. It was still there, an ugly brown stain, when the snows melted into spring.

SIX

ZENTA

1941

Zenta stirred the clothes through the boiling water, her breath misting before her. Spring was limping to life through the city, tiny buds of new growth dotting the trees, but ice still whistled on the winds. Pausing her stirring she poked the fire beneath the washing pot, stoking the flames. The bright red lick of heat surged momentarily, comfortingly warm as it flashed over her face, before settling down into a smaller dance. She continued stirring the clothes. They had running water inside, but not heated. So the weekly job of boiling water to wash clothes and sheets and tea towels fell to Zenta or Estere... if her sister was ever around to do her chores.

Zenta sighed as she continued working. There was no point complaining, the washing had to be done. Above her head a sparrow landed on a bare tree branch, turning his head to the sky, but did not sing. The season was still too new. Soon the small birds would rejoice, opening their throats in beautiful song as they wove and danced about the green of new growth.

But for now they were silent. Only the distant cry of seagulls carried on the wind.

Zenta paused, looking up at the little bird, and smiled. Soon, she thought.

The back gate creaked, making her jump. She looked around. Aleks slinked through the opening, closing the gate gently behind him.

"I thought I saw washing steam," he said by way of hello, coming to stand close beside her, seeking not just her closeness, but the warmth of the washing-fire.

The long, hard winter had been made worse by the wood rationing that had left them on the brink of freezing. Just last week Zenta's teacher had relented and allowed them to keep their gloves and hats on inside.

"Will you come to the river, when you are done?" Aleks asked, without much hope in his voice.

Zenta didn't look up from her washing. "I can't."

Aleks nodded. Since the Russians had arrived, Zenta always said no, but he wouldn't stop asking.

She glanced up at her friend, regret slicing her heart. Many had faced loss and hardship under the Reds and Aleks had not been spared. Seeing the sorrow that traced his eyes reminded her of just how lucky she was to still have her family intact. They were an untouched bubble in the middle of a city of loss.

The fire dipped low, the clothes would be done. Zenta leaned her stick against the wall then plunged her hands into the water, gathering up a shirt, wringing it as dry as she could before pegging it to the single washing line that looped across the yard. Without a word Aleks rolled up his sleeves to help.

"Mr and Mrs Tannis left today." He spread out one of her father's shirts and pegged it to the line.

Zenta looked up at her friend. "Where did they go?"

Aleks shrugged. "They are the third family this week. Mother says it's because of the Nazis."

Nazis. That word again. Zenta had heard it before, whispered between her parents when they thought she wasn't listening. Recently people had started leaving. By choice, not forced onto trucks by the Red Army soldiers. But packing bags and slipping away in the night.

The two friends stood in silence, their hands busy with work, the gentle sounds of the fussing sparrow searching for nesting materials overhead touching the edge of their thoughts.

The back door opened and Dārta bustled out, arms loaded with the next round of dirty clothes to wash.

"Aleksandrs?" she said, surprised. "Why are you helping my daughter and not your mother?"

"The chores are done. There aren't so many, now it's just the two of us. Mother is sleeping..."

Dārta's drawn face softened as she looked at Aleks. The whole city was gaunt from winter's harsh hand, but Aleks was bordering on skeletal. They all knew how badly Lauma had taken her husband's "removal".

"It's icy out," Dārta announced suddenly. She turned back inside with the dirty washing. "Come inside, you two, let's have some pudding."

Zenta blinked in surprise at her mother's uncharacteristic offer. There was still light for at least another round of clothing, and more to do besides. But she knew well enough not to question her, and, with a skip in her step, followed her mother and Aleks into the warmth of the bakery kitchen.

They were ushered upstairs to the family kitchen. Dārta made straight for the cupboard. Grabbing a pot, she placed some of the morning's breakfast bread inside, then covered it with milk and a sprinkle of sugar before placing it on the stove to warm into rye pudding. Zenta and Aleks sat close together; it was warmer inside than out, but it was still cold enough to raise goosebumps.

Soon, two steaming bowls of rye pudding were placed

before them. Grinning like the little children they still were in their hearts, Zenta and Aleks tucked in. Dārta watching on with an expression of motherly warmth.

Zenta filled her mouth with the doughy, milky-sweet pudding, the stale bread falling apart on her tongue and slipping down her throat. Footsteps sounded on the stairs and Nikolai poked his head in.

"I thought I smelt pudding!" he exclaimed, walking to embrace Dārta, casually ruffling Aleks' hair as he passed.

"Who is minding the shop?" Dārta asked, momentarily bewildered by her husband's presence during the working day.

He paused before her, pressing a kiss to her forehead. "I will be soon enough. Aleks!" He turned to face the young boy. "Will you give me a hand with the afternoon customers? There is often a rush just before closing."

Aleks quickly swallowed his last mouthful of pudding and stood up hurriedly. "I will. I would like that," he said.

Zenta's father glanced at her, then grinned in approval. "Good boy, come."

Nikolai led Aleks from the family kitchen, leaving mother and daughter alone.

"Quick then, child," Dārta prompted, "Let's clean these dishes and return to the washing. The sun will be lowering soon."

Dutifully Zenta piled up the plates and helped her mother wash up. Then she headed back outside into the cold and Dārta followed with even more clothes.

As Zenta worked to hang the last batch of washing along the line and the last rays of the sun kissed the gathering clouds, Aleks loped out from the bakery, his face calm, settled. He paused beside Zenta.

"You have a wonderful family," he said simply, once again dipping his hands into the washing pot to help with the hanging.

Sadness pressed down on her at the unspoken, obscured sorrow his simple words masked. She didn't know what she would do without her father; it was a loss too great to imagine. Zenta continued her work in silence, not knowing what to say, but wishing she could somehow soothe his pain.

When all the clothes were strung along the line, Aleks waved goodbye, making his way home to his mother. Zenta stood a moment in the yard, watching the gate through which her friend had disappeared. He moved differently now, his pace slower, his tread heavy. The loss of his father weighing on his every step.

Zenta realised how lucky she was that her family were all still together.

The dress cracked as Zenta folded it into the basket. The washing water had frozen into tiny little ice balls through the weave of the cotton as the fabric dried in the cold air. It wasn't as bad as in the depths of winter, but still a cold and stiff task. Laying the ice-hard clothes into a basket, she moved to the next item, breath misting before her. She would lay them in the bakery kitchen to finish drying. It was the warmest room in the house.

Her mother appeared at the back door, large cooking pot in hand. By the way she held it Zenta could tell it was full of something, soup, stew... but from here she could not smell it. She watched curiously as her mother navigated the steps from the house, offering her daughter only a passing nod as she crossed the yard and disappeared onto the street. What on earth was she doing? No time to wonder, there were chores to complete.

But Zenta didn't have to wait long to learn what her mother was up to. That evening as Dārta served out a thin cabbage broth, adding the last chunks of the morning's leftover breakfast bread to make the meal more substantial, the answer came.

"Wife," Nikolai ventured gently. "I thought we'd potatoes left from the weekend market?"

"We did," Dārta confirmed, taking her seat at the table. Her voice was firm, but Zenta heard a note of uncertainty hiding in its timbre. "But we have bread. I thought Lauma and Aleksandrs could use a good stew."

"You are a good woman," Nikolai said, reaching to take his wife's hand. "Girls, your mother is a good woman, never forget it." He eyed Zenta, but his gaze lingered on Estere, who turned away, focusing on scooping her cabbage soup into her mouth.

"Zenta, pass the bread," Dārta said, breaking the tension that had settled between Nikolai and Estere. Zenta did as she was bid, wishing her sister would do the same.

"Soon there will be too many potatoes to eat," Nikolai said, voice boisterous and warm. "The season is turning, the crops are greening. The time of plenty is fast approaching."

As he spoke a single water drop wended its way down the kitchen window, cutting a path through the fog of misting moisture that had condensed against the glass. The world outside was warming, but slowly.

Zenta could not wait for spring.

SEVEN
ZENTA

"They are coming! They will be here within the month!" Tomass burst into the family kitchen. Throwing his cap onto the table, he stood before them all, feet set wide apart, hands on hips, eyes triumphant. He was still dressed in his dock worker clothes, smears of grease across his shirt, sweat patches at his armpits from the heat of the newly arrived summer sun. Somehow he still looked handsome, despite the grime that marred his face.

Zenta blinked in surprise. Since the Soviets arrived last summer, Tomass only came home for Sunday dinner, staying in lodgings near the docks to avoid contact with late-night patrols. But today was a weekday. Excitement and concern warred within her. Seeing Tomass was always a joy, but this was a change in routine, and change was rarely a good thing these days.

Nikolai looked up from his meal, body going unnaturally still. Taking the time to wipe the sour cream from the corners of his mouth, he eyed his son.

"Sit down, Tomass. Eat. Your mother has made borscht."

"Did you not hear what I said?" Tomass replied, eyes

ablaze. Beside him Estere tensed, her body going rigid as if ready for flight. "This year of terror is coming to an end. The summer sun has hardened the soil, now our saviours can come."

"Sit down." Her father's voice was hard, he would brook no argument.

Reflexively Zenta curled into herself. She had learned to make herself small these past months, a skill that was becoming more and more useful.

"Father," Tomass continued, "it will soon be over. The Germans are coming. They will drive the Reds out. They will free Latvia from under the boot of Russia, once and for all—"

"Enough!" Nikolai's fist smashed down on the wooden table with such force their bowls of soup would have sloshed and spilled, had they not been so poorly filled. Zenta started, pulling back even further from the table. She looked at the stairs, wondering if she should run up them and escape the building conflict.

Tomass stared at his father, daring his ire.

Everyone went still as tension zapped between father and son.

"Father, it's true," Estere piped up, her voice high and tight. "Valdis says—"

"Do not speak that man's name in this house! Do not speak it anywhere. What have I told you about fraternising with rebels?" Nikolai shouted, breaking eye contact with Tomass to glare at Estere, who had pushed away her food.

"Valdis is not a rebel!" Zenta shrank from the dangerous look in her eyes.

"He is a rebel and a fool and asks for his own death."

Estere shot to her feet, her slender body quaking in rage. "At least he is willing to fight for us. To fight for Latvia!"

"I am going to join up." Tomass' voice cut through the room, and instantly silence fell.

Bewildered, Zenta looked from father to brother to sister.

Utterly lost and confused, she hunched in on herself more, flinching away from the passionate anger building before her. The world she knew seemed to be spinning away.

Voice low and menacing, Nikolai addressed his son. "You will do no such thing."

"I am a man now, Father. You cannot stop me. I will join the Germans and I will fight to free my country. If you were a man, you would too."

Nikolai recoiled as if slapped, his mouth going slack with shock.

Rising suddenly to her feet, Dārta screamed, "Enough!" She rounded on Tomass. "Get out!" Her hand flew to point at the door. Tomass' head snapped to face his mother. He paused. The flush of colour that had stained his face in anger drained from his skin, leaving him pale. For a moment it looked almost as if he were about to cry. Then he squared his shoulders and, spinning on his heel, strode from the room.

Zenta's mother began collecting the bowls, soup still sloshing inside them. "Dinner is finished, go to your rooms."

"But, Mother..." Estere began.

"Go!" she roared.

Zenta didn't need to be told twice. Rattled and confused she bounced to her feet and scuttled to the room she and Estere shared at the top of the stairs.

Flinging herself on the bed, Zenta buried herself beneath the covers seeking comfort, warmth, safety. Soon she heard the clip-clop of her sister's heeled shoes as they crossed the wooden floor to the bed.

"Here." Estere drew back the woollen covers and pulled Zenta into her arms. "Shhh." She stroked Zenta's hair.

Tears spilled from Zenta's eyes, sobs bursting from her chest. What had just happened? She didn't understand. What had her brother decided? The world around her had turned upside down, a pall of fear falling over them all. But home had remained safe, predictable. She didn't want that to change. It was all she had to lean on.

Estere said nothing, breathing softly as she rocked her sister, hoping to calm her.

When Zenta's confused sobs came to rest, Estere pushed her sister back so she could look her in the eye.

"Did you take bread?" she asked gently.

Zenta frowned, shaking her head.

Estere released a heavy sigh. "You need to be smarter, Zee. These are not normal times."

She drew a thick slice of bread from her pocket and handed it to her little sister.

"Eat. Always eat. You don't know when your next meal will be coming."

"At breakfast, tomorrow," Zenta said, unthinking.

"If there is still a bakery to bake in," Estere answered, lips pursed in fury.

"I don't understand," Zenta cried. "You are all talking in riddles." She buried her face in her hands, a fresh wave of tears threatening to start.

Estere pressed her eyes closed, taking a deep, calming breath.

"Europe is at war, Zenta," she began. "We are at war. The Red Army came and took too much and now the Germans are coming too. Tomass is right, the Germans will force the Reds from our borders. The Nazis are powerful, successful. Russia is no match for them, at least not now. But that doesn't mean Latvia will be free. Valdis says—"

"Father said not to speak his name."

"Father is old and afraid!" Estere shot back.

Zenta recoiled. Estere often snapped at their mother, their father, even Tomass. She was intense, and outspoken, unwilling to bend to the will of others, even their parents. But Estere never snapped at her. What was wrong with everyone?

After a moment of silence, Estere softened. Reaching out she feathered her fingers over Zenta's gaunt cheek. "Calm, oh my sweet, sweet Zee," she said, her eyes looking past Zenta as if staring into a different time and place, her voice wistful. She shook her head and clutched Zenta's hand. "Zee, you must listen to me. Things are changing. Father's war won Latvia freedom. He fought then, alongside his brother, to push the Russians out and reclaim Latvia for her people, you know this history."

She paused, fingers smoothing the skin of Zenta's palm in a soothing gesture before continuing, her expression hardening. "You also know it wasn't enough. We thought it was, but the Reds returned. You have seen the horrors they have inflicted on our people. On our friends..."

Zenta lowered her eyes, the sting of fresh tears burning her lids as she thought of Aleks and his missing father. She thought of the hope that still rang in her friend's voice as he spoke of his father, Boris, and the sorrow that now permanently lined his eyes. Aleks would never stop missing his father or give up hope that he would return. Her friend was changed forever.

"So," Estere continued, tucking her blonde hair behind her ear, "Father is scared. He believed his days of war were done, buried his head in the sand, ignored the signs. And now once again we are enslaved, not to a Tsar, but to an idea, a movement. We have been forced into the Soviet Union. And Father believes there is nothing to be done. He is afraid of what *must* be done." Her eyes darkened, angry and sad at once, her focus turning inward. Zenta swallowed.

"But that doesn't mean he is right. It is up to us now, the younger people, to stand up and reclaim our freedom. Tomass believes the Germans will help us. He may be right. Others, like my Valdis, believe liberation must be won by our own people. Either way, Latvia must be free. But it won't come easy. There will be fighting in the streets. There will be scarcity, worse than now even." She gently guided the bread in Zenta's hand towards her mouth. "So, eat... never leave food if you can take it."

Zenta listened to her sister with an honest and open heart, but it was all too much, too big, too wide-reaching for her to understand. Unsure what to say, she did the only thing that made sense, and bit off a large chunk of her bread.

"Good girl."

"I will halve it for you..."

"No," Estere rose from the bed and gathered her cloak, "I will eat with Valdis."

Without another word she crossed to the window. Drawing it open she swung a leg into the gathering evening.

"You are leaving?" Zenta squeaked, after swallowing her bread. "It's still light, Father will see you."

"He always sees me," Estere replied. "But he will never stop me."

With a final flash of her beautiful smile, Estere disappeared over the windowsill and into the summer's purple dusk.

EIGHT

ESTERE

The moment she saw him, he took her breath away. Tall, dark-haired, with a presence that drew you to him, inviting you close with a warm, open smile, Estere had known then and there that her heart no longer belonged to herself, but to him.

He was giving a talk at a student meeting at Riga University. Estere wasn't a student, of course, but, drawn by the undercurrent of social rebellion all new adults crave, she followed her friends to the small meeting hall on the West side of the city, and she listened.

The hall was small, the air inside thick and musty from the worn carpets. She took a seat in a chair on the edge of the circle of listeners, nervous to be there, but excited.

His voice was resonant, clear, his tone friendly. Though she understood little of his message back then, his delivery did not make her feel small or stupid, only curious to learn and grow.

"Latvia for all Latvians!" he'd concluded firmly, inspiring a round of applause from the gathered students, some shouting their agreement. "Equality." "Food for every mouth." "No man left behind."

The room buzzed with energy the way rooms of young

people always do; a charge of passions, both ideological and something more primal. Desire. Dressed in their neat shirts, collars open with their belted trousers firm about their slim waists, these university students represented a different part of Latvian society than Estere had encountered before. Those with money and time to pursue education.

Estere ran her hands nervously over her faded dress, cotton so worn in parts that her skin almost showed through. It had first been her mother's; most of her dresses had. At least this one was yellow, Estere loved yellow. But her hair was neatly pinned at her nape and her friend Elina had let her borrow her red lipstick to paint her lips. She was beautiful, she knew that, and refused to be cowed by anyone. So, despite her fear, she held her head high and acted like she belonged.

"You sound like a Communist!" A voice cut through the cheering. After an audible gasp, the audience of students fell silent.

The man before them smiled calmly, nodding as if in thought as he walked closer to his circle of listeners. His steps brought him almost to her side. Estere's breath quickened at the closeness of him, so close she could see the light sheen of sweat on his forehead, the twitch of his eyelid as he paused before her. He looked right at her, their eyes locked. She thought she was going to faint and prayed her body would not betray her so. She smiled nervously. Then he winked.

Swallowing hard she gripped her skirts, willing herself to hold it together. Who was this man? She had to know him better.

He turned to the crowd, stepping away, and she released a gush of breath. Her fingers trembled.

"You say that like an accusation," he said, looking at the man who had spoken. "But what is so bad about it? Communism is for the people."

"It is a method of subjugation. Of holding people down. Just look at what Stalin is doing in the name of 'Communism'!"

"It is a philosophy of equality. Isn't that what you want? What we here all want?" he paused, gesturing to the gathering of students. "A more equal Latvia?"

"I doubt most Russian farmers felt so equal when their farms were taken from them."

"But that is not a failing of ideology. That is a failure of delivery. Lenin's work, his goals for Russia, there is purity there. A way for all to be equal and valued in society. But change always comes with mistakes. Don't judge an idea by the people who implement it."

The objector scoffed. "So how do we implement it fairly?"

"We learn from the mistakes of others."

The man nodded at this and a murmur of agreement spread through the crowd.

Later, as the gathering slowly dispersed, Estere hung back. Emboldened by his eye contact she now hoped for more, she wanted to speak to him. As she sat on the edge of the small hall, her eyes scanned the room, quickly finding their way back to him. Standing near the doorway he chatted amiably with the man who had challenged him. A small woman, long red plait down her back, lingered by their side. Estere blinked in surprise. There had seemed such hostility between the men, and yet now they spoke as friends. They embraced as they parted. Then his gaze once again fell on her.

A slow smile, filled with intent, spread over his lips as he approached her.

"I saw you as I spoke, you seemed interested in my message," he said.

She nodded, swallowing hard.

"Your name?" he prompted gently.

Embarrassment, red and hot, flushed her face. She glanced down, hoping to hide the blotchy patches of colour she knew now stained her face. She was such a foolish girl, so unsophisticated, so unworldly. And this man...

He waited patiently, his eyes never leaving her face. Finally, she managed, "Estere."

"Estere." He rolled the "r" ever so slightly, drawing out the sound of her name. "A beautiful name."

"Thank you," she whispered, throat tight with nerves, deeply pleased at a compliment that really was owed to her parents.

"I am Valdis," he continued, smiling warmly. "Are you a Communist too, Estere?" he asked.

"I... I like the idea of equality."

He nodded sagely. "A Latvia with a place and a role for everyone. Where all are valued, children never go hungry, and everyone can prosper..."

She wasn't sure about being given a role. She'd been born into that expectation already with the bakery. Once Tomass had made it clear he would forge his own path on the docks, her parents' expectations had fallen to her to take on the store. Estere could think of little worse.

"That man..." she interrupted, unthinking. "He disagreed with you, but you seem, friends."

He released a small laugh. "This is Latvia, we are a country of different opinions. That should not stand between friends. Dāvis and I were in school together. We may have differing ideas about the method, but we both believe in Latvia. He and Olga are good people, we need more passion like theirs in our nation."

Estere thought of her family, her father and uncle, from the same womb yet almost always at odds. But beneath it all, love. His words made sense of that strange dynamic in a way she'd never been able to find. A wistful smile curved her lips.

"Can I walk you home?" he asked, voice lowered just for her, eyes sparkling in the flickering light of the hall.

She looked up. "I'd like that."

After a walk through the warm spring air, he kissed her cheek at the back door of her home, his dark eyes gleaming.

She slipped inside, creeping up to her room as silently as she could, hoping her parents would not stir from their slumber. Easing between the bedsheets she ran a seeking hand over her body, tingling in new and unexpected places, remembering the feel of his mouth on her skin. Warm, soft but reserved, a vibration in his body suggesting he was holding something back. A promise of more.

Sliding into sleep the thought popped into her head, unbidden. Perhaps having a role wasn't so bad after all. If that role was to be by Valdis' side.

As they began their courtship, Europe fell to war and they fell in love. Valdis opened his heart and mind to her, sharing his fervent belief in equality and hopes for Latvia. Swept up in his rich voice, the feel of his hands on her skin and the warm breezes off the Daugava caressing the new summer air of the city, anything seemed possible.

His parents, Tekla and Adukis Dreimanis, opened their home to her willingly, seemingly unconcerned by the patches on the elbows of her cardigan or the worn leather of her heels. Things between them advanced at speed and Estere was soon dreaming of marriage, her first child, a new life, a new role: wife and mother.

And then the Soviets had invaded, and once again, everything changed.

It was late. She'd risked much to be there. Sparing a moment to glance behind her, she paused, savouring the deep purple of the darkening sky. It was peaceful at night, fewer soldiers marched the streets, fewer trucks filled with soldiers, their sharp eyes always watching. Taking a deep breath, she knocked on the double-sized wooden door to Valdis' home. Silence greeted her, and she waited, drawing her cardigan closer to her body as the evening chill seeped through her clothes. She was about to knock again when footsteps sounded in the hall on the other side of the door. The door opened a crack revealing a sliver of Tekla's face, her eyes narrowed in suspicion. Until she saw Estere.

"My dear!" she exclaimed, hauling the heavy door open and ushering her inside. She quickly scanned the street beyond before she pressed the door firmly closed, key turning in the lock to secure them safely within.

"I am sorry, Mrs Dreimanis, I know the hour is late."

Tekla eyed her warily, the loose skin of her jawline trembling slightly as she ground her teeth. Occupation had everyone on edge, even the wealthy, or perhaps especially the wealthy. "Has something happened?"

"No, no." Estere rushed to relieve the worry she saw breaking over the older woman's face. "I simply needed to see Valdis."

Tekla visibly relaxed, a smile curving her lips at the thought of her beloved son. He'd been hard won, Estere knew. A late pregnancy, the only one of many to come to term. Wanted desperately and utterly adored by his elderly parents, her Valdis.

"Of course. Come, he is in his sitting room. Have you eaten?" she said as she led Estere into the cavernous home.

She reached the lamplit aura of his reading room, and saw him in profile bent over a book, taking notes. He still took her breath away. No doubt he was working on a new newspaper article. There were a few going around. After Russia took over the press, some citizens had decided to fight back, circulating their own Latvian news, hoping to counter Soviet propaganda and lies. Of course, Valdis was one of the first to offer to contribute, no matter the risk to his safety.

"The people need to know the truth," he'd proclaimed. Estere agreed, though she doubted this paper could do much, and by producing it he risked a great deal.

His mother cleared her throat loudly, bustling forward to collect his supper plates. He looked up at the old woman and smiled warmly.

Noticing Estere, he placed the book down on the table and rose, coming to take her into his arms.

"I'll bring soup," his mother called over her shoulder as she left the room.

"Thank you, Tekla," Estere replied.

Valdis had yet to move out of his family home. And really, with the number of rooms here it was no wonder. A big name in the shipping industry of Latvia, the Dreimanis had money in abundance, even if Soviet control had meant the company was no longer theirs.

"I did not expect to see you tonight. All is well, I trust?" Valdis pressed a kiss to her hairline, his breath warm against her temple. She wondered idly how he felt about Communism now that his father had been forced from his own company. A pointless, bitter thought. She pushed it away.

"Father and Tomass had a fight. It was... hard. I needed some space."

"It is a difficult time in Latvia. Clashing beliefs and hopes, family against family. Arguments are normal."

"It is more than a clash, Valdis. People don't have the same desires here anymore. Some want the Russians to stay, others are imprisoned. Some want to leave, others welcome the Germans, thinking they will bring our country back."

"The Germans won't give us back our Latvia."

"Tomass believes they will..."

"Then he is a bigger fool than even I was!" He broke away

from her, crossing the room to gaze out at the rapidly advancing dark.

Tekla came in, bearing a tray of soup and bread for Estere. "Thank you very much, Mrs Dreimanis, I truly appreciate your hospitality."

Tekla waved away Estere's thanks. "Of course, darling. You are always, always welcome here."

Placing down the tray she retreated once more. They were good people, Valdis' parents. Rich, and good. Estere would be proud to be their daughter-in-law. One day.

Crossing the room, Estere wrapped her arms about Valdis' waist and rested her head against his back. She could feel the tension thrumming in his body, the anger and disappointment, too.

"He promised our people would be safe," he whispered.

He was referring to Vilhelms Munters and his speech to the university the year before, when Latvia was still free. He said the Soviets were no threat and Valdis had believed him.

When the Reds first came Valdis had not been afraid, trusting in the possibility of positive change. A new approach to government, a more equal society. He believed the philosophy that guided the Soviet Union could be purified here in Latvia. So when the Soviets had replaced the Latvian government he wasn't worried, nor had the state seizure of companies and lands troubled him. But then they had come for the university. Professors forced from classrooms onto the backs of trucks, never heard from again. New lecturers instated, all courses changed to Russian. Valdis spoke the language fluently, of course; he read history at university, and the history of Latvia was bound to Russia. But this was not the equal Latvia he had believed was coming.

Despite the tension in his body, to Estere he felt strong, solid and real. An anchor to grip fiercely against the changing world that spiralled unpredictably around them. She felt him breathe deeply, expelling a long sigh.

"You will stay tonight."

It wasn't a question, she always stayed if she could. He drew her against his chest, one hand twining through her hair.

"The Nazis are not the answer. Just as the Russians were not. The only answer is the same as it's always been."

She waited, silent. He would explain when he was ready. Estere had learned a lot in the months since they had met, and she still had lots to learn.

"The only answer is Latvia herself." He stared at her for a moment with fire in his eyes, then his shoulders slackened. "Come, eat your soup. I must keep working, this article is needed in the morning. But when I am done, we can read together if you like."

Estere smiled. "I would like that very much."

NINE

ESTERE

Shouts rang through the thick humid air. Estere and Zenta huddled at their window, watching, bare knees pressed to the cool wooden floor, eyes peeking over the windowsill. At an hour when all would normally be abed, the streets below were alive with action.

Trucks and armed soldiers moved through the hazy night, the moisture-laden summer air a miasma, blurring the glow of the streetlamps and headlights and casting all in dulled orange. The sisters watched as trucks of soldiers pulled up outside the house across the street. The soldiers decamped, almost running to the door before knocking, loud and furious. A sleepy Mr Liepins had barely opened the door before the soldiers barrelled in, shoving him back out of sight. A few minutes later he emerged with his wife, Asenka, each clutching a small suitcase, their boy, Olivers, on his father's hip. They were marched to the waiting truck and loaded into its bowels. The soldiers climbed in behind them and the truck moved on, down the street, before stopping again, the soldiers racing for another door.

Out across their quarter of the city the sounds of more trucks, more shouting soldiers echoed.

Estere looped an arm around her sister, drawing her close. She could feel the trembling of her frail body, and Estere tried her best to conceal her own fear.

A knock sounded on their door.

Both girls jumped, turning as one, eyes wide. They hadn't seen a truck at their own front door... had they somehow missed it?

Their mother's head appeared around the door, and she entered swiftly, closing it behind her. In her hand she carried a plate topped with buttered bread, baked that morning. Without a word she placed the plate on Estere's bed. Then, motioning the girls from the window, reached up and drew the curtains firm against the night.

"I am going to lock you in. Open this door for no one. No one. Understand?"

Estere nodded, drawing herself up taller, her arm still wrapped about her little sister.

"I will keep her safe, Mother."

Dārta eyed her daughters, a moment of indecision crossing her face, as if she doubted Estere's promise, or her own decision, before she stepped forward and drew them into a tight hug.

"Be silent."

She slipped from the room. The clack of the key turning in their door was impossibly loud in the silent, still space. Against her side Zenta shivered. Estere looked down at her sister. She'd grown tall this last year, the final softness of childhood stripped from her bones by hunger. New curves showed through her nightdress. But she was still a child.

"Come," Estere said. "Sleep in my bed."

The sisters climbed under the sheets, snuggling close. Estere passed Zenta a slice of bread, thick-cut, slathered with butter. A treat. They chewed in silence, pressed close, legs entwined, listening as chaos continued outside.

· · ·

Dawn broke silent and cool. Estere jolted awake, surprised to find she had drifted off in spite of the noise from outside. Beside her, Zenta still slept, snoring softly. She didn't know what had happened last night, or the extent of it, but she knew she had to get to Valdis. Clearly the Russians had been rounding people up. Why? She didn't know, but Valdis was always a target; his work with the underground newspaper saw to that.

Against her Zenta stirred. Then, she heard the gentle footfall of her mother on the landing and the click in the door.

Dārta's face was pale and worn, her eyes rimmed with deep black, like bruises. It was clear she'd not slept.

"Your father wishes to speak with you. Tomass is here. There is bread baking. Dress quickly."

Estere and Zenta made fast work of their morning routine, dressed and were at the kitchen table in record time. There their father sat, hunched in his chair, eyes as dark as their mother's. No sleep for him either. He didn't smile as they approached, didn't even nod at Zenta. He was exhausted.

A tousled-haired Tomass sat beside him. Their brother must have come in the early hours, the events of the night drawing him home for safety. Estere watched as her brother smiled up at their mother, his eyes seeking her comfort, their recent conflict forgiven. Dārta patted her son on the back as she moved to her place by her husband. The sisters took their usual seats.

The family together at the breakfast table, the warm scent of baking caraway seeds filling the air, so familiar, so normal. Yet everything had changed.

Nikolai cleared his throat and, resting his hands flat on the table before them, he spoke to the wall opposite, meeting no one's eyes.

"The Russians came for the resistance last night, and the poor and the Jews, and the strong workers. I can see no solid connection between the families targeted. But many served in the War of Independence." He paused, ran a hand through his hair. Dārta rose, coming to stand beside him, a hand on his shoulder in solidarity.

Briefly Nikolai looked up at his wife, placing a hand over hers in thanks.

"Trucks took people to the railway, loaded them onto carriages bound for Siberia. I don't know how many were taken, or if they will come for more. But for now, it seems, we are safe."

"They are running!" Tomass suddenly exclaimed. "They know the Nazis are close. They are getting out."

"Perhaps," Nikolai conceded. "But we must be smart. I am closing the bakery until further notice. No school. No work. No visiting." He stared at Estere as he spoke these last words, hoping his point stuck. Estere swallowed. There was no chance she would obey. She would not be kept apart from Valdis for long. Beneath the table Zenta reached across and gripped her hand. Estere's heart cleaved, her sister so small, so scared. She wrapped her fingers about Zenta's palm and squeezed tight.

"We have a virus, that is our story," Nikolai continued. "We are all abed. Until this madness calms. Until we can be sure."

"But what of Uncle Artūrs?" Tomass said. "Surely Riga is not the only place they have raided?"

Nikolai paused, face sombre. Thoughts raced across his brow, as he fought with an internal conflict. Finally, he nodded, expression heavy.

"I will travel to Jekapils today and bring him here – if I can. Tomass, he can share your room."

"But, Father," Zenta interrupted, "that cannot be safe. What if you are stopped on the streets? They will think you are trying to escape!"

"She's right," Dārta said softly. "It is too dangerous, Nikolai."

Nikolai frowned, eyes linking with Estere across the table. "I will take Estere. Then we are just a father and daughter visiting family. We will travel light and fast. And return swiftly."

Beside him Dārta stiffened. "Husband," she said, her voice panicked, questioning.

"I have spoken. Estere, gather your things, some bread, gifts you would give an ageing uncle, a coat, umbrella in case of rain. We leave in an hour. It will do you good to see the danger you play with."

The last words landed hard and heavy in Estere's heart. The danger she played with, the freedom of Latvia. Wasn't that worth any price? She met her father's eyes, heart defiant, but what she saw in the milky blue of his irises broke her heart. And she knew, with a certainty she rarely experienced, they would not find Uncle Artūrs alive.

The streets of Riga were silent and still, doors firmly shut, curtains drawn. Everyone had withdrawn, the fear of a knock on the door a black cloud over the city.

Nikolai kept a swift pace as they wound their way through the twisting streets, heading for Riga Central Station, his limp heavy and pronounced. It did not slow his determined stride.

Breaking through the tight cluster of the central city, the tracks opened before them, leading away into the country beyond.

Nikolai stopped. At his side Estere gasped, her hand flying to her mouth.

Littered along the tracks that led from the city were sheets of paper, hundreds of them, white and gleaming in the morning light. Nikolai walked forward, bending gingerly to gather one from the track.

"What is it?" Estere asked, coming to his side.

"A letter." Nikolai stared at the page in his hand, the lines of his face deepening with sorrow. Blinking fast, he folded the page carefully, before slipping it into his pocket.

"A letter?" Estere was confused.

"The taken. These are letters of farewell, to family, loved ones. They must have thrown them from the train."

Estere looked out along the track, realisation dawning.

"They knew they would not be coming back. They wanted to say goodbye."

Estere swallowed, her throat tight with the horror of understanding.

"Come." Nikolai started moving slowly along the track, gathering page after page after page and slipping them into his cloak.

Estere joined him.

The soldier at Riga Central Station paid them little mind, checking their papers and waving them on. The train was late, but it came. The walk to Artūrs' farm look longer than usual, her father's limp impeding his progress. It had worsened significantly over the course of the day, as if in beat with the growing fear in their hearts. Estere wondered if it was more a mental ailment than truly physical, a way to slow time before he faced what had happened to Uncle Artūrs. She made no comment, simply keeping pace at his side.

From the street the farm seemed normal. All was still, quiet.

But as they got closer, she saw that the front door was unlatched, open. The curtains were drawn against the bright light of day. No one inside had opened them for the morning.

The usual call from brother to brother across the drive never came. They approached the house with caution.

Inside was chaos. Overturned furniture, a broken table, splintered as if someone had been thrown onto it with force. Footprints, large and muddy, were in a matted crisscross over the floor. A few summer leaves, blown in through the open door, dotted the floor with bright green in the curtained gloom.

"Artūrs!" her father finally called, his voice breaking over his brother's name. "Artūrs!"

They checked each room, under the beds, in the cupboards. Nikolai even limped out to the sheds that lined the back of the farm. He returned in silence, saying nothing as he led his daughter from the farmhouse and back to the station. They did not speak the whole train ride home, nor when they finally arrived back at the bakery. Nikolai ascended the stairs without a word, heading for his bed.

There was nothing to say.

"Please stay."

Estere paused at the window, one leg already in the warmth of the summer night. She was exhausted. The poor sleep she'd had the night before and the long journey to and from her uncle's home had sapped all her reserves. But the emotional turmoil she'd shoved deep, deep in her belly would not let her rest. Time enough for that later.

When she and Nikolai had returned home, Zenta had burst into tears. Overwhelmed, her parents had retired immediately to their bedroom. She and her siblings followed not long behind to their own rooms. But Estere could not rest. Not yet. So many had been taken; the broken doors and drawn curtains she'd passed on her way to Jekapils a silent proof of mass abduction. She had to know if Valdis had been one of them.

Sitting in the window, she forced a smile to her lips, trying to show strength for Zenta.

"I will be back swiftly. But I must see Valdis. I must know that he is safe."

"You never come back quickly. You always stay all night," her sister sobbed. The terror and grief of the last twenty-four hours had well and truly stolen Zenta's usual calm compliance, replacing it with desperation.

Guilt twisted in Estere's gut; she knew she should stay and comfort her sister. But she would not. Another emotion, more powerful and possessing, had her in its grip: fear. Fear that Valdis had been a target of the night's events. She could not wait for the morning to find out if he was alive, she'd already paused too long. She had to go to him. Crossing the room, she took a moment to hug Zenta close.

"I will return before sunrise. I promise."

Zenta wrapped her arms around her, pulling her close, burying her face into Estere's body. After a moment, Estere pulled away, squeezed Zenta's shoulders once, her gaze focused over her sister's head. She could not bear to look into Zenta's pleading eyes. She retreated, out the window, down the drainpipe and into the terrified silence of the mid-June night.

Estere crept along the cobblestones, the clack of her shoes too loud in the quiet that had engulfed the city. A warm night, slow to darkness, had once meant gatherings, laughter and shared food. Now, only the insects sang into the gloom. Coming to a row of impressive houses, she paused. Her eyes scanned the street, watching for movement, fearing soldiers and prying eyes. In a nation ruled by fear, neighbour could turn on neighbour, to secure the favour of the oppressors. And after last night everyone would be looking for a way to ensure their own safety.

She waited. Ears straining to hear if soldiers lurked nearby, shivering despite the mildness of the night, Estere wrapped her arms around herself. She should return home to the safety of the bakery, console her sister, be there for her father. She should leave... she could not leave.

Taking a deep breath, she stepped onto the street.

TEN

ESTERE

The front door was ajar. A single light shone in the hallway beyond, casting through the open doorway to illuminate the manicured front lawn. She could see the mantelpiece over the fireplace, the glint of golden picture frames.

Estere's breath caught in her throat. Despite her desperation to find Valdis, in that moment she wanted to run away. She wanted to pretend she didn't already know what had happened here, hold onto hope and ignorance for as long as she could. But she knew she had to go inside. She had to be certain.

Gingerly she stepped over the threshold. The door swung freely on well-oiled hinges. The entrance hall was chaos. The wooden coat rack had been knocked over, presumably caught by the rushing body of an enthusiastic soldier. A gilded mirror lay smashed across the tiles, an overturned lamp by its side. A more privileged mirror image of the destruction she'd just borne witness to at her uncle's home.

Moving further inside, her heels echoed as they struck the hard floors. No other sounds emanated from the house to muffle them.

"Valdis? Tekla? Mr Dreimanis?" Her voice rang out unanswered, just like her clicking heels, but she walked on. She mounted the staircase, taking the steps two at a time, rushing up towards the bedrooms. They were empty, untouched.

Racing back down, she burst into Valdis' reading room. It had been destroyed. The shelves were torn apart, cupboard doors ripped from their hinges. Panic, hot and trembling, seized her in its fist as she surveyed the room. Books lay strewn over the floor, spines snapped, dirty boot prints over the covers. One bookshelf lay on its side, its wooden door partially split. Drawers had been pulled from the writing table, and the contents thrown about the space seemingly at random.

They'd come here for his writings. They'd come here for Valdis.

What had they read in his notes? His newspaper articles praising Lenin and ravaging Stalin? His love of equality and his anger at what Russia had brought to Latvia? Could the soldiers read Latvian? Did it even matter?

Whatever they'd found, Valdis wasn't here.

They had taken him.

A cry tore from the very core of her body, rough and pulsing. She pressed her eyes shut, fingers digging into her lids, trying to block out what she had seen. Red light burst through her senses, panic pure and raw as her limbs began to shake. She had to leave, to get home to the bakery, her family, to her terrified little sister. She had to go.

Valdis was gone.

Her mind fought the truth, desperate to find an alternative reason for his absence. Yet there was none. The Soviets had taken Valdis, and with him all her dreams of their future together.

Her knees gave way. The horror of reality crashing down around her she slumped to the floor as tears cascaded down her cheeks.

· · ·

It was days later that the pebbles pattered on her window.

She didn't bother to get up, she knew it wasn't him. Nothing mattered anymore, her love was gone. She doubted she would ever leave her bed again; there was no point pretending to care. Closing her ears to the shuffling sound of her sister opening the curtains, she pulled her blanket up over her head, as tears welled in her eyes.

"It's Valdis," Zenta chimed.

"What?" she muttered in disbelief. "What did you say?"

'It's Valdis," her sister repeated.

Estere didn't consciously move. Before her mind had even registered Zenta's words she had reached the window and was throwing herself outside it and down the drainpipe, almost slipping in her haste before collapsing into Valdis' arms.

"I thought you were gone. I, I thought you were..." She couldn't say it. To voice her fear was simply too great. She melted into hysterical tears. She'd thought she would never feel his touch, smell his scent, again.

"I'm so, so sorry, my darling," Valdis soothed, holding her firmly against him. "We heard the Reds were rounding people up, so Dāvis and I ran. We hid at Olga's – her place is on the edge of the city, where it meets the forest. I wanted to send word, but it wasn't safe. We had to wait."

"They took my uncle."

She felt his exhale of breath. "Why harm an old man? It's barbaric."

She squeezed him tighter, trying to close every space between them, to know he was really, truly there with her.

"I must return home. Mother will be worried, too. Come with me, stay the night—"

"Home?" Estere pulled back, face turning to his. "You haven't been home yet?"

"No, I came here first." He gently ran a finger down her cheek, soft smile on his lips.

Estere blinked hard, forcing away the selfish surge of pleasure that flooded her body at his presence. He didn't know, she realised. He hadn't yet discovered his parents' fate.

"Valdis," she started, "they are gone."

His head twitched slightly. "Gone? Gone where?"

Her heart broke for him. "They were taken."

"No, no, darling, that's not right. My parents would never have been a target. They complied with all the Soviet orders. You must be mistaken."

Estere shook her head sadly. "Valdis, I went there, the night after everyone was taken. I went looking for you. There was no one there. They were gone."

"They must have been visiting a friend, stayed late."

"The house was trashed..."

But he wasn't listening. Moving away from her down the street, he kept repeating, "No, you must be mistaken." Sorrow heavy in her heart, she followed.

They stood together on dust-kissed cobbles before his parents' home. A warm breeze skittered leaves across the road, blowing the front door wide open.

"Your reading room was ransacked. Books torn apart, papers thrown about..."

Valdis stood in silence, eyes trained on the open doorway.

"Valdis," Estere gripped his arm, turning him to her. "You can't stay here. It's not safe. Come back to the bakery with me. You can stay in Tomass' room..."

He turned from her, striding for the house. "Valdis, please. You don't need to see what's inside."

He didn't heed her warning, walking ahead alone. She held back; she couldn't face it again. Folding her skirts, she sat on the front steps to wait. It wasn't long before his polished shoe scraped the wooden floor behind her. She took a deep breath.

Stepping down, he lowered himself to sit beside her. Thighs pressed together, they sat watching the still early-summer night.

His tears were silent, glistening golden in the fading light.

Reaching over she took his hand in hers, felt the sweat of panic clinging to his palm, then, wrapping her hand around his neck, drew him down to rest his head in her lap. He didn't resist; the reality of his parents' fate had taken the last of his strength. Head in her lap, he stared out at the street. The tears flowed, hot and streaming and silent as he bled his sorrow into the night, wetting her skirts and cutting her heart. His breath came in short gasps, his chest heaving as he gave in to his emotion. She remained silent, hand pressed to his crown, throat bobbing as she struggled to hold in her own sorrow and grief. This was not the time for her pain. Valdis needed her strength now, she knew.

Eventually, he drew himself up. Wiping his face with a shirtsleeve he gazed out at the row of trees that lined his street, branches shifting gently in the evening breeze.

"The Nazis are coming," he said, not turning from the road.

"I know."

"They won't give us our Latvia back."

"No."

He heaved a sigh, his breath wobbling at the edges as he worked to contain his grief.

"Where will you go?" she asked.

She wanted him to say the bakery, to agree to come and live with her, to be with her always. They could marry, work in the store, slowly take over as her parents aged. They could build a life. Perhaps not the one they'd dreamed of together, but a life, good and safe.

Had this horror not shown the danger they dabbled in? The folly of their actions?

But she knew these thoughts were foolish, she knew he would not agree. Perhaps could not. At least not yet.

"I will return to Olga's. Dāvis is still there. We need to talk, to make a plan. This change is an opportunity."

"The Nazis are strong," Estere cautioned. "They are conquering Europe. They took Paris in a month! How can Riga stand where Paris could not?"

"Armies cannot win forever. Latvia's time will come. We must prepare our people. The newsletter, the truth, is more important now than ever."

Estere closed her eyes, resigned. His choice would be to fight on for Latvia. With his parents now lost to the cause, he would never give up. The life she had pictured for them once again drifted away from her reach.

It would mean months apart, only seeing each other in secret, Valdis living on the edge of danger. But she would not argue. How could she? A free Latvia. It was a dream she believed in, too. It was the answer to her desires just as much as it was to his.

And he was right, change was coming. The Nazis would be in the city within the month. Change could be opportunity.

They had to go on. They had to fight for each other.

One day, a long time afterwards, Estere would learn the truth of what happened that fateful night, the 14th of June, 1941. A night that would become known as "The Night of the Disappeared", when over fifteen thousand Latvians were stolen. Men separated from women, husbands from wives, fathers from children, deported to Siberian work camps to toil away the war and pray for the liberation of death, while their families struggled to survive in remote Russian villages on the edge of the Union.

But that night, as she sat on a stair before a ruined home, the only soul she cared about was the man held tight within her embrace. Nothing would part them, she swore to herself fervently. She had known what it was like to lose him once, and would never let that happen again.

ELEVEN

CRISSY

2018

Crissy sits on the bed flicking through her phone. Mamina-Zee has been napping on and off for most of the day. That turn she had was quite a scare. Crissy closes her eyes, steadies her breath. Zenta is old now, very old. Crissy knows she has to prepare for the inevitable. But she's just not ready yet.

Her phone bleeps. A message from Neil.

> See you at Mamina's by 2pm tomorrow. Kids will be fed. Xx

Her heart stutters at those two little crosses.

Stupid. Neil's made his position clear. Their marriage is over.

Checking the time, nearly 5pm, Crissy rolls her neck and propels herself off the saggy mattress. Her back aches from sleeping on it, the springs have well and truly seen better days. But Zenta won't buy a new one, she knows that, there's no point asking. Her great-aunt dislikes change.

Crissy definitely takes after her on that one.

She slips quietly into the kitchen; she doesn't want to disturb Zenta. Opening the fridge, she collects salted mackerel, pickles and soured cream, places them on the table.

Her hand lingers on the supermarket cream. Such a shame, she thinks. In her youth, Mamina had always made her own. Old Bill would bring fresh milk from his dairy farm and together she and Mamina would churn it until it thickened. The dairy had been part of everyday life. As a girl, with no father, and in the absence of her mother, Aina, Old Bill had filled a gap in her life. She loved the old man.

Sighing, she collects potatoes from the pantry.

She lights a match and sets the water to boil for the potatoes, turns to the sink to peel them. Zenta likes them peeled. Aina, Crissy's mother, does not.

Crissy always peels her potatoes.

She watches the backyard as she peels, the galahs are pecking through the grass, searching for insects in the cooling earth. Zenta's canaries chirp, the tinkle of the small dangling bells she hangs for them to play with rises gaily. The trees are shaded in the gentle pastels of sunset. It's peaceful. It's home.

Crissy was only four when Aina left her here. Terrified, confused. She didn't know she could cry so many tears, didn't understand where they all came from.

But Mamina-Zee had wiped them all away. Gave her rye pudding, and ice cream. Read her a bedtime story from an old book with dog-eared pages, torn edges on the cover.

It had been her mother's book, she learned later. Crissy pauses her peeling, idly wondering where that book is now. No doubt Zenta has it stored somewhere.

Running the potatoes under the tap to clear the last of the dirt from their white flesh, she moves to the stove, plops them in the bubbling water. A small splash flies up from the pot, lands on her hand. It sizzles, and stings. Crissy rubs it roughly with her other hand.

She needs dill.

Out in the yard she bends over Zenta's small vegetable garden. It's overflowing with greenery, beetroots, potatoes, carrots, parsley, dill, rosemary. As she flicks her knife to slice off the stalks of dill for the salad, the herby scent floats up to her nose. Familiar, comforting.

She's struck again by how calm she feels here. It has always been the way, from the first night she spent on this land.

Crissy never wanted to leave, not permanently at least. The plan was always to return after her teacher training, get a job in the local primary school in Renmark, or a little further on in Berri. Teaching the children of farmers and townies, to become part of this Riverland community forever.

But the city lights were dazzling, the energy of the people intoxicating. And then she met Neil, fell in love and that was that. She found work in the city, until she had Lily. By then Neil made enough at his firm for her to stay home with the kids.

Now Neil had moved out, and Mamina-Zee was old.

And who was going to hire an almost fifty-year-old teacher who hadn't worked in fourteen years?

Crissy felt adrift. Lost. Just like she had as a child when Aina left her here.

Straightening from the vegetable garden, determination settles across Crissy's face. Her own children won't know the uncertainty of having unreliable parents. Crissy won't let that happen, whatever Neil decides.

Back inside, the potatoes have softened, she drains the pot, sets them to cool. She's boiled too many for just her and Zenta to eat. There will be leftovers. There should always be leftovers, her great-aunt had taught her that.

The soft scuff of socks raises her head. Zenta appears in the archway. Her face is drawn, tired. Somehow she looks even older than her eighty-nine years. Crissy's heart lurches.

"Mamina-Zee!" she says, voice light. "Dinner is almost ready, you can rest in the lounge while I finish."

Zenta looks at her, eyes still sharp, despite her age. "You are my guest, I cook for you."

Crissy grins at her stubbornness. "It's no bother. You cooked for me my whole childhood. This is the least I can do to repay you."

She laughs. "You make me sound like a project."

"No, like a beloved relative." Crissy crosses the room, presses a kiss to Mamina's forehead. Her skin is papery, dry. But hot.

"If you'd rather sit with me?"

Zenta nods, allows Crissy to take her arm and help her into a chair at the kitchen table. Her legs are still wobbly from her turn earlier in the day.

What did that woman on the phone say to her?

Crissy wants to ask, but she knows Zenta well. Gently, gently.

She brings the potatoes, dill and pickles to the table, then starts assembling the salad.

"The day is still so warm, I thought a cold dinner. Salted fish, potato salad. Sound good?"

Zenta eyes the potatoes. Sniffs. "I suppose it will be enough."

Crissy ignores her grumbling, chops the potatoes and pickles, adds a healthy dollop of cream, sprinkles it all in dill. It smells amazing.

As they plate up their meals, she broaches the elephant in the room.

"So," Crissy ventures, "you took a nasty turn there, Mamina-Zee. Are you going to tell me who that was on the phone?"

"No," Zenta says simply, hands shaking as she slices into her mackerel.

Crissy watches her chew, the movement is awkward and Zenta pauses. Probably her dentures slipping a little in her mouth again. She should get new ones fitted, another thing she refuses to consider.

"Mamina." Crissy sighs. "She obviously upset you. After you got wobbly and I put you to bed to calm, she was still on the phone... she was worried about you."

Her hands stop dead over her plate, hovering above her potato.

"You spoke to her?"

"Of course. I went to hang up the phone and she was still there."

Crissy sees the bob of her throat, the flicker of her eyes. "What did she say?"

"She just asked if you were all right. I said you'd had a funny turn and needed rest. She understood, wished you well. Was sorry to have bothered you."

"That was all?"

"Of course. Why would she question it? You are an old woman, Mamina."

Her body relaxes, limbs going slack and loose. Reaching forward she pats Crissy on the hand, smiling at her. "Thank you for taking care of me."

"Mamina." Crissy looks directly at her great-aunt, eyes sad. "I will always take care of you."

The old woman turns away, knife and fork clattering onto the table.

"I must feed the canaries," she announces, pushing herself to her feet.

"Mamina... I can do that."

"No, no. It is always me. How will my babies sleep if they don't see their māte before bed?"

She shuffles for the door and Crissy sighs.

No answers tonight then. She gathers up the plates, covers

the leftover potato salad in plastic wrap and finds a spot in the fridge. The kids can enjoy it tomorrow.

As she runs the hot water tap, filling the sink for the dishes, she ponders. That woman, her voice kind, nervous, her accent heavily American.

What on earth could she have to do with Mamina-Zee?

PART TWO

UNDER THE NAZI FLAG 1941–1943

TWELVE

ZENTA

1941

Barely two weeks after the Soviet's mass deportation of citizens of Riga, the Nazis arrived. The ring of machine-gun fire and the pounding of explosions rattled Riga for hours as the soldiers fought to cross the Daugava. In the end, the Soviets retreated, leaving behind a battered city, the town hall square, Rathaus-platz, razed to the ground, the spire of St Peter's Cathedral engulfed in flame.

And yet the city celebrated.

High beaming rays of orange sunlight kissed the streets as young women in polka-dotted cotton and young men with sleeves rolled up gathered to usher the Nazi soldiers into Riga. The Germans marched in neat rows, buttons gleaming, as they passed the Brīvības piemineklis, the swastika raised against the memorial. Heroes, saviours, liberators. Cries of joy rang loud and happy to the beat of the Nazi boot.

The German army pushed the Reds out of the rest of the country within a matter of weeks, the Russians broken easily under the mechanised might of the German War Machine.

As the Germans advanced, the Reds fled, along with many Latvians, Communists in fear of retribution and Jews in fear of labour camps. Many carried nothing more than the thin summer shirt on their back.

But on the whole, Latvia celebrated. And Nikolai retreated into himself even further.

Tomass, buoyed by a belief that freedom was at hand for his people, signed up for the German-administrated Latvian Auxiliary Police almost immediately. On the day the soldiers marched into central Riga, he raced to the Freedom Monument to watch their liberators arrive. Zenta and Estere followed, drawn by the energy of the gathering crowd of revellers. Nikolai remained at home, in bed.

Zenta stood silent, watching as the young Rigan women, hair freshly curled, lips painted bright, chatted and flirted with young, fresh-faced soldiers, beaming smiles on everyone's faces. People danced and cheered, pinning the startling red and black of the Nazi flag to the Freedom Monument.

At her side Estere was restless, scanning the crowd before making her excuses and heading away. Tomass whooped with delight and fell in with the excited throngs. Zenta stayed on the edge of the celebrations. She'd been drawn to the square by the promise of hope and joy, but surrounded by the jubilant people of her city, she felt more alone than ever.

The change in her father since the disappearance of Uncle Artūrs, and her own grief at her uncle's assumed fate, pressed against her heart and slowed her step. Nikolai had not worked in the bakery for weeks now. He remained in his room throughout the daylight hours, only to shuffle out for a quick supper, before returning straight after. And Estere was barely home, slipping out nightly, often not even returning for breakfast.

Their absence left the running of the bakery entirely to Zenta and Dārta. It had meant a reprieve from school for Zenta,

Dārta needing her home to help with the daily tasks of running a home and business. But it was hard to be glad of it as she moved through the unnatural quiet of her family home. Her mother said nothing of her husband's missing presence, nor her daughter's nocturnal activities. Face set, she simply pressed on, eyes tight and tired. Grief affected people in different ways, Zenta knew. Nikolai was the last of his family left. She could not imagine how she would feel if she lost her family...

A warm hand slipped into hers.

Glancing at her side she found Ava, large brown eyes round with apprehension.

"Mumma wanted to leave," Ava whispered, lips almost pressed to Zenta's ear to be heard over the din of celebration. "But Father says we are Latvian and have nothing to fear."

Zenta squeezed her dear friend's hand tight as they watched more and more soldiers march into their city. The rumours of the Nazi treatment of Jews, of labour camps and imprisonment, were so well circulated even children had heard them, driving many to take their chances with Russia. But more remained than left. Memories of the "polite" Germans of the Great War and their gentle treatment of all Latvians were still fresh. As were the scars of Soviet control and the horrors of the deportations just weeks ago. What could possibly be worse than that?

Returning home that afternoon Zenta found her parents deep in conversation. It was the first time she'd seen her father out of bed in days. White shirt creased and yellowing at the armpits, hair uncombed, he hunched over the table, hands out in supplication to his wife.

Tension fizzed in the air between them. Zenta hung back, listening.

"You have to talk to him, Nikolai. Karlis listens to you. You have heard the rumours, you know the danger Rosa and Ava face. It passes down the maternal line. Karlis is safe, but his daughter..."

"I tried, Dārta. Please. He would not hear of leaving his home. And why should he? He fought for this country, just as I did."

"You are not a Jew."

Her father grimaced at that. Raising a shaking hand to his hair, he ran nervous fingers through the thinning blond strands.

"It is too late, you know this," he said, reaching for Dārta's hand. "The Nazis are here. The borders will be closed. It is too late."

Her mother pulled her hand from his grip, moving to the window, turning her back on her husband.

Silently Zenta slipped back to the stairs, heading up for her room. All she wanted was to be alone. Away from a world of ideas and hopes and fears. Away from opinions and possibility. To just exist, silent and safe beneath her woollen blankets.

That night as she hid beneath her covers, eyes pressed tight against the outside world, Riga burned. The stink of smoke, thick and acrid, pulled her from her cocoon and she knelt before her window, trembling. Fires lit the summer night, a brilliant and terrible orange; buildings across the city burned.

She saw him approach through the hazy streets and shimmied down the drainpipe to meet him.

His breath was fast, eyes filled with fear. "They are burning the synagogues. Quickly, we must go!"

Hand in hand, Zenta and Aleks rushed through the smoked-out streets to Ava's home. It was empty, the lights off, the door unlocked. Shock rattled through her body as she worked to slow her breathing.

Aleks could not meet her eye. "Perhaps they got out."

Zenta nodded. "Yes, perhaps." A shiver travelled up her spine and she closed her arms around herself in an embrace.

Her father's words loomed in her mind: "Too late." But she pressed them down. The hope in Aleks' face was too fragile, too raw. She would not shatter it.

The two friends stayed together to watch as the first rays of the sun broke over the smoke-filled city, the fires still raging, the air a palette of grey and ash. The coals of the synagogues smouldered for days afterwards.

A new newspaper began distribution, one stamped with the Nazi symbol, its pages filled with articles encouraging the good people of Riga to name their hidden Jewish neighbours. One article reminded the citizens of Riga of the ways in which the Jews had hurt Latvia. Worse, it was declared no longer a crime to attack a Jew. The Nazis' efforts to turn Rigan against Rigan horrified Zenta.

And their efforts worked. Under the domes of Riga Central Market, as Zenta trailed behind her mother on shopping day, she saw a tall, thin man, dressed all in black, begging the fishmonger to serve him.

"Please, sir," he cried, "I have money."

Rows of fish lined the market, the smell thick and close. There was no shortage, no reason to deny this man his purchase. And yet...

"No Jews," the fishmonger proclaimed, turning his back on the man while his stall brimmed with fish flesh.

Zenta stopped in shock, mouth gaping at the scene. The man, the Star of David bright against the black of his cloak, hung his head, eyes to the floor. The urgent tug of her mother's hand pulled Zenta from her gazing, and she allowed herself to be hurried away by Dārta's swift pace.

Within a week the ghetto was erected. Not much more than strands of barbed wire held up by wooden stakes. But it was intimidating nonetheless. The people of the Moscow Quarter were moved out, and Jewish citizens rounded up and moved in. Zenta watched as the soldiers went from house to house collecting the Jewish owners, then, after the civilians were moved out, the soldiers returned to take their belongings. Paintings, furniture, jewellery, boxes and boxes and boxes of possessions, loaded onto trucks and driven to the German barracks.

Zenta started a new routine. Aided by the early light of a particularly hot summer, she made her way to the ghetto each morning, seeking a glimpse of Ava or her family, and at the same time hoping desperately that she would not succeed. From a laneway near the edge of the camp she watched. People milled behind the wire fence, black armbands adorned with a yellow Star of David on their upper arms. Groups would be let out in the morning, mostly men being led to work details on the outskirts of the city. Some were taken to the town hall square where they toiled, clearing the ruins of the House of the Black-heads with shovels and their bare hands. Women and children remained within.

The men became grubbier and grubbier, the women and children gaunt. The quarter was one of the oldest in the city. Unlike her own home, few of the houses in the Moscow Quarter were plumbed so there was little running water, and no electricity. A trench was dug in the centre of the ghetto for the residents to dispose of their bodily wastes, becoming an open pit of excrement in the heat of the summer sun, the stench blown out through the old town by the breezes off the Daugava.

The people of the city complained. The Nazis did nothing.

Zenta watched as the people grew dirtier, their clothes worn and torn, their faces drawn, eyes hollow. As the cool winds that whispered of coming autumn blew through the quarter, the first coughs of disease rang out from between the barbed wire. Soon bodies began to appear, wrapped in rags and piled by the makeshift gates to the ghetto. Collected by soldiers, placed in trucks and driven away.

As the first snows fell, the filth of the pit froze, bringing relief from the stink of piss and shit. Zenta still had not spied her friend. Each night she sent a prayer to God that Ava and her family had somehow, against her father's belief, made it out, and had gone East, away from this hell the Nazis had created in the heart of Riga.

Watching the men return from the workday, bloody hands bright red against the black of dirt on their skin, eyes gazing far away, Zenta didn't think it could get any worse for the Jews of her city.

She could not have been more wrong.

THIRTEEN
ZENTA

"The Jews are all lined up. In rows. They have spotlights out. Something is happening," Zenta cried as she burst into the bakery. She'd snuck out early, before her mother rose to start the working day, and had made her way to the ghetto. The Jews were always up early, to prepare for work detail, but the soldiers were slower, cold and tired from the night watch. The perfect time to stand in the shadows and search for Ava.

But this morning had been different. Large, bright spotlights lit up the barbed-wire fencing. And within, huddled in neat rows, was the population of the Riga Ghetto. Zenta raced home to tell her mother.

Dārta, working the morning flour, looked up, concern writ large across her pale face. She turned, deftly wiping the wet flour from her hands, and made her way to the door. Collecting her coat, hat, gloves and securing her scarf in place with a knot at her throat, she led her daughter back into the frozen November pre-dawn.

"Show me."

In silence, mother and daughter linked arms, pressing their bodies together against the icy wind and the rising fear.

If they'd learned anything from the Soviet occupation, it was caution.

Their heels slipped treacherously over ice-coated cobbles. Piles of snow, dirt-stained from the road, lined their path as they made their way down to the riverside and the Moscow Quarter. About them the early morning was still and silent; a few lamps glowed in curtained windows, but most were dark, the occupants still asleep. Bed was the warmest place to be.

They paused in the darkness of a laneway, peering around the brick wall of someone's home to watch. The ghetto was a hive of activity. Soldiers, guns held before them in open threat, paraded up and down row after row of lined-up Jewish citizens. The people stood still and close, drawing their coats tight against the light feathers of snow that had just begun to fall.

Zenta felt her mother's body suddenly relax.

"There are women and children too," she said. "And they all have a suitcase. It is all right. They must be moving them to a more suitable holding. The sanitation here was never good enough."

It was a measure of how bad things had become for the people of the ghetto, that even the possibility of a new prison seemed hopeful. As if to highlight the understatement, a gust of wind off the Daugava pressed the stench of unwashed bodies against their noses. Zenta ducked her face beneath her scarf, seeking respite from the foul air. But her mother's words had soothed her. The ghetto had always seemed rushed, makeshift. It was good that the Jews would now have a nicer place to stay.

Maybe the Nazis were even going to let them return to their own homes?

Zenta and her mother stayed and watched. Despite the presence of women and children, and her mother's reassurance, she was still nervous. Occupiers were rarely to be trusted.

As the sun rose tentatively over the Daugava, casting a pale yellow light over the waiting Jewish people, more German soldiers marched into view. They lined up along the railway track that led south, out of Riga. Suddenly, shouted orders echoed through the air, and the Jews startled into motion, walking, row by orderly row out of the ghetto and along the soldier-lined railway tracks.

"They are walking. Wherever they were going must be close. That is good," Dārta said, a quaver in her voice revealing her tension. They watched in silence as the Jews of Riga were marched out of the ghetto, down the track and into the distance, until the last couple, old and hunched, shuffled slowly out of the barbed-wire prison.

"Have hope," Dārta said, though she squeezed her daughter's hand too tightly, and pulled her away.

Zenta nodded, and they made their way back to the bakery and their daily chores.

The darkness of winter had come early that year, bringing strong frozen winds and deep black nights. It was as if the season was screaming its anger at the war and the cruelty inflicted by man.

For Zenta and the people of Latvia, it simply meant further hardship, scarcity and fear.

After their morning at the ghetto, mother and daughter had worked in the bakery, using the familiar daily tasks to busy their minds, a distraction from the gnawing fear for their friends and fellow Rigans who now marched out of the city. To where? To what fate? There was no way to know.

When the final rays of pale winter light left the sky and no customers came, Dārta left Zenta to close up. Zenta watched as her mother plodded up the stairs, back hunched, step slow. She could feel Dārta's fatigue, sense the effort even this everyday task cost her as she made her way to the little room she shared with her husband, to find sleep and some short respite from this world, so weighed down by occupation and sorrow.

Zenta felt her own eyes droop and she longed to snuggle beneath the covers and escape into the world of her imagination. But she was responsible; she would finish the bakery tasks first.

After packing away the unsold bread, wiping down the kitchen benches, ovens and the sales counter, then setting out the flour for the morning baking, she took up the broom to give the floor a final sweep. Bending down with the dustpan to collect up the tiny pile of dirt she'd swept from the wooden floor, movement outside the storefront window caught her eye. Zenta looked up sharply, watching the darkness beyond the window, frowning. A trick of the light? Her own nerves playing with her senses? She remained still, crouched on the floor, eyes on the window and the night beyond. There! A flash of movement in the dull light of the streetlamp, the scuff of footfall. Rising slowly, Zenta paced to the door and poked her head out into the night.

There before the shop was her brother, his tall frame encased in the green coat of a soldier. It had been months since she last saw Tomass. His duty for the Latvian Auxiliary Police, and Nikolai's frank disapproval of his son's choice, kept him from visiting. He bent over himself, as if pulling into his body, to become smaller, to shrink, as he paced back and forth, back and forth in tight marches beneath the streetlamp. His movements quick, jerky, tense, leaving a path of footprints in the snow-dusted street, crunching as he trod. His pale blond hair, cropped tight to his scalp, peeked out from beneath a woollen beanie. The air before him misted with his breath.

Zenta stepped into the night, closing the door softly behind her. Something told her not to startle Tomass. Wrapping her arms about herself against the cold – she'd not thought to draw on her coat – she stepped from the light of the shop window towards her brother.

"Tomass?" she whispered softly.

His head snapped round, wide eyes glinting yellow like a wolf's in the darkness. He saw her, recognition contorting his face in anguish.

"Tomass," she said, "will you come inside?" She gestured towards the shop.

As if only just considering the idea, Tomass looked up at the door to the bakery. Tears welled in his eyes, his mouth quivered.

"I..."

They heard footsteps down the street, and both their heads turned.

"Hello, soldier?" A German soldier stepped into view. Uniform freshly pressed, pristine, eyes shining, skin unlined. A boy, barely older than Zenta.

Tomass whipped around, arms flailing, stepping back from the approaching German.

"No, no, no..." he stammered, hands out before him.

The German stopped, confusion flitting across his face.

"What is wrong?" he asked, his Latvian heavily accented as he addressed Tomass.

"Nein!" Tomass screamed, reaching into his coat and drawing out a small pistol.

Zenta gasped in horror as her brother brought the gun up. But he did not point it at the young German, instead he pressed it to his own temple, his hand shaking so badly Zenta feared he would drop the gun, or worse, pull the trigger accidentally.

Tomass screamed again. "Nein, nein, nein!"

Bewildered, the young German glanced at Zenta. But her eyes never left her brother.

'Stop!" she shrieked. "Tomass?" Her throat closed over, choking her words as she reached towards her brother.

Behind her the bakery door opened and closed.

A presence, solid, dependable and familiar stepped up beside her.

Nikolai stood in silence, taking in the scene before him.

Then he stepped to his son, hands wide before him, stance hunched, unthreatening. Zenta's relief at her father's arrival quickly turned to fear for his safety.

"My son," he said, "it is all right. I am here."

Tomass whirled around, gun still at his temple, and looked at his father.

His face cracked, tears cascading down his face. He wobbled.

Slowly Nikolai stepped forward. Reaching out he took his son's head in his hands, bringing their foreheads together. There, surrounded by light flurries of snow that settled in a blanket of white over the cobbled street, father and son stood, foreheads pressed together in the dark. Nikolai murmured something to Tomass, too low for Zenta to hear. Suddenly Tomass slumped forward bodily. Deftly, Nikolai stepped into his fall, catching his son, pulling the gun from his hand and throwing it into the now mounting snow.

Seeing his chance, the young German spun and ran, his heavy boots pounding the street and echoing through the night.

"Zenta, get the gun," Nikolai said. "We can't have it left on the street."

Zenta stood staring, too shocked to move.

"Zenta," her father repeated, the urgency of his tone breaking through her fear. She obeyed, warily picking up the cold metal object, holding it far from her body. It was surprisingly heavy for such a small item.

Behind her Nikolai was crooning to Tomass.

"It is all right, my son. It is all right. Come inside. Come inside."

Sobbing heavily, Tomass allowed his father to lead him from the frozen dark of the city into the warm light of the bakery.

Zenta followed, gun held gingerly before her, pausing only to lock the shop door. Even inside, out of the cold air, she was shaking.

The sweeping could wait.

They gathered in the kitchen on the second floor. Dārta boiled water for broth, Zenta cut thick slices of day-old bread. At the table Tomass sat, head in hands, shoulders shaking. Nikolai at his side, an arm around his child's waist, as though Tomass were a boy again.

Zenta buttered the bread and placed it before her brother. Then she took a seat. Dārta, cup of broth now at Tomass' elbow, stood behind her son, one hand on his neck, fingers running soothing circles through the nape of his light hair. They waited in silence as Tomass' sobbing eased. Until he was ready to speak.

"I was wrong. I..." His voice broke, tears once again flooding down his cheeks.

Behind him Dārta placed a hand over her mouth, holding back the grief of a mother as she watched a child of her body in so much pain.

"Speak," Nikolai said gently. "We will listen."

Tomass swallowed loudly, his throat bobbing.

"We were called from our barracks in the middle of the night, to round up the Jews. 'One suitcase per adult. Warm clothes.' We were moving them, I thought."

Zenta met her mother's eyes over Tomass' head. The ghetto.

"After they were woken and organised, my battalion was driven out of town. We were stationed in a line along the railway. An unbroken wall of soldiers from Riga into the forest at Rumbala. It was dark, and so, so cold. My breath clouded before me. I stomped my feet to be warm." He paused, fingers flexing subconsciously, continued.

"Then, as the sun shone over the tops of the pine trees, I saw the first people.

"They were in a line, walking slowly. They passed me, weary, tired, wide-eyed. A small boy looked up at me as he passed, his hand clutching his mother's skirts, a toy hedgehog hugged to his chest.

"I... I smiled at him. To reassure him. He, he looked scared, unsure. I wanted him to feel safe. He smiled back, gave me a little wave..."

Tomass stopped, face contorting into a rictus of anguish.

"I didn't know!" he screamed, voice breaking. "You must believe me, I didn't know!"

Lurching forward, Tomass clutched Nikolai's hands, gripping onto his father as if his life depended on it.

After a short time, he was composed enough to go on. "A motorbike went by, an old man on its back, being driven along the train line, into the forest beyond. Where the people were walking.

"It was only a few minutes later that I heard it. Gunfire. Screams. They rang out through the forest."

Dārta gasped, clutching her chest.

"The Jews stopped walking then, looking around them, afraid. The men started shouting. Next to me a German soldier ordered them to keep walking. To keep walking towards the sound of gunfire. One man tried to run. He pushed past us, breaking free of the line. The German shot him in the back. Then he raised his gun, I thought he was going to..." Tomass swallowed, head shaking.

Zenta gripped the table, bracing herself against the horror of her brother's words.

"He fired into the air, screaming at the Jews to walk. We were ordered to point our guns, at the Jews. To make them walk.

"I... I... unslung my gun. The little boy was just ahead, he looked back at me. At me, with my gun. But the Germans kept shouting, forcing the people forward. They killed them. They killed them all."

Wild-eyed, Tomass looked up, spit collected on his lips.

"And I ran. The screams, the guns, the terrified faces, the little boy. I couldn't. I ran and ran and ran. Then I was here."

Tomass collapsed into hysterics again. Horror descended over them all.

Zenta's heart pounded in her chest, so fast it felt it would burst from her skin. It was too much. Children gunned to death. Her stomach roiled, nausea flooding her senses, threatening to make her sick.

The Jews of Riga had been massacred.

Loud banging rang up the stairs, replacing their frozen shock with molten fear. Nikolai stood swiftly, shoulders braced, face set. "Zenta, the gun."

Quickly she passed the awful item to her father. He held it with a familiar calm.

"No," Tomass whispered. "I must face this."

"I will tell them you are in bed. Sick with fever," Dārta suggested, voice begging.

"No." Tomass stood and embraced his father, his mother. Both parents went still in his arms, accepting his decision, savouring this last moment.

The banging grew louder. Shouted demands. Threats.

"I must go."

"No," Nikolai choked. "We will tell them..."

"I love you," Tomass said, cutting him off.

Then he turned. Meeting Zenta's eyes he curved his lips in the imitation of a smile, winked at her as he always did. There was no joy in the gesture.

"Tell Estere I love her," he said, then, face filled with sorrow, he made for the door. Dārta stepped forward, but Nikolai stopped her with a touch of his hand. She burst into tears and Nikolai wrapped his wife in his arms, and they both sobbed.

Zenta followed her brother, head reeling, mouth opening and closing as she sought the words to stop his tread, to turn him back to them, and keep him from the Nazis waiting at the door. No words came. She watched as he opened the bakery door, as black-gloved hands reached in and grabbed him, pulling him from the shop and into the unknown.

She never saw him again.

Daylight brought the full story of the horrors of that night. Spread fast on the whispered breath of a city in shock, the cruel and calculated extermination of the Jews of Riga was shared first by soldiers and ghetto workers, then the people of the streets, the families left behind, everyone. Told to pack a suit-case, to line up in family groups, fed lies to keep them calm. Then they'd been marched to a killing field. Set on a hill in the Rumbala forest, a pit had been dug, deep into the hilltop. The Jews, forced along by guns and threats, had been marched into the forest, forced to strip off their clothes then climb into the pit where they were mowed down by gunfire. Group after group forced into the pit to stand on the bodies of those who went before them and be shot. Men, women, children, the old. All but the healthiest workers, those of value to the regime, were put to death. Twenty-six thousand lives taken over two days of slaughter, November the 30th and December the 8th.

When the full extent of what had happened made it to the bakery door, Nikolai closed the store, disappearing upstairs once again, Dārta's hand in his.

Tomass was not the only Latvian man who deserted. Faced with the true horror of what they had joined, many ran.

But most stayed. Too afraid for their own lives and their families to do anything else.

Those that ran were labelled Traitor. Executed.

Those that didn't were broken men, hollowed out by the shame stitched into the lining of their souls. Locked forever in an internal battle, searching for a forgiveness their hearts could never accept.

FOURTEEN

ESTERE

"It's too much." Valdis paced before Estere, eyes wild with horror. So many lives, almost the entire population of the ghetto, machine-gunned to death in a frozen pit, only a two-hour walk from their city.

"And your brother."

Her chest tightened. Tomass. Not only her brother, her first best friend. When her mother had told her she had broken down, unable to stifle the heaving sobs that racked her body. Dārta had gathered her in her arms, but even the familiarity of her mother's smell, her firm touch, had not brought comfort.

Just one year her senior, she'd grown up beside Tomass, in his presence. She closed her eyes, picturing him, his pale hair and straight nose a mirror of her own, his eyes shining with humour. For as long as she could remember, he was always there.

And when it had mattered, she wasn't. Away from home as she so often was these days, Estere had missed her brother's final moments with the family. Could she have helped him? Convinced him to run, to hide? Would he still be alive if she had just been there?

She closed her eyes, steeling herself against the anguish in her heart.

His sunny smile, his easy laugh.

Gone now. Gone forever.

"We should have stopped this," Valdis continued. "But we stood by and watched while our citizens were slaughtered!"

"Valdis, please." Estere stood from the small worn couch and moved to her lover's side. She needed his warmth, his strength, his comfort. Not his anger.

They were at Olga's, in the spare room she'd set up to keep Valdis hidden from the Soviets. The house was set on a small plot of land on the city's edge. Old but solid wooden slats coated in peeling white paint, wooden floors in need of a polish, Olga had inherited it from her father, and raised chickens and grew beets there. When the Nazis came the men had stayed small, unnoticed, the loss of Valdis' parents looming large over every choice. But none of them were good at following the orders of occupiers.

When the new underground newspaper, *Brīvā Latvija*, Free Latvia, began sharing articles defending the Jews and promoting independence, Valdis took up his pen once more. But cautiously, taking care not to draw attention to himself or his friends.

Now these actions seemed insignificant. Cowardly. What did it matter if they wrote a few words when thousands of Rigan citizens had just been slaughtered? What had they done to stop it?

Turning Valdis around to face her, Estere smoothed his hair gently, hoping to still his fluttering rage.

He pulled away from her touch.

"We'd heard the rumours. The stories from Poland made it across our borders. Why did we think our people would be treated any differently?"

Estere closed her eyes, as pain throbbed in her chest. Not

knowing the full truth was the worst part. Neighbours, friends, her sister's darling Ava, were they all lost now? Buried beneath the blood and frozen flesh of the next row of prisoners marched to their deaths? Or did they get out? Make it to the borders before the Nazis closed the country?

It was a pitiful, unlikely hope.

Valdis paced to the small, cracked window and gazed out at the ice-tipped trees of the surrounding forest.

It was not only Jews put to death at Rumbala, but also the Roma, the disabled and the resistance. Men like her Valdis.

Pushing down the flare of dread that threatened to turn her guts to water, Estere followed Valdis to the window. Cold air seeped through the poorly fitted frame; the ice of Riga would not be held at bay. She wrapped her arms around his waist, seeking his warmth and the solidness of his presence. For now, at least, he was safe.

"There is a way." Valdis spoke suddenly, breaking the gentle moment.

"A way?"

"A way to make a difference."

He pulled from her arms and took her face in his hands.

"It is a grave risk. Dangerous," he warned.

"Whatever it is, I am with you," Estere interrupted, fervour racing on her blood. They had taken her city, they had taken *Tomass*, her own flesh and blood, her big brother.

Nothing and no one was safe. They could not go on pretending that compliance was enough to keep the Nazis from the door. They had to do more.

For Valdis, for her brother, for Latvia, she would risk it all.

"Dāvis knows a man, from when he worked at the docks. Žanis Lipkes. He is nothing special, just a man who has seen too much and done too little. As have we all."

"Go on."

"When the Nazis first came he hid a Jewish family at the

local theatre, to keep them from the ghetto. But a conspirator told on him. The family were put to death. Žanis was lucky his own name was not shared."

Estere took a deep breath, and held it. She wanted to block her ears, to turn the conversation away, to stop the inevitable tide that was now in motion, from what she knew Valdis was about to suggest.

"It won't stop him. He has a network of other hiding locations: cellars, attics, sheds, barns. He plans to rescue the men who remain in the ghetto and hide them in safety. They might have been spared Rumbala, but they will face the same fate soon enough."

"But how?"

"Smuggling. Žanis has a history... he used to smuggle moonshine from the docks. Small things, so he did not lose his job. But he is persuasive."

"I don't understand."

"He has a job, working for the Nazis transporting the men from the ghetto to their work detail. Every few days, he smuggles one away."

"To a cellar?"

"To wait out the war. There are plans to get them out of the country. But for now, he must hide them. Indefinitely."

Estere watched her lover's face, saw the passion and hope there, read the fear he worked hard to conceal.

He was right, it was dangerous. But if they didn't try, those men in the ghetto were already as good as dead.

She made her decision.

"What can I do?"

Valdis paused, swallowed, then said, "Žanis needs food to feed the hidden men. Olga, Dāvis and I will work to help with supplies, through the black market and... donations."

A whoosh of air escaped Estere's lungs. Of course. It would be months, years possibly before a route out of Latvia could be cultivated. A long time to keep hungry mouths fed. But Estere's family ran a bakery. Their supply of flour and grain was assured, to help feed the city.

"I know the Nazis keep strict tallies on supplies..."

"I can do it," Estere interrupted. She didn't know how, but she would find a way. "Mother is a wonder at stretching food, I can skim from our rations. And with the bakery, I can alter the numbers... make smaller loaves."

"We can all go with less, give you our ration cards to fill but give the supplies to the Jews. Do you think it can work?"

Estere thought a moment, then firmed her shoulders, standing tall. "We have to try."

"It will mean hardship for you, and your family."

"It is the right thing to do."

Valdis closed his eyes then drew Estere in close and tight. "Bring the supplies here. I will take them to Žanis. The less involvement you have, the safer you will be."

He touched her cheek, and smiled softly. Her heart soared with love for this brave, brave man. Her man.

"You must be safe."

"I will," he promised.

The morning air felt as though shards of ice floated on its currents, pricking her flesh like tiny frozen needles. Estere rubbed her face in the dark, willing life into her skin. She was out of practice. How long had it been since she'd joined her family for the morning baking? She was a selfish daughter.

But not today.

Forcing her cold-cramped body from her bed, Estere stumbled on numb feet to her wash basin. Splashing freezing water over her face certainly woke her up. Dressing quickly, she headed down to the bakery kitchen. There Zenta was, sleeves rolled to her elbows, a sheen of flour already floating about her head as she kneaded a ball of dough. On the bench before her sat five perfectly prepared loaves, left to rise before baking. The oven fire was not yet lit, so the room was still cool. Estere paced to the great oven, pulled open the steel hatch and started adding kindling to the coals that simmered in its bowels, the remains of yesterday's fire. Zenta paused her kneading, looking over at her sister.

Estere smiled. "Thought you could use a hand."

The sisters' eyes met across the room. Pure gratefulness flooded Zenta's face. She looked like a small girl again, her open expression full of happiness at the simple pleasure of her sister's company. Estere turned back to the oven quickly. It was all she could do not to burst into tears at the relief in her sister's eyes. The weeks after Tomass was taken had been hard on them all. Each family member suffered the loss in their own way. Her mother still ran the house, but she'd slowed down, her focus likely to drift. More than once Estere had found her standing idle in the yard, eyes turned to the ash-grey sky, face slack. Her father now spent his days in bed. Last time she saw him the unmistakable scent of alcohol had clung to his sweat-stained clothes. She hadn't seen him out in days.

But the bakery had to keep going, or all would be lost. That responsibility had fallen largely to her little sister, who shouldered the burden without complaint.

Swallowing her guilt, Estere stoked the coals, igniting the kindling and preparing the oven to work. She would do better, she promised herself. But deep inside she acknowledged the thought as the lie it was. After all, she was only here for the morning baking to siphon rations for Valdis. Still, she could also help her sister. Two things could be true, she decided.

Turning to the workbench, she took up a spot by Zenta and measured out the flour for a roll; a little less than normal.

"I was thinking," she began conversationally, "if we make the loaves slightly smaller the flour can go further. I know it means less for all, but it also means more people get some." She held her breath, eyes fixed on the flour before her. Waiting.

She heard Zenta pause her rhythmic kneading once more, could feel her thinking. She didn't dare face Zenta: she was sure her expression would give away her guilty conscience.

"You mean smaller loaves, but more of them? So, more people can at least get some bread?" Zenta said.

"Perhaps even some who can't afford it..." Estere stopped abruptly, not trusting her voice to speak the deception further.

Silence fell between them. Then...

"It is a good plan. It will help the city."

The rhythmic bop of Zenta's kneading began again and Estere breathed out heavily, adding water to her flour and starting her own rhythm.

Later, when Dārta made her way into the kitchen, eyes bloodshot from lack of sleep, puffy from tears, Estere let her sister explain the plan. Dārta simply nodded, gathering up a tray of fresh loaves and carrying them to the storefront for display, habit moving her through the actions as she barely processed what was around her. Zenta followed her mother to the store, ready to open for the first customers.

Estere hung back. Guilt churned within her belly. She had done what she had set out to do, but fooling her mother and sister filled her with shame.

Then, as the ring of the doorbell announced the first customer, she steeled her emotions and sprang into action. Hands clad in oven mitts, she pulled the tray from the oven, the flash of steam from the buns blurring her vision. Working quickly, she sectioned off four loaves, not quite cooked, but close enough, moving the others about to cover the missing rounds, then pressed the tray back into place. Shoving the loaves into a bag, she gathered up the sack of flour they'd been using. Enough remained at the bottom for perhaps a loaf and a half. Zenta would surely use it tomorrow, but would it really be missed? Estere hoped not as she rolled the sack closed and added it to her bag. She heard her sister's voice, high and sweet, calling good day to whomever had just collected their morning bread. No time to dawdle. Racing for the back door, she pulled on her coat and made her way out into the icy morning light. Time to get these first supplies to Valdis, before Zenta or Dārta could miss them. She could claim ignorance later if anything was noticed.

As her heels hit the cobbled lane, she slowed her pace. It was daylight, people were expected to be out and about, purchasing food, checking on relatives. She needed to blend in, not rush, even if her legs burned to run. Drawing her coat tight around her neck, partly to stave off the icy winds that lifted from the Daugava, and partly to obscure her face. She walked calmly across town towards Olga's unassuming home. In her pocket her papers, neatly folded and ready should she be stopped and questioned by a patrol. In her mind she prepared her explanation for the loaves in her bag: delivery for an ageing friend.

Soon the all too familiar sight of a pair of soldiers on their city rounds moved into view before her, the grey of their trench coats blending with the street. She lowered her gaze, focusing on the dirty snow that clumped along the gutters, pretending to be distracted by the challenge of not slipping on the ice.

They passed, eyes boring into her, looking through her flesh and bone and into her soul.

But the soldiers did not stop her, only walked on, their warm breath puffing clouds of mist before them.

Estere snorted a sigh of relief and picked up her pace.

Her plan had begun.

FIFTEEN

ESTERE

The room still smelt of him. Musky, familiar. If she tried really hard, she could pretend he was just at work, that Tomass would soon stride through the door and demand to know why she was in his bedroom. Like old times, before he started working the docks, before the Soviets, before the Nazis.

The room was dimly lit, only the palest sun peeking through the space between the drawn curtains. She dared not turn on the light. It might alert her mother.

Padding softly across the bare wooden floors, she placed an open suitcase on the freshly made bed. Dārta must have been cleaning the linens when she did the rest of the house. A routine born in futile hope.

Tomass was not coming back.

It was an undeniable truth, Estere had accepted. But standing in this room, the scent of her brother still on the air, she felt her heart rebel. She wished she could believe in another fate. An unending pit of sorrow threatened to open up within her, dark, consuming, total. Estere straightened her back, shaking her head, forcing herself back into the moment. She had a task to complete.

Estere moved to the cupboard, treading carefully, aware that her parents' room lay below. She did not want the creaking floorboards to wake her father. However unlikely that the sound of her work would rouse him from his day-drinking slumber, it was a risk she was not willing to take.

Easing the cupboard open, she began. Pulling coats, jumpers, shirts and trousers, all still neatly hung and folded, from the wardrobe, she placed them in her suitcase. Dārta would notice, but it was unlikely that suspicion would fall within the household, or so Estere hoped. Ultimately, once it was done, it was done. What came next was less important.

Next, she stripped the bed. The worn but sturdy sheets and blankets were useless here. Tomass would not be needing them. But the living did.

She had to press her full weight down on the suitcase to close it: she'd stuffed it to the brim with Tomass' things. Warm clothes and blankets for the hidden men of Riga. Dwelling in frozen cellars in groups of three to seven. In the dark, for the most part. Chilled, afraid, hungry and totally dependent on outside support for food and supplies. The men Žanis had rescued. But only if they took care of them.

Tomass had been horrified by the events at Rumbala. Powerless to stop them, he'd deserted, and the Nazis had taken him. In death he could help those survivors, men he could not help in life. Even if it was only in a little way. It was fitting. A tribute to his sacrifice.

Hauling the suitcase into her arms she crept from the room, closing the door with exaggerated care. No point getting caught red-handed now.

Door shut, she hurried down the stairs, through the bakery kitchen and out the back of the home into the shattering cold of January.

Snow lay in a thick blanket over the city, silencing everything, including her secret mission.

It was the right thing to do. It had to be.

"How could you do this!"

Estere sat bolt upright in her bed. Darkening mid-afternoon light filtered through her window. She'd fallen asleep. Exhausted after staying late with Valdis the night before, she'd practically sleepwalked through the morning baking. After lunch she'd snuck to her room. She'd intended just a small lie-down, to gather her strength. Clearly, she'd fallen asleep.

She blinked her bleary eyes, trying to focus. Before her Nikolai loomed. The weight had fallen off him in the months since Tomass was taken, flesh stolen from his bones by grief. Where his belly had once been rounded between his braces, his trousers now hung loose. His cheeks were concave, his greying whiskers unkempt and patchy. But he was no less imposing.

And right now, he was furious.

"Father?" She swung her legs over the bed, feet clicking on the floor. She hadn't even removed her shoes.

"Pack a bag and get out."

"What...?"

"Don't you try it. Don't you even speak it!" He stepped forward, wobbling slightly on his bad leg as his rage tensed his muscles. Jabbing a finger in her face he screamed, "You took it all! And for what?"

Estere breathed out in understanding.

Tomass' things. She looked up, hands gripping her skirts, and tried to explain, "Father, listen."

"I know you have been sneaking bread," Nikolai said, fury driving him on, the skin of his face purpling with anger. "You aren't as clever as you think. The numbers don't add up. You are lucky I noticed before the audit. I figured you were helping someone, doing some good. I covered for you. And you..."

His voice cracked with emotion, his face falling into trenches of pain. His torment was unbearable to see. Estere's heart twisted in her chest, an ache so deep she thought it would break in two.

"It was all I had left of him." His sob tore her asunder. His knees gave, and he crashed to the floor, hands splaying over the rough wood. Arms shaking as he succumbed to his grief, Nikolai wept, uncaring that his daughter was watching.

"Father, I had to. I had to do something…" Estere begged, tears springing to her eyes. "Please, listen. We are hiding them, the Jews. We are trying to save them…"

Quick as a flash his rage returned. His head snapped up, teeth bared in warning. "Enough! You have gone too far. You have risked us all with your folly. Your little sister, your own mother! No more. You will leave."

Anger burst through Estere's chest. "Coward," she hissed, glaring at Nikolai. "I tell you, we are saving lives and you think of no one but yourself."

Her father recoiled, features tight with hurt. "How can you say that? I think of my family. Our family."

"Latvia is about more than these walls."

Nikolai stared at her, shell-shocked. "Has he so turned your head that you value his word over the blood of your sister?"

"Valdis stands for something," she shouted through eyes blurred by anger. "I am proud to stand with him."

"Get out," Nikolai cried, pointing towards the open doorway. "Get out and never, ever come back."

"Don't worry, I won't stay another second in this house of weakness," she shrieked as she strode for the door.

She did not look back.

The door swung open. Olga, small in the backlit opening, stepped aside. Estere walked in. Valdis met her in the entrance-way, eyes wide.

She held her head high, feigning a strength she did not feel. "Father has kicked me out."

Strong arms enveloped her. His chin resting on her crown. She knew he mouthed something to Olga. She didn't care.

Fired by her fury at her father's reaction, Estere had packed her bag and trudged the two-hour walk to Olga's farm. Through ice-coated streets, then layers of snow, slick from melt and dirt, her stride was strong and sure, but as the trees opened out into the forest that enveloped the farmhouse, the weight of the situation had begun to gather in her heart.

Valdis didn't ask questions. Without a word he led her upstairs to his room off a corridor. He took the coat from her back, hung it on a hook by the door, slipped the shoes from her feet and buried her beneath the blankets. His own warmth soon joined her as he pulled the blankets tight around them and gathered her into his arms.

Only then did her resolve break. "He will never forgive me," she sobbed, face pressed to his naked chest.

"Shhh, be still," he smoothed her hair, his fingers gently tugged the knots the wind had knitted from its length.

"I had nowhere else to go," she repeated, heart desperate to know if she had a place here, with him. As she hoped.

"You are safe," he crooned. "You always have me."

He kissed her forehead, turning her body to cup into his. Wrapped in his smell, his warmth, his skin, her eyes drifted shut and she slept.

"She isn't one of us."

"She is my partner. You know her. She is part of the supply network."

"Valdis, I've never met her. Not really."

Estere hovered in the doorway to a large central room. It took up the majority of the ground floor of the farmhouse. Upstairs was little more than a hall and two rooms, one of which she had awoken in.

The bark of an excited dog had called her from her slumber. Warm in a cave of blankets, she'd stretched. The cold of the space beside her, long empty, had shocked her awake. She was not at home in the attic she shared with Zenta. Blinking in the half-light of dawn, memory had filtered through the curtain of her waking mind. She was at Olga's. She no longer had a home.

Pulling her coat from the door she'd descended the stairs, seeking Valdis.

Olga's voice had stilled her step.

"This house is not a refuge. It is a place for the resistance. You are only here because Dāvis vouched for you."

"And I vouch for her."

A pause. "You trust her?"

"Olga, I love her."

Estere's heart spasmed. Words she'd longed to hear echoing to her ears, spoken to another. But about her. He loved her.

A door banged shut. Estere jumped, turning as Dāvis approached from the yard.

"Good morning, sleepyhead." He smiled. At his feet a large black and white dog pranced, tail high and wagging.

"Oh," Dāvis said, "this is Bruno. Don't worry, he's more size than teeth!" As if on cue Bruno rushed forward, shoving his head between her legs, paws scratching at her shoes.

"Bruno!" Dāvis' voice alerted Olga and Valdis, who appeared in the doorway.

Olga's eyes narrowed at Estere.

"Breakfast?" Valdis asked, a smile hovering about his lips as he regarded her and Bruno.

She was led into the main room. Table and chairs in the

centre, wood-fired oven and sink against the outer wall. Condensation licked down the windows. But here, it was warm.

Estere allowed Valdis to draw up a chair for her, bring her bread and hot water. She chewed carefully, eyes focused on the meal before her. Valdis sat close, a hand resting on her thigh.

She could feel Olga watching her, assessing. She knew she should look up, should speak, say something, anything, to argue her case. But her mind was blank. Between her father's rage and grief, her own guilt and fear, Estere had nothing left to give.

She returned the slice of bread to her plate, her appetite suddenly gone.

A warm, soft pressure pushed at her calf. Her leg rose, Bruno's head suddenly appearing at her knee.

A laugh erupted from Dāvis, who, clapping his hands, walked forward and patted Bruno as he sat between Estere and Valdis.

"Dog's a good judge of character," he said, looking meaningfully at Olga.

Estere looked up, meeting Olga's eyes for the first time.

"Your girlfriend can stay. But she works for it," Olga said, before turning and striding from the house into the yard.

Stillness settled over Estere's limbs and a quiet peace came into her heart. For the first time since the Soviets had invaded more than two years before, she felt calm.

Another thing she would fight for had been taken from her: her family.

That left only one thing remaining: the man before her. The man who had owned her heart since the first day she heard him speak of revolution. The truth was, she had chosen Valdis over her family a long time ago. She had thought she was caught between the two. But Nikolai had only made her see the truth. It was a choice she'd long borne guilt for, guilt that cut her deep every time she looked at her little sister. But now there was no turning back, she no longer had to feel burning shame every time she crept out the back door of the bakery, arms laden with goods. Though finding enough supplies for their network would be harder, the emotional burden was less. Now, there was only Valdis. Valdis and their fight to help as many Jews as they could to hide from the terror of the Nazis.

It was good to have no other choice. It set her free.

SIXTEEN

ZENTA

1943

Zenta rode her bike, bouncing gently along the cobbled streets of the city, ice cracking beneath the wheels. A cold rush of air propelled itself under her skirts, and she was thankful for the extra-thick stockings her mother had mended for her just last night.

Hooked to the crook of her arm, a woven basket filled with rye bread, the warmth of the freshly baked loaves wafting up her sleeve.

It was mid-March, and the ice was thinning on the streets. But it was still fiercely cold. Latvia was a land of six-month winters. And this winter had been brutal.

More than a year had passed since her brother was taken.

And her sister had disappeared.

At first, she'd searched for Estere. As she rode through the ruins of her once grand city, delivery basket tapping against her thigh, Zenta's eyes scanned those she passed. She'd visited the university grounds often, some memory of Estere's rambling stories telling her it was a place of importance to her sister. But the university was long deserted, and the streets mostly empty. In truth, she'd no idea where to look for Estere.

She'd given up, placing her trust in her father's insistence that Estere had run away to the countryside, joining the others of the city who fled Nazi eyes. It was preferable to the alternative. If she'd run away, she could return.

At the beginning of 1943, as the cold of January set the streets in ice, rations were halved, and sickness rose. To make matters worse, the Germans divided the stores, some for German patrons, few for Latvians. Unsurprisingly the best and the bulk of the produce went to the German stores. The rest of Riga made do with what was left. It meant long lines for basic staples: milk, bacon, bread.

Zenta and her mother did what they could for their customers and friends, baking smaller loaves to make the flour go further, "more for some" as Estere had once said, putting some loaves aside and braving the bitter winds to deliver what little they could to those in most need.

When the hacking cough that echoed through the streets made it into their bakery, taking root in the lungs of both her parents, Zenta tended them, scooping cabbage broth into their mouths, laying wet cloths over their fevered brows. When her own temperature rose, there had been no option to slow down. Throat raw from coughing, lips chapped from fever, she struggled on working in the hot bakery, shouldering most of the housework.

Many a night as she lay in her small bed, breath misting in white clouds as she struggled to breathe in the frozen attic room, she'd almost wished for the end. To close her eyes and drift into an eternal sleep, warm and safe and ignorant.

But she always woke, called from her swaddling to care for others.

After all, she had a bakery to run, a line of patrons around the block, ration cards in freezing hands, hoping for a daily staple.

Now, as the first buds of the new season pushed their way into the light, Zenta pedalled her bicycle, a wisp of spring on the wind a timid promise of better times ahead.

She traced the edges of an empty square, heading down towards the Daugava. She avoided the ghetto now. It was full again; the puff of steam from arriving trains signalled each time a new delivery of Jewish prisoners, mostly from Germany, pulled up at the station

But the Latvians were gone. Ava with them, had she been inside on that horrific day. Zenta pressed the memory down, the hope that Ava had somehow survived too hard to believe anymore, now that her brother was also gone.

And her sister.

So much had changed. As she rode through the streets, she passed empty houses; curtains open, doors unlocked, their occupants forced out in the night by Russian or German hands. There was Mr Bērziņš' small apartment building, that had long been left empty and cold. There were the barracks. Once a schoolhouse, now home to the foreign and Latvian soldiers who policed the city streets.

Cycling past Rathausplatz where the town hall once stood, now reduced to rubble, she averted her gaze. The Nazi flag, proud, red, dangerous, blew in the breeze atop the newly declared German-controlled town hall, the capital of Reichskommissariat Ostland. The Latvian flag, maroon and white, was long gone. She turned off the square back into the rambling lanes of the old town proper. Rows of terraced buildings of brick and stone. The paintwork, once fresh and bright, now dulled to beige and grey. Flecks peeled from the doors to float in the wicked winds that whipped along these man-made funnels.

Her next stop was Mrs Petrova. Almost ninety, the old, wizened woman had seen too much in her time on earth, so God had taken her sight. Cataracts clouded the once sparkling blue of her irises. But her smile was still warm, still genuine as she greeted Zenta at her door, hunched and shaking. Zenta handed her a parcel of bread. Mrs Petrova brought it to her nose, breathing deeply the scent of baked rye.

"Not like my mother's, but very, very good."

Zenta smiled, nodding. Then remembering herself, she said, "Our mothers all make the best morning loaf."

It was true. Or at least tradition. There had been a time when every family baked their own bread. Mothers teaching daughters the secrets of the knead, the rise, the oven heat; the ratio of flour to water to egg; the handfuls of caraway. But over time, as cities grew busier and homes smaller; as rural life yielded one too many failed crops and forced second sons and daughters to the city seeking work; as life in Latvia changed, more and more people sourced their bread from bakeries like her parents' store.

But no one would ever make bread like a mother.

Gently squeezing the old woman's arm in farewell, Zenta mounted her bicycle and continued on.

Before her a line of soldiers came into view, marching beside them a ragged group of Jewish workers, on their way to a day of forced labour. Subconsciously, she slowed her pedalling. The men moved at a stilted, shuffling pace. Impossibly thin, hipbones jutting out against threadbare trousers, cheekbones sharp beneath hollow eyes. A man looked up, his hair hanging in limp ringlets across his stretched forehead. In his eyes she saw emptiness, a void without hope. Pity opened a hole in her chest, raw and aching, and she turned away, his pain too much to bear witness to.

Guilt slayed her heart. Quickly she turned back, a sorrowful smile on her lips. But it was too late, the man had dropped his head back down, eyes locked on the icy cobbles beneath his bare and bloody feet.

There were less of them now. It seemed their number decreased almost daily. Taken out to work, some gone for weeks, months, before returning even thinner than before. Walking skeletons. The Nazis had used them to build a new camp down in Salaspils to house more prisoners of Nazi Germany. Zenta wondered what that would mean for the men who remained in the Riga Ghetto. Would they be transported? Or something different? A shiver raced up her spine, the memory of Rumbala so fresh in the hearts of all Rigans. Mrs Petersone said these prisoners survived on no more than a roll of bread a day, dipped in water. How they kept on, toiling the days in physical labour, freezing at night, bellies empty of real nourishment, Zenta could not imagine.

Perhaps that was the point... She was aware that Nazi cruelty knew no bounds.

How had they believed them heroes?

How could they be so much worse than the Soviets?

Heart heavy, Zenta angled her bike away, turning her back on the Jews of Riga. Shame crawled over her skin, digging through the sinew and bone, burrowing deep, deep into her gut. There it curled into a tight, hard ball, held together by fear, at its core, cowardice.

Before her the expanse of the Daugava came into view. Its waters rippling gently. Large chunks of ice floated towards the docks and the Baltic beyond, broken free from the banks as the temperatures began to rise and the thaw commenced. A single rowing boat glided through the dark currents, its oars churning through the ice-thick water. Zenta filled her eyes with the river, a memory of laughter and fishing poles, of green grasses and warm smiles calming her heart.

A flash of light caught her eye, and she looked up at the rusting railway bridge that joined the two sides of her city.

Rebuilt after the Great War, the bridge had once been a symbol of possibility and power to Zenta. Now, a lone soldier, Nazi swastika on his arm, marched along the tracks, head facing firmly forward, gun resting against his shoulder. The sun reflecting off his bayonet.

Tired and cold and heartsore, Zenta turned back for home.

SEVENTEEN
ZENTA

Her father's laughter rang through the garden. A shadow of the rich, glorious sound that had filled her childhood, but a balm to Zenta's heart nonetheless. It told her that her friend was visiting.

She rested her bike against the back wall of the house and hastened into the bakery kitchen. There her father sat at the small table, Aleksandrs by his side, his hands raised above his head, his face alive as he recounted some story.

Zenta leaned against the doorframe, not wishing to interrupt them, but to just watch this moment of simple joy between two people she loved. The warmth of the morning sun radiated through the window, illuminating the room in a golden glow. She felt a grin forming on her face.

Aleks had a way of doing that.

"They hid the pig in the coffin!" Aleks was exclaiming, smacking a hand down on the table. "It was dressed in an old wedding gown. Totally fooled the guards."

Nikolai, face red from laughter, threw his head back, a full laugh, right from his belly, erupting from his throat.

"They shared it with their street. Everyone got a cut of the wedding pig."

Nikolai wiped tears of amusement from his face, a glisten of moisture sticking to his unshaven cheek as silence settled over them. The thought of roasted pork made everyone's mouths water.

It was good to see Nikolai happy, even if it only lasted a moment.

Since that spring when Dārta had surprised them with pudding, Aleks had become a regular visitor to her father's bakery, sitting in the downstairs kitchen drinking warmed water (there was no tea anymore) beside the large bakery ovens, chatting away the hours with Nikolai. Aleks' visits were the only time her father ventured from his rooms. While he'd still not baked a loaf since Tomass was taken, at least when Aleks was there he smiled from time to time.

Brought together by love for Zenta, the two had grown a bond.

Aleks needed a father figure.

Nikolai needed a son.

And Zenta needed Aleks.

"What on earth is going on in here?" Dārta strode into the room, hands on hips, but her voice was light, playful.

"Aleks here tells a fine story, my love," Nikolai said, breathing heavily as he calmed his mirth. "However unbelievable."

"It's the truth," Aleks protested, eyes gleaming.

"It is a good story," Nikolai agreed amiably.

"Well, now, young man, don't you tire my husband too much," Dārta said, patting Aleks on the shoulder, expression of mock severity on her face.

"Yes, yes," Nikolai called to his wife.

Aleks turned, seeing Zenta. His smile broadening as he nodded in hello.

Slipping her scarf from her neck, Zenta crossed the kitchen

to press a quick kiss to her father's greying temple. The change in her father when Aleks visited was remarkable. He was still weathered beyond his years, thin and grey, but a small light would return to his eyes. A tiny flame of hope reignited deep inside, the rebellion of finding moments of joy in spite of the world about them.

Zenta felt that same spark within her own heart.

Turning to wash her hands, ready to relieve her mother in the store, her lips curved in a small, secret smile, just for Aleks.

He grinned back, eyes shining.

Despite it all, hope remained. Life went on.

The patter of stones sounded on her window. Zenta's stomach flipped in excitement. There was no longer the need for these clandestine meetings; they saw each other regularly in the bakery. But, it seemed, it was never enough, so they kept to their secret evenings on the street beneath her bedroom window.

Flinging off her sheets, Zenta practically bounced out of bed, rushing for the window.

She pushed up the awning and looked down, blonde hair spilling out like a fairy tale. Below her Aleks grinned and waved. She swung out a leg and made her way down to his side.

They embraced. She felt his warm breath against her neck, the soft press of a chaste kiss to her cheek.

The heat of her body rushed up her face at the touch of his lips to her skin. Her legs weakened in anticipation. Pulling back, Aleks looked into her eyes.

Zenta frowned. Something was wrong.

Where his mouth would normally twist in a wry smile, eyes dancing with excitement over their innocent deception, only shadows fell.

"Aleks?" Zenta said, placing a gentle hand against his cheek. "What is it?"

He closed his eyes, leaning into her touch, savouring the moment.

"My service letter came today. They call it 'volunteering', but there isn't a choice, not really."

"Volunteering? For what?"

"I must join the German army."

Zenta went still. Her body suddenly ice cold.

"But you are only fifteen!"

"The order came through this week. Hitler has broadened the age range for soldiers. I won't even be the youngest, not by far..."

"You can't go. You can't fight for them!" The heat of panic flushed her face, burning her skin. She couldn't tell if she were angry with Aleks, or just afraid.

"I don't have a choice."

"But, Aleks! They are the enemy. Think about it. Lowering the age for younger soldiers... Hitler must be desperate. They are losing, you know they are losing. The rumours..."

He took her hand, pressing it to his chest. "It doesn't matter. I don't have a choice."

Zenta paused, eyes scanning his face in desperation. An idea, sudden and thrilling, burst from her mouth.

"We can run. We can escape into the forests. Find the rebels and the other deserters who have fled to avoid the army. Find my sister. We can hide..."

"I can't," Aleks said simply. "I would never put you at that risk..."

"...It would be my choice..."

"I would never!" Aleks' voice was firm, eyes going hard. "That is a fool's errand. We don't know if your sister is even out there."

Zenta stepped back, turning away, arms clamped about her waist. It hurt her to hear his words, however much it was the likely truth. Estere had not sent word. Not even once.

The warmth of Aleks' body wafted up her back as he stepped close, hands coming to rest on her shoulders.

"I'm sorry," he said simply, "I spoke without thinking."

Zenta turned into his warmth, wrapping her arms around him, pressing close. He was solid. Real. He was here. How could she go on without him? With him in danger? Her brother had already become a soldier and had been killed. How could she lose Aleks too?

Aleks ran a hand down the length of her hair, breathing softly.

"Please don't go," Zenta whispered. "You can still say no."

She felt his body sag in defeat. Fingers came up under her chin drawing her eyes up to his.

"If I say no, they will send me and my mother to the labour camps. You have seen the men who return from work detail at Salaspils."

Zenta swallowed, images of walking ghosts flashing through her mind.

"Mother would not survive it." He looked at the ground, watched his shuffling feet for a moment before continuing. "The Russians killed my father. I won't let the Germans take my mother."

Zenta closed her eyes, tiny tears escaping to track down her cheeks, and nodded. She knew. The moment he'd told her, she knew. There wasn't a choice, not here in this Latvia controlled by a foreign power.

"When do you leave?"

"At sunrise. I have been assigned to the 5th Battalion. We are being sent to train."

"And where will you fight?"

"I don't know. But the Soviets are amassing to the east. Germany is engaged on both fronts. I suspect I will face the Reds."

Zenta tried to suppress the cold shiver of fear that snaked

up her back. The Nazis were incomparably cruel. But so were the Soviets.

"The war is ending, Zee," Aleks continued, pulling her into his embrace once more. "You are right, Hitler is desperate. Pressed between two powerful armies. West and East. He cannot hold out forever. Germany will fall. And then we fight!"

His voice rang with hope, causing Zenta to look up at him, a question in her eyes.

"Like our fathers, Zee. After the Great War they stood tall and won Latvia her freedom. We can do so again. Now it is our turn."

Her breathing shallowed. Was it possible? Could these years of bloodshed and horror really end with a free Latvia? Was it worth risking Aleksandrs? Her father had returned from the War of Independence but many men had not. Their fight for freedom had come with a terrible cost.

She didn't know. And ultimately there was no alternative.

"It is a wonderful dream, Aleks."

"Soon it will be true, Zee. You will see. I will win you back your Latvia."

Zenta smiled, lips quavering, blinking rapidly to hold back the tears that threatened to rush from her eyes. It was a good dream.

He drew her to him once more, his arms strong, his embrace firm. As he pulled back their eyes met. Their breath mingled before them in the spring night air. Aleks' eyes dipped to her lips, then he swallowed, stepping back.

"Goodbye for now," he said. "Be safe."

"You too," she whispered. She stayed there, watching the empty street long after Aleks had disappeared around the churchyard corner.

Despite the fear that trembled throughout her body, her soul, she chose hope.

And she prayed it would sustain her.

EIGHTEEN

ZENTA

The months after Aleksandrs left for war echoed like an empty shell of time. Spring blossomed in the trees that filled her city, but its warmth could not reach her heart. Nor could its bounty fill the concave stomachs of the citizens of Riga.

War on two fronts was pressing Germany hard, the breakdown of their supply lines into a heavy Russian winter stalling their progress in the east, and an invigorated Allied Forces forcing them back in the west. They needed more soldiers, more munitions, more food and supplies. As the long hot days of summer began, the deliveries of produce from the fields of Latvia slowed, the soldiers siphoning off greater and greater portions for their war effort. The stalls of Riga Central Market thinned to nothing, and the Nazis took over most of the space for weapons storage and workshops.

The logistical challenge of feeding the nation was worsened by Hitler's ever-increasing recruitment programme. More and more young men were conscripted, leaving in weekly allotments for basic training and then the front line, somewhere to the east or west. At first, letters from those who went to fight made it back to tearful families, all praying for word from their loved ones.

It wasn't long before the letters stopped.

So desperate had the drive for more men become that even her father was forced to prove he could not fight.

Two soldiers, smooth-cheeked with youth, uniforms in the green of the Latvian Auxiliary Police, faces thinning like those of the rest of the citizens of Riga, demanded Nikolai uncover his leg. His features arranged in cold fury, Nikolai unclipped his braces and dropped his trousers to the bakery floor. Dārta turned away, hand pressed to her mouth in grief. Zenta stared. There her father stood, trousers about his ankles, the pale flesh of his bowed legs exposed. The left twisted in at the knee at an unnatural angle, the flesh withered almost to the bone. The soldiers at least had the decency to flush with shame. It didn't stop them from helping themselves to loaves of bread.

Everyone was going hungry.

As the first frosts covered autumn's brown leaves in icy white, the radio proclaimed that Germany was nearing victory and the war would soon be at an end.

The faces of the new recruits sent to support the Latvian battalions across Europe grew younger and younger. In their gentle flesh she saw her Aleks, in their fear she saw her brother.

She was nearly home when she saw him. Dressed in the field-grey trench coat all German soldiers wore, he was standing by the old library, hip against the stone wall, cigarette at his full lips. He was waving, Zenta realised. Waving at her. He pushed off the wall as she drew near, walking straight to the roadside, hand outstretched, mouth smiling. Unwillingly, Zenta slowed. Her mind raced. What had she done to draw his attention? It was well within daylight hours, she had not disobeyed curfew.

Heart thumping, she drew her bike to a stop, placing one leg on the ground to steady herself. She did not dismount.

He walked onto the street, stopping right at her elbow, looming above her. She looked up, smiled, through quivering lips. He was young. Could not be more than a few years her senior. Fresh-faced. Smooth-skinned.

His eyes, so pale their colour was almost lost to the whites, stared at her.

"Guten Morgen."

"Guten Morgen," Zenta replied. She spoke very little German, only the few pleasantries she had picked up when running the bakery. They were needed to survive.

He smiled, eyes tracking down her body. Returning to her face, he looked at her expectantly. Zenta swallowed. She'd heard stories of the soldiers and young women of Riga and had been warned to stay far away.

Tapping his chest he said, "Otto."

Oh, Zenta realised, he wanted her name.

Voice shaking, she tapped her own chest, "Zenta."

His grinned widened. "Schöne."

Zenta frowned, the word unfamiliar.

He leaned back, stance suddenly casual, and took another drag of his cigarette before offering the bud to her.

Startled, she shook her head.

He laughed. A puff of breath, barely a sound, but the humour swam in his eyes.

He reached into his coat, fingers diving into a pocket hidden in the lining.

Zenta froze as a memory flashed before her.

A frozen night, years ago, a dark street, a single lamp's light, her brother's shaking hand.

As his hand withdrew, she braced herself to flee. But it wasn't a gun that dangled between his long, oddly elegant fingers, rather a small bar of chocolate.

He held it out to her, nodded, gesturing for her to take it.

"Paldies, please," he said, the Latvian surprising her. The word sounded uncomfortable in his mouth, too flat. But his meaning was clear.

Zenta looked at the chocolate bar. It was open, more than half gone, just a stub in foil remaining. Instantly her mouth began to water, her tastebuds alive with the memory of the delicious, creamy treat.

Why on earth would this soldier be offering it to her? And yet, he was.

She shouldn't take it.

But it would be rude not to.

She shouldn't take it.

But oh, chocolate.

The year had been so tough. Food limited. Bellies barely filled. Rations halved. And winter was fast approaching once again. Lately, it seemed it never really left.

And chocolate...

Hunger won out and Zenta reached timidly for the bar.

She took it swiftly, the brush of his finger as he relented his hold on the bar making her skin crawl. Briefly she held the tiny foil-wrapped parcel before her, then flushing with embarrassment, she pushed it into the pocket of her coat.

The soldier's face split in two, what seemed to be genuine joy spreading across his features. It made him look... sweet.

Stepping back, he nodded down the street and Zenta understood she had been dismissed.

She pushed off the cobbled street and, on shaking legs, rode home as fast as she could.

She did not look back.

"Where have you been?" Dārta asked, eyes sharp, as her daughter entered the bakery kitchen.

Zenta blinked, surprised at her mother's tone. "I've come from Lauma's. I always visit Aleks' mother on Wednesdays."

Since Aleks had left for the front Zenta had made a point of checking in on Lauma. The older woman welcomed her warmly, but her smile never lit her eyes and Zenta often sensed relief when she said it was time for her to go. But she kept going. She owed it to Aleks to watch over his family. He'd have done the same for her.

Dārta stared at her daughter. "You are late."

"Sorry, Mother," Zenta said, hurrying to the tap to wash her hands for work.

"See it doesn't happen again."

As she rinsed her hands under the cold water, Zenta worked to slow her racing heartbeat, the small portion of chocolate burning a hole of blackest guilt in her pocket.

Dārta didn't know about the chocolate. She couldn't possibly. That was just irrational. And she wasn't late back, she was sure of it.

As her nerves settled, understanding came to her. Aleks' recruitment had left them all bereft. His absence a physical, pulsing thing that hovered at the edges of each day. A space that refused to be filled, no matter how they tried to distract themselves.

Of her siblings and friends, Zenta was the only child left. No wonder Dārta fretted.

She could not be angry with her mother for fussing; it was only natural. The whole of Riga been living in a constant state of heightened anxiety since the Soviets came four years before; a lifetime ago.

Yet tensions had mounted still further, the currents of fear increasing as the days shortened and the rumours of Russian advance grew. Zenta could feel the shift on the wind. It sat in the furtive glances of neighbours, the flutter of curtains as she passed on the street, the increased patrols at night. The new arrests.

The soldiers grew desperate.

Desperate men do desperate things.

Drying her hands on a tea towel Zenta turned to her mother. "I am sorry, Mother," she said, voice sincere. "I will be sure to mind the time better next time."

Not ready to relax, but somewhat mollified, Dārta nodded, lips pursed.

Later, in her room, alone, Zenta crawled under her blankets and carefully unwrapped the morsel of chocolate. It was small, the marks of teeth, presumably the soldier's, scored the hard chocolate. It should have disgusted her, seeing the outline of his teeth. But it didn't. Biting into the hard, cold bar her eyes closed. A groan of pleasure sounding deep in her throat as the bitter, sweet flavour coated her tongue. It was even better than she remembered.

As she chewed, she wondered idly if she would see him again. The thought filled her with unexpected excitement.

She did see him again.

Weeks later she spied him. As she cycled closer the scent of ice and woodsmoke danced on the air, familiar and comforting. He stepped forward, eyes shining.

She pulled up a few paces away.

"Sveiki," he waved, "hello."

"Sveiki," she replied.

Glancing left, then right, he strolled over, shoulders hunched against the chill, hands deep in the pockets of his trench coat. Coming to her side he paused, a sly grin snaking across his face.

"You work hard."

Zenta nodded. It was only the truth.

"Very thin."

Again, a simple truth. She cocked her head at him in question.

"My mother..." He paused, seeking the right words. A huff of irritation. "Deutsch, ja?"

"Slowly," Zenta agreed in German.

Face relieved, he continued, "My mother, she says you need milk to grow stark."

Zenta frowned, her German vocabulary not strong enough to follow fully. "Stark?"

"Ja!" He grinned, raising an arm and squeezing his biceps. "Strong!"

He wiggled his eyebrows outrageously. Zenta couldn't help but laugh. As her giggles quieted Otto grew serious. "For you." He held his hand before her, a small parcel wrapped in his palm.

Zenta hesitated. Then, reaching forward, she took the offered gift. It was larger than the chocolate square, heavier, thick.

"No milk, but this is close enough I think."

Carefully she unfolded the wax paper wrapping. Neat and yellow and hard, a square of cheese sat in her palm. It must have been a week's ration. Instantly it made her mouth water.

She looked up at Otto in surprise. "You are sure?" she asked.

He nodded vigorously. "You need to be stark!"

She smiled, honest and open. Gratitude for his thoughtful gift flooded through her. "Paldies, dankeschön."

Otto grinned, stepping back. "Labrīt, good day."

"Labrīt," she answered and cycled away.

NINETEEN

ZENTA

2018

Crissy has brought me a cup of tea, weak, milky and sweet, just as I like it.

She nestles into the lounge beside me, drawing her feet up under her, just as she did as a child. I smile at the memory. A small Crissy in her bright pink pyjamas, long fair hair neatly braided down her back.

My second chance.

The sound of tyres crunching over my dry driveway draws our attention. Crissy glances at her mobile, checking the time. No one wears a watch anymore. I never did, I've never had the money.

"He's early," she says, a hint of frustration flushing her face. It passes quickly, however. Early or not, her children are here. Crissy adores them both, as do I.

The split with Neil has been hard on them. Learning to live between houses, between parents. But Crissy has been masterful in her care and understanding of their transition. She lived it herself, after all.

It was like history repeating itself. Long ago I had opened my front door to my niece Aina, just like I had many times before, welcoming her home after another long absence. Only this time she was a mother, with Crissy, small and bewildered, at her feet. Aina had stayed three months the first time. Then one morning, without warning, it was just Crissy and me. When she returned, she brought stories of a retreat in a forest, a rebirthing ceremony, a search for inner peace. And the cycle continued. Aina would stay a while, then leave, always seeking, never settling. She never did find herself, not after her mother, Estere, took her away.

But she always comes back, my Aina. Unlike my sister. When Estere left, it was forever.

The bang of the front door slamming shut pulls me from my memories. Sandalled feet slap on the lino flooring as two children, on the border of adolescence but still with the free souls of childhood, race each other to be the first to embrace Crissy.

"Mum! Look! I painted this for you!"

"That's lovely, Peter, thank you."

"We saw the new Avengers movie with Dad."

"Did you?"

"It was boring."

"No it wasn't, Lily, you lie! You loved it."

"Now, now, Peter. Your sister can have her own opinion."

"I'm hungry, is there lunch?"

"I need to put a brick on your head, you are growing so fast."

"Grand-mina!"

Like a sudden storm breaking over drought-ridden farm-land, their focus snaps to me, and within seconds I am enveloped by their arms, swallowed. Limbs, uncoordinated from quick growth, wrap clumsily around my neck and shoulders, two heads vying to press kisses to my cheeks, wet and soft on my parched and sagging skin. Fingers clasp at my sleeves for better purchase, as if clinging to me to test I am real. They smell of soap and sweat and family.

The smile that breaks across my face is true. It reaches not only my eyes, but my very core. My babies are home.

"Peter. Lily. It is good you are here," I say, cupping each of their eager faces in my hands in turn. Holding their features in my eyes. I see them often, but they change so rapidly these days, growing taller, developing new obsessions, new hobbies. It is almost like meeting them anew every time they visit. Almost.

Peter's face has thinned, not from malnourishment, just the sluicing of youth on his trek to his tenth birthday, his eyes are bright and quick, his smile easy. Thirteen going on twenty-one, Lily has dyed her hair a new shade of blue, lighter this time. It brings out her eyes. Hideous fashion, if you ask me, but if it makes her happy... Her body has new curves, the burgeoning of puberty. A smile teases at the corners of her mouth, then breaks across her face. She wants to be too cool for me, but she isn't quite ready to go through with it. Not yet. I still have a few years left.

My heart feels light, floaty.

"It is good to see you well, Zenta." Neil has come in from the car. He leans down to press his own kiss to my forehead and I let him. His face has also thinned, though more from grief I suspect. Divorce is a fool's game. He turns to Crissy and the energy of the room evaporates immediately, replaced by an uncomfortable silence. For an awful moment I think she will reprimand him for being early. I see the thought flow over her features, her raw hurt at their separation still there for all to see.

She didn't want this. I know. But he made his choice, for all it seems he regrets it now.

Thankfully Crissy smiles. "I appreciate you bringing them all the way here. Can I offer you a cup of tea?"

Neil shuffles nervously, runs a hand through his hair. "It

was nothing, really," he says. "We made a day trip of it, didn't we, kids?"

"We stopped at Murray Bridge and saw the billabong monster!" Peter enthuses.

"It's called a bunyip," Lily corrects.

Unfazed, Peter continues. "It would be so scary at night-time." He gives a pretty good impression of shivering from fear. I laugh. His eyes turn to me. "Have you heard of bunyips, Grand-mina?" he asks, eyes wide.

"Of course Grand-mina knows about bunyips," Lily defends me.

"But she wasn't born here," Peter protests. "Bunyips are Australian."

"I am Australian too," I interject, coming to my feet to put the kettle on. Crissy moves to take the kettle from me, but I wave her away. Deal with your husband instead, I think to myself. She busies herself moving the children's bags into their room, as Neil stands awkwardly by the kitchen table, body turned on the side, half coming, half going.

"Sit," I order firmly. "I made pīrāgi."

"Oh yes!" Peter exclaims. He loves my pīrāgi. Actually, I think he likes any food. The children take a seat, but Neil still hesitates. I stop my preparations and face him squarely.

"I've a long drive back..." he begins.

It won't do, I know this. Whatever silliness he and my Crissy are playing at we are still family, and it is nearly Independence Day.

"So, you need food. Sit. Eat. Then you can go." It is not an offer; it is an order. A small knowing smile crosses his lips. He's always liked it when I get bossy. Men often do.

I place the pīrāgi in the middle of the table, Crissy prepares the teapot. I watch as the children fall on the little baked pastries, eyes wide, mouths grinning as they bite into the soft bacon and onion stuffing, pastry flakes coating their lips. It is the food of celebration; I always make them when I know the children are coming. Hesitantly Neil reaches forward, taking a small bun. They are still warm from the oven, their scent filling the kitchen. It is the smell of family.

The house feels too quiet after the bustle of the children's arrival. Crissy has taken them for a walk in the evening cool, to aid digestion after dinner. They finished the potatoes. I knew Crissy needed to cook more.

The setting sun casts the land in a vivid red, the white of the gums reflecting pale crimson, the shadows tinged in scarlet. It is utterly beautiful. I leave the curtains open; I love the dusk. Cockatoos call to each other as they prepare to nest, my canaries trill and flutter against their cages. It is a beautiful time on my land. I savour it, drawing in the stillness to strengthen my bones, my soul.

The phone rings.

I knew it would.

Rising slowly, I pad to answer. I know who it will be.

"Hello, Mrs. Bradford," I answer.

"Hello – I, oh," Heather stammers on the other end of the line, her surprise at my greeting obvious. But I knew it was her. No one else calls me.

She clears her throat. "Hello, Mrs Vanaga. So sorry to call again, but I felt dreadful after our call. I wanted to check that you were all right."

"Quite fine," I reply crisply. Honestly, all the fussing over my well-being these past days is becoming a bore. I know I am old. They don't need to keep reminding me.

"I know the past must be unsettling. My grandparents told me stories of Latvia..."

I press my eyes shut. I don't want to hear this.

"...but it would mean a lot if I could talk with you. Perhaps I can buy you a coffee?"

"It is nearly Independence Day. One hundred years since my father and the men of Latvia first liberated my country. I am old and busy. I don't have time for you." I go to hang up the phone.

"I understand, but, Mrs Vanaga, please, wait!"

I pause. Listen. "I am sorry my timing is so poor. But I am only in the country for the next few days. I can come to you. Please, I just want to understand."

"The past is past. There is nothing to understand. Goodbye, Mrs Bradford."

I slam the phone down harder than I mean to and turn my back to the phone. The sunlight has leaked from the sky, the red hue faded, casting the room in grey shadow. The stillness seems sinister somehow, oppressive. I move to the couch, collecting up the TV remote in a shaking hand and press the "on" button. The plastic tab gives under my finger and the screen flicks on. A woman with neat brown hair and a bright blue suit jacket is talking at the screen, her face impassive to the details she recites. "The cost of living crisis is deepening. More than sixty per cent of households are now experiencing food insecurity, according to new reports..."

Subconsciously my hand moves over my belly, full now of potato salad and pīrāgi, but it was not always so. For many years my choices have been simple: bake bread or pīrāgi, cake or soup, pick apricots, plant beetroot or potato, or both.

Can the children visit? Yes.

Can we stay the night? Yes.

Will you tell me about my mother?

I sigh heavily, hand patting my full belly. A part of me knew this choice would come. That no matter how deeply I'd buried the past, it would return.

I have carried this burden for so long and I am old now, my

time is almost through. Perhaps it's time to make a new choice. Perhaps they all deserve to know the truth?

I rise to my feet and walk to the phone.

I press redial.

"Hello." Her voice sounds wary, surprised.

"Do you know the cemetery at Paringa?"

"Mrs Vanaga? Um, well, I can look it up."

"Meet me there tomorrow at 11am."

I hang up the phone.

PART THREE

REBELLION 1944

TWENTY

ESTERE

1944

The oars strained through the mush of the Daugava. Deep winter chills moved down from the north bringing the ice of the Arctic and freezing the edges of the mighty river. Dirty clumps of ice lined the banks, breaking off at random to bob through the ice-flecked brine. Valdis leaned back, arms sure as he cut a line through the layer of ice that had formed over the river's surface. The water was glassy, still, reflecting the pale winter sun.

Soon the freeze would deepen, icing over the river. In some places the ice would be strong enough to walk upon. Then the pole fishers would come, cutting round holes in the ice in search of fish. A seasonal activity, a necessity in wartime. When that happened, Estere doubted the children would venture out to play. It would be too cold.

They were making their way along the river from the old town towards the docks. A common route for locals, quicker than walking on market day, easier to transport goods, too.

But their purpose was not to purchase supplies, but rather to smuggle them.

She drew her coat closer around her. The afternoon was cold, the breeze off the frozen river icy. She'd felt the chill more acutely lately. She guessed it was hormonal.

"Are you all right?" Valdis asked.

Estere patted the new swell of her belly. "The baby is fine," she replied.

He drew the oars through the water slowly, a shard of ice slipping along the paddle. "I am asking about its mother too."

She smiled. "I am well, my love. The cold air helps the sickness."

She'd been nauseous for months, bedridden, struggling to hold down simple broth. Olga had been a Godsend, rubbing her back, cleaning her mess, but Estere had wanted only one person, her mother.

The pregnancy wasn't planned. She could still picture the shock on Valdis' face when she told him. That shock had melted to purest love quicker than she'd dared hoped, and it had made her love him even more. They'd celebrated with Dāvis and Olga, breaking out a ration of sugar for cake, singing and dancing before making their way to bed with the moon. And then life had just gone on, as it had to. They had work to do.

Coming to Kīpsala, a small island nestled against the opposite bank of the Daugava, Valdis drew the rowboat up to the edge of the river, tying it firmly against the shore. Offering his hand to help Estere from the rocking hull, the two slung packs to their backs and began the trek to Žanis' small tree-lined dwelling on the island's edge. Their cargo today: shoes. So hard to come by now that the Germans had made it illegal to own more than two pairs per person. But children grew, and leather wore, creating an infrequent supply for the black market, where worn heels and boots with holes could still fetch a high price, or be traded for food to feed their hidden refugees.

The sky was grey with winter, the birch branches bare and tipped with frost. Estere's breath puffed before her, white and cloudy. Several paces before Žanis' gate, Valdis took her bag. Leaving her hovering between the bare trees that lined the dirt road, he knocked three times and entered. It was always this way. She waited on the outskirts, a lookout for soldiers, but also separate, so that should anything happen, she could melt into the forest.

As she waited, the clouds in the sky dissipated, shifting the sky from grey to the deepening blue of winter dusk, the pale yellow of the setting sun a dividing line across the horizon, blue on yellow between the trees.

The gate creaked. Valdis and Žanis approached, their heads pressed close in conversation. They paused several steps from her. Žanis looked up and gave her a small wave.

She nodded back. He was an unassuming man, shoulders sloping steeply like her father's, hair dusty brown. Perhaps that was why the Germans had overlooked him. He looked nothing like a hero from the great stories, but he was the saviour of some thirty Jewish lives. A true hero.

The men shook hands, then parted. Valdis strode past her fast, head down, aiming for the river. Estere quickened her step to follow as he cut through the surrounding neighbourhood, feet crunching over frozen mud. He helped her back into the rowboat, but did not look her in the face, keeping his own head low, his shoulders hunched.

He did not speak throughout their journey back across the river, nor as they made the lengthy walk to Olga's home. Estere knew better than to ask what was troubling him. He was wrestling with something, no doubt a request from Žanis that he was unsure of. He would not talk about it until his own mind was set. She would find out what soon enough.

Valdis' pitch came after dinner, as Estere and Olga were clearing the table. A traditional meal of boiled potato, soured cream, dill pickle. Simple, but plentiful here on Olga's farm.

"The ghetto is being closed down."

"Yes," Dāvis nodded, lighting the stub of a cigarette he'd be savouring for the best part of a week. "We've known this for months. Why do you bring it up?"

"Žanis has a plan, to get more men out, before they are shipped away, or worked to death... he has asked for our help."

"We already give all we can," Olga said, returning to the table and the conversation. Estere hung back, standing by the sink, listening. The trio would discuss and decide what to do, they always did. And she would agree to whatever they chose. "I don't think we have anyone else we can pressure for rations or items for trade."

Valdis shook his head, accepting a puff of the cigarette Dāvis offered to him. He blew out a long stream of smoke, coughed. "He needs housing for the rescued. Somewhere to hide them until the threat has passed."

"Valdis, it's been more than two years since Žanis started hiding Jews, we've no idea how much longer this will continue."

"Exactly." Valdis passed the cigarette back, stood, hands held before him as though he was giving a lecture, like that very first moment Estere had laid eyes on him. His face came alive. "Don't you see? Žanis has had those men in his tiny bunker for years. They are safe, well hidden. But there is no more room."

"No one is going to agree to harbour Jews, Valdis," Olga said.

"But we can."

Estere's hand flew to her mouth, pressing down the gasp of shock that threatened to escape. The trio fell silent.

Valdis continued. "We have worked so hard, collecting supplies, encouraging our friends to donate food and clothes. Estere even gave her brother's belongings." He looked up at her, eyes full of pride.

Estere swallowed her guilt. Her father's anguished cries rose afresh in her ears.

"But it isn't enough. More men are still languishing in that ghetto, moving closer and closer to death with each work detail. Žanis can get more out. But he needs help, our help. Can we really turn our backs on them? At this critical moment?"

"Valdis, be reasonable!" Dāvis said, rising from his own chair to challenge his friend. "Smuggling is one thing. Frowned upon yes, but expected, tolerated. But hiding Jews! If we get caught..."

"We will be shot. Yes."

Dāvis blinked, silenced by Valdis' frank admission of the risk. Olga shuffled in her chair, tugged at the end of her braid.

"Look," Valdis said. "I know it's a risk. A great risk. But if we don't try, those men *will* die. We have a cellar, we can access supplies. This is something we can do. We can make a difference."

"You are asking us to risk death."

"We haven't been caught yet."

"*Yet* is the key word there, Valdis. And what about Estere?" Dāvis spun to face her. "What about you, and your unborn child?"

Estere curled inward, instinctively protecting herself and her baby from his scrutiny.

Valdis paused, mouth working as he sought the right words. "My child is my responsibility, Dāvis," he said, voice low, firm. "And one I take seriously. Estere and I are as one on this. We will not use a baby as an excuse to turn from our duty."

"Your duty? Valdis, what are you saying? You are going to be a father! What other duty is there?"

"The duty of a Latvian, to all Latvians."

"You can't be serious."

"What do you want me to say to my child when he or she asks? That I stood by and watched thousands of men be worked to death? That I hid? That is not who I am. And it is not the Latvia I want to raise my child in."

"That is very noble. But..."

"Enough." Olga stood, hands pressed against the tabletop. "You both forget yourselves. This is my house, not yours. I allow you to stay here. I agreed to be part of your resistance. All of this is moot without my say."

The men lowered their heads sheepishly, and fell silent.

Estere stepped forward. "And what do you want to do, Olga?" she asked.

Olga sucked in a deep breath and straightened her shoulders. Head held high she said, "I want to save them all."

Valdis' face split into a grin.

Estere closed her eyes.

Dāvis and Valdis spent a week preparing the cellar. They lined the walls and ran an unconvincing wire for electricity into its depths. It was rigged to a simple heater. Estere and Olga prepared blankets.

Estere straightened from folding the final blanket over a small cot and took in the completed space. It was tight and cold, the electric heater barely strong enough to take the chill from the air.

"We will have to make sure they turn that off if the Nazis come," Olga said, following Estere's gaze. "It makes the meter in the kitchen whirl like crazy."

"It's not very nice down here, is it?" Estere said, hand rubbing her belly.

"Better than the ghetto," Olga replied, turning to climb back up into the house above.

Estere couldn't argue with that.

TWENTY-ONE

ESTERE

The truck idled at the crossroads, its old engine struggling in the frozen air. Before them the soldiers guarding the checkpoint stomped their feet, willing blood flow and warmth to reach their toes. Estere hoped they got frostbite.

She sat on the passenger side of the vehicle, her rapidly rounding belly pressed firm against her dress. She needed to let the dress out again; it was impossible to keep up with her growing size. Beside her at the wheel, Valdis scanned the checkpoint. So basic. Just a wooden barrier set across the middle of the main road. They could drive straight through it at speed. But then they would definitely be shot.

Valdis turned to her. "It's time, are you ready?"

She nodded, not trusting her voice to speak through her jangling nerves.

"Don't worry." He reached over and squeezed her hand. "Žanis has done this dozens of times. All we need to do is say we are clearing rubbish ready for the baby. You are the perfect cover. Simple."

Unable to face his open faith, she turned her eyes to the road.

He released her hand, returning his to the wheel. "Here we go."

He slid the truck into gear, the engine coughed and spluttered angrily then the truck lurched forward, seats bouncing on the unstable suspension. It rattled round the corner, turning right and straightening to aim directly for the checkpoint. Estere's teeth rattled in her head along with the truck's passage. She clamped down her jaw and prayed to God they would succeed.

A soldier stepped out onto the road before them, a gloved hand held up to stop their passage. Valdis pressed down on the brake pedal. The truck shuddered to a stop, the furniture burdening the trailer tipping dangerously. Estere gasped, ears alert for any cries of alarm.

It was natural, after all. No one liked to feel they were about to be tipped out of a truck.

For it was not only furniture they carried in their load, but people. Stuffed inside old cupboards and between piled tables and chairs squatted men of various ages, heights and former occupations. All were thin, now, if not before. And all were Jewish.

They'd been hiding at Žanis' for months, but his back garden bunker was too crowded for this last push to save the prisoners. So, they were taking these men to Olga's cellar. Žanis had rowed them across the Daugava obscured by the light of dawn, huddled beneath a blanket; now they crouched inside the furniture on the truck. The soldier stepped up to the driver's side of the truck, eyes scanning the tray of furniture. Valdis quickly wound down the window.

"We are setting up a nursery," he said. "A friend was kind enough to give us these pieces..."

"Papers." The soldier held out his hand. Valdis pulled out a set of documents belonging to Olga's father. The soldier took them, reading quickly, then passed them back. His eyes lingered on Estere, taking in the swell of her stomach beneath her dress. He seemed to be considering.

He turned, waving over a fellow soldier.

Estere's heart leaped into her throat, her breathing quickening.

"It's just old furniture..."

"No one goes through. Only supply trucks. You are not on the list. I have to check with my commander."

"But..."

Estere placed a calming hand on Valdis' knee, squeezing gently. Don't argue, she pleaded, just wait.

An older soldier walked over, legs stiff, hands hidden in thick black gloves. He scanned the truck, thin lips twitching beneath a drooping moustache that hid the expression from his face.

"They are setting up a nursery, for the baby."

The older soldier took their papers, eyes running over the fabricated details of their lives.

"Married?" he asked. "I see no certificate."

Estere felt Valdis bristle. He acknowledged no government here, only God above. Marriage under Nazi rule was out of the question.

"Yes," Estere stammered, voice unsure. She couldn't let him lose control, she couldn't let him say what he really thought. Honesty hovered too close to the edge with Valdis.

"We lost our documents when the Soviets came. It has been a blessing to have order restored under German leadership."

The old man eyed her. His large red nose had dripped snot onto his whiskers. She doubted he could feel it, his face likely too numb from the cold to have any feeling.

He nodded once, stepping back and waving to the remaining two men who manned the makeshift checkpoint gate. They waved back then pushed down one end of the wooden barrier, raising the other to the sky.

Estere released a long breath through her nose, forced a smile of thanks to her lips.

Shifting the truck gears into drive, Valdis pressed down the accelerator and drove beneath the barrier, heading for Olga's home.

Olga and Dāvis met them at the gate. Nervous and wary, they fidgeted as the truck ambled onto the yard. Dāvis shut the gate as soon as the rear had crossed into the property.

Together they helped the men from the furniture, leading them inside Olga's house and down into her freezing cellar.

"Thank you," one old man said as he passed Estere, his too-thin torso caving in on itself as he walked.

Skeletal and overworked, they simply didn't have enough food to rehabilitate their health. Living underground, out of the light surely didn't help. It wouldn't be much better here. But it was safe, at least for now.

Estere smiled at the old man.

"I'm Emil," he said.

"Estere."

"Thank you, Estere."

She watched him ease himself unsteadily down the small ladder into the cellar. He didn't even blink, just accepted his new subterranean home.

It was all so wrong.

Frustrated and angry, she strode out into the cold. Snow trimmed the dirt drive, glistening in mounds that weighed down the boughs of the trees. February was a horrid month in Latvia, the coldest of them all, the end of a long dark season. Food was always scarce, and because of the war it was scant. People had so little to sustain themselves, how could they afford to ration even further to help these refugees? And yet people did, and somehow through the small but trustworthy network Žanis had built they kept these people alive. It never felt enough, it wasn't enough. And now, with the baby growing in her womb, Estere was out of time.

She felt him step up behind her. His warmth seeped through her back as he drew her into an embrace. His hands rested on the bulge of her belly.

"You have to decide, my darling."

"I know," she replied. "I will."

She felt him nod against her head before his hands slipped from her body and he walked out towards the trees that lined Olga's home. Watching the forest, he seemed lost in thought. She waited, allowing him the time to reflect.

"The war is changing, Estere," he began at last. "The Nazis are overstretched. They grow weak, distracted. It is time to shift the plan."

Estere frowned. "What do you intend?"

Valdis eyed her. "Our network of supporters, they don't just believe in the plight of the Jewish survivors. They believe in a free Latvia. As do we. With the Nazis harried on two fronts, they are vulnerable. The time to strike is coming."

"You are talking about rebellion, open fighting."

"I am." His eyes shone. "We need a way to communicate, to rally the people, to reach their hearts and prepare them to fight... If we could circulate messages of strength, show people that we are all together in this..."

She believed in his fervour, she wanted to help, but her back was aching abominably and her heartburn was making her nauseous. She felt defeated.

Valdis turned to her, eyes fevered with passion. He was energised, buoyed by their success in bringing the Jewish citizens safely across the city, ready to think even bigger.

Estere sighed.

She couldn't help it, her exhaustion was too much, and the baby was kicking again.

His face dropped, eyes darkening. "Have you lost your faith in me?"

Estere blinked in surprise. "How can you ask that? I follow your every plan. I came today, even though I was afraid. For me, and for our child..."

"Ah, of course." His expression softened and he paced back to her, placing a gentle hand over her belly. She breathed in the moment, holding his expression in her mind. They had so few moments like this, just them and their love for their unborn child. "It is a natural distraction. And a valid reason to be wary. It is instinctual. You have our child to think of now. Not just yourself."

And you, she thought. *I always think of you. I left my family to be with you. That was my choice.*

"It is time you returned home. You need to rest and prepare for the birth."

Estere worked to keep her features calm. How could he want her to leave already? Had she become a burden so quickly, now she was with child? "I am months yet from being due," she stammered.

"But you need to rest..."

"Soon, all right. Soon." She clasped his hands, pressing them to her heart. "I am not ready to leave you. Not yet."

Valdis smiled, placing a hand on her cheek to cup her face. "You aren't leaving me. We are always together, in our hearts and minds," he tapped her forehead, "you must remember that."

The tension in her shoulders slackened. There he was, the man she loved, her Valdis. "I will remember," she whispered, a secret smile on her lips.

"Not yet then," he relented, pulling her close once more. "But soon, for the baby."

"For the baby," she agreed.

TWENTY-TWO

ESTERE

They came with the sunrise, during the softness of the spring thaw. They did not knock, or call their arrival, but strode onto Olga's land as though it were their own. Silent, fast, they had mounted the porch before Bruno awoke to bark.

It was that bark that roused Estere. Digging sleep from her eyes she crept to the window, and stopped dead.

"Valdis!" she hissed, racing to his sleeping form. "The Germans are here!"

He rose like the wind, banging on the thin wall that separated their room from Dāvis and Olga's. Pulling his trousers over his sleeping trunks, braces dangling at his hips, he raced from the room. The house erupted. She heard Dāvis' heavy tread as he raced down the stairs, the four sharp bangs of a chair on the hatch to the cellar to warn their hidden Jewish survivors, the rattle of the door handle and the shout of German demands.

"Ja, ja, ja," Olga's voice rang through the house. Estere paused in the doorway, worked to still her breathing. Drawing on her dressing robe, she slowly descended the stairs.

The soldiers were already inside. Standing, legs wide, faces grim, guns slung over their shoulders, crowding the central living space. Dāvis sat at the table, his foot resting over the hatch to the cellar. Valdis was to the side. It was Olga who stood before the soldiers, her small frame braced as if to hold them back from the hidden cellar hatch by the sheer force of her will alone. A small, pale hand reached up and smoothed her hair as she forced a smile to her lips.

Estere's eyes flicked to the electricity meter. It whirred fast, out of control. She sent a silent prayer that the men hidden below would remember to turn off the heater. Or that the Germans would not notice the unusual draw of current spinning the meter.

"Guten Morgen, I was not informed you would be visiting."

The soldier at the front nodded, doffed his cap and nestled it under his arm in a ludicrous parody of polite behaviour. "Guten Morgen, Fräulein. Not a bother. You were not informed. This is a surprise inspection."

Estere's body flashed hot as panic tremored along her limbs. Somehow, Olga remained calm, at least outwardly. "An inspection? Whatever for? We are just a smallholding. I have only two chickens, not enough to share..."

"You misunderstand, Fräulein. We have no interest in your stocks. But more in your activities." Olga swallowed, the bob of her throat pronounced.

"Please, tell me what activities you wish to know more about and I will detail them."

"No need," the soldier said. "We will just take a look around."

He turned behind him to the three waiting men, flicked his fingers and they dispersed through the house. Two strode through the main room, one headed upstairs. The thud of their feet echoed through the small farmhouse, the walls quaking with their strides. Estere huddled against the doorframe, arms instinctively wrapped about her stomach.

Her heart sought Valdis. Across the room they stared at

each other, eyes locked. Around them the house banged and crashed, cupboards thrown to the floor, windows smashed, doors kicked open, but they kept their eyes on just each other, never turning as Olga's home was ripped asunder.

The soldiers returned, another nod from their superior and they flowed outside. Bruno barked. A shout of aggression, a whimper, then silence. Estere snorted in fear, but Valdis held her focus. More crashes, the shot of a gun. Then silence.

Tears flowing freely down her face, Estere held firm, eyes fixed on her lover, hands gripping her unborn babe.

The soldiers returned, gathering in a row behind their leader. One stepped forward. The officer inclined his head, listening to the report. A nod. The soldier stepped back.

Silence fell.

Estere ran her hands down her dressing gown, trying to dry the sweat from her palms.

The officer stepped forward. Valdis broke eye contact. Estere turned.

Somehow, through it all, Olga had remained still and stoic on the threshold of the room. Her head was high, her shoulders back, holding space before the might of the German army, embodied in this one man dressed in grey.

Behind her head the electricity meter had slowed.

"All seems in order," the officer said, voice soft, expression aloof. "But don't get comfortable," he continued. "We will be back to check on you."

"You are welcome any time," Olga said, a tiny quaver in her voice.

The officer bared his teeth in a grin, more menace than convivial.

"Good day, Fräulein."

The soldiers filed out. Olga shrank. As the front door closed behind the last uniform, her knees gave. Dāvis was on his feet in an instant, gathering Olga from the floor. Wordlessly, he turned for the stairs, but before he ascended, he stopped. Olga's face appeared over his shoulder.

"She goes," she said, pointing directly at Estere.

Dāvis mounted the stairs.

Estere shuffled to the kitchen table, eased herself down to sit. The door banged again. Estere looked up in fear, but it was only Bruno. The old dog waddled across to her, coming to rest his head in her lap. Hands deep in the scruff of his neck, she buried her face in his warmth and softness.

Silently Valdis came up behind her, placing a hand on her shoulder.

There was nothing to say, no debate to be had. The Germans were watching, and Olga wanted Estere gone. So, she would go.

They stood beneath a hundred-year-old oak, foreheads pressed close, cheeks wet with tears. Above their heads drops of dew fell from new buds, green and tender. Hopeful.

"We knew this day was coming," Valdis said, fingers digging into the flesh of Estere's upper arms.

"It came too soon."

"I won't stop, Estere. I promise. I will find a way to free the men in our care. I will bring our people together to fight. There is a Latvia for us. You believe me, don't you?"

"I always have."

Estere calmed, savouring the warmth of his breath on her skin.

"But we are always together, in here." He tapped her chest, above her heart.

Estere closed her eyes. The platitude was dust against the reality they now faced.

"I will write," she said. "I don't know how I will get letters to you."

"You will find a way." He cupped her chin, breaking their foreheads apart and staring into her eyes. She would, she promised herself.

"I still want to help, to contribute. I can send supplies—"

"You have done enough," Valdis said, eyes on her stomach. Estere looked down at the swell of her dress. She loved the life that stirred within, but she would not stop. Valdis needed her.

"Father will be furious."

Valdis huffed, body going rigid. "Estere, you know I would marry you. *Will* marry you. But not now, not like this."

"I know, I know..." she soothed. And she did. Her man of principles. She would have him no other way. "It's the least of my failings."

"No part of you is a failing."

A soft smile curved her lips, her eyes closing.

"Estere?"

"Hmm?"

"I love you. And now, here, beneath this tree that has stood for longer than either of us has lived. That has seen Latvia fall and rise, and fall again. That, God willing, will see her rise once again, one final time. Beneath this oak, I vow. My heart is yours and yours alone, for all of my days and any beyond this mortal life. Estere, you are my wife, in heart, in body, and before this great creation of God." He gestured up at the sprawling tree. "I am yours, if you will have me?"

The tears flowed freely, salt lining her lips. Heart swelling with joy and hope, she drew his face down to hers and kissed him.

Her answer and her promise sealed, flesh on flesh, forever.

TWENTY-THREE

ZENTA

She brought with her the scents of the forest. New pine, fresh grass and dew, apple blossom and sun-warm hair. Her eyes were wary, darting. Her mouth tight. Her belly, full and round, pressed against her dress.

"Estere!"

Zenta gathered her skirts and raced to the bakery door. There, standing pensive, one foot in the bakery, one still on the street, stood her sister. Without hesitation, Zenta threw her arms about her sister's neck, pulling her close, drawing her within, relief pulsing through her, a physical rhythm beating from her heart.

Estere was home. Joy and relief rushed through her veins.

Pulling back, Zenta scanned her sister's face. Thin, worn, tired; like everyone in Riga. Her eyes drifted to Estere's bulbous waist, a smile curving her lips. "Let's get you fed."

Arm wrapped around her sister's shoulders she led her inside, the door closing gently behind them.

Zenta's cry had brought their mother, who met them at the stairs. Dārta's eyes filled with tears as she beheld her first daughter.

Wordlessly the women embraced. Dārta released a gasping sob as she gripped the worn woollen cardigan that Estere wore. They moved up to the family kitchen, Dārta's hands still clinging to Estere, her grip like a vice, holding her daughter tight so she could not disappear again. They sat and Zenta went to light the stove, and boil water. Kettle on the hob, she gathered the morning's bread and the lard from last night's fry, bringing them to the table.

"There are apples too," Dārta said, not taking her eyes from Estere's face. "And sugar..."

Zenta nodded. Her mother's instructions were clear. Use their rations. Her sister was home.

Zenta arranged the fruit and sugar, poured warm water into a cup, flavoured it with fresh peppermint, Grandma tea as they called it. When it was ready, the food and tea set before Estere, she took her own seat, hands folded before her, and stared: bread, shrivelled fruit, cold lard. A single tear leaked from her eye.

"Eat," Dārta urged, finally releasing her grip on her child to take up the bread knife and carve a thick slice for her daughter. Slathered in lard, Estere brought the bread to her lips, bit and chewed. Her eyes closed, more tears pushed from her lids to run freely to her chin, gathering together in a large droplet that threatened to spill onto the collar of her dress. A gasp ushered from her throat, and she looked to her mother, her sister, a smile, wobbly and thin, forming on her face.

"We missed you so," Zenta said. Estere nodded.

"You've been gone so long."

Estere swallowed, eyes focused now on her bread.

"But you are home now."

"Thank you," Estere whispered. "Thank you." Dārta gripped her daughter's arm, taking hold once more, as if to secure her in place.

Silence fell between the women, and they sat together, still and patient, as Estere finished her meal.

After eating, Estere retired to her bed, still freshly made, sheets clean, blankets mended and ready. Dārta had never stopped hoping. She was clearly exhausted after her journey home, from wherever she'd come.

Back in the bakery, Zenta reopened the shop, ready for the customers the fine spring afternoon might coax from their homes. For the first time in months, Dārta joined her. Mother and daughter smiled at each other, hearts lifted. A sense of hope shining between them in the warmth of the sun that filtered through the windows.

It was days before Estere spoke. First, she slept, long and deep. Then she washed. Zenta boiled water for her to wipe down her face, hands, legs and feet. Dressed in fresh clothes, faded but clean, she appeared in the kitchen at breakfast. Nikolai looked up. His eyes unfocused. Standing, he walked towards her, and, without a word, pushed past and made his way up to his room.

"He is in shock," Dārta said by way of explanation.

Estere nodded, taking a seat beside Zenta. She ate heartily. Zenta secretly plated her own morning ration for her sister. She would fill up on water, it was surprising what tricks you learned to fill a hungry stomach. After eating Estere returned to bed and rest.

"We must be patient," Dārta said. "She has been through much." She busied herself clearing the table.

Zenta watched the empty doorway through which her sister had once again vanished and suppressed a sigh. How long she had prayed for her sister's return, imagined her coming home with the rebels, ushering in a free Latvia.

This was not what she had pictured.

It was that night Estere finally spoke. Zenta lay in her bed, eyes closed against the night, mind giving way to rest.

"I missed you too."

Zenta's eyes snapped open. She blinked at the darkness, swallowing and waited.

"It was hard, living away from you."

Quietly, Zenta rolled onto her side. Bringing her arm up to cradle her head she watched her sister in the faint moonlight. Estere rolled over too, their eyes met.

"Where were you?"

"I can't say. It is still a hideout."

Frustration flared in Zenta's gut. She deserved the truth, after all this time. They all did.

Estere smoothed a stray lock from her eyes, before rubbing her temple. Face softening, she relented. "It's about a two-hour walk from here, on the edge of the city, where it meets the forest."

"Which forest?"

"Believe me, Zee, I wish I could tell you. But it's not safe. If the Germans were to find us... please understand."

"I looked for you," Zenta said. "But I didn't know where."

"I am sorry. We had to be so careful."

"We... you and Valdis?"

"Yes, and some others."

She fell silent. Zenta waited. Questions building up within her, pressing against her lips to be asked. But she remained quiet. She knew to let her sister tell her tale, in her own time.

"I didn't want to leave you," Estere continued. "But after Tomass... and Valdis' increasing underground activities. If I stayed, I may never have seen him again."

You may never have seen us again by leaving. Zenta pressed her eyes shut against the uncharitable thought. Who was she to judge her sister in this time of war? The choice was not Estere's fault. Just as it wasn't Aleks' for leaving also.

There were few good choices left in Latvia.

"I understand," Zenta said, reaching out a hand between the beds.

Estere took her proffered hand, squeezed it tightly.

"I got pregnant. That changed things. I can't move fast now. I am a risk to everyone and to the baby. Valdis was right, I had to come back. For our baby."

Did you come back for us too? Zenta hugged herself in the dark. "It's not long then... until the baby will come?"

"A few months, maybe less."

Excitement fizzed in her belly. "I am going to be an aunty."

A small laugh escaped Estere's lips. "And I am going to be a mother. God help me!"

The sisters giggled, a shared moment of lightness.

"Will he come for you? When the baby is born?"

"Valdis will come. Once it is safe. Once the war is won."

"He believes that time will come?" Zenta asked, warily. Years of occupation had taught her not to trust to hope.

"It draws close. Closer than you think."

Zenta had heard that before, but she kept her doubts buried deep. What good was guesswork anyway? The Soviets and the Nazis had taught her that much.

"Then we must keep you and the baby safe until he does."

Squeezing Zenta's hand once more, Estere released her sister and rolled onto her back.

"She's kicking."

"She?"

"A guess."

"Can I feel?"

"Of course, come."

Zenta rose quietly, crossing to her sister's bed, slowly reaching out a hand, cautious, afraid she might startle the baby within Estere's womb.

"Here." Estere took her hand and pressed it firmly to her belly. Her flesh was taut, hard. The roundness of her stomach tight like a balloon. Zenta fell still. Waited. Nothing. Then... light like the touch of a feather or the passing of butterfly wings, tiny taps.

She released an involuntary gasp of wonder.

The sisters' eyes met in the moonlight. Estere smiled. "I hope she will be just like you," she whispered. "Good, right to her very centre."

Zenta smiled, pride swelling in her chest. "I know she will be strong like you."

TWENTY-FOUR

ZENTA

Zenta leaned her bike against the back wall of her home. She was late to work this morning. Estere had come down to help Dārta, so Zenta had taken the opportunity to visit Aleks' mother at the end of her delivery run.

She had already lost so much in these years of war. But Zenta could see she still had hope that her son would return. The same prayer nestled within Zenta's own chest. The women had shared rye pudding and warm water. Lauma often gave her tea ration to an aged neighbour. She was a good woman. Selfless, kind. Zenta saw so much of Aleks in her gentle warmth, her shining eyes. He was his mother's son, as Zenta was her father's daughter.

Standing in the shared garden behind the bakery, Zenta stretched, enjoying the warmth of the early-summer day, the positive energy of the bright sun, despite the reality around her. These moments alone, without the burden of the bakery, the rations, the stories of loss and despair that were written in the greying walls of her city, these moments kept her going.

That and the thought of the impending arrival of her niece.

Estere had seemingly doubled in size since she arrived home. As the sun drew higher and stronger, Estere's belly swelled, her face plumping on the extra rations they all shared with her. Estere tried to refuse, of course. But Dārta would hear none of it. Nikolai had still not spoken to his eldest daughter, but even he gave up his slice of morning bread for the baby in her belly. Zenta had caught him watching Estere as he sat by the window with his pipe. A softness filled his tired eyes as they fell upon the swell of her stomach. His anger at Estere's choice would thaw, in time. New life healed much, especially in a world of loss.

Smiling at the thought of the baby, Zenta made her way into the back of the house, into the bakery kitchen. Estere was there, kneading bread.

"I can take over," Zenta offered.

Estere straightened slowly, wiping sweat from her brow with the back of a flour-covered hand. "Would you mind? I know you've been out on delivery, but my back is aching dreadfully."

She grimaced, emphasising the point.

"Not a problem." Zenta rolled up her sleeves, washed her hands, then plunged them into the dough Estere had begun to work. Estere took a seat, picking at the sticky dough that had lodged in her fingernails. Zenta fell into the routine of the dough, kneading, mind going still, empty, timeless.

She was pulled from her trance by the sound of footsteps and voices. One the familiar cadence of her father's, the other speaking German. She stopped her work and, wiping her hand on a tea towel, made her way to the front of the store. What was going on? Their ration of flour was late, perhaps it had finally arrived.

Coming into the bakery proper she stopped in her tracks.

There, in the middle of the shop, stood Otto. She hadn't seen him for weeks. No little chats, small gifts. No uncomfortable stares. She'd wondered if he'd been moved to a different patrol, or a horrid thought, sent to fight... she'd hoped not. He was the enemy, true, but he had been kind to her. Despite her wariness, it had felt nice to know his admiration, to receive his little gifts. In his absence she'd found herself looking for him, scanning the streets of Riga for his easy smile. Clearly, he had not left.

He was talking with Nikolai, words calm. Nikolai gestured back to the mostly empty racks of bread they had for sale. They were making do as best they could without their delayed delivery, but by mid-morning most of their stock was gone. Zenta and her sister were preparing the last bake of the day.

The German looked up. He spotted Zenta immediately and his face split into a wide, boyish grin.

"Guten Morgen, Fräulein."

Nikolai's head whipped around. Zenta froze.

Otto walked forward, his step light, almost bouncing. "Beautiful day," he said in his awkward Latvian.

Zenta tried to smile, but her lips wouldn't cooperate.

Still grinning, the soldier turned back to Nikolai. "You have a beautiful daughter," he said, returning back to German.

"I am a lucky man," Nikolai replied, his eyes narrowing on his daughter.

Zenta felt Estere come up behind her, the touch of her sister's hand on her back a small reassurance in the turmoil.

"Mein Gott!" the soldier exclaimed, taking in Estere's swollen belly. "You are to be a grandfather!" It seemed even young German soldiers were excited by new babies.

"A *very* lucky man," Nikolai replied.

The room fell silent. The young soldier smiling genially at them all, seemingly unaware of the mounting tension. At length he nodded, turning to Nikolai, "I will check on the ration delivery."

"Dankeschön."

Then Otto fixed Zenta with a stare. Tipping his head in a mime of doffing a hat, he grinned. "Auf Wiedersehen."

No one spoke until the door had shut behind him.

"What was that?" Nikolai's voice was soft but vicious as he addressed his youngest child. "How do you know that man?"

"He patrols near the square." Zenta's mouth had gone dry, she worked her tongue, trying to lubricate her throat. "I see him sometimes, on my rounds."

"*See* him? What do you mean, *see* him?" Nikolai demanded.

"I..." What to say? Zenta's eyes fluttered about the shop, the room suddenly both colder and hotter at once. The walls pressing in as her father advanced towards her. "He sometimes waves."

"He spoke to you in Latvian!"

"I believe he knows a few words..."

"What has he promised you to make you turn from Aleksandrs?"

"What?"

"Have you shamed yourself? Have you turned from your country?"

"Nikolai!"

Dārta stood at the staircase, eyes wide, hands planted firmly on her hips.

"That is enough!"

Nikolai recoiled, eyes snapping up to his wife. Dārta's face was red with fury as she stared down at her husband. "You will listen to your daughter. You will not assume! Zenta is a good girl. You know this."

Beside her Estere sucked in a sharp breath; the words an unfortunate comparison between the sisters.

"He spoke to her in Latvian..." Nikolai repeated, flinging a hand out to point accusingly at Zenta.

"He is barely a man," Dārta snapped. "Young men are all

the same. And your daughter is a pretty thing. She was bound to turn his head. That does not mean he turned hers!"

"It will not matter if that is true or not – if people start to believe it."

"You, it seems, are the only one who does."

Nikolai stood still, face furious. Then, "Fine," he huffed, turning to Zenta. "The truth, now. Tell me and I will listen."

Zenta took a deep breath... and lied. "It is as I have said. He waves sometimes as I pass. He stopped me once, said hello. But that is it. Nothing more."

She couldn't tell him the full truth. Of the chocolate, the cheese, the kindness in his eyes. The loneliness in his smile. There was no way her father would understand.

"You are telling me the truth?" It was a demand.

"I am."

Nikolai stared at her for the longest moment, eyes cold and hard. Then, nodded once.

"Change your route," he said before turning on his heel and storming out of the shop.

They knew he wouldn't be home until curfew.

Zenta released a heavy breath, her heart hammering in her chest. She felt weak. Light-headed. She'd done nothing wrong and yet guilt snaked its way through her gut, thick and shimmery.

Her father was right. Even if she wasn't sneaking about with the young soldier, his familiarity with her would cause talk. And talk could be deadly.

"Well." Dārta spoke as she moved into the bakery kitchen. Zenta and Estere followed. "I see the bread is not completed. Back to work."

Zenta met her eyes, a silent thank you passing to her mother before Dārta retreated back upstairs, leaving her daughters to their toil.

.   .   .

That night Estere sat on the edge of Zenta's bed and gently combed the knots from her long fair hair. Zenta's eyes drifted shut as the rhythm of the brush strokes soothed away the tension of the day. She was thankful to her sister for this moment of affection. She needed it. Nikolai's anger had stayed with her all day, filling her with shame and fear.

"Thank you," she said.

"Of course."

The sisters sat in silence, enjoying the peace of the evening and the time alone. Just like old times.

"Zenta." Estere's voice had changed. An edge coming into her tone, shattering the calm of the night around them.

Zenta stiffened reflexively, before turning to face the question in her sister's voice.

"I told the truth," she said. "Well, mostly. I am not seeing that soldier."

Estere's eyes held her face in the lamplight. The brush was now limp in her lap. Their moment of peace gone.

"I know," she said finally. "That is why it is you I must ask."

Zenta frowned. "Ask? Ask what?"

Estere heaved herself to her feet, taking a moment to balance the weight of the baby in her stomach before pacing to the dresser and placing the brush back in its drawer. She paused, facing away from Zenta. Suddenly, her shoulders squared and she turned, fixing Zenta with a stare.

"I need you to do something for me. For Latvia."

Zenta blinked. She had been about to confess to her sister about Otto's little gifts that she had concealed. She'd not expected the conversation to take such a turn. "For Latvia? Estere, what are you talking about?"

Estere crossed the room swiftly, sitting back beside Zenta and taking hold of her hands. "It is dangerous, but important. Believe me, if I could think of any other way..."

"Estere, stop talking in circles. Speak plainly."

Estere's eyes flicked side to side.

"The Russians are coming, Zee. Germany is being squeezed between two armies, one to the West and one to the East. The war is ending. There is an opportunity. It starts right here, in Riga."

"What opportunity?" Zenta swallowed, watching as Estere paused to find the right words.

"We need to get the news out there. To tell the people the truth. We need to spread the word."

"You want to tell the people of Riga that the Russians are coming? Estere. We already know that."

"No," Estere shook her head. Standing from the bed she began to pace. "We want to get them to fight. To join us. People are afraid. And we only hear the news the Germans want us to hear. So, we do nothing. Men cower at home, women hide their faces in the streets. We are held down by Nazi threats and propaganda. But they are breaking."

She turned to face Zenta, eyes ablaze with fervour, arms outstretched. "They are losing. And now, now we can start the revolution. We can rise up and take back our country. Force the Germans out. Stop the Russians. And you can spread the word."

"Estere, slow down. I don't understand. Spread the word? What word? What are you talking about?"

"Valdis knows others, men and women who believe as he does. As I do. If we can rally our men, we have a chance. The time is coming, Zee. Like it did at the end of Father's war. The moment when the armies are weakened and we can strike. We can take back our country. But we need believers. We need fighters."

Zenta blinked. Estere's vision an eerie echo of Aleks' fevered hope.

"How?"

"We need to connect the links. Send messages, organise."

"Estere, you are talking about sharing secrets. If we were caught..."

Estere answered quickly, her voice high, agitated, "If we want to be free, we have to stand against them and their rules and controls. We have to speak for Latvia."

"You have heard the rumours about the labour camps. You remember the Jews..."

"I will keep you at arm's length," Estere cut in. "We can add the messages to your delivery run. If anyone suspects you can just say you thought they were notes between friends. But no one will suspect you." Returning to the bed she took her sister's hand. "Your soldier friend won't suspect you. It is the perfect cover. There is risk, yes, but the reward is our freedom, Zee. What can be worth more than that?"

"This puts us all in danger. Estere, what about your baby?" Zenta gestured at her sister's growing bump.

Estere took her belly between her hands, holding its round-ness firmly. "My baby is the very reason I must risk this. Don't you see, Zee? We are slaves in our own land. Occupied, repressed, starved and afraid. I want more for my child. I want what we had. What Father won for us. Now it is our turn. We must act. We must fight for our country. And now, now is the time. But we have to gather our men. We have to join together. We have to tell our people the truth: that we can."

Zenta stared at her sister, breathing slowly. There was more to this request, she could feel it. Estere was hiding something.

Yet her words were still true. Life in Riga was a dance of fear. The Soviets had taken the laughter of children from the streets. The Germans had killed the hope. And now, the Germans were faltering. But the Russians advanced.

There was a moment, an opportunity between armies, to

rise up as the people of Latvia and fight. To take back their laughter and their hope. To free their nation.

Zenta looked into her sister's pleading eyes, read the desperation and fear that Estere's words tried to hide. Saw too the hope. It strengthened something within her own heart.

"What do you need me to do?"

TWENTY-FIVE

ZENTA

Well, her father had told her to change her route.

Zenta pedalled along the renamed Hitler Strasse, away from the old town and heading into the groups of houses that were dotted between the trees of the forests that surrounded Riga. Part of the city, but also part of the forest. Perfect for those who wanted to remain less visible to Nazi eyes.

The delivery plan was simple. Her basket full of bread, Zenta would collect a stack of messages, interleaved with bakery orders, at her first stop, then, circulate the food and the information across a selected network of Valdis' contacts.

What the letters contained, Zenta didn't ask. Her sister had trusted her with some information, but there was more. Much more.

But she didn't need to know. Ignorance was a protection.

She just hoped her sister would be able to doctor the books to account for the missing supplies to the Nazis. She'd have to ask about that when she got home. It wouldn't do for the soldiers, or their father, to realise what they were up to.

Nikolai still hadn't spoken to Estere, at least not to Zenta's knowledge. There was still a barrier between them, large and edged in shadow. But Zenta remained hopeful. The new baby on the way would surely bring some perspective and healing.

Not if Nikolai noticed the missing bread, however...

Zenta made a mental note to check with Estere. How would they keep their careful father from noticing?

Her first stop was at the end of a long dirt track. Birch trees rose high in the sky around her, the bright green of their full leaves glinting gaudily in the summer sun. A smile came to her lips. She loved the change of season, the joy and hope of rebirth that was June in Riga.

The property came up quickly, a high wooden fence lining its boundary against the countryside. Swinging from her bike she approached the gate. Loud barking erupted from within.

No need to knock then.

She waited.

Soon a woman of similar age to her sister approached, hair bound back by a patterned shawl. She peered at Zenta through a gap in the wooden gate, eyes flitting, furtive.

Zenta gave her biggest smile.

"Bread from the city," she said loudly. "As you ordered."

Understanding came over the woman's face. Nodding quickly, she unbolted the gate, opening it just enough for Zenta to squeeze into the perimeter. Inside she was met by the full weight of a large fluffy hound as it bounded up to her, jumping to place a paw on each shoulder, before smothering her in hot, wet licks. A laugh escaped her lips. Joy at the dog's exuberance overtaking the tension of the moment.

"Ah, Bruno. Stop! Stupid mutt!" The woman grabbed the animal by a collar and pulled him from Zenta.

"It is all right," Zenta smiled. "He is a darling."

The woman's expression softened as she pulled back the panting Bruno, who was still struggling to get to Zenta for more kisses. "He is that. But not much of a guard dog. Still, perhaps it is a good thing that some of us have not lost our innocence."

She ruffled Bruno's mane then turned her attention back to Zenta.

"The bread for the men?"

Zenta took a deep breath, "men" plural. It confirmed her suspicions, more was already in motion than Estere had let on. "Yes."

"And you will be back next week? Same time?"

"I will."

The woman took the package of bread. "Thank you. Sorry to be so short. Our rations have been running very low... the men are getting tense."

"It has been a long war. It must be hard when they long to fight."

The woman gave a humourless laugh, "I doubt this lot would have the means to fight, not after all they have endured." She paused. "I'm Olga."

"Zenta, but everyone calls me Zee."

Olga smiled. "I will look out for you next week, Zee. Keep this mutt away from your pretty face. It is a brave thing you are doing. Helping us... and them."

"For Latvia."

"Yes, yes, I suppose it is. These are for you, I presume?"

Reaching into her skirts, Olga produced a small stack of papers, to be handed out with her remaining deliveries. She took the bundle.

"They are in order of delivery. The bottom one is for Estere," Olga said, stepping back with a brief smile. "Until next week."

The next few stops were much the same, a handover to a man or teenager, confirmation of next week's delivery. With each stop Zenta's confidence grew. These were good people. Valdis had planned this well. Finished in the forests, she made her way back into the city to deliver to her regular customers.

Soon only one message remained in her basket: Estere's. It had been a long and taxing morning, finally it was time to go home.

But first, a detour for herself.

Turning from the city she pedalled along the banks of the mighty Daugava, savouring the salty brine that wafted to her nose. Above her head seagulls called, their long wings spread across the blue sky. She cycled past the now empty central market arches, further down the riverside until the banks returned to mud. There she stopped, laying her bike in the dirt.

Pressing her hands into the small of her back she stretched, easing the tension that gathered there during her long delivery journey. Stillness settled over her. Sun on her face, salt breeze caressing her skin, she allowed herself to just be. Alone and quiet on the banks of the Daugava.

She closed her eyes.

For a brief moment, surrounded by the sound of the river as it rushed to meet the sea, she could imagine things as they once were. That she was eleven again and here to play with Aleks and Ava. That the Soviets had never come, the Nazis either. That the buildings that lined the river were not blasted to rubble, that the streets still rang with the echo of children's laughter, the rocking rhythm of the tram, the cry of the market sellers offering their wares. The real Riga, coming to life again after the cold of winter kept all indoors. Blossoming with the flowers. Her city.

Opening her eyes she reluctantly returned to reality. The grey haze of smoke that clung in the air from new industry, the road churned to mud by tanks and cannon. The dead trees, torn by the roots from the earth by explosions, the burned-out husks of synagogues, the blasted walls of people's homes, the hell of the ghetto. War had scarred her city at its very core. She didn't know if it could be repaired.

"Good morning, my friend."

Zenta jumped, turning swiftly and coming face to face with Otto.

Her jaw dropped in shock, throat tightening with fear. What was he doing here? Had he followed her? If so, for how long? She brought her hands together in front of her, clutching them tightly, willing herself to calm. She realised her mouth was hanging open and snapped it shut.

Otto laughed good-naturedly, misunderstanding her flustered reaction. "Don't worry, I won't tell." He winked conspiratorially.

Zenta's eyes went wide with fear, her mouth suddenly dirt dry.

"T-tell?" she stammered.

Otto grinned. "I won't say I caught you here, resting in the sun. I think it is all right to have a small break. You do work so very hard."

A break. He was teasing her about slacking off by the river. He can't have discovered how she'd spent her morning. Relief flooded Zenta's limbs, threatening to collapse her knees beneath her. She gave a breathy laugh.

"Come," Otto said, moving to her bike. "I will walk you home."

Swallowing hard as his hands hovered over the breadbasket, Estere's message inside. Zenta sprang into action. "No, no, it is all right. I can manage." She reached for the handlebars, just as he did. Their hands met on the cool metal rim. Otto smiled. His eyes met hers as he slowly and purposefully ran a finger across her flesh. She froze. He broke the contact, taking the bike into his control and moving it back up to the path. It left Zenta no choice but to follow.

"I often come to the river on my breaks," he explained as they walked. "Especially on beautiful days like this. Perfect for spending time with a beautiful lady."

Zenta gave him a smile, eyes flicking briefly to Otto's face.

She saw red blotching up his neck from his collar and knew he was nervous too. But for an entirely different reason. She fell into step beside him. The bread and letter sitting like a ticking time bomb in her basket right under Otto's nose.

But he wasn't interested in what she was delivering, only in her.

And that was a great advantage.

Swallowing her nerves, she spoke. "Do you enjoy summer? I think it is my favourite season."

Otto looked over to her in surprise. It was the first time she had engaged in a conversation with him. Delight curved his lips as he answered, "It is my mother's favourite season too. She would like you."

Zenta smiled. Her heart softened at the wistful tone that had come to Otto's voice. "You miss her? Your mother."

He nodded. "And my baby brother. He would be five now. He is too much like me. I think he would be up to all mischief with Mother."

An unexpected laugh bubbled up in her chest at the thought of a little version of Otto, tormenting his mother. "I think you were a good son," she found herself saying and realised she meant it.

Otto remained silent, eyes forward.

Zenta licked her lips, reading the sorrow in the slump of Otto's shoulders. "You will see them again," she said simply. She hoped it was true.

"Ja," Otto said, flashing her a quick smile. "One day things will return to normal."

They passed the remaining walk in silence, both lost in their own thoughts of the war and what it had cost them, the squeak of her bicycle wheel the only sound. Coming to the bakery, Otto stopped.

"Your sister is well?" He gestured the shape of a rounded belly.

Zenta smiled. "Yes, very well. It won't be long now until the baby comes."

"It is good." He said, eyes intense, nodding.

"Yes."

They paused, sudden awkwardness rising between them.

"Oh! I forget!" Hands diving into his pockets, a grin, pure and excited, lit up his face. Zenta's stomach twitched.

He held his hands before him, cupped carefully, obscuring whatever he was offering from her view. A half-smile tugged at the corner of her mouth.

"For your sister. And for you." He opened his hands. There on his palm rested a small cardboard box, inside it four strawberries, red and plump and perfect. Zenta gasped.

Strawberries were a seasonal delicacy, enjoyed throughout Latvia, in normal times. But this year, the crop was sparse, and the farmers sold only to German stores, leaving regular citizens of Riga to go without. But Otto was German, he had saved and bought strawberries. And he was offering them to her.

It was an outrageously kind and thoughtful gift.

Zenta's lips parted in shock. She looked at Otto, eyes questioning.

He smiled. Taking her hand, he carefully tipped his bounty onto her palm. Wiping the sticky juice from the berries on his trousers, he straightened.

"Well, good day, Zenta." His eyes met hers.

"Good day, Otto."

She felt his eyes on her back as she made her way to the rear gate. Once inside the yard she released a long, heavy sigh of relief. She leaned her bike against the back wall of her home and collected the remaining bread, and Estere's message.

Their plan had worked.

Otto had not even thought to search her basket. The baker's daughter delivering bread, as she always had. What was there to be suspicious about?

But there was more. As she placed the strawberries in a bowl, careful not to further bruise their delicate flesh, Zenta realised she could deny it no longer. Otto had not simply ignored her, dismissed her as no threat and moved on. He had taken a moment to spend with her. Helped her, in fact. Out of some belief of friendship, or the need for connection, she wasn't sure. But it was clear that Otto liked her.

And despite herself, she realised, she liked him too.

Estere was right, it was the perfect deception for their plan.

TWENTY-SIX

ESTERE

As the cramps of labour began racking her body, Estere thought that she wasn't ready. She hadn't done enough.

Zenta took her hand and helped her up the stairs.

"You must not miss the deliveries tomorrow," Estere had said, panting with the effort to speak above her pain.

"You must focus now, sister. Your baby comes. All is well. I have it in hand."

As the contractions that contorted her belly intensified, Estere had accepted she had no other choice.

It was all right. She had done her part. Unexpectedly, Zenta had been the key. Catching the eye of a young, naive soldier, her sister was the perfect cover for the messages that Valdis needed circulated to try and mount a resistance. She hadn't liked to bring Zenta into it, to risk her little sister. But Estere could see no other way. Now, she had to let go and trust.

The baby came easily. Or so Dārta said. Estere was of a rather different opinion. Small and red and screaming, she slipped out in the early hours of an unseasonably warm day in early June.

Estere had never seen anything so perfect in her life.

The baby was cleansed then wrapped in a woollen blanket and placed on her mother's chest. Instantly, she nuzzled, seeking sustenance. It was the way of Latvia that summer. Heat and hunger hung over them all. Estere bared her breast and guided her child to suckle. She would give all she had, and more. She would keep her baby alive.

"Her name is Aina," she whispered to her mother and sister.

"A beautiful name," Dārta had said.

Healing took longer than she expected. The fatigue of her labour, the hot burning between her legs, a sense of general malaise that just wouldn't lift.

Dārta saw that her daughter was as well fed as possible from their meagre rations. Extra portions of cabbage soup, larger slices of bread, all made their way up the stairs to the room Estere still shared with Zenta. Part of her wanted to refuse the extra food, knowing it would otherwise have been going to those she and Valdis strove to hide and supply. But a greater part, the mother she now was, took every extra she could, knowing it would pass to her precious Aina.

In truth, with the birth of her baby, the fight had gone out of her. The moment she looked into the perfection of her child's sleeping face, it sluiced from her shoulders, and she drifted into her own rest, deep and heavy, exhausted. She wanted to stay cocooned with her newborn forever, away from danger, away from the fight.

But it couldn't last.

Pebbles sounded against the window. Valdis waiting in the darkened street below. Zenta snuck him into the bakery kitchen and Estere made her way, silent as a mouse, to introduce him to his daughter.

He waited, body pensive, a small posy of yellow daisies clutched in his hands.

"For you, my warrior," he said. Estere thought her heart would burst.

He reached for Aina instantly, eyes welling with tears, wonder stitched through his smile.

"She looks just like you," he said, voice barely a whisper.

Estere smiled, she thought Aina looked like Valdis.

She watched as he held their daughter to his chest, cradling her head in his large palm. A perfect moment, kept secret from Nazi watch.

Valdis didn't stay long. And as she watched his back disappear out the door, Estere knew her time of convalescence was through. This was not enough. Moments stolen, marred by the fear of discovery. No, Aina deserved to know her father. Aina deserved to be free.

As the sun rose the next morning, Estere left a dreaming Aina sleeping in her crib and made her way down to the kitchen.

"I will see to the deliveries today," she announced to a surprised Zenta.

Her sister blinked, then swallowed. "It is all right, Estere, I have it under control. You need to rest."

"I am going, Zee. I have wasted enough time at rest."

Zenta must have seen there was no point in arguing, and accepted. Together they packed Zenta's supply bag of bread and flour. Much smaller than those from only a few months before as rations continued to dwindle. With a quick hug, Estere set off.

Though it had only been a matter of weeks since she had walked the streets, a new tension rode the winds.

When she reached the farmhouse, Olga explained it all. Opening the door, she threw her arms around Estere. The friends embraced. Estere was held by the small woman so tightly she worried her ribs might crack. Any tension between them from the day Estere had left evaporated in that moment.

Finally, Olga released her, eyes brimming with tears.

"I hear she is a hearty one," she smiled.

"Growing fat on my milk," Estere replied.

They laughed, a moment of joy.

The moment passed. Olga turned away.

"What is it, Olga?" Estere asked. "Something has changed. I can sense it, out there."

Olga gestured her inside. Estere sat in silence at the thick wooden table as Olga fussed over water for tea. Estere waited patiently, she knew Olga would speak when she was ready.

The words finally came. "They are losing."

"Who is losing?"

"The Nazis. Winter in Russia is bad. You know this. But it was even worse than Hitler expected. The Soviets have them on the run. Pressing them back... towards Latvia."

Estere sat still, mind sifting through this information.

"They are pushed to the west also. A war on two fronts and they are not doing well. The reports from the front deny it, but it is plainly true. You see it in the soldiers. There have been more... incidents."

Estere closed her eyes. She knew well what men were capable of when they were angry and scared. But this was the weakness Valdis was banking on. So why did Olga seem so afraid?

"Have we been discovered?"

"No. All the hideouts are still secure. But Žanis has started moving Jews out of the city, into the countryside proper."

"Risky."

"Yes. But it's the only way. We can only push our luck so far."

They fell silent as Olga poured hot water into two mugs, before adding fresh mint from her windowsill garden to the cups to steep.

Suddenly Olga turned, her mouth forming a hard line before she spoke, "You should get out."

Estere looked up at her friend. "What do you mean?"

"Your family, you should go. The Germans have started evacuating families to Danzig. There is a civilian camp there. The Kristaps went last week. You would be safe there."

"What are you talking about? Why would I leave my city? Now, as the invaders are on the brink of failure."

"Because it will be the Soviets who return! Your brother joined up with the Nazis, and your uncle..."

Estere rose to her feet, pacing to the sink, cup of tea forgotten. She watched the world through the grimy lace of Olga's window dressing. Outside the forest was still, silent. She understood Olga's meaning. The actions of Tomass and Uncle Artūrs had made her family a target for Soviet retribution. And the Soviets were coming.

"I can't leave. Now more than ever Latvia needs us to be strong. This is the opportunity Valdis has been preparing for, the gap between invasions. We must support our men to overthrow both powers and claim our nation once again."

"Estere, Latvia isn't strong enough. You know this."

"Valdis will not leave." She hadn't asked him, but she knew it was true.

She'd long ago realised just who the man she loved was in his heart: a philosopher, an immovable idealist in a world of imperfect humans. He dreamed of more for the people of Latvia, believed in this possibility, and nothing would stop him fighting for it. Even when there was little hope. Estere had accepted this; it was the essence of the man she loved, her Valdis. So, he would continue to fight for beliefs he'd read about in books and she would stand by his side. Always.

Olga didn't argue. It seemed she knew it too.

"Thank you for the tea, dear friend. I must be going."

Olga nodded, pulling Estere into a last embrace. "Be careful, my friend," she whispered. And Estere understood, all Olga had ever wanted was for Estere and her baby to be safe.

"You, too."

As Estere made her way back to the bakery she felt the weight of her limbs like sacks of potatoes, pulling her to the ground. They'd come so far. It had been so long. There was still a long distance left to travel.

Yet there was no choice. Their course was set long ago. There was no turning back, whatever the odds.

She had to keep going. Just a little longer. She had to see Valdis, make a plan.

Lost in her own thoughts and fears, she didn't notice the piercing stare that watched her from across the street.

Stubbing out his cigarette on the pavement, Otto followed Estere at a distance all the way back to the bakery. He wondered where a woman, so newly from childbed, had desperately needed to go so early on a midweek morning...

Estere closed the back door quietly behind her and made her way up to her room. Passing her parents' floor, she heard the soft cooing of Aina and her mother's soothing words. She should go into the family kitchen, collect her child into her arms and give her mother a break. But her meeting with Olga had unsettled her, and the walk had worn through her reserves: she needed her bed. Slipping into her room she eased the door shut behind her. She didn't see him waiting for her.

Turning, she came face to face with her father and flinched instinctively.

"Oh, Father," she exclaimed, raising a hand to her heart. "I didn't see you."

"But I see you," Nikolai replied. He sat on her bed in an undershirt and braces, hands placed neatly on his knees. A pose of waiting. Patience.

Estere swallowed. It was obvious why he was there. He must have seen her, known she was returning to the fight. She drew herself up tall. She would not allow him to throw her out, not this time.

Nikolai didn't speak for several moments. He simply sat, watching her, eyes scanning her face. At length, he sighed.

"I have tried to find peace with my choice. But I cannot. Daughter, I was wrong. Can you ever forgive me?"

Estere blinked in shock. Her mouth fell open. She had not expected this.

Nikolai shook his head. "I was afraid. Losing Tomass... but what is a life lived in fear? That is no choice to make." He looked up, meeting her eyes, sorrow warring with hope in those deep, sad pools of blue. "I fought for Latvia once. I am ready to do so again. Will you let me help you?"

A gush of breath raced from Estere's lungs as tears of happiness sprang into her eyes. "Father," she said, racing to his side and wrapping Nikolai into a tight hug. His arms came around her, pulling her close and firm. They stayed like that, father and daughter, forgiveness and hope surging between them. At length Nikolai gently disentangled himself from her embrace. Subtly wiping the mist of tears from his cheeks, he smiled cautiously, lips trembling.

"Your mother cannot know. Nor your sister. We must protect them as much as we can."

So, he had seen her. Of course, her father could not be fooled. Estere hesitated, then confessed, "Zenta has been delivering letters, passing information through the network. But I have kept her ignorant of the details... She doesn't know the extent of our work."

She watched the emotions flare across her father's face, the pulse of his temple as he worked to control his fury that Estere had involved her little sister.

Gaining control of his anger, he nodded. "It is a clever ruse. She has always delivered to our older customers. It is unlikely suspicion would fall on her. But it stops now. I know some men, friends of your uncle, Nationalists. Once I make contact the danger grows greater still. Zenta can be no part of it."

"I understand."

"Good."

Estere sucked in a quick breath, braced herself and said, "There is more. You know we are hiding Jews. But the Germans grow suspicious. We need to move them somewhere safe. Especially now that things are advancing."

Nikolai's eyes flicked side to side, his mouth twitching in thought.

"Then together we will find a way."

Estere swallowed, gratitude and hope flooding through her.

"Thank you, Father." Estere pressed her forehead to Nikolai's brow. "Thank you."

Estere's resolve strengthened within her. With her father by her side, anything felt possible.

TWENTY-SEVEN

ESTERE

Was it the same soldier at the checkpoint? Estere couldn't be sure. In their grey uniforms, to her they all looked the same, Germans.

A trickle of sweat ran down her spine, but the truck was too hot for it to bring any relief. As it pooled in the small of her back with the other droplets that wet the back of her dress, she stretched her neck, willing herself to be calm. Pressed on her left sat her father, his hands deftly manoeuvring the truck. To her right, Valdis.

Her lover smiled at her, wiping the beads of moisture that gathered on his brow with a quick strike of the back of his hand. He was nervous, she could feel the tension of his body pulsing with her own heightened heartbeat.

Nikolai slowed the truck as a young soldier paced forward, upper lip moist in the beating sun.

"Papers."

Promptly her father handed over his documents, a calm smile on his face.

"Beautiful day, isn't it?" he said conversationally, his German flawless.

The soldier blinked in surprise. Many Latvians spoke German, but few so well as Nikolai.

"Ja, beautiful but hot."

Nikolai grinned. "Better the sunshine than the snow."

"True, true," the young soldier agreed. "So, why are you heading out of the city?" His eyes returned to their papers, but he didn't seem overly focused on the details, more interested in chatting with Nikolai.

"My daughter and her husband are new parents," Nikolai explained, beaming a proud smile at Estere. "I think our little house is too small for a growing family. We have land, out of the city. Time to consider options for my granddaughter."

A wistful half-smile curled the soldier's lips. "Ah, babies are loud."

"So loud." Nikolai chuckled, the perfect image of the doting grandfather. "But I will miss her giggles. Still, city life... it isn't the best option for a newborn."

Estere grimaced. What a risk her father was taking, openly criticising the state of the capital. *Oh God, please let it be overlooked*, she prayed.

The young soldier stared long and hard at Nikolai. Her father's face remaining a mask of calm.

Then, he stepped forward. Valdis grabbed her hand, their sweat-drenched palms squelching together.

The soldier passed their papers to Nikolai, then raised his hand to wave them through. The edges of his eyes looked moist, as though gathering tears, seemingly caught by some memory of his former life.

For a moment Estere felt her heart lurch, some instinct, natural and unexpected, drawing her to the emotion on the young man's face. But Nikolai fired the engine, the truck burped loud and rattling and lurched forward unsteadily, breaking the moment and moving them forward, away from the soldier and his memories.

Her hand fluttered to her chest and Estere breathed deeply. She had yet to properly recover from birth, that was all. Her body was all out of sorts. Yet she found herself watching the young soldier in the rear-view mirror, heart heavy as Nikolai pressed the accelerator, moving them further apart, fast.

Blinking back the sudden tears that gathered along her eyelids, she settled back against the torn leather seats. There was still a long road ahead before they would reach Jekapils.

The house was almost exactly as she remembered it. The garden, however, was overrun with weeds and failing spring growth. Untended for three years, the vegetable patches had been overtaken by grasses, and there were no chickens scratching around, long since scavenged by hungry neighbours or foxes, no doubt.

Nikolai pulled up right by the front door, wheels crushing the rotting leaves and twigs of years past. They alighted together, subconsciously drawing close as they stepped into the echoing hollow of the house.

The years had not been kind. Untended leaks, open windows, and the nests of all manner of forest creatures had rendered the wooden floors water-damaged and soggy. Piles of bird poo littered the ground, as well as fox scat and food scraps. Estere stepped gingerly through the central room. The crushed table, the overturned chair remained untouched. She looked away sharply.

At her side, her father moved slowly along the external walls, hand running its length. Valdis followed, watching his every move, trying to help. A petty huff escaped Estere's lips. What would Valdis know about the structure of a house? Yet, he was here. Trying. She resolved to be more understanding.

Her father stopped at the end of the wall. He paused. Then paced out the back door. Looking at each other in surprise, Valdis and Estere followed. They picked their way across the back stretch of land, Estere unsteady in her heels.

Valdis slowed to take her elbow, she felt overwhelmed with gratitude.

Soon they made it to Nikolai, standing, hands on hips before the small group of wooden sheds that made up the property's barns.

"They need work, but they are salvageable," he said.

Valdis stepped forward, pressed his hand against the wall of the closest shed, and gave it a shake. It shuddered under his palm. Not convincing.

Nikolai nodded once, then, without a word, strode back towards the main house. A furtive glance between them, Valdis and Estere followed.

Back inside, Nikolai righted an upturned chair and offered it to his daughter. Suppressing a shudder over whose hands had last gripped the wood, Estere took a seat. It was a relief to be off her feet. Her body was aching, legs sore from walking, crotch still raw, breasts filling uncomfortably with milk. She was beginning to regret insisting she came along.

Nikolai cast a concerned glance over his child. The sweat on her brow was telling. But Estere straightened her back. She would not allow him to cast her as the weak one. She refused. She'd given birth, for the Lord's sake!

Accepting her determination in silence, Nikolai turned to Valdis.

"There is much work to be done before they can be moved here. But it is doable. I have already contacted my friends in the area. We were together as children, and in the fight for liberation." A pause, heavy with unspoken torment. "They will help. And be silent."

"And transport?"

"The truck, filled with furniture and... cargo. Your idea is a good one. You just needed a story to carry it further from the city. A new family is a dream of the future. It can sway the most hardened heart." He glanced at Estere, eyes misting. She smiled at her father, love solid and true flowing between them, as it had when she was little. It was a balm to her ravaged soul. Nikolai continued. "It will work. If we are careful."

"Thank you," Valdis said, honestly. "Your contacts, they will be invaluable to our plans."

Nikolai nodded stiffly, visibly uncomfortable, but accepting the gratitude.

Hope soared in Estere's chest. It could work. Setting up Uncle Artūrs' old farm. Transporting the Jewish escapees here. A safer place to plan resistance, to gather men. It was a whole new opportunity for all she and Valdis had been working towards for so, so long. If only Nikolai had listened sooner. She suppressed the thought. He was helping now. It was enough. It had to be.

She stood, crossing the room to Valdis.

Their hands clasped at their chests. Pressing their foreheads together they paused, savouring this moment of hope and joy.

"And we will be together, as a family," he breathed to her soul.

"Yes."

"What?" Nikolai rounded on them, legs spread wide, eyes fierce. "No, my granddaughter cannot be here."

Estere blinked in surprise and faced her father. Confused, she said, "But, Father, that's the plan, isn't it? The ruse? We are a young married couple, coming to set up a new home. It's the perfect cover. You said so yourself."

"For today, yes. But as we put things into action. Absolutely not!"

Estere pulled back her head in surprise.

Nikolai stared at her, dumbfounded. "You think I would put you in this danger?" his voice a whisper. "You think I care so little for you?"

"Father, no!" Estere cried, rushing to his side and gripping

his arm. "I think you value me. And what we are trying to do."
She gestured wildly at Valdis.

Nikolai looked at her, mouth opening and closing, head
swaying side to side.

"He does value you." Valdis stepped forward, placing a
calming hand on her shoulder. The warmth of his palm spread
through the cotton of her dress, settling her nerves.

She looked at him, a cautious smile hovering on her lips.

He faced Nikolai. "I understand."

The two men nodded at each other.

Estere's stomach dropped. Fury, hot and primal, shot
through her core. They were deciding without her. How dare
they!

"I am a part of this," she said, voice fizzing through clenched
teeth. "You cannot discard me!"

"No one is discarding you," Valdis said.

Estere rounded on him, eyes aflame, angry words building
like lava behind her teeth. But he smiled. So pure. So simple.

Her flame stuttered. Gradually, it went out.

A hand on each shoulder Valdis braced her, forcing them to
stand parallel; together but apart.

"Your father is right. The risk is too high. We have Aina to
think of."

"She can stay with Mother..."

"Aina is a baby. She needs you."

He cupped her face, eyes sad.

It was true. She knew it. In her heart, in her gut, in her
rapidly filling breasts. Even today, only a few hours from the
scent of her baby, her body ached to return to Aina. To hold her
child close and safe and warm. To feed her from her body. To
know she was safe, now and always. She could never be apart
from her daughter.

Estere closed her eyes, a single tear tracking down her

blushed cheek. The dream of starting their family life was gone. Once again, she had no choice but to wait.

Seeing her capitulation, Valdis turned to Nikolai. "I will come here with Olga and Dāvis. A German soldier won't know one Latvian woman from another. We can do the repair work. As we do, we can transport our cargo."

"And my friends can help you with food and tools. Any supplies you need..."

As their voices droned on Estere made her way back to her chair, her body spent, the throb of her milk-full breasts a deepening ache underscoring the truth. She was a mother now. Her life was no longer her own to give.

As the truck rattled back towards Riga, Estere rested her head against Valdis' shoulder, and watched the deepening dusk. Shades of orange and pink lit up the space between the leaves of the forest, creating a kaleidoscope of pastels across the landscape. It was peaceful here, beautiful. Separate from the ruined homes and bomb craters of the capital. She would return to the countryside one day, she promised herself. And she would take Aina with her. Her daughter would grow up in the sun, with grass between her toes and flowers tucked behind her ears. She would be free.

Estere would see it so.

Whatever she had to sacrifice to ensure it.

Snuggling closer to Valdis, her breathing slowed as the rattle of the truck bouncing along the country roads of Latvia rocked her to sleep.

TWENTY-EIGHT

ESTERE

The morning air was crisp, the sky clear blue. Already the promise of heat blushed on the breezes off the Daugava.

Valdis pulled Estere into an embrace. By then Dāvis and Olga were loading the last packages from her old farmhouse onto the trailer. Bulk supplies of bread, flour, bedding, petrol all hidden within old furniture, cupboards with loose doors, chairs without stuffing, a collection of junk to hide their true purpose.

"Be careful," Estere whispered into Valdis' neck as she breathed in the familiar scent of his wind-roughened skin.

"I will. Kiss Aina for me every day. Soon, we will all be together. Soon."

"Yes," Estere said, keeping her voice light to cover the doubt that tugged at her heart.

Releasing her, Valdis joined Dāvis to help secure the large wardrobe that wobbled in the tray.

Olga came to her side. "The men will be safe at your uncle's farm. They have been here too long. And your father has set it all up perfectly. An old comrade is already there, waiting to greet us. It will be all right." She took Estere's hand and squeezed.

Valdis disappeared into the house. He returned leading their Jewish survivors, Emil's frail elbow in his hand. The four men ambled into the morning light, blinking, unaccustomed to the brightness after their months below ground, steps unsure. Olga moved over to help them onto the truck and behind the various cupboard doors that would obscure them from Nazi eyes. It had worked when they brought them here; Estere prayed it would do so again.

She forced down the tears that misted her lashes. This day had been coming for years. Now was a time for bravery.

Valdis returned to her side one last time. They kissed. The touch was both soothing and painful to Estere's soul. She broke away, heart too raw for this goodbye.

If she'd known what would come next, she may never have let him go.

Forcing a smile, she patted Valdis firmly on his shoulder. "Go swiftly and return even faster."

"I will."

He turned for the cart, his step sure and firm.

Estere watched him go, pride and hope filling her heart. And then it happened. Without warning, a horrifying bang tore through the air. And Valdis' head exploded.

Reflexively, Estere fell to the ground as the loud blast of gunfire filled her ears. The grass was crunchy beneath her fingers, dried from the heat of the summer sun. Chaos had erupted around her. Shouted orders, screams of horror and pain, the rattle and pop of gunfire. By the truck Olga fell, body limp. Dāvis, crouching behind the cart, was screaming and waving at Estere. Heavy footfall sounded around her as soldiers materialised out of the trees.

But all she saw was Valdis. Slumped on the ground before her, a mess of red and grey where his head should have been. She crawled forward, aiming for his lifeless form. Surely her eyes deceived her.

As she blinked a veil of red dripped from her lashes. She sat up, hands coming to her face to wipe away the stickiness she felt running down her cheeks.

Her fingers came away red. Staring at the stark scarlet against her white skin, reality crashed in on her. She was covered in blood splatter. Not her own. It had come from Valdis.

The horrific realisation of what had happened crashed down on her and a guttural scream of horror erupted from her throat. Scrambling to his body, she rolled him over. Only half his face remained, the right side obliterated by a Nazi bullet.

"Estere! Run!"

Dāvis' shouts cut through the chaos and Estere's eyes snapped up. The yard was a war zone. Soldiers approached from all sides, guns raised and firing. Dāvis threw open a cupboard door, reached up to try and help Emil from the truck. Red erupted from Emil's chest and they both collapsed to the earth. Two other men had jumped from the truck and were making for the house. Bullets found both their backs before they mounted the stairs. Bruno raced from the farmhouse, maw wide, barking frantically until a bullet found him too.

On the edge of the scene stood a tall, young soldier. Their eyes met. Otto.

The world went still.

Otto knew. And he knew where she lived.

Aina.

Scrambling to her feet, she turned and ran. Seeing her flight, Dāvis struggled up from under Emil's dead weight, arms waving high above his head, drawing the Nazi guns. They mowed him down in an instant.

But it gave her a chance. Racing now, she reached the edge of the trees and hurled herself into the overgrowth. Heels catching on the dried twigs that had fallen from the canopy, Estere pumped her legs, willing herself to move. Faster. Faster.

Behind her the sounds of the shouting soldiers grew softer, more distant.

She risked a glance behind her.

No one was following.

They didn't need to.

Otto knew where to find them all.

"Where is Aina?" Estere burst into the bakery, breathing heavily. "Where is Aina?"

The heat in the little shop was almost unbearable, the air thick with the steam from the fires of the grand bakery ovens, trapped inside by the late-August warmth.

She saw Zenta, broom in hand, a sheen of sweat glistening on her brow, as she turned on Estere's command.

Wide-eyed, Estere paced towards her. She hunched over to slow her ragged breathing. She had run there as fast as she could, but there wasn't time. The Germans would be here any moment.

Dārta came into the room, a wriggling bundle nestled on her hip. Heaving a sigh of pure relief, Estere rushed to take her baby into her arms. There was no time, but she hesitated, took one last moment to hold Aina close, to breathe in the scent of her: milk, warm and sweet. If only she could pause time. If only this moment would last for eternity. Her eyes flicked open, wide and wild.

Spinning on her heel, she advanced on Zenta. During her escape, over the miles she'd covered between the farmhouse and the bakery, Estere had worked out what she had to do. It was too late to save them all. But she could save her daughter.

"Take her." She pressed Aina into her sister's arms, watching as Zenta instinctively pulled Aina close. Acceptance of her choice washed over her. Yes, this was the right decision. Zenta loved Aina as her own, she would protect her.

"Estere... what is happening? Is that blood on your face?" Her sister stepped forward, a hand reaching to touch Estere's cheek.

Estere dodged her touch, stepping to her sister's side. "There is no time to explain," she said, hands forming a prayer position before her. "Zenta, you have to go..." Estere gripped Zenta's upper arm, turning her, propelling her towards the back door.

"Go? Go where? Estere, what are you talking about, what has happened?"

Dārta looked on in horror as a shadow fell across the floor.

"There is no time..."

The bell above the bakery door chimed.

It was already too late.

TWENTY-NINE

ZENTA

The bakery door swung open, bringing with it another blast of the intense summer heat. Heavy boots fell on the now well-worn wooden floor. Otto led them, his grey cloak pulled tight despite the heat of the day. He surveyed the scene before him, calculating, angry. Standing exposed in the centre of the store, Zenta swallowed as his piercing stare landed on her. Something new swam within those glassy pools, a passion Zenta had never seen from Otto before. Gone was the easy-going joy of the boy she had come to know on her bread rounds, replaced by rage. She pulled Aina closer, drew in a deep breath and tried to still her nerves.

Otto didn't move his eyes from her face as he crossed the space between them with slow determination, stalking like a wolf. Stopping uncomfortably close before her, he drew himself up slowly, coming to his full height. He towered over her. She'd not realised just how tall he was.

Staring down at her, he paused then said in a quiet, steady voice, "Did you know?"

Confusion furrowed Zenta's brow. In a snap of sudden

understanding, her eyes widened. Giving away the truth before she could hide it. *He knew.*

Behind them, Estere launched into action.

"She knew nothing. No one here knew anything but me. It was only me..."

Otto rounded on her, advancing menacingly. "Silence!" he shouted, pitched almost as a scream. He was ashamed, Zenta realised. *He knows we used his good nature against him. We have made a fool of him. I have made a fool of him. God save us.*

Estere recoiled but did not back down. "It was just me. Valdis and I have long worked to stop you and your brutal regime. We would do anything for the people of Latvia." She paused, defiance flooding her face. "I am proud of what I have done."

"Estere!" Dārta gasped in horror, covering her mouth as she watched her eldest daughter sign her own death warrant.

A cruel smile spread over Otto's lips. He stepped closer to Estere. Cocking his blond head to the side, he said, "I believe you, partly. Women are frail and stupid, they will do anything for love." His voice cracked on the word "love". He glanced at Zenta and she knew he was talking about himself too. He raised his head, looking across the family, one by one, "But you could not have done this alone..."

"Valdis helped me..."

"No, no," Otto pressed a finger to Estere's lips, silencing her. "No more lies. The network is too vast. You passed messages between dissidents, stoking resistance against the Reichskommissariat Ostland. Gathering an army. You smuggled out Jews," he shot a glance back at Zenta, "but the messages. The plans, however hopeless. A mere woman would not be trusted with those."

Zenta held her breath. An army? Jews? This was far greater than she had suspected. Why had she not been trusted to know about it? She could have helped. She had proved herself worthy.

Estere bristled visibly at Otto's insult.

"I have ways," she announced bravely.

"Then you will be invaluable to our investigation," Otto replied before grabbing Estere by the hair and forcing her to her knees.

"No!" Zenta cried out, unable to stop herself. "Otto, please! It was just a few letters... we stopped weeks—"

"My sister doesn't know what she is saying," Estere cut her off before Zenta could further incriminate herself.

"I want to believe that," Otto said, his words almost a whisper on his plump lips. "Make me believe it!" His eyes lit with a brutal light as he forced Estere down to the floor, pressing her face against the hard, rough wood, one knee in her back, applying his full weight to her torso.

Estere began to struggle as Otto's weight forced the air from her lungs.

"Otto, stop!" Zenta pleaded. "She can't breathe, you are killing her."

Otto looked up. Their eyes met across the room. "Tell me you knew nothing," he said, voice cracking with emotion.

Zenta froze, reading the hurt in his face. Despite the violence he'd unleashed on her sister, guilt ripped through her core. Otto had been good to her. He wasn't much older than she was. But she had chosen her country, would again.

Her mouth went dry. What should she do? Confess her part and maybe spare her sister? Or lie and protect Aina?

Her mouth opened...

...And Nikolai's voice boomed across the room.

"Unhand my daughter!"

They all looked up. Nikolai stood by the kitchen door, clothing dishevelled and stained, unwashed, unshaven, yet his stance held a power long missing from his body. Head held high, Nikolai advanced on Otto.

"Release her and I will confess it all."

"You will confess now," he whispered, pressing harder into Estere's back. Beneath his weight Estere gasped for breath, emitting a tight wheeze as her skin paled.

Something glimmered in Nikolai's hand. He tossed the object across the floor. Tomass' gun.

An offer, a surrender.

He planted his feet and spoke, low and firm. "Let her go."

Otto eyed the weapon on the floor before him, then looked up at Nikolai.

As if bewitched, he complied. Standing up from Estere's prone body, he reached out, gathering the gun. Dārta rushed to her daughter, pulling Estere into a sitting position, cradling her against her breast. Estere blinked rapidly, her breathing ragged.

Cocking the weapon, Otto pointed the barrel at Nikolai. "Speak, old man, and fast. My patience is almost spent."

"My youngest is innocent of this," Nikolai replied, "let her go."

"You have made enough demands. Explain yourself to me now or you will all face the camps."

A chill raced through the oppressive heat of the room. Zenta's knees wobbled, but she forced herself to stand strong, clutching Aina to her chest.

Nikolai grimaced. Zenta watched his thoughts shifting across his features, his internal battle writ large there for all to see.

It was clear he'd made a decision. It was time to tell the truth.

"I am a Nationalist. I believe in Latvia."

Zenta gasped. Her father was involved in this?

Nikolai continued. "Estere..." His voice cracked on her sister's name as he fought his instinct to protect his child. But there was nothing he could do for Estere now. "Estere and I worked with them to save our fellow countrymen. Jews are our people too. Zenta," he glanced up at his youngest child, his sunlight and heart, a soft smile smoothing away his sorrow for a moment, "and my wife, Dārta, knew nothing of this. Nothing."

Silence fell. Otto stood perfectly still, eyes on Nikolai. Then, one short nod.

"All right."

He lowered the gun.

Nikolai released a heavy breath, the power of his stance rushing from him, returning him to the husk of a man he had been since Tomass' death.

"Soldiers, secure the old man and woman, and her." He pointed at Estere.

Zenta's head snapped up. They were taking her mother?

"My wife knew nothing!" Nikolai raged as the soldiers advanced on his wife.

Rough hands pulled Estere from Dārta's embrace, forcing both women to their knees, hands pressed to the backs of their heads. A single cry escaped Dārta's lips.

Nikolai surged towards his wife, but two young soldiers forced him into submission.

"Tsk-tsk, comrade," Otto said, straightening his stance. "You seem to think you have some say over what is happening here." He reached down and gripped Nikolai's chin, wrenching the old man's head up to face him. "I am in charge. For what it is worth, I believe you."

He dropped Nikolai's head, stepped back. "Your connection to your brother and his... treachery, was always suspicious. And with your daughter's actions... it is clear you have been working with dissidents, sending messages of sedition. But," Otto paused, pacing slowly towards where Zenta stood cradling Aina, "with so many lies under one roof, you cannot expect me to believe neither your wife, nor your beautiful youngest daughter, knew of your deceit." He ran a single finger down Zenta's cheek. His skin was soft and smooth, and clammy. Zenta tried to conceal her revulsion. "And, as we all know, not reporting a crime is as bad as committing it. Is it not, Nikolai?"

As he spoke Otto had moved behind Zenta. Now he stood, body so close to her back she could feel the heat emanating from his flesh, smell the sweat and rage on his musk. Zenta was frozen, her arms tight around her baby niece, who somehow knew to keep quiet despite the noise.

"Who knew, Nikolai?" Otto continued. "Your loyal wife? Or your pretty daughter? Which one is a traitor? And which one is innocent?"

He fixed Nikolai with an ice-cold stare. Panting, Nikolai looked between his family, his beloved wife, his precious child. He met Dārta's eyes. There was only ever one choice.

"Dārta knew. What wife would not? Zenta is innocent."

"Father!" Zenta cried, stepping forward. But Otto stopped her, his hand a vice pinching into her shoulder, rooting her to the spot.

"Thank you, Nikolai," he said. Then, face beside her own, lips so close they brushed against her ear, Otto whispered to Zenta, "Run."

His meaning was clear. Otto knew she was guilty of passing messages. He knew she had used his affections to blind him. But he was willing to believe Nikolai's lie, for now. She had to run, to get out and disappear, before he changed his mind.

Zenta hesitated for one dreadful moment, filling her memory with the sight of her family one last time. Her mother, her father, forced to their knees, their eyes full of love, willing her to go. Estere gave her a tiny nod, unspoken understanding passing between the sisters. Words were not needed.

Zenta knew what she had to do. She had to live to save Aina.

Clutching her niece to her body, she turned and raced for

the door. Yanking it open, she spilled out onto the dusty, over-heated streets. The door slammed shut behind, the ring of the bell following her as she raced down the lane as fast as she could. Aina, wriggling in her arms, started crying.

Zenta pressed her eyes tightly shut to hold in her own tears, and did not look back.

THIRTY

ZENTA

2018

Aina, the woman I raised until my sister returned, the mother of Crissy, has come home. She walks through the front door as if she still lives under my roof. I wish she did. I wish I'd never ever let her leave. Never let Estere take her.

"Aunty Zee!" she exclaims as she bustles into the kitchen. She is dressed in old brown corduroy trousers, a black shawl embroidered with bright pink flowers wrapped about her shoulders, her hair a mess of grey bunched into a loose tail at her nape. "I brought wine, and scones. Oh, and I found these new chocolate biscuits at Coles on my way. I needed petrol. But they look delightful so I bought three packets. Hello, children!" She turns from me to Peter and Lily, her grandchildren, embracing them warmly. It's understandable, they are her future, but it still hurts to be discarded so quickly.

Peter and Lily hug her back enthusiastically, eyes shining. But she releases them quickly, moving to the fridge and setting about rearranging the contents. "Just making room for the wine.

Oh, you don't have cheese? I can grab some later. We need cheese."

She is still intense, despite being in her early seventies.

As a child she was taught by my husband's fists and Estere's abandonment to be silent and small. Now Aina can't stand still-ness. Instead, she fills a room with talk and action, a wave of energy to stave off the anxiety permanently nestled in her chest. Her never-ending fear of rejection.

Crissy comes in from the back garden, where she's been collecting fresh rainwater from the tank. I see her pause just out of sight and take a deep, steadying breath as she sees Aina.

Her mother has always unnerved her.

Her features arranged into an approximation of a smile, she walks in.

"My baby girl!" Aina exclaims, clasping Crissy to her in a fierce grip. The hug is swift, fleeting, then Crissy is held at arm's length and examined. "You need to dye your hair more often."

Crissy's face falls, but Aina doesn't see, she has already turned back to the fridge.

I hear the clang of jars, the scrape of pots, the crinkle of packaged lettuce, then Aina's wrinkled face appears over the rim of the fridge door. "You don't mind if I leave these out? I need room for my brew, and this lettuce looks old anyway."

It's not old, Crissy bought it yesterday. But I nod, there is no point arguing with Aina. Like a river in flood, you avoid it, or go with the flow.

Crissy bangs the kettle onto the stove, tension radiating from her. Peter and Lily have slunk away to their room. Prob-ably for the best. Their mother and grandmother always need a moment to reconnect. I settle myself at the table and smile.

There may be tension between them, but they are here. The two women I love most in all the world. The children of my family.

I have been mother to them both, from time to time. An

imperfect mother, true, but always with their best intentions in my heart.

But is that true? Or just something I tell myself to feel better about my decisions? The question surprises me, rising from deep within to torment my mind. I clasp the table to steady the shaking that has overcome my limbs, tremoring down my arms and legs. I feel unsteady, woozy.

You are just old, I tell myself, every year of my near nine decades of life creaking in my joints.

But I know it's not that. The past is surfacing again, pressing against my resolve, its weight heavy, its presence scolding. It wants out. And for the first time, I am planning on letting it.

Aina closes the fridge with a firm smack and joins us at the table. She is slowing now, her energy drained from the whirlwind of her arrival. She always takes some time to settle. It has long been her way. Ever since Estere left for good.

I shake my head, the past is clawing at my shuttered teeth, working to pry my mouth open so it can pour out into the world of sound.

But not yet, it's not quite time.

Aina stands behind me, her hands hot on my shoulders. "So," she says breathlessly, "when do we visit Mumma?"

A warm breeze stirs the eucalyptus leaves that dangle overhead, pushing the remaining tufts of my hair out of place. We plod from the car park towards the wide, flat cemetery, the earth red beneath us. My feet ache, they have swollen nastily today, pushing over the rim of my worn leather court heels, the shoe cutting into my skin. My breathing labours, my step slows. Lily appears at my side, takes my arm. "Ah, why so many steps?" I groan as I always do on this pilgrimage.

I feel the laughter fizzing through her body, pressed as it is to mine. I hope she never loses that easy joy. I smile at her. She is a good girl, Crissy should be proud.

The graveyard is quiet, only one couple, a husband and wife of middle age, are visiting a grave. A dead parent I assume, I hope. The alternative too raw to consider.

We stand together, me, Aina, Crissy, Lily and Peter, arms wrapped round each other as we face the small plaque, engraved with my sister's name.

It took years to petition the cemetery for this space. There is no body, after all. Estere walked out of my front door in 1956 and never came back. Disappeared. Aina hoped she'd return, of course, waited, searched. But Estere wasn't coming back, I knew.

After twenty years when no trace of my sister could be found, the police pronounced her legally dead and the cemetery allowed us this plaque. A small marble box with a shining silver plate.

It is good. Aina needs a place to mourn. So do I.

"Ah, Mumma," Aina breathes, stepping forward and placing a bouquet of flowers to rest against the silver plate. A bright yellow daisy lands against the neat engraving of Estere's name. The flowers aren't special. On the drive here she made Crissy pull in at a petrol station so she could rush in and buy them, the price tag quickly peeled off and dumped on the floor of Crissy's Honda. But the gesture is sweet, and Estere loved yellow, so I choose to be happy.

I miss my sister. I've been missing her far longer than she has been officially gone.

She never really escaped Latvia.

"I never saw Riga again." The words escape my lips before I realise it. The past is leaking out, already.

"Why didn't you go back? At least to visit," Crissy asks.

"There was no reason to return... and every reason to stay away. You know the history."

She nods solemnly. Latvia was only freed from Soviet occupation with the collapse of the Union in 1991. Though they declared independence the year before. I remember the scenes on the TV, the celebrations at the Freedom Monument.

But I never wanted to return.

Like many who escaped Latvia, striking out across the globe for the hope of a foreign land, the war never really left me. The memories, the fear, the pain, it takes its toll. The soul is not strong enough to weather it all. I had a new life here.

It was more than enough.

A figure appears at the edge of my vision, moving towards us. I brace myself; I know who is coming. Peter spies her first.

"Who is that lady?" he asks, pointing.

"Don't point, love," Crissy says, pressing his hand down.

"She's definitely looking at us," Lily says.

I look up.

My vision blurs, my breath coming in rapid bursts, I feel like I am falling through time, back, back, back...

Heather is dressed head to toe in black. Black dress, black shoes, black handbag. In her hands she clutches a bouquet, a Renmark Florists sticker is still attached to the plastic wrapping. Around the same age as Crissy, she makes her way across the graveyard with a familiar confidence.

I glance at Aina; she is watching Heather's approach wide-eyed. Shocked.

"Hello?" Crissy says, stepping forward. We must look an odd bunch to Heather. She's dressed smartly, an act of respect. But not us. Crissy and Lily are in loose jeans, both wearing bright T-shirts of the same cut. Crissy's too tight, Lily's too loose. I think they bought them in a multipack. Peter's head is topped with a bright purple football cap, some East Coast team, I don't remember. And Aina is in her hippy shawl. Only I am in a dress, but dresses are all I've ever worn.

Heather smiles nervously but stands tall.

"This is Heather Bradford," I say.

Crissy shoots me a look, shock and surprise written over her face.

"Who?" Aina asks.

"My mother was a Latvian refugee, like yours," she gestures to me.

"Oh, Aunty Zee isn't my mother. My mother is gone," Aina points at the plaque.

"Oh, sorry, I lost my mother recently, I am sorry for your loss." Heather's gaze turns inward, a wobbly smile on her lips, then she raises her head, holding it high, focusing on us once more.

"Why are you here? You don't sound like an Aussie."

Heather smiles. It reminds me of her grandfather. "No, I am American, from America," she amends. "I believe we have a connection..."

Again, she looks to me, a question in her eyes.

The past is scratching my throat, filling my mouth, pressing against my teeth.

I swallow, sweat has broken out over my face, I can feel it pooling on my upper lip.

"I knew Heather's mother," I say. "Back before..."

My family turns to me, heads moving as one.

The past has broken free.

THIRTY-ONE

ZENTA

1944

"I didn't know where else to go."

Zenta stood at Lauma's door, dressed in only her light summer dress, a near-naked Aina snug to her chest, the day at her back rapidly turning to night. She'd done as Otto had ordered. She'd run. Out onto the summer-dusted streets of Riga, no destination in mind. Behind, her family on their knees, and Otto's accusing eyes. She could not yet make full sense of what had happened. The scene had unfolded so fast, so hideously unexpectedly.

What her father had confessed about the full extent of their underground activities...

"Come in, quickly," Lauma said, gesturing Zenta into her small ground-floor apartment. Inside was cool and dark, but welcoming and familiar. Zenta followed Lauma down the hallway, worn, faded carpet silencing their steps. On the walls hung photos framed in wood. Aleksandrs. A lump, hard and cold, formed in her throat. But she pushed away her sadness and longing for her childhood friend. It was not the time to dwell on what could not be changed.

Lauma led her to the little kitchen at the back, indicated that she sit and went to the stove to boil water for tea. Hob lit and kettle on, she returned to the table, small buns of pīrāgi on a tray. She offered them to Zenta, but her stomach recoiled. The image of her sister's face, covered in blood...

"For the baby then," Lauma insisted.

Nodding, Zenta took a small roll, still oven-warm, and handed it to Aina. She took it in a chubby fist, waving the bun in the air before mashing the soft pastry in her gummy mouth. Small pieces of finely chopped onion escaped the bun to settle on her naked chest. Zenta brushed the crumbs away absently, thoughts far away.

Lauma brought her back to the moment.

"By the state of you I suspect you left in a hurry. Which can mean only one thing. They came for you."

Zenta blinked, focused her eyes on Lauma and nodded. "We were delivering messages. Estere didn't tell me much, but I knew it was people who did not want to be found. I thought they were just intellectuals, academics like Valdis who said too much. But then Father said, oh..."

Her voice quavered, tears spilling down her cheeks. She pressed a hand to her throat, a sudden tightness there threatening to halt her breath.

Lauma reached over, placing a hand on Zenta's arm. "Be still. Focus on your breath. It will calm."

Zenta did as instructed, trying to slow her breathing, to find stillness in the panic that enclosed her heart.

The kettle boiled, Lauma rose to prepare a brew. Zenta pressed her forehead to her niece, breathing in the milk-sweet scent of her. She was all that mattered now.

Lauma placed a cup before her, then plucked the wiggling Aina from her arms. "I'll find something to clothe her. The evenings are growing cooler. Drink your tea. I will return."

It was not long before she did, bearing a thick woollen jumper for Zenta and an Aina now clad in trousers and a knitted cardigan. Taking her squirming niece back, Zenta smiled. "Aleks'?"

Lauma nodded. "I have kept them all. For my grand-children."

The hope, spoken aloud so brazenly, silenced both women.

"Thank you," Zenta said.

Lauma gazed down on Aina, a sad smile on her lips. "She is a happy one, despite it all. My Aleks was like that. Always laughing."

Fresh sorrow flooded Zenta's chest as she watched Lauma sip her tea and she snugged her niece closer, drawing comfort from her softness and innocence.

"Now tell me," Lauma said. "What did your father say to the soldiers?"

Zenta looked at her through wide, terrified eyes. "He said we were passing messages between rebels, raising a resistance... and that we smuggled out Jews."

Lauma breathed out a heavy breath. Rising, she paced the kitchen "Salaist grīstē!"

She was right, they'd made a terrible mistake, and now they all faced the consequences. "Did you know of this folly?"

"I knew there were messages, but I had no idea of the extent of it. I thought they'd stopped." Zenta looked down, ashamed.

"I had seen him around town. Out visiting his old friends. I should have suspected, but... I presume Estere and Valdis are involved in all this?"

"Otto," Zenta said before stopping herself. "The German soldier said he discovered what Estere had been doing to help the Jews. He ordered them all taken prisoner. Even Mother. Only Aina and I were allowed to leave. I ran. I didn't know what to do, where to go. But my feet guided me here. I am sorry, Lauma. I wasn't thinking. My presence here puts you at risk. If we could just stay the night, I am sure I can return to the bakery in the morning..."

"Your home won't be there in the morning," Lauma said ominously, eyes hard. "You will stay. Both of you. I have the room. This home has been too empty since Aleks enlisted. I would never turn you out, Zenta. You must know that?"

Relief flooded through Zenta, her gut suddenly watery. In truth she'd no idea where else she could go. "Thank you," she managed on a soft breath.

"Dinner will be potato cakes. You can peel. Then I will show you to your room, Aleks' room, it is the warmest in the house, best for the baby. I think it would be sensible for you stay inside, do not venture out. At least for now. Until things settle."

Zenta nodded. But both women knew, nothing was even close to being settled.

She woke wrapped in his scent. Aleks. A visceral reminder of the fear that rode her heart every waking moment. She didn't know where he was. And she didn't know what had become of her parents. Burying her head into the sheets of his bed Zenta fought the rising terror that gripped her heart. It was too much. She had to do something.

Despite promising to remain indoors, Zenta swung a leg out of Aleks' window into the early-morning light. On the bed, a peaceful Aina slept, tucked safe and snug between pillows.

Foolhardy or not, Zenta had to know. She wrapped her scarf carefully around her head to disguise herself the best she could and shimmied outside, just like she used to from her own attic room when Aleks came by.

Striding quickly, cursing the click of her heels on the pebbled streets as she passed the Three Brothers buildings, the oldest dwellings in the city, she made her way through the warren of laneways that curved through central Riga to the bakery. She smelt it long before she saw the glowing embers. The acrid scent of burned wood and charcoal coated her nose and mouth. Where once her parents' store, and her home had stood so proudly, was now an ash-heaped ruin. Embers still glowed red, flamed to life by the morning breeze. Ash rose from the centre of the rubble, where the roof had caved in, taking part of a wall with it. Burned to the ground.

Zenta wondered briefly where their adjacent neighbours had fled to. She prayed they had escaped the flames. She longed to cross the road, to walk the blackened shell of her home in the rising daybreak. To search for anything that might remain. But the heat of the fire still pulsed into the pre-dawn sky and the burgeoning sunrise posed too great a risk. What mattered was gone anyway. Her mother, her father, her sister. Loaded into the back of a Nazi truck and driven away. Somewhere. To face questions. To be judged without trial. To be found guilty and thrown away like trash.

Would they be sent to Salaspils? Would they be given that chance to survive? Or simply shot dead. Had they already been executed, killed on the bakery floor, their bodies mingling with the ash of the floorboards and ceiling, the furniture and family portraits?

Zenta heaved a sob, pressing her hand to her mouth to silence her fear and pain. Perhaps it didn't matter what the details were. The only question that mattered was, would she see her family again? Her lungs heaved as she fought to control her rising terror. She spun on her heel and rushed away through the misting city streets.

On her return, Lauma was waiting for her in the kitchen, sitting in the gloom of the curtained room, Aina cooing in her lap.

"I am sorry," Zenta blurted, stepping into the small space. "I had to see, to know for sure..."

"It is gone, yes?"

"Yes," Zenta lowered her head, tears leaking from her eyes.

Lauma stood, bouncing Aina on her hip as she crossed the room to Zenta's side. A gentle hand on her shoulder. "Take a moment alone. Allow the tears to flow. Then, wash your face, straighten your hair and return to me. Never cry in front of Aina again, you understand? We move on, yes?"

Zenta sniffled, nodding.

"Go now."

Obediently, Zenta drifted from the kitchen. She buried herself beneath Aleks' blankets. Her strength cracked and sobs exploded from her soul. She felt her heart had been shredded, her chest torn open, her insides laid bare for all to pick through. It hurt, so, so much. How could she carry this? How could she go on? Eventually her tears slowed, her cries calmed. Exhaustion weighed down her limbs, writhing through her muscles, her sinew, leaden to her very bones. Her eyes, puffy and sore from the salt of her tears, blinked heavily, before closing. Her pain released, pouring wet and hot into the blankets of Aleks' bed, a damp pillow for her head, her body's resilience was obliterated. Eventually, Zenta fell asleep.

Hours later, in a fitful half-sleep, she heard Lauma creep into the room. The older woman stood in silence above her for a moment. A heavy breath rushed from her nose as if she were steeling her resolve, fighting her own despair. Gently she pulled back the blanket exposing Zenta's curled body to the air. Zenta stayed very still, not ready to talk, too exhausted with grief to move. Carefully Lauma tucked the sleepy Aina into the curve of Zenta's belly, wrapping her limp arm over the child before tucking the blanket back securely over them both. Aunt and niece, warm and safe, together. At least for now.

She watched over them until Aina's soft coos silenced, her

small body relaxing into sleep, before quietly leaving the room, pulling the door shut behind her.

When Zenta woke later the baby was still beside her, the soft warmth of new life a promise of hope, a reason to go on.

Lauma must have known Zenta would need that.

THIRTY-TWO

ZENTA

Another blast echoed through the streets, they were growing louder, closer.

Cradling a screaming Aina, Zenta risked a peek out the front window of Lauma's apartment. The months since she'd fled her bakery home had been filled with fear and uncertainty for Riga as the Soviets advanced upon their city once more. But tonight was different. The wait was over.

The sky was red with flames. The low clouds of gathering winter reflected the angry red of fire. Fire that was destroying her city. Even here, on the outskirts of the city proper, they were not protected. Smoke laced the air, seeping through the cracks in the apartment windows, dulling her vision at street level. But not in the sky. There the full vibrancy of the flames wicked against the darkening blue of day.

Aina held back her scream, vibrating in Zenta's arms, as she built up to release another raging cry. The sound of blasting bombs was terrifying. At least Zenta knew what was happening. Her niece had no understanding of the world she had been born into.

"Shhh, shhh, my love. Calm. I have you. It will be all right," Zenta cooed, smoothing her hand over Aina's soft crown, her feathery hair plastered to her scalp by the cold sweat of fear.

Zenta heard her approach, despite the blasts that tore the city apart. Lauma came up beside her, paper-dry, cracked fingers gripping her cardigan, pulling Zenta close.

"You must go."

She heard the words, read them on lips white-tight with fear. "They are here."

As if to underscore the moment, the windows of the apartment began to shake as the heavy tread of tanks rolled along the street outside.

"The Germans will be running. They cannot withstand this. The city is ablaze. Here..." Lauma grabbed Zenta's hand, pressing something cool and round to her palm. "Take this, buy your passage."

Zenta looked down at her hand. There, cradled in her palm sat a long chain, its golden hue shimmering in the blazing red of the burning city outside.

"I can't..."

"You can. It came from my German family." Lauma sniffed. "I would have it save you, for my Aleks."

Eyes bright with unshed tears, she folded Zenta's fingers over the heirloom, already turning for the door.

"I've packed a case. It isn't much. Some woollens, hats, pīrāgi. Take my coat."

She wrapped the dark red garment around Zenta's shoulders, helping her into its warm embrace.

"Go straight to the docks. Avoid the queues. There will be many trying, we should not have left it so late."

They'd reached the door, but Zenta pulled back and stopped their rapid movement.

"Come with me," she said.

Lauma paused, her eyes flickering in the half-light of fast approaching dusk. "No," she replied simply. "I must wait here... for Aleksandrs, for my husband."

"Then I must stay too. We will all stay together and wait for Aleksandrs."

Lauma's head shook vigorously, tears of despair spilling from her eyes. "No, child. You must go. Find safety."

"I can't." Panic, pure and primal, gripped Zenta's throat. "I can't leave you. I can't do this alone."

"You will be safer alone. Only you and the baby to think of."

She stopped, taking Zenta by the shoulders, forcing her to look into her eyes. "Avoid the soldiers. Get to the docks. Find a fisherman and bribe him. Get out. Get to safety. Come back once our country is free again. We will be here, waiting for you."

A huge blast erupted outside, so close they could hear shattered glass pinging on the cobbles down the road, could feel the pressure of the explosion in their bowels.

"Go," Lauma whispered.

Zenta stood frozen, mind whirling. Once again she had to run, to leave behind someone she loved. To face the unknown alone. The soft bulk of Aina on her hip reminded her, there was no other choice. She swallowed and set her jaw. Nodding once, she wrapped the coat about herself and the clinging, crying Aina, fastening the buttons tight. Then, one hand still cradling her niece, the other clasping the suitcase Lauma had packed, she launched herself onto the streets.

Glancing back through the grey-tinged air, Zenta saw the tears begin to slip from Lauma's eyes, smudging grey and greasy with the soot that settled on her cheeks. Her heart lurched back, to the woman she might have called "Mother", to the dream of a life with Aleks. Would she ever see him again? Would she ever see anybody that she loved?

The loud blast of an explosion ricocheted through the streets, snapping Zenta back to the present.

Once again, she ran.

Smoke, black and thick and choking, curled around her, enveloping her body, diving into her lungs. But she ran. Heels slipping on the smooth cobblestone paths, lungs protesting the smoky air, she ran.

She tucked Aina further into the coat, holding her niece's small head against her breast as she drove forward, on, on, on through the streets of Riga, racing for the docks.

The sun still shone, its sunset orange adding to the hellfire palette of the Soviet invasion. For invading they were. Driven out by Wehrmacht guns four years before, now the Red Army had come for revenge. And the people of Latvia were nothing more than collateral.

The dockside was full to the brim with citizens of Riga: women, babies in arms, children clutching at their skirts; old couples, heads pressed close; lanky youths, socks loose at their ankles exposing the filth of living on the streets. They all crowded together, a heaving mass of fear and desperation, hoping for a seat on one of the large evacuation vessels. Along the dock's edge a row of soldiers fought to maintain order as people pushed and shoved, desperate to put distance between themselves, their families and the city burning at their backs.

Zenta hitched Aina higher on her hip, pressed a quick kiss to the soft curls on her head. Stealing her resolve she edged around the crowd, aiming further along the river where the fishermen bobbed. Anyone with something to trade, and others with nothing but desperate hope, had the same idea, and she joined a thin line of willing refugees as they made their way to the boats beyond to try their luck.

A soldier's shout echoed over the feverish crowd. A surge of movement passed through the line. Zenta was shoved to the

back. Losing her footing she pitched sideways, tumbling straight
for the water's rippling edge. A gasp escaped her lips, she tried
to roll, to angle Aina above her to save her niece from the
Daugava's cold embrace. She closed her eyes, waiting for the icy
slap of the water to swallow her whole, but something stopped
her fall. Her eyes sprang open. Two hands, large and covered in
ship grease, gripped the shoulders of her coat. The fisherman
hauled her to her feet.

"Thank you," she stammered.

His eyes scanned her, pausing over Aina's small face that
peered from beneath her coat.

"You can trade?" he asked.

Zenta blinked, momentarily confused. The line of hopeful
Rigans stretched before her.

"No? Okay. Good luck." He turned his broad back, started
moving away.

"Wait!" Zenta pushed forward, gripping the rough wool of
his knitted jumper. "I can. I can pay!"

He turned back and grunted. Quickly she dug her hand
into her pocket, producing the chunky golden chain. The fisherman took it from her, holding it close to his eyes.

"Come," he said. Wrapping a heavy arm about her shoulders he pulled her close and, shoulder lowered, forced his way
through the throng. He led her to a small wooden vessel, its
deck already covered in shivering passengers. Another fisherman stood on the dock, feet wide, a large spanner clasped
before him. He held it high, a barrier between the desperate
citizens and his overladen boat. The man looked at her, then
spoke to the fisherman at her back. "We can't take any more,
Pēteris, she's almost at the waterline already."

"She's a scrap of a girl, Milhails. She'll fit," Pēteris replied,
pushing past his companion and shoving Zenta along a
wooden plank that sat between the dock and the boat. The
plank swayed under their weight, the boat dipping closer to

the water. The passengers on deck shuffled, moving aside to make a space. A woman, hair secured beneath a bright blue scarf, smiled up at Zenta, patting the deck beside her. Zenta sank to the deck, legs cramping from running and the gathering cold. On the dockside an old man was arguing with Milhails, hands gesticulating wildly; behind him stood an old woman, two small children obscured in her skirts. The fisherman held his spanner up, shouted something, then brought it down against the old man's shoulder. He fell back into the pulsing crowd.

"Time to go," Pēteris called. His companion spun, rough hands unwrapping a thick rope from a pylon before racing over the plank, pulling it away from the dock. Rope in hand, he placed a foot against the dock and shoved. At the rear Pēteris fired an engine, a loud explosive sound kicking up across the waves, the smell of gasoline flooding the cool night air. The boat drifted through the Daugava currents, set in motion by Milhails' shove. Soon the engine settled, its cadence lowering to a rhythmic hum as the vessel lumbered, low and slow into the channel.

They cut out over the darkening waters, the smoke of the burning city churning around them as the breezes of the bay lifted off the currents. At her breast, Aina began to cry, a low exhausted whine. Zenta pressed her forehead to her niece. "Shhh, little one. Be still, be still. We are safe now. We are safe." She rocked Aina gently, whispering softly, until Aina settled, head heavy against her shoulder.

Huddled in the close press of travellers Zenta looked back towards her city. In the distance Riga burned. Flames of red and yellow sparking high along rooftops reflected off the Daugava's currents, bright and shining, like Christmas lights, the spires of cathedrals enveloped in smoke. She closed her eyes. Tucking her head back beneath the collar of her cloak, Zenta spoke a silent prayer for Lauma and the remaining citizens of her home.

And for her parents, her sister. She prayed for the hope of reunion she could not yet relinquish.

The boat motored, the currents parted as they headed for Riga Bay and the Baltic sea beyond.

To another city, another country, as Riga went up in flames.

THIRTY-THREE

ZENTA

The motion of the boat made her sick to her stomach. Zenta pushed down her scarf, holding her face up to the icy winds rising off the Baltic sea to buffet their vessel. The cold air was the only thing keeping her from being sick. Still tucked snug beneath her coat, Aina stirred. Zenta looked down and feathered her fingers over Aina's bright red cheeks. The poor thing was teething.

"A beautiful boy."

Zenta looked up at the woman squeezed against her side. They'd left in such a rush last night, the dark of the sky obscuring their faces. Only now, as the first rays of morning peeked over the horizon, could Zenta really see her fellow escapees. The woman's dark hair curled out from under a simple headscarf. Her kind eyes, like deep pools of black, were bordered by fine lines. She squinted as she smiled.

"I am Alma, this is my husband Stefans." She pointed to the man beside her, a large, red scar poking from beneath his cap, an old injury from the Great War, Zenta presumed.

"I am Zenta. And this is my niece Aina. A girl. I had to borrow clothes for her..."

"We all left in haste."

"Yes."

Alma gazed lovingly down on the restless Aina. "Teething?"

"I think so."

"Here, this might help." Alma reached into a sack tucked tight between her and Stefans and produced a heel of rye bread. "It's a little stale, so tougher for her to chew against her gums. It helped my Lote."

A shadow flickered over Alma's face, a small shake of her head before she rearranged her features and passed the bread to Zenta.

"Thank you." Zenta handed the heel to Aina, who promptly popped it into her mouth, chewing contentedly, saliva glistening on her lips and pudgy fingers.

"I have pīrāgi. Will you share it with me?" Zenta said, pulling the paper bag of rolls from the suitcase Lauma had packed her. She passed two across to Alma, one for her and one for her husband. "No bacon, but lots of onion." They all knew how restricted meat rations had become in Riga.

Alma nodded her thanks. "The onion keeps them moist," she said. "I almost think I prefer them this way." They lapsed into silence.

Around them the cold waters of the Bay of Riga lapped gently against the fishing boat, a soft orange glow spreading across the tips of the current. The toxic scent of motor oil wafted over them from the chugging engine, forcing the fresh air from Zenta's reach, choking her with fumes. Zenta pressed her eyes closed, willing herself not to be sick.

"Don't close your eyes," Alma said, a gentle hand touching Zenta's arm. "Focus far away, look at the horizon. It will help with the seasickness."

Zenta did as Alma suggested – at this point she would have tried anything. "You know boats?" she said. Talking helped to distract her from the roiling nausea in her gut that threatened to burst from her lips. And from the pain that stabbed in her heart as she remembered Riga wreathed in flame.

"My father worked on the docks. You pick up some tips."

"Where is your father now?" The moment the words left her lips, Zenta regretted them. They'd all lost so much, asking after loved ones was a hazardous topic. "Forgive me, you don't have to answer that."

Alma smiled sadly. "It is all right. It is good to talk of him. And my Lote." She paused, adjusting her coat around her slim shoulders. "Fever took them both the first winter after the Nazis came. It was a horrid time. Their cries of sickness echoed through the house. We needed a doctor, but, well..."

"Yes." Zenta nodded sadly. It was not just food that had become scarce with the invasion. Her family had been fortunate to be spared such serious illness, though not much else.

"And where are your family?" Alma asked.

Grief plunged through Zenta's core as the image of her parents and Estere forced to their knees flashed through her mind. "Gone," she croaked.

Alma accepted this in silence, the tired lines of her face falling into an expression of understanding. "They live on, in her," she gestured to Aina, her little fist now holding a soggy mess of rye bread, brown pieces of half-chewed bread dotting her cheeks. Zenta smoothed Aina's soft hair and pressed a kiss to her brow. Hot and sticky.

Alma was right. Aina was all she had left of her family, her home. Aina was the future.

They sailed for three days and three nights. Alma shared more rye bread and Zenta more pīrāgi. At night they snuggled under the same blankets, sharing body warmth to stave off the deepening chill off the water. By day they chatted, of everything and nothing, whiling away the hours, pushing down the red-hot grief that lurked just below the surface, two whispering voices in a crowd of closed-off silence. More than once Zenta caught their fellow passengers watching them, listening intently. The normalcy of conversation held them all together as they travelled from the only home any of them had ever known, into an uncertain future.

On the morning of the fourth day Pēteris turned the fishing boat down a river. Chugging slowly, hull dangerously low in the water, they motored into the port of Danzig. The air was thick with the smoke of wood fires. The docks teemed with German soldiers. They raced up and down the docks, directing the vessels, all laden with people from across the Baltic: Estonia, Latvia and Lithuania, as they arrived. The Nazis had designated Danzig as the port for those fleeing the Baltics months before, an acknowledgement of the mounting threat from Soviet Russia. Now, the soldiers looked strained as they worked to control the influx of civilians seeking shelter.

She left the boat with Alma and Stefans. Stefans helped Zenta to step from the rocky deck onto the solid dock. The currents at the dockside churned, the wash from the arriving boats creating bulging waves that threatened to tip their vessel on its side.

As her feet landed on the hard wood of the dock, the slats seemed to sway beneath her feet, and Zenta swayed with it. Stefans held her firm until she found her balance, before turning to assist his wife. Days at sea had left her body wobbly. At least now the nausea in her belly should begin to settle, she hoped. They stayed together as a group as they followed the soldiers' orders. Stefan took the lead in interpreting the rapid-fire German words, and they were directed from the docks and into a large warehouse for processing. The queue moved surprisingly quickly. Inside they were separated, women and children directed left, men right. Zenta gave her name to a thin young German who barely glanced up at her from his record book. She was allocated a bunk in the barracks at the edge of the city that housed the people fleeing their homes. People like her.

"We are in building five," Alma said as they came together once more outside the warehouse.

"We are in ten."

"Not so far apart then, we can look out for one another," Alma said, an expression of motherly warmth on her face.

They followed the stream of other refugees through the outskirts of Danzig to the barracks, a long slow march of hunched backs, patched cloaks and furtive eyes, to a series of square buildings set in rows, well-trodden muddy paths between them.

Alma and Stefans' building came up first.

"I will see you to your bunk," Stefans said, kindly. Zenta didn't argue, it was nice to have someone at her side, to feel watched over, even for just a moment. He walked her to building ten.

"You know where we are if you need anything."

"Thank you."

Zenta climbed the wooden steps and entered the building. Bunks lined the walls, lit by the open windows that let in the pale October sun. A group of women, cotton scarves tied snugly over their hair, sat on a bunk opposite the door, chatting companionably. They looked up at her arrival and smiled.

Smiling weakly in response, Zenta walked past them in a daze, found her bunk and collapsed onto to its squeaky mattress. Aina tucked securely between her and the wall, she plummeted into sleep.

It felt like she'd slept for days. Her body and mind had been ripped apart by loss and fear. Alma came periodically, bearing porridge and taking a wriggling Aina out to get some sunshine while Zenta slept. Her dreams were foggy, as though veiled in smoke. Dark visions of trees and roofs, the bright flash of a fired gun. She woke drenched in sweat, her mother's name on her lips, before sinking back into unconsciousness once more.

When she finally came to, Alma was perched on the end of her bunk, bouncing a giggling Aina on her knee.

"How are you feeling?" the older woman said, reaching over to smooth Zenta's hair from her face.

"Better," Zenta replied, pushing herself up into a sitting position. "Thank you for watching her. I just... I couldn't..."

"It catches up with all of us. It is no problem. Aina is a darling. We have been enjoying discovering the city below."

"Thank you."

Alma smiled and stood. "I will let you freshen up, there is a basin and soap by the window." She pointed across the barracks. "Then we can take Aina for a walk into town. Show you the sights. Some sunshine will do you good. Wrap up well though, it's icy out there."

She left, patting the doorframe as she passed, the tap a prompt to Zenta: it was time to move.

Zenta rolled her neck, setting off a series of loud cracks along her spine. She stood, padding over to the wash basin to splash her face. Pulling on stockings and a fresh dress from the bag Lauma had packed, the material hanging loose from her withered frame, she grabbed her coat and joined Alma outside. The sun was slanted, glowing pale yellow across the browning grass, frost lacing the soil.

"The season has definitely changed," Alma said. "It is cold here."

"We are Latvian," Zenta said as she secured her scarf over her hair, the knot tight to hold against the wind that whipped between the barracks buildings. "We understand the cold."

Alma eyed her, lips curved into a grin. "We are," she agreed simply.

Zenta reached out to take Aina, tucking her niece into her body. "Hello little dove," she cooed, pressing their foreheads together. Aina giggled, then, losing control of her head, proceeded to head-butt Zenta, hard.

She laughed.

Alma laughed.

It felt good.

Danzig was beautiful. Rows of terraced buildings lined the cobbled streets, their roofs stepped in flights of four or five. Bright red brick and white window frames. It glowed in the autumn light, a beautiful city. Just as Riga had once been.

They walked along a main street, the deep red and black of the Nazi flag flapped from the lampposts. Zenta felt herself cower beneath that black symbol. Would she ever get away from Nazi reach? It didn't matter how often she saw the flag, it still made her guts turn liquid in fear. Even Otto, before he had revealed his true nature, hadn't eased that initial panic. *Otto.* She pushed the memory of his fury aside, the impossible choice he offered her father. He'd never been her friend, not truly. A lesson in trust, learned in the worst possible way.

Guilt clawed along her ribs, squeezing her lungs, forcing her to puff as she struggled to take in enough air as the beginnings of a panic attack threatened to take hold. Alma, seeing her distress, linked an arm through Zenta's, her unspoken message clear: I am here, we are in this together. It wasn't much, but it was something. Another person to cling to as the world around them swirled out of their control.

The two women paused. Zenta felt Alma's eyes on her, but the woman didn't speak. Zenta was grateful for the silence, she needed a moment to collect herself. Her body longed to return to the barracks, to snuggle beneath the rough woollen blankets and hide from the world. But she could not. This was her new reality, here in Danzig, and Zenta knew she had to face it. She had to be strong.

As her nerves settled Zenta released a long breath, glancing up gratefully to her new friend. Alma patted her arm and faced forward.

Continuing, they turned a corner onto a road lined with shopfronts. Women in long cloaks and children in thick knee-high socks lined up along the footpath, waiting their turn to buy their rations.

"It would be best to come earlier," Alma said knowingly as they passed an old woman, back so hunched she was almost bent double, the swelling of her feet pressing out over the edges of her heels. She should be home by a fire, Zenta thought, tended to by her daughter, a laughing grandchild on her knee. Yet here the woman stood, eyes cast down as she waited for food. They walked on, the streets of Danzig at once familiar and also foreign. But no sound of gunfire echoed between the buildings, no shouted orders, or sudden blasts of mortars. Nazi rule was solid here. And that meant stability, for now.

A group of soldiers in grey marched down the middle of the road, guns nestled on their backs, distracting her. Subconsciously the two women stepped closer to the buildings, putting as much distance as possible between them and the marching men.

She didn't know how she saw him. Even years later as she replayed this moment over in her memory, time and time again, it seemed an impossible coincidence.

But she did see him.

Aina cried. Overtired and sore from teething, she was letting her displeasure be known. Zenta looked down at her niece, turning her face towards the marching soldiers. Aina cried again, louder, protesting. Her cry caught a soldier's ear and he looked up, just as Zenta looked up. Taller now, broader, and his face had hardened, but it didn't matter, Zenta would know him anywhere.

Across the street their eyes met.

Before Zenta realised what was happening, the soldier had broken away from his line, running across the road, directly for her.

A sob escaped Zenta's throat. Her eyes welled with tears as he approached, arms open wide. He enveloped her, crushing her body against his. His familiar scent filled her nose, pine and salty air. Could this be real? Was it really him?

Aina screamed in protest at being pressed against a stranger, but Zenta didn't hear her. Her senses were full of him. Clutching him to her with her free arm, Zenta breathed out. The tears overwhelmed her eyes, wetting the grey of his uniform jacket. Neither of them cared. He had returned to her after all this time, changed in many ways, but still the same, still hers.

She looked up, water lined his eyes too.

"Aleksandrs," she breathed.

"My Zee."

THIRTY-FOUR

ZENTA

He collected her from the barracks that evening. Trusting Aina to the capable care of Alma, Zenta allowed him to take her to a small cafe in the city. The cafe owner showed them to a small round table, the paint of the chair peeling, the seats rickety. Leaning over them, she struck a match and lit a small candle that nestled on the simple red tablecloth between them, her stern features softening as she observed the two young people. Zenta didn't notice. She couldn't take her eyes from Aleks. They shuffled their chairs close, thighs pressed together, fingers entwined, faces inches from touching. The pale glow of the candle encircled them, a cocoon of light between a world of Aleks and Zenta and the world of reality.

Zenta studied the new lines of his face, the sharp cheekbones and faded freckles, the split on his bottom lip. His green eyes usually so bright, seemed dull, sunken, tired. But when he smiled at her the changes fell away, revealing the spark of light that brightened a room, the beautiful soul within him that called to her own. Despite it all, whatever he had endured in the year since they last spoke, huddled close on the street below her bedroom window, Aleks remained the boy she'd grown up with. The friend she knew.

"You are thinner," she said.

"So are you."

"I cannot believe you are here."

"We were evacuated from Leningrad," he said, eyes tracking away from her, haunted.

What horrors had he seen? What brutality? Open battle. It was another level of fear in this time of terror. Zenta stayed quiet, allowing him a moment to regain his composure.

"They are using us to support the evacuation effort," he continued, voice soft. "Thousands of people are fleeing the advance of the Soviets in the East. So, my battalion was sent here, to relieve the men who are managing the barracks. And to regroup." He paused, swallowed. "Riga has fallen."

"I saw," Zenta whispered. Aleks squeezed her hand.

"You are safe here."

Zenta looked down. She didn't know if she would ever feel safe anywhere ever again.

"Do you have any news of my mother?"

Zenta breathed, pity washing over her face. "She was well when I left. She packed my suitcase, some of your baby clothes for Aina, a mountain of pīrāgi."

Aleks released a laugh, an affectionate smile tinged with sorrow on his lips. "She always has a supply of pīrāgi."

His eyes returned to her, seeking more. Zenta gripped his hand tightly. "I didn't want to leave her, but she wouldn't come with me. She is waiting for your father, and for you."

He nodded in silence, processing her words. Zenta held her breath, shame and guilt twisting her stomach. She didn't know how he would handle the news, especially knowing that Riga was now in the control of the Soviets once again.

After some time, he blinked, and looked her straight in the eyes. "I am glad you got out. I am glad you are here."

"Me too."

"And you are alone? Just you and the baby..."

"Her name is Aina. She is Estere's child."

He held up a hand to placate. "I wasn't judging."

"I know," Zenta paused. "I left alone. There was no one to come with me. There is no one left."

Aleks leaned forward, face set with intensity, eyes glowing in the candlelight. "There is me."

"Yes," Zenta whispered, unable to trust her voice as his words settled over her heart. She'd lost so much, her family, her home. Yet somehow, despite the turmoil of this hideous war, she had found her way to Aleks.

Zenta didn't question him as he led her from the cafe to a small hotel two streets over. Hands clasped together, she followed him up the stairs and into the small attic room, floral wallpaper lining the walls. She did not resist when he closed the door and came to stand before her. The light from a street-lamp spilled through the open curtains, warm and comforting, illuminating the green of his eyes, the red of his mouth.

His lips were soft and warm on hers. His touch gentle and confident.

As he pulled her dress over her head, she smiled. Standing before him in only her silks, she felt whole. As his shirt fell to the floor, she allowed her eyes to roam his body. Then her hands. As he laid her gently on the narrow bed, his hips coming to rest between her thighs, she pulled him close, face burying into his neck as she breathed him into her lungs. When he entered her, slowly, carefully, he paused, eyes searching her face before a smile bloomed on his lips. As she threw her head back in ecstasy, she knew she would love him forever.

Zenta rolled over on the bed. Beside her Aleks lay on his back, one arm behind his head, dozing. She'd been meeting him here at this hotel for three weeks now, leaving Aina in the loving care of Alma. The older woman always happy to have more time with Zenta's giggling niece. Aina's innocent joy was a welcome respite from the reports from the front shared from the lips of the ravaged refugees who still poured into Danzig daily. Watching the two of them together soothed Zenta's heart. She could see the peace that settled over her friend as she cuddled Aina close, a balm for her own lost child, Lote, a hope for the future.

Watching Aleks in the lamplight, his skin glowing warm and inviting, Zenta felt her belly fizz. She would never get enough of him.

Sensing her eyes, Aleks turned to her, a smile instantly on his lips.

"Good morning, beautiful one," he said.

Reaching over he drew her body against him, pressing his hips into her. A request she was happy to oblige. As they made love, Zenta felt light in a way she barely remembered experiencing before.

After, she lay in the crook of his arm, her head against his chest, she sensed the rise and fall of his breath, savouring the gentle beat of his heart.

"What are you thinking about?" Aleks asked, one hand tracing slow, lazy circles down her bare back.

"Nothing much," she lied, her mind wheeling away on the heel of her thoughts.

She'd learned about herself from these stolen moments, fleeting and precious. The truth of her heart and her love, and an understanding of Estere. To be with the man resting beside her, she realised she would have made the same choices as her sister.

In these uncertain days, she didn't know how long they would have. She would take whatever she could get.

. . .

That week Aleks' battalion received orders. He left for battle in two days. The Soviets were advancing through Latvia. Hitler, railing against enemies on both sides, was running out of options. Aleks and his battalion would be sent to fight the Russians once again.

They were tucked in their hotel hideaway, naked, flushed, beaded with sweat. He'd waited until after to tell her. She felt angry at that, some ill-defined resentment curling along her limbs, making her agitated. Later she would be thankful he waited. That they had this moment of bliss, pure and immediate, untainted by the horrors that hovered over their heads. She would understand his choice. But in that moment, it stung.

She needed to move. Rising from the bed, she paced to the little window. Perching her bare flesh on its narrow sill she gazed out over the cobbled street below. Silent, still, unseeable shadows lurked on the edges of the pale glow of the streetlamps. She wanted to douse them in water. Plunge the whole of Danzig into darkness. To hide them all from official eyes.

Aleks slipped out from between the rough sheets. He knelt before her, uncovered and raw. Taking her face between his palms he stared into her eyes, unblinking and open.

"I will be all right, Zee. I have made it this far."

Zenta wanted so desperately to believe him. She swallowed. "The Nazis are losing. They are falling apart. Don't go, Aleks. Stay here with me."

"You know I can't do that."

She panted, hands flailing at her sides as she fought against the expectations of fate.

"Then we run. You, me and Aina. We leave Danzig, make for somewhere else, somewhere the Nazis have already lost."

"I will not abandon my country," Aleks said, voice low, eyes dropping to the splintering wood at their feet. "You wouldn't love me if I was that kind of man."

"I will always love you, Aleks." How could he not know that?

He leaned forward, pressing a kiss to her forehead before gently nudging her aside, making room for himself to sit beside her on the windowsill. Crossing an ankle over a knee, he rested his arms on his thighs and regarded her, his face serious.

"We are a Latvian troop," he began, "being sent to fight Russians on the Polish border. The Reds have driven the Germans to the very edge of Latvia. They have cut off the fighters there, a small pocket of soldiers in Courland are holding them out. If we succeed in Poland we can push north and join them. Under pressure from our side, the Reds will fail. We go to fight for Germany, yes, but we are Latvian men. When we win it will not be for Hitler. It will be for Latvia. Then we will face the Reds on our land, and turn them back, force them from our borders and take control of our country. Once and for all."

Zenta straightened, her hair sliding over her shoulder, the cool of the night beyond the open window pimpling her bare skin. Looking directly at Aleks, she whispered, "Can it be done?"

"Our fathers did it. Now it is our turn."

Zenta's composure cracked. "I don't want you to go," she sobbed, desperation clutching her heart.

Aleks turned, cupping her cheek. "After this, I will never leave you again."

Zenta watched his face, eyes glistening with tears. It was too much. She couldn't let Aleks leave, not again. But it was not her choice to make. It never had been.

"I will go and fight under the banner of Germany, as a part of the 5th Battalion," he continued. "But I do so for Latvia. For us. You must stay here, safe from the fighting, and wait. When the Reds are defeated, finally flushed from our nation, you will come back to Riga. We will meet under your bedroom window..."

"I told you, the bakery is gone…"

Aleks huffed a laugh. Leaning forward he pressed his fore-head to hers. "Then we will build our own bakery. I will find you, Zee, wherever you are in the world, I will find you. And bring you home, to our Latvia. Wherever we are, whatever happens, we will always find each other."

Zenta pressed her face into his chest, breathing in the scent of him, sealing it in her memory. She could not change Aleks' mind, but she could choose to believe his hope.

So, she did.

THIRTY-FIVE

ZENTA

"We have to go."

Zenta looked up sharply as Stefans thundered into her bunkhouse. "Stefans?"

"The Germans are pulling out, the Soviets are nearly here. They will not defend us. We have to go."

Terror, sharp and cold, sluiced through Zenta's heart. "They are here?"

"Not yet, but they soon will be. The port is already flooded with people trying to flee by boat. A group of us are leaving on foot, we leave today. You must come with us."

Nodding, Zenta began to fold up her bedding, stuffing her belongings into her suitcase. Aina watched, gurgling happily on the bed, feet splayed above her head, hands reaching for her chubby toes.

Zenta's mind whirled. Where would they go? Where would Aina be safe, warm, fed? Danzig had been the answer, the safe harbour from the Reds. But like every place of safety in Zenta's life, it was being stripped away. Aina was so small, so vulnerable. She couldn't survive on the road. Winter lay around them, thick and cold, the ground iced over, the trees covered in frost, snow flurries bursting from the sky coating the fields. She couldn't take a baby into the countryside. And what about Aleks and his promise? Would he find her if she ran? How would he know where to search for her? Could they find their way back to one another?

Zenta didn't know what to do. She froze, paralysed by indecision and fear.

Stefans stepped up to her side. He reached down, gathering one of the cloths Zenta used as nappies for Aina. Folding it carefully, he placed it in her open suitcase.

"We will stick together. Move as a collective. The plan is to get into Germany proper. Then we will head beyond Berlin. Get as far from the advancing Soviets as we can."

Zenta huffed, looking up at Stefans. "But we are not Nazis."

"We are whatever we need to be to be safe. Get ready quickly. We want to leave with the sunrise, get as many miles between us and the Reds as we can before nightfall."

"But..."

Stefans gripped her hands. "I know you are scared. I am too. There is no good choice here, Zenta. But Danzig will fall, and soon. We have to get out."

Chest heaving, she nodded, turning to gather her last few items.

Pulling her scarf up over her head with one hand, Zenta descended the steps of her building, with Aina tucked beneath her cloak. She'd grown so long in the months since they'd fled Riga, Zenta hadn't noticed until now. Her roly-poly thighs, still fat and juicy, stretched down Zenta's side. Reaching down she drew her niece up into a ball, firm and tight against her body.

The whole of the barracks was in motion, women, children, the elderly all racing between buildings, packing bags, wrapping coats, jumpers, blankets, anything they could to stave off the winter ice, gathering together to leave. Word had got around. It was no longer safe in Danzig.

"Darling," Alma greeted her with a tight hug. "Ready?"

They fell into step with a line of other evacuees stretching from the camp out into the countryside that surrounded Danzig. Trucks piled high with soldiers sped past them, racing towards German strongholds further inland. Not even one slowed to help the civilians. This was not the organised evacuation of Riga, nor the desperately cobbled-together fleet of ships for citizens as the Reds advanced on their capital. This was every man for himself. The Germans were decamping, their bright red banners and Nazi flags left behind to flap in the winter winds. They held no loyalty to those they left behind.

And so, they walked, this line of Estonians, Lithuanians, Latvians, Poles, the very old and the very young. Fleeing another home, another sanctuary, striding into the unknown, a mass of human fear and despair.

Behind them, dim but undeniable, came the deep thud of explosions and the buzz of rapid gunfire. Fire lit the horizon in flame and smoke. Shouts echoed through the trees around them, cries of pain and abject terror. But they did not turn from their line, did not break rank to run back to the wounded soldiers they heard begging the night for mercy. Did not even pause their stride.

No, they picked up speed, widening their gait, quickening their step, putting as much frozen earth as they could between them and the battle at their backs.

Once again, the fight was upon them. The Reds encircled Danzig. They could not stop. They had to get out.

They marched all day along the dirt road, its edges sowed with ancient trees, and into the dark of winter night. Zenta's feet throbbed, her heels rubbed, blisters rising on her flesh. Her calves spasmed. But she kept going, following the line of people illuminated by a half-moon, slung low in the star-bright sky. Bare tree branches reached out from the darkness, their twigs like fingers groping in the night, catching the edges of jumpers, the exposed flesh of a cheek. They trudged on. Behind them the lights of Danzig had long since faded from view, before them lay nothing but black.

"We will rest here," Stefans announced.

There was no obvious reason to choose that spot, the side of a dirt road lined by farmland, but Zenta was too exhausted to care. She collapsed against a fence post, the splintering wood of its sides digging into her side. Alma sat beside her, tucking her legs up under her skirt, pressing their bodies together, while Stefans worked to light a fire. Without it, they'd never wake from the night-time cold. Fire lit, Stefans joined them, a pile of bodies and cloaks against the winter dark. They nestled Aina between them, snug and warm, and soon found the oblivion of sleep. A soft fall of snow began from the grey sky above, covering them in a thin white blanket of winter.

The coughs began on day five.

The line of evacuees had thinned, elderly folk falling behind, others racing ahead, boots crunching through the ever-deepening snow. Alma, Stefans and Zenta had found themselves in a group of about seven, all keeping pace, sharing resources and the warmth of their bodies and firelight at night. Unfortunately, they also shared the sickness. It started in Mr Jansons' lungs, subtle and soft. Easily mistaken for a winter tickle brought on by the dripping nasal passages they all suffered in the frosty chill. But it grew in strength and depth and, aided by their proximity, ripped through them all, from nose to throat, soon landing heavily on Zenta's chest.

At first, she shrugged off the tickle in her throat, chewed ice or snow from the roadside to ease her burning fever, and pushed on. After all, she'd done so before, caring for her parents and running the bakery. What was the difference now, really? Yet, weak from years of malnutrition, fatigued from their trek and cold to the bone from sleeping in the dirt, the truth was her body couldn't fight infection like it once had. Before the sun set on the first morning of her symptoms, she collapsed. Stefans raced to the bundle of clothes and blankets that pooled about her on the road, Alma close behind. A look passed between them. Without a word Stefans gathered Zenta and Aina up in his arms and moved them to the roadside. Alma gathered twigs for a fire. The rest of their little troop plodded on. No one even paused to offer aid. No one had anything more to give.

Stefans stoked the unstable flame. The twigs were too damp from frost to properly catch alight. Alma melted snow in a cup over the fitful flame, pouring the freshly defrosted liquid into Zenta's gasping mouth. Her fever raged throughout the night. Sweat ran in rivulets down her chest and back, yet she quaked with cold, frozen to her core despite the blankets, cloaks and bodies Alma and Stefans piled upon her. Throat parched, lips sticky with dried saliva, her mouth gaped, desperately sucking at the air between the coughing fits that ravaged her weakened body.

"We must find shelter," Stefans said, while Alma looked on in fear.

He set off with the first rays of dawn, striding through the fresh blanket of snow that dusted the countryside. Alma remained by Zenta's side, her body wrapped around her young friend, the damp of melting ice seeping through their blanket den as the sun slowly rose to bathe the land in light.

He found an old barn. Run-down but solid and better than the side of the road. Scouting through the deepening snow, a fresh fall just starting from the darkening sky above, Stefans spied no other farm buildings, no main homestead that might hold a farmer who would come checking. Sure the old shed was long abandoned, he gathered Alma, Zenta and Aina.

Inside the barn Stefans built a fire while Alma rearranged

their blankets and coats over a shivering Zenta, before curling her body around her once again, cradling her like a child.

Zenta shivered, aching into her very centre, her skin a fire of pain as her body was racked with streams of coughing so violent they threatened to choke her.

Alma, her voice laced with fear, said, "She needs a doctor."

Stefans' answer, empty of hope, was, "There is no doctor. Keep her warm. Pray. That is all we can do."

Delirium, thick and vivid, plagued Zenta's senses. She imagined herself buried alive, the ash and ruins of her bakery home collapsed above her. Her father's sobbing echoed from the darkness that enveloped her. Her mother's voice pleaded for mercy. Estere screamed.

Zenta started. Body going rigid, she sat up, eyes blinking blindly into the darkness of the barn. Her flesh was ice, her core a furnace, her muscles spasming in pain and strain, sweat cascading from her every pore.

"Peace, child, peace. Rest. I am here," Alma whispered, running soothing hands over Zenta's fever-scorched brow. She drew her back down beneath the blankets, holding her close to her breast.

Zenta drifted back into a fitful sleep.

Blackness enveloped her. She turned her head, left and right, but nothing, not even the speck of a tiny star shone before her. Here, the dark was everything. It spoke to her, a tempting siren's call, the promise of peace and rest, forever.

A new cough, small but moist cut through her delirium to pierce her heart with terror.

"Aina is sick." Alma's voice swam through the pressure that pressed against her mind. "She has a temperature."

Zenta's eyes fluttered, she tried to swallow but her throat was too dry.

"Here," Alma pressed a cup of melted snow to her lips. She drank, rivulets of liquid coiling down her neck as she slurped, desperate for relief from the coals of her tongue, before slumping back to the floor, panting from exertion.

"Aina needs a doctor, or she will die. She is too young to fight this."

Zenta understood. She had to move. Bracing herself she pushed up from her arms, bringing herself into a sitting position. The movement rocked the inside of her head, her brain pulsed with pain, her lungs burned with the effort to breathe. She swayed in place, eyes open but unfocused. The room around her spun. The cough snuck up on her, rattling her body, tearing her lungs. She collapsed back into the cave of blankets.

Alma nestled close, her cool palm soothing as she stroked Zenta's forehead.

"Let us take her," she said, her voice barely a whisper. "We can get her to a town. We can try to save her. There is still time."

Save Aina. It was all that mattered. Zenta tried to rise again, but her body betrayed her. The last of her strength was gone.

She nodded feebly. Tears leaking weakly from her eyes.

"We will leave you food, a bucket of water," Stefans said. Zenta barely understood. The raging pulse of her blood had returned, her fever spiking, her mind disconnecting.

"When you recover, walk straight down the road. You will find us. We will register our names, and Aina's. Walk down the road, Zenta. Walk down the road. We will be waiting."

Even as she heard the words, she knew it would not be possible to follow Alma's instructions. The rest of her family was gone. And now she was dying, too. It was too late for her. But not for Aina. Not yet.

"Go," she whispered, voice hoarse. Alma's face appeared before her. "We will love her as our own," she promised. A tear fell from her eye, landing on Zenta's cheek and Zenta knew she spoke the truth.

Acceptance and relief settled over Zenta's chest. She had come so far, battled so long, fought to protect her niece.

She could not go on, but it was all right. She had done all she could. It was enough. Now she could rest. She had kept her unspoken promise to her sister.

Aina would be saved.

THIRTY-SIX

ZENTA

2018

"No, no, Mamina-Zee. You are confused," Crissy says gently, her hand coming to rest on my forearm. She scans my face, sees how I've paled, the effort of retelling the past has taken my strength.

"You didn't let them take my mother. We all know the story of your winter in the barn, it was your salvation. You and Aina recovered, then you brought her here. You saved her life…"

The ground beneath me sways, my head feels light, floaty. I begin to pant, panic seizing me by the throat.

Crissy is by me in an instant, arm wrapping about my waist, holding me up on my feet.

"Peter, take the keys, get the water bottle from the car, quickly now. Lily, help me. Come, Mamina, let's get you to the bench, I think the heat has given you a funny turn."

Crissy to one side, Lily to the other, I am guided gently to the cemetery bench, simple wooden slats held together by a concrete casting, deep green paint flaking from the wood. I sit, eyes pressed closed as I gather my composure. Aina trails behind.

I lean back against the park bench, the wood hard against my fragile ribs, focus on my breathing, slowing the dizzy panic that has gripped me. I open my senses to the space around me, the shuffling of a magpie digging through the dirt for worms, the scent of hay on the wind, the radiant heat of the sun. It feels exactly the same as it always did. The past hasn't changed the world around me. It is just the past. It can't hurt me now, or so I'd thought.

Regardless, it is almost out. Released from where I've pressed it, deep, dark, repressed, its presence a physical weight, edged with razor blades. Now it is escaping.

I am not sure that I am ready.

There is the scuff of footfall and Peter is before me, water bottle in hand. I accept the bottle, take a sip. The water is lukewarm from the heat of the car, not at all refreshing. But it helps to steady me. I open my eyes.

Heather is still standing at the grave. I watch as she slowly turns towards us, her eyes are scanning side to side, thinking. She approaches with caution, her step light.

"I am sorry, I think... I think this is my fault," she says.

"It is no one's fault," I say, looking down at my hands. "Some things just are."

I turn to the rest of my family. They are watching me with confusion. They are still wondering how I know this woman, why she has come here. I breathe in through my nose, draw myself up taller, or at least straighter.

"There is more," I say.

"Mamina," Crissy interrupts, voice laced with worry. "It is a hot day, and you've not been well. I think it's enough for now. Let's go home, have a cup of tea. I am sure Heather will understand..."

"There is more," I repeat, louder, firmer.

Crissy falls silent, watching me.

"I would hear your story," Heather says. "Of what happened next. How you came to be... here. I'd like to know everything."

I pause. I have released a lot of the past already this day. I am weary, fatigued to the bone. But not to my core.

And there is more to share. Of course there is more.

My teeth are no longer clenched and my throat is open, and the words are ready.

I regard my family standing before me, a mix of confusion and concern.

Then I lean forward, focusing on Aina.

"You need to know," I say to her.

It is her story too, after all.

PART FOUR

OUT OF EUROPE 1945–1951

THIRTY-SEVEN
ZENTA

1945

She should be dead.

Zenta flopped onto her back, pushing the pile of blankets from her body, suddenly desperate for a breath of cool air. Pulling her dress open she exposed her chest to the barn. Sweat drenched and pale. Breathing heavily, she blinked, trying to force her thoughts into order.

How long had she been lying here alone? Days? Weeks? Months?

Time had dilated, stretched and snapped as she'd suffered. Coughing from deep within her lungs, gasping for air, body a rictus of aches, pains and shivering, her temperature soaring, then plummeting to freezing, and always, always the wrenching fist in her heart that reminded her of what she had chosen.

Aina was gone. Her niece was lost to her. Zenta should be dead. She had thought she wouldn't survive. She shouldn't have. She'd been ready to let go. Aina, little Aina, had started coughing... There had been no choice.

There was always a choice.

Zenta pushed herself up into a sitting position and surveyed the barn. Old and run-down, but solid. Beside her lay the remains of a fire. She vaguely remembered tending it in her fevered state, keeping it alight. Now nothing but ash remained. A small sack of oats and a pot of gruel had been left for her. Fingerprints marked the shiny film that coated the surface of the greying remains. The water pot was empty. That at least she had finished, or perhaps the water had evaporated, given the urgency of her current thirst.

Zenta listened. Outside was still and silent, the absence of sound a promise of a snow blanket that muffled the world. Her head ached abominably, the throbbing at her temples thumped in time with her heartbeat. She longed to lie back down, bury herself beneath the blankets and fall into oblivion. But her throat was dry, raw, and the cold had seeped into her bones. If she slept now, she would never wake.

The needs of her body overrode her exhaustion and bewilderment. She needed water, and that meant going outside. Driven by instinct, she rebuttoned her dress and, drawing her coat tightly around her, forced her body into action. Coming to her feet her knees wobbled, and her head spun dangerously.

Slowly. Slowly.

She picked up the water pot and, putting one foot in front of the other, padded for the barn door.

Snow lay thick and glistening over the open fields around her. In the distance trees stood stoic, their limbs weighed down precariously by piles of shining white. No wind blew, not even a breath of breeze. Pale sunlight peeked between the tree trunks. But it was disappearing. She'd only just awoken, but night was gathering. Not much time then. Bending down she scooped handfuls of snow into her pot, her hands burning from the icy touch. Then, cloak tight about her neck, she trudged out towards the thicket of trees that bordered the clearing. She needed kindling, small twigs to start a fire, and a log. Rifling through the undergrowth she found what she needed, but everything was thickly covered in snow, soaked through, too wet for use. She hauled it inside anyway. Perhaps she could dry it out.

Exhausted now, she pulled the barn door closed and collapsed onto her blanket pile. Cold slithered over her skin, seeping into her muscles. She needed a fire to melt the snow for water. She needed its flaming warmth. But fatigue was winning, her eyelids drooping, mind disassociating. Stuffing a handful of snow into her mouth to try to quench her thirst, she fell back beneath her blankets, eyes shut, mouth chewing ineffectively. Her teeth burned from the ice, but liquid dribbled down her throat, cool and soothing on the cough-ravaged membranes. She knew she should not eat snow. She knew it would bring her core temperature down too low, especially in this cold. She couldn't find the strength to care. Burying herself beneath her blankets, she shivered and gave in to sleep.

The farmer trudged through the snow, his booted feet sinking as he surveyed the deepening dusk.

All was quiet across his lands. They'd been lucky, he knew. The ravages of war had pressed at the edges of his holdings, threatening his farm, but never encroached directly. That could change now as the Allied Forces advanced across his country. But there was nothing Heinrich could do about that. He was a farmer, spared conscription due to a heart condition and his ageing bones. His task lay in the here and now. Running his farm – and getting his family through the winter.

On the opposite side of the field his grandson Dieter performed his role, eyeing the perimeter, ensuring all was as expected. He was small for the task, snow coming well up his thighs as he waded along the fence line. Better this trudging work than marching as a soldier to his death. The image came unbidden, Heinrich's heart clenching at the thought of his own son, Oskar, long since forced into the war. They'd heard nothing for months. And with the news of the collapse of the German lines, to both the west and east, that silence became oppressive, a physical presence bearing down on their small homestead. Surely there was no need for the Western forces to press this far into Germany, or for the Reds to cross from Danzig?

Heinrich shook his head, burying the thoughts deep inside him, adding to the growing stone of icy panic that poked against his intestines.

He had work to do. No point imagining things he could never know. Turning back towards the house his eye caught a flicker of movement at the far end of his fields. He hadn't trekked out that far all season. No need. Those barns on the outskirts of his property were for summer crops, and in need of repair; war meant rationed supplies. He kept the animals in the winter barn, adjacent to the house. Nothing should be out there. He paused, eyes scanning to the edge of his lands. Had he imagined it? Almost certainly. And yet with the advancing invaders...

"Dieter!" he called across to his boy. Dieter looked up, face open, ready. Warmth and love flooded Heinrich's heart. He was a good lad.

"Come." He gestured to the far fields and started making his way towards the summer sheds. Dieter followed.

He spotted the footprints well before he reached the barn. Impossible to tell the size of their maker in this dense snow. But he was fairly sure there was only one set. He stopped, waiting for Dieter to catch up.

"Wait here," he said. "If you hear me shout, run."

Dieter stared at his grandfather, eyes wide. He nodded.

The barn door was closed. Heinrich eased it open, the dim light of the fast-setting sun spread across the dirt floor. Set just off-centre, between the tool racks and a rusting tractor, lay a pile of cloth, likely blankets. Beside it some pots, the remains of a fire. Carefully Heinrich paced forward, arms out wide, eyes alert. The pile remained still, unmoving. He was almost upon it before he saw her face. Small, pale, gaunt. A girl. Her starvation was obvious in the hollows of her cheeks, the black smudges beneath her closed eyes.

Swallowing, Heinrich bent forward, pressing a hand to her forehead. Warm. Too warm given the barn's winter cold. She murmured, lips twitching, but did not wake.

Fever. Heinrich was a father and grandfather, he knew the signs. Without a second thought he squatted down and gathered the girl and her nest of blankets into his arms. Years of farm work had grown powerful shoulders, well used to hauling barrels of hay, strong despite his advancing age. But this girl felt like a feather, insubstantial. Her eyes fluttered and Heinrich paused. But they fell closed again and she remained asleep.

"Opa?" Dieter rushed to Heinrich's side as he exited the barn.

"A girl. She is very sick. Run ahead and tell your grandmother. We will need hot broth. Stoke up the fire."

The boy paused, mind whirring. Then, spinning on his heels he threw himself across the snow, making for home.

Ponderous, Heinrich followed.

Entering his home, warmth enveloped him, the scent of bubbling soup permeating the small entranceway. By the built-up fire sat a cot, freshly made up. His Frieda was a good woman. Heinrich crossed the room and laid the fitful girl on the cot. Frieda came to his side, bending to place a hand on the girl's forehead, just as he had done.

"Too warm," she announced.

Heinrich only nodded.

"Leave us. Watch the soup."

His granddaughter Karoline entered with a bucket of soapy

water and a sponge and Heinrich and Dieter retreated to the kitchen, leaving the women to nurse the girl.

Later, after his wife and granddaughter had stripped the girl of her filthy clothes, wiped her clean and dressed her warmly in some of Karoline's garments, he stood with Frieda watching over the sleeping girl.

"She barely woke," Frieda said. "It was a challenge to get any broth in her. It will have to do."

"She is very ill."

"Very."

"I wonder who she is?"

"Whoever she is, she is a victim of this stupid war," Frieda spat bitterly.

Heinrich's curiosity softened into care, and he wrapped an arm about his wife's shoulder. "We will take care of her."

"There is more," Frieda said, leaning her solid frame into her husband's embrace.

Heinrich turned to her, cocking his head.

"She is with child."

Zenta woke with a start. Her body tensed as her eyes flew open. She lay still, adjusting to the dim light around her. It was tinged with orange. A soft crackle sounded to her right. Turning her head she saw the soft pulse of coals, a glowing log smouldering in the fireplace.

Fireplace.

She ran her hands down her chest. Her clothes felt different: soft. Carefully she sat up, her hands sinking into a thin mattress. She wasn't in the barn. She was in a room. She scanned around her. Hearth, two armchairs, some picture frames glinting in the half-light. A low-slung roof, dark wooden beams encroaching on the room making the space small, but warm and cosy, the smell of cooking lingering in the air made it a home.

As her eyes adjusted, she noticed a girl, possibly around twelve, sleeping on one of the chairs. She looked peaceful, calm, her blonde hair curling softly, cupping her face. A smile touched Zenta's lips. She hadn't seen such rested features in years. So innocent.

Where was she?

The girl stirred, rolling over on the small space of the chair, pinching her arm beneath her. The discomfort disturbed her slumber and her eyes popped open, landing on the also awake Zenta.

The girl paused a moment, fuzzy from sleep, then she sat up and smiled.

"Guten Morgen," she beamed. "Are you well?"

German, not Russian. So, she was still in Germany. That made sense.

Zenta nodded her response.

"Where am I?" her voice croaked, her throat raw from sickness roughening the sound.

"Our farm. Opa found you in the summer barn. I'm Karoline."

Ah, so her hideout had been discovered. She had not moved that far after all.

"Zenta," she tapped her chest.

"Where are you from? You don't sound German..."

"I am from Latvia."

The girl frowned. "Where is that?"

"A long way away."

"You have been sick. Oma and I have been caring for you."

"How long have I been here?"

"A few days."

"Karoline?" A deeper voice, feminine and kind, sounded

from the doorway and Zenta looked up to see an older woman, round and strong, standing there.

"Ah," she said, "you are awake."

"Her name is Zenta. She is from Latvia," Karoline piped.

"I see. I am Frieda," Frieda said to Zenta, before making her way through the room into an adjacent space. The clang of pots, then the blooming scent of food told Zenta it was a kitchen. Frieda soon returned, a bowl of soup in hand.

"Eat," she ordered, handing the bowl to Zenta. "You are skin and bone. The baby is taking everything from you."

Zenta started. How did this woman know about Aina? How could she know that Zenta had been going without for months to ensure her niece had plenty? Was Aina here, somehow?

"You know about my Aina?"

The older woman chuckled. "Named her already, have you? I was the same with my first." A wistful look came into her eyes, "My Oskar." She took a deep breath. "You wish for a girl. That is good. Girls stay." She sat down beside Karoline, wrapping an arm about her granddaughter, a secret smile on her lips.

Zenta pressed her eyelids together, confused. Her German was obviously not strong enough to follow, their dialect was quite different from Otto's. So, Aina wasn't here. Of course not. Alma and Stefans had taken her down the road, towards the city. They had not stopped so close to the barn; if they had, they would have come back for her... No, she'd misunderstood the kindly woman. Swallowing her disappointment and sorrow, she followed Frieda's instruction and took up her spoon and scooped soup into her mouth.

It was delicious. Simple root vegetables and pork, and the best thing she had tasted in months. She breathed an audible sigh of joy. "Thank you, for all you have done for me."

Frieda nodded, coming to her feet. "We aren't all monsters," she said, padding from the room. Zenta fell silent, savouring her soup. As she ate the household slowly came to life. A older man entered with a younger boy. "My opa, Heinrich, he found you," Karoline supplied, "and my little brother, Dieter." Frieda served a breakfast of bread and eggs, actual eggs! And Heinrich and his son headed out to the farm, following the gentle lowing of a cow. Zenta supposed there were many tasks for a farmer to perform, even in winter. Frieda called to her daughter and Karoline left the chair to join her mother in the kitchen. There would be much work to do to prepare food, that Zenta understood.

Soup finished, Zenta lay back on her cot and nestled down into the blankets. She cupped her hands about her belly, thinking of how deliciously full it felt, how round and substantial. Shock shot through her. She sat bolt upright. Pulling her dress tight about her waist, she stared down at her stomach. What was once so flat as to be nearing concave now rounded softly against the cotton dress. Frieda's words clicked into place. Shock washed over her body in a hot wave as realisation dawned.

She was having a baby.

Zenta spent the months of winter and spring with the family. At first, she simply rested, eating and sleeping and crying. But as she healed she began to help out around the farm. Initially in the kitchen, where she baked daily bread, her loaves earning her grudging approval from Frieda, who had to admit Zenta made a superior loaf. When the cows were released from the barn into the tentative sunshine of spring, jumping with the joy of freedom as they raced into the fields, she joined Dieter on the morning trek to milk the cows. It was difficult work. Dieter's small hands made the movement seem swift and easy; Zenta's hands, so used to kneading, struggled with the subtle touch. But she persisted. These people were helping her. They were unfathomably kind.

And she had no choice but to stay.

Alma's last words to her, "Walk down the road,", echoed through her mind. She prayed she had not imagined them. She longed to leave, to search for Aina and her friends, but the swell of her belly and the ache in her back demanded she stay put, for now. When she could, she would follow the road, find the place where the people of Danzig had fled to, and search. She had to believe she could find her niece. Until then she would work, her stomach a heavy weight and source of constant surprise. She knew a baby grew within, her baby. Yet it felt disconnected, separate from her, a challenge to work around as she milked the cows and carried the buckets, warm with fresh milk, to the storage shed in the next field.

The war continued around them, she knew, but here on this isolated farm it felt distant, remote. As neighbours brought the news of the fall of Berlin and Germany's unconditional surrender, Heinrich and Frieda worked on, ignoring the outside world, and Zenta, growing bigger every day, did the same.

When her time neared, Frieda ordered her to rest again. "Alwine, my daughter-in-law, did not heed this advice. She should have..." The outcome was left unspoken, but the absence of the children's mother in the farmhouse told its own story.

Part of Zenta wanted to argue. It was important for her to contribute to this place of safety. But the larger part of her knew she had to stop. The baby was large within her now, the skin of her belly stretched paper-thin across her stomach. She couldn't imagine getting any bigger. And yet, she did. As the skies cleared and the heat of summer began to press down on northern Germany, she swelled and swelled until she thought she might burst. Her waters broke over supper, flushing Zenta with purest panic. This should not be happening, and yet it was. Somehow it was.

Frieda talked her through the birth, Karoline held her hand. Time and again she thought she would die from the pain and exertion, yet her body continued, finding some power, some reserve from deep within. For a day and a night she pushed, and screamed and sweated and bled. Karoline wiped the sweat from her brow with a damp cloth and a smile. And then, miraculously, her baby was born. Frieda placed the tiny infant in her arms. The child was quiet, likely exhausted after the trial of her birthing, but her eyes were open, watching. Zenta stared at the little face, red and wrinkled, and felt nothing. Numbness enveloped her, limb by limb, until her head was buried in fog. Lying back against the sweat-drenched sheets, she rolled away from her daughter and slipped into an exhausted sleep.

Brow furrowed in concern, Frieda collected up the child, and, taking a cloth dipped in cow's milk, dribbled liquid into the baby's sucking mouth.

"Won't Zenta feed her?" Karoline asked.

"She will. But she needs rest."

Zenta stirred, glancing up at Frieda and her child before sliding back down into the darkness of unconsciousness.

THIRTY-EIGHT

ZENTA

She walked out of the farmhouse into the warmth of a German summer. Frieda and Heinrich waved her goodbye, Karoline and Dieter trotting beside her until she reached the roadside.

"Where will you go?" Karoline asked, eyes brimming with tears.

"I must find my people," Zenta replied. "They won't know to look for me here." *Aleks won't know to look for me here*, she thought silently.

The girls embraced. Karoline pressed a small kiss to the baby's forehead. The child stirred, nose snuffling against Zenta's chest.

Smiling to Karoline and gently ruffling Dieter's hair, Zenta turned and began her walk down the road, Alma's promise ringing in her ears. "Follow the road. We will be waiting."

After so many months it was a fool's hope. But hope was all Zenta had left.

Baby clasped to her breast, she followed the road, eyes forward, walking slowly, each step shooting pain through her groin. Her body was still healing from childbirth, but she would rest no longer. She had to be going.

Sometime after the sun had crossed the peak of the sky, a jeep appeared before her. Three young soldiers rode inside. Instinctively she withdrew from the road, walking in the long grasses that edged the dirt track, shoulders hunching, making herself small. They pulled up beside her anyway.

She faced the soldiers, fresh-faced, clean. An unfamiliar uniform was on their backs. A young passenger leaned out of the jeep, smiled at her and spoke. Zenta had no idea what he was saying. She stared at him blankly. A third man, in the back, leaned forward.

"Deutsch?" he asked.

"Ja," Zenta replied.

"You look like you need help," the man said, in slow, deliberate German.

"I am looking for the evacuee camp."

"Where are you coming from?"

"Riga."

The man eyed her in surprise. Taking in her thin but clean appearance, disbelief flickered over his features. "Latvia is a long way from here."

She nodded, fell silent. He could not know the fortune that had seen her and her child through the winter, and she would not risk explaining. Heinrich and his family would remain her secret, she would protect them from the armies of man, at any cost.

The man nodded. "A Displaced Person then." Zenta blinked; it was the first time she had heard that term, "Displaced Person". It would not be the last time.

"Come." He opened the jeep door. "There is a camp nearby, we will take you."

Zenta stiffened, stepping back. She knew not to trust the kindness of soldiers. She had learned that lesson the hard way.

"Calm." He held up his hands in a soothing gesture. "Not Germans. English."

"English?"

"Yes, miss, that's us." He grinned.

They drove her to a camp on the outskirts of Bergen in the British Occupied Zone. Dazed, Zenta allowed herself to be led to the processing building.

"Name and date of birth."

She stared blankly at the soldier before her. The one who had brought her spoke a few fast, unintelligible words and the soldier nodded.

"Name and date of birth," he said in heavily accented Latvian.

Zenta breathed, then the words rushed out of her in a flurry, "Zenta Kalnina, 18th of September, 1929. And my niece, she might be here. She came with friends, her name is Aina. Is she listed? Can you find her?"

"Slow, slow." The soldier held up a hand. "Zenta Kalnina. And Aina. Here." He handed her a slip of paper covered in letters in combinations she didn't understand.

"Building seven." He pointed out the door.

"But, Aina..."

"Yes, Aina," he tapped the paper, "building seven. Next."

A woman with three children stepped up behind her and Zenta was moved along.

Confused, she followed the direction the man had indicated. Before the exit she came to a table where another soldier stopped her. He looked her over then handed her a pile of blankets, a tin cup balanced on the top, before gesturing her on. She was led to a shower block. As the water washed the dirt of the road from her skin, she felt her shoulders relax. Carefully, she wiped her baby over, a tiny smile tickling the edges of her mouth as she marvelled at her perfect little fingers and toes. The baby stared back at her, mouth forming the shape of a tiny

"O". Zenta searched her features, seeking something of Aleks, a twist of lip, the shape of an ear, but found nothing. The numbness returned, dulling her interest and turning her thoughts away. Dressed in fresh, albeit ill-fitting clothes, she made her way to her new building and her new bunk.

Later she would learn of the mix-up. The intake officer, having only rudimentary Latvian, had not understood Zenta's desperate query about her niece Aina. He had believed her tension had been to protest that the baby in her arms was in fact her niece. Her niece Aina.

Now, she had papers. Stamped and approved by the British Army Administration. She was Zenta Kalnina of Riga. Occupation, baker. And her child was Aina Kalnina. Zenta's niece. By the time she realised the mistake, it was too late. Perhaps she could have tried to correct things, perhaps she could have faced the reality of her choices: that her niece was gone. But the weight of it all was too great. Besides, it was better to be considered an aunt than an unwed mother.

In her cot that first night, sitting on rough cotton sheets, in the airless, stuffy barracks space, the deep breathing and coughs of her fellow survivors sounding around her, the heaviness of hopelessness pressed down on Zenta.

Sometime between letting her niece go and birthing this new child, Zenta realised she had given up. Given up on the hope she'd harboured for her parents, for Estere. The reality of Nazi cruelty was too brutal to overcome, even in her dreams. She'd given up on her country, too. In the face of Soviet advance, what hope could there be for Latvia? She'd given up even on herself.

The salt of her tears mixed with the sweat of her body as Zenta gave in to her pain.

And the truth, horrid but honest, swelled in her chest.

This child in her arms, flesh of her flesh, blood of her blood, was a stranger. Born outside it all, yet mingled in, inextricably linked. Emotions blanked by loss, Zenta could not feel the love she knew she should for this new life.

It was all gone.

Aleks' promise was all that remained.

A tiny spark her soul clung to. The only way back from this empty place she now inhabited.

Silently she prayed, sending her words out into the world.

Aleks was all she had left.

THIRTY-NINE

Over the first few days she adjusted to the ebb and flow of camp life and came to know some of the women whose fate she shared. Sisters, Desna and Vanya, chose her as their friend, helping her to secure cow's milk for Aina by day, while Zenta secretly fed the baby from her breast at night. But mostly, Zenta kept to herself. It was easier to keep up the lie if she maintained a distance. The hole within her, black and hungry, refused to be filled by the smiles of others.

Subtly she made enquiries after Alma and Stefans, querying the soldiers who ran the camp. They came to nothing, and Zenta soon accepted that her beautiful niece was lost to her, disappeared in the turmoil of war.

The camp sat on the edge of Bergen, formed by a set of repurposed Wehrmacht barracks, originally taken over to house the survivors of the nearby concentration camp, Bergen-Belsen. Zenta had seen the impact of the Riga Ghetto, the skeletal men, eyes sunken, expressions empty, having been worked day in, day out until they collapsed. But she had never seen what a concentration camp could do. Somehow the Jewish survivors were even thinner than those from the ghetto. They moved with slow, shuffling steps, heads cowed, eyes furtive, nervous. And not just men, but women and children too. Impossibly small.

They were kept in a separate section of the camp. Zenta watched medical staff coming and going from their quarter. Too often soldiers came to carry away bodies. Swaddled in cloth to protect their dignity. Some so small a single soldier cradled them in their arms alone.

They had survived the war, but not all had the strength to recover.

September brought news that the war in the Pacific had also ended. The British soldiers cheered and sang, dancing through the streets of Bergen, steins of beer in hand. No one else joined in. Events so far away seemed unreal in the fog of their own displacement.

Quickly the camp filled to bursting as more and more people arrived, fleeing the long arm of the Soviet Union. Soon, the soldiers gathered together the people from the Baltics and assigned them to larger, more established camps across Germany. Some went to Stuttgart, others to Foehrenwald.

Zenta, her child, Desna and Vanya all landed at the processing camp set up within Hamburg Zoo. They and the other "dipīši" were split into groups of fifty, dusted with DDT to prevent lice and sent to spend a night in the barracks of a former forced-labour camp. The next morning they moved on to the national Latvian camp in nearby Fischbek; a new building and new bunk. The camp was another set of repurposed barracks nestled on the edge of the war-ravaged city of Hamburg, but already it was far more established than their accommodation in Bergen, where the rehabilitation of the Jewish survivors had rightly been the primary focus.

Several churches were set up, Sunday worship quickly establishing itself in the social calendar. Staffed by teachers brought from the United Kingdom, a school for the children was started. Small at first, with all ages mixed together in one room, it quickly expanded as more and more families grew confident enough to be separated from their children for a few hours of lessons. As the refugees settled, former teachers came forward to return to their professions. Watching the groups of children trot to their lessons, their voices high and excited, brought a smile to Zenta's lips. If she narrowed her eyes, blurring out the barracks at their backs, she could almost pretend she was on a normal street, in a normal town, watching the schoolchildren head to class. A memory of cool breezes, green grass, a warm hand in hers fluttered in her chest. A promise of return that she clung to.

Rations were plain but plentiful, in even greater supply than the food provided for the local population, with some enterprising refugees trading food for other goods and services in the city. Children started to play, racing down the dirt paths of the camp with balled-up socks for a ball. It wasn't long before the socks were replaced by an actual ball, gifted by a local woman from Hamburg. It was a rare interaction between the survivors of the camp and the people of Hamburg who generally kept a distance from the refugees, whether from shame or fear, Zenta didn't know.

As she walked through the blasted city, she saw the pain and loss that hung over the streets like a pall. It reflected her own heart. She thought of Otto and his easy smile, his homesickness and desire to see his mother. Of Frieda's sad smile when she spoke of Oskar. How many of these women awaited the return of sons, husbands, brothers? War had torn lives apart on both sides. She awaited news of her Aleks, his promise a constant beat in her heart. The war had been finished for months now. How long until the women of Hamburg would give up hope? How long until she would?

. . .

Her answer came with the first winter frost, delayed by the slow tread of survivors across a broken Europe and the natural passage of war. A new arrival to the Fischbek camp stood in a ring of mothers, his voice soft, solemn.

"They were holed up on the edge of Poland, they had nowhere to go," he said. Drawn in by the hush that fell around him, Zenta approached, Aina in her arms.

He stood tall and strong, in spite of the white and grey that peppered his hair. Wrinkles ran deep like trenches across his skin.

"They fought for Latvia, and the Reds slaughtered them like hogs," he continued.

A breathless woman cried out in sorrow, her trembling hand coming to her mouth. "How do you know?"

The man faced her, tears welling in his eyes. "It was my town, once. My wife was a Pole. Now it is nothing but rubble." He paused, voice shaking, face going still, before continuing. "The Germans sent no more supplies, no more reinforcements. The soldiers were unarmed, but the Reds didn't care. They massacred the 5th Battalion."

Zenta sucked in a breath. Shock shot through her body.

The 5th Battalion. *Aleks.*

Her arms subconsciously tightened on her child as she stepped closer.

"The men surrendered. But it was a bloodbath."

"What do you mean?" Zenta's voice loud, high-pitched, cut through the crowd's cries of horror. "They are prisoners of the Soviets?" Memories, vivid and painful, flashed through her mind. Of a night of darkness, and stolen fathers, of carriages, of wooden slats, her sister's hands full of letters collected from the railway, floating on the wind of their passage to Siberia.

The old man looked up, meeting Zenta's stare, his eyes red with fatigue and unshed tears. "No, my daughter," he whispered. "The Soviets killed them all. The Latvians fighting for the Reds did nothing to stop it. Brother against brother, they lined them up, forced them to their knees and shot them in the head. An execution."

The ground beneath her fell away, the world itself shuddered, twisting around her. Zenta forced air into her lungs, fighting the physical convulsion that gripped her – a pain that started in her heart and radiated through her soul. She saw Aleks' face in her mind, as the boy she'd known, who threw rocks at her window, and then as the man he'd become. She pictured his bright eyes so steadfast, determined to do the right thing for Latvia, and heard the promise whispered from his lips as they'd said goodbye.

"But they surrendered..."

"The Soviets didn't care."

Beside her Vanya touched her shoulder, an offer of comfort. Voice firm, she said, "They will be remembered, as the heroes they were."

Murmurs of agreement rolled around her, like a mounting thunderstorm. Zenta could hear the pounding of her heart, the rasp of her quavering breath.

"Take Aina," she pushed the child into Desna's arms.

"Wait, Zenta? Where are you going?"

Her companion's call faded behind her as Zenta streaked across the camp, eyes a blur of tears, limbs pulsing with a need to run, to flee, to escape the old man and his hideous words. She broke out of the line of buildings that made up the camp, feet moving fast, chest heaving. She crossed the grassy plain, the frozen land silent and still around her. Breaking into a run, she galloped over the icy world, her feet pounding to the rhythm of her pain. At length, exhaustion claimed her and she crashed to her knees. Fingers curling in the winter-hardened earth, she braced herself and, head tilted to the sky, screamed her terror into the night.

Worse even than the fate of a Siberian camp.

Lined up.

Shot in the head.

Executed.

Aleks.

It could not be true. It could not be. He escaped. Somehow. Perhaps he wasn't ever there, but was in another town, separated from his battalion, but alive? Her mind raced, her body trembling from cold, from horror as it rebelled against the knowledge that lodged itself in her guts.

"You promised," she screamed at the sky. "You promised you would come back. You promised you would find me!"

With that final cry she collapsed to the ground, body racked with shuddering sobs, face a mess of tears and soil. "You promised," she whispered to the white-tipped grass that cradled her. "You promised."

There she lay, unable to move, stuck like a statue of mourning as the sun streaked the sky in the pastels of dusk. She stayed long after darkness claimed the day, until the cold of the earth had reached its tendrils up, up, twining with her skin, her bones, her soul. The ice embedded itself in her, until it became part of her.

Forever.

That night, breasts weighed down by a full day's worth of milk, Zenta snuggled her daughter to her chest. Hidden by a rough woollen blanket, she fed her child from her body, her soul heavy with despair.

She wanted to give up. To stop. It was too much loss to bear.

She longed for the release she'd felt in giving her niece away to Alma, in giving up on her own life. There was nothing left. No one was coming.

Gazing down at the child suckling at her breast, her small fists pressing against the white of Zenta's flesh, blue eyes, tinged with green from her father, shining in the moonlight that peeked in through the ill-fitting curtains, Zenta realised she could not follow that path. Not this time.

This child only had Zenta. Her father was gone, like her grandparents and aunt. She needed her mother.

Leaning down, Zenta pressed a kiss to her daughter's brow, the wispy tufts of her baby hair tickling Zenta's nose.

"I will protect you, small one. Always."

A new reason to go on. A new promise.

One that Zenta would fight to keep.

Impossibly, life went on, day, by day, by day. Aina started babbling, then crawling, walking, her first tentative steps made in a stumbling run across the new grass of spring. Zenta watched as Desna and Vanya and the other women of the camp shrieked in delight at her daughter's progress, smiling at the collective joy new life seemed to inspire.

It was a tentative joy. One built on a foundation of truest sorrow. But for a few moments, Zenta's child allowed them all to pretend.

Time passed in the camp on the edge of Hamburg, and refugees continued to integrate into the ecosystem of the region. There were courtships and marriages. Babies born. New schools and churches, choirs and cultural activities. A thriving mini-city developing on the outskirts of the port city, an oasis of Latvia, Lithuania and Estonia, safe from the reach of the Soviets who now ruled the Baltics.

By the next summer the university in the city had agreed to take on a number of refugee students, allowing them to take up previous degrees, or start wholly new ones. The entry requirements were relaxed to improve access, and groups of young people took up the opportunity. As the summer sun shone down on the people of the Baltics, some of the tension of displacement began to thaw.

But as time stretched around them, wide and unending, cracks began to appear as the trauma of years of occupation broke through the initial shock of displacement. An increase of petty crime, scuffles between men on the streets, women pulling back from burgeoning friendships.

As more refugees arrived, others became restless, choosing to risk a return to their homeland over the uncertainty of this existence.

Return was never an option for Zenta. What was there to return for? A blasted city. A family gone. And her last hope, Aleks, lying dead somewhere on the edge of Poland, his body rotting into the ground.

Aina, *her* Aina, was all she had left.

The governments who ran the camps realised the programme was unsustainable. These people could not go home, but they also could not stay in this temporary state indefinitely.

In 1947 new agreements were drawn up with Allied countries, different nations agreeing to take in refugees for permanent resettlement. Britain was first, committing to take skilled labourers. Many women were selected, including Desna and Vanya, their seamstress skills precious in these post-war days. But not Zenta.

Her turn was soon to come.

She was called into an office. An older soldier, with a stern face and unruly moustaches, sat behind a large wooden desk. He spoke to her in heavily accented Latvian as he informed her of her future.

"Australia."

"Australia?"

"Australia."

It seemed there wasn't really a choice. Within the week she was packed and on her way to Bremerhaven, the port where she would embark. The docks were wide and flat, the ground low-lying and eerily bare. A huge metal crane loomed above her, blocking out the sun. She and her fellow passengers were guided up a steep plank onto the large former troopship USAT *General Stuart Heintzelman*, its hull rising tall and imposing from the murky waters that churned below, children gaping in wonder while their mothers fussed anxiously. As the vessel powered its way along the Weser River heading for the sea beyond, resignation settled over Zenta. She had been at war for seven years. First the Reds, then the Nazis. Forced from her home, her family destroyed, her lover killed, her niece lost. Looking back towards the coast of Germany she realised she was leaving Europe, finally, once and for all. The choice had been made, the die cast. There was nothing for her here but loss and misery.

Australia.

An island on the other side of the world, impossibly far away; impossibly different. Miles away from her family's bakery, from the comfort and love she'd known within its walls. That world had been destroyed, torn away by brutality and terror, existing now only in her memory.

Now they would travel to a new world, untouched by the horror of war.

A new beginning for her and her child.

FORTY

ZENTA

The open sea had swallowed them whole. Zenta stood on the deck of the *Heintzelman*, Aina on her hip. Her daughter's sleepy head rested on her shoulder, her breathing soft and peaceful, her lengthening limbs heavy against Zenta's side. She'd grown again, another quick spurt. She was always changing, always discovering something new. Her child was a wonder. It helped, in the long dark of night.

She'd been drawn to the deck by the promise of sunrise, a daily ritual, a moment of new hope Zenta clung to as the days of their passage expanded before her. She looked out over the railings. Open ocean stretched out, reaching from the deck where she stood to the horizon where the first rays of sunlight climbed over the curve of the world.

The boat trip had been long and fatiguing. Zenta spent the first week fighting nausea, sitting on the deck staring out to where the water met the sky, as Alma had once advised her to do. It helped, a little. At first they'd hugged the coast of Europe, then turned inland through the Suez Canal. But since they'd broken through the long man-made cut that divided a continent there had been nothing to see but water. Their vessel that had seemed so impossibly large as it reared up against the docks of Bremerhaven, now enveloped by the cold and eerie press of the ocean currents that stirred below.

As the sun began its journey across the sky, its touch glinting golden off the tips of distant waves, other migrants began to appear on deck. They collected in small groups, chatting in their native tongue, Latvian, Lithuanian or Estonian, washing past Zenta's ears. She could have turned, could have made her way to the cluster of Latvian women who settled by the stairs each morning. But she didn't. There was nothing she wanted to say, nothing she wanted to hear. She stayed by the railing, watching as the *Heintzelman* sluiced through the waves.

She spied him after lunch, making his way through his daily circuit around the deck. Fair-haired as her brother had been, he was short and round-shouldered like her father. His eyes were fixed on his feet, watching his tread as he moved around the edge of the boat. He never looked up.

This was his routine each day. Circuit complete, he'd slink over to sit on the deck, back resting against the central wall that rose up from the hull. Settling his body, knees up, forearms crossed over his stomach, he would stare out over the waves as the day limped on. She never saw him with the other groups of men. But she didn't question it. She also sought solitude. He was just another displaced person watching the horizon, seeking oblivion from the past.

Over the last few days, he'd moved closer, closer. Last week he'd smiled at her in passing, yesterday he gave a small wave.

Now as she sat with Aina, clapping her hands as her daughter sang a nonsense rhyme for toddlers, she felt his eyes on her.

She looked up, smiled.

His lips trembled, his eyes flicked down then back to her face. Taking a deep breath he said, "Hello, it is a good day, yes?"

His presence had become so familiar that talking felt as natural as breathing.

"It is," she replied.

He shuffled closer. "I am from Riga."

Zenta felt the smile hit her lips, unexpectedly. "Me too."

He nodded.

"Timurs Vanags." He tapped his chest.

"Zenta Kalnina, pleased to meet you."

"You too." He glanced away, fingers picking at his nails.

"How did you escape?" she asked.

"I was in a labour camp in Germany. The Americans liberated us."

It was an explanation, but it left much out. Why was he in a German labour camp? Did he refuse to fight? Where was his family?

But Zenta didn't press. No one did. They all had losses to bear, histories filled with guilt and shame.

"I took a fishing boat."

He nodded quietly, didn't ask for details. She'd known he wouldn't.

"Your baby?" He gestured to Aina. "But no wedding ring." A note of accusation in his tone. Or was it just a simple question? Zenta struggled to tell the difference these days, her nerves so frayed, her world on its head. She blinked, decided it was a natural thing to ask.

"My niece," Zenta said.

He seemed to relax. Aina looked up at him, fingers pointing, fat arm wobbling.

He laughed. "Very sweet."

"She is."

They lapsed into silence, but it was a comfortable one, borne of long days on the water with nothing but the edge of the sky to watch. After years of keeping herself apart from others, it felt good to watch it with him.

November the 18th, Latvian Independence Day, came and went. No one celebrated. A few men spoke loudly of reclaiming their country, but when met with the silence of disbelief, fell quiet. Ten days later, they docked at Fremantle.

The heat hit her like a physical blow. Intense like the bakery oven, but dry and coarse. It sucked the air from her lungs, making her gasp for breath. Timurs, at her side, took Aina from her so she could steady herself. Her daughter secured on his hip, he gripped her elbow to help her walk. The gesture was familiar, and protective. She realised she had formed a bond with this man from Riga whose pain echoed her own.

They were processed, then loaded onto a new ship bound for Victoria and purpose-built housing on the outskirts of a town named Bonegilla. The camp consisted of a set of thin-walled, flimsy buildings, surrounded by an endless expanse of rugged bushland. Tall, white-limbed trees stretched up into the burning sky, dusty green shrubs scratched at ankles, catching on stockings, slicing at exposed flesh. The air smelt of eucalyptus, floral and sharp.

Men and women were housed in separate buildings. Aina and Zenta were assigned a bunk in a building that pressed on the edge of the forest: yet another new building, new bed. The heat of the land leaked through the plasterboard, inspiring a sheen of sweat permanently slick on their pale European flesh. By day they drew the curtains against the wall of heat that rose from the earth and radiated from the sun; at night they threw open the windows, dresses open, their skin seeking the touch of the cooling breeze that rustled through the gum trees that lined the camp.

They were told to report for language classes.

Gathering in the morning in a set of rooms at the far end of the camp, the Baltic refugees shuffled nervously in their seats. A young woman stood before them, her fine blonde hair set in ringlets that cupped her round face. She smiled, and began.

English made no sense. Nothing like the Russian she'd been forced to learn in Riga; foreign even to the German she'd picked up throughout occupation. The room murmured, a collective confusion of Latvian, Lithuanian and Estonian, they hadn't even separated them by mother tongue for the lessons.

"Stop!" the young woman snapped. "English only."

The bushland and the language weren't the only challenging things. The food was different, too. Gone was the expected daily rye bread, the potato cakes and soured cream. Replaced with mutton stew served on a tray, the chunks of meat heavy and chewy. Pickles were non-existent. Fish, on the rare occasions it was served, tasted of the muddy floor of their inland river home, not the salty brine of open sea.

Her father would have hated it. At least they were fed. After living through the food rationing in occupied Riga, Zenta knew to be grateful for any food on her plate. But it was still hard.

Everything was different. Every day a fresh and bemusing challenge.

The unfamiliar food, the oppressive heat, the headache-inducing language, it was all too much. Timurs was all that felt familiar. They passed their free time together, talking of Riga, of Latvia, of pīrāgi and rye pudding; of the time before the Soviets. Or they simply sat, still and silent, the whistle of a honeyeater calling overhead as they watched Aina toddling around on increasingly stable, but still pudgy legs.

Six weeks later they were assigned jobs. Most of the men were sent to New South Wales to work on the Snowy Mountains Scheme. Zenta had no idea what that was. Some protested.

"But I'm a doctor."

"I lecture at university."

"I am not a labourer."

They were ignored. The conditions of their arrival were

clear: two years of service to the nation, in whatever role they were assigned. No arguments, and only a few exemptions for mothers like Zenta with small children. Branded "The Beautiful Balts" by the Australian media, they were celebrated for their contributions to the nation, but only if they did as they were told.

Timurs was sent to South Australia with a group of twelve other Latvians. Zenta went with him. Somehow the authorities had paired them, and they didn't correct the assumption. Loaded onto a boat, shipped to a port in Adelaide, the others were assigned work on a pipeline outside the city, and later irrigation or fruit picking roles in the Murraylands. Timurs, having a family, needed stability, so was sent to the railways. The trip overland was long and hot. As the ocean had enveloped them as they crossed the Pacific, now red soil, scraggly trees and dust-filled winds swallowed their passage. The sky overhead seemed higher, further from reach, its striking blue looming large above them. Daunting in its size.

They were assigned a small railway cottage in the heart of the Murray Mallee, a thriving farming district half a day from the capital city of Adelaide. Thick sand-coloured stone, a raw tin roof, bare soil stretching behind their little row of houses, a man-made barrier against the encroaching bush.

The heat continued. The high burning sun beat down from a bright blue sky without cease. If Latvia was a country of long winter, Australia was one of never-ending summer. Days stretched into weeks, the very stone of their home seeming to boil, radiating heat even into the midnight hours. During the afternoon, at the height of the scorching temperatures, Zenta would strip to her silks and lie on the bare stone floor, arms and legs akimbo, a naked Aina toddling beside her. Body slicked with sweat, the hair of her forehead and nape damp, she closed her eyes and dreamed of snow.

Shopping was another challenge. The walk into the town

centre was long and dusty, her throat parched and raw before she'd even sighted the main street. There was one general store, little more than a front room and a cash machine, the walls lined with shelves of tins. Zenta's English was weak, the words on the labels a jumble before her eyes. She gathered items at random, hoping the poorly printed images of round orange fruit or green leaves indicated the produce she expected. Some foods were easy to find: potatoes for cakes, beetroot for soup. But rye was nowhere to be found, and the wheaten flour she could source baked differently. At the till a friendly smile from the ageing woman who ran the store, rapid-fire words and a mounting headache. Zenta poured her coins onto the counter, watching the woman as she counted out the pounds.

Tired, dripping sweat, streaked with mud, Timurs would return from his day on the railway, mouth drawn, eyes hooded. He ate her food in silence, filling himself to the brim before visiting the washroom to clean away a day on the tracks. His passing words were always the same, "Not like my mother makes it."

Zenta understood.

Companionability. Familiarity. Proximity.

When they found themselves in bed together, naked limbs entwined, it felt like the next natural step. Two displaced persons, far from home, in a barren foreign land. They were the last of Latvia for each other. A lodestone to cling to in a world that was racing away from memory. Looking into his pale blue eyes, swimming with sorrow, so different from the warm green hue of Aleks', she gave herself to him, binding them together against this place so far from everything they knew.

Slowly Zenta began to find a grip on this new land, this new life. Words started to take shape and meaning, faces on the main street becoming familiar. Feeling brave one morning, she baked a fruit cake, sweetened with the plump dried sultanas she'd found at the store. It was an experiment, but the cake looked passable. Aina on her hip, she walked to her neighbour's home. A small, pale woman answered. Zenta had seen her in passing, her head always lowered, her eyes furtive. It seemed they were two women alone in this tiny railway outpost. Zenta had hopes for a friend.

Despite her broken English, she managed to introduce herself, and learned her neighbour's name was Bethan. They shared tea and Zenta's cake. It was surprisingly good, but Bethan barely touched it. As Zenta said her hesitant goodbyes, making her way back out into the bright day, a feeling of doom enveloped her.

That night, as she lay spreadeagled in bed, Timurs beside her, the window thrown open sneaking even the tiniest puff of breeze, she heard the commotion.

At first it was little more than a raised voice, a bang. Then the loud crash of shattering plates followed by the heavy tread of stomping feet. A cry and then screams, long and drawn and desperate.

Zenta sat bolt upright in bed, hand gripping Timurs' arm.

"That's Bethan, next door."

Timurs lay still, but he was awake, she could feel the alertness of his body.

"Timurs, we should do something."

"It is not our business," he said. "Go back to sleep."

When Zenta knocked on Bethan's door the next morning, no one answered. She didn't see her neighbour until church that Sunday, the yellowing blue blotch that marred her white cheek unmistakable. Zenta watched as Timurs shook hands with the man at Bethan's side. He was tall and dark-haired, an easy smile on his lips. Beside him Bethan cowered.

"How could you be so friendly with him?" Zenta hissed as they walked along the dirt track back home.

"He works the railway. He's one of the few who are friendly to me."

"But you know what he did to Bethan. You heard him put that bruise on her face."

"It is not our business," Timurs replied.

Breathless from disbelief, Zenta watched his back as he walked ahead of her. How could he turn his back so easily from cruel reality? He was Latvian, like her. He had seen the horrors of war. How could he not understand? A new uncertainty flickered within her.

But life rolled ahead, dragging Zenta with it.

When the pause of her monthly bleeding told Zenta without a doubt that she was pregnant, they married.

She borrowed a white dress from the church organ player and said her vows before God. Timurs a silent, tense presence beside her, the swell of her stomach still too small to be noticed.

That night as they lay in bed together, Timurs rested a hand on her belly.

"I can't wait for there to be three of us," he whispered to the night.

"Four, you mean," Zenta replied.

"Sure," he said, rolling over to sleep.

Zenta swallowed, cold unease coiling in her gut.

Soon after their wedding Timurs earned a promotion to "Ganger", managing his own crew of men on the railway. They moved to a small house on the northern edge of a town called Renmark in the Riverland. "We need more room for a family," Timurs insisted, though honestly Zenta didn't understand.

Land was never something she had growing up in Riga. Neither had Timurs. But she hadn't protested, thinking it was his way of finding acceptance of this new life. The house stood alone in a sea of cleared farmland, dry and barren. Along the rear of the property ran a line of bush, trees and shrubbery rising up from a small tributary of the Murray River that ran through the centre of town. That small run of bush-land, rising dusty green from the water at its roots, became a beacon for Zenta, a little piece of beauty in a vast foreign space.

And for a time, things were good. Timurs toiled on the railways, Zenta started a vegetable garden, and the new general store sold rye flour. Aina talked more and more, finding English words far quicker than her mother.

In the quiet of their new home Zenta discovered the birdsong of Australia. The warble of a magpie, the raucous caw of a galah. It was not the gentle choir of Latvia, but held its own beauty. It matched this land, this new home that Zenta was building. Far from Latvia, but safe.

That was all that mattered.

She lost the baby.

Standing in the backyard, hands deep in soap suds as she wrung out Timurs' work shirt for the coming day, a flood of red, hot and metallic, gushed down her legs. Pain, sharp and piercing, ripped through her belly. It was nothing like the cramping pull of childbirth, this was something else entirely. Zenta slumped to the ground, gasping for breath. She was in trouble, she needed help. She had to move. But her legs wouldn't cooperate, her head suddenly groggy.

"Aina, inside," she ordered, breath panting. "Inside, now!"

Her child obeyed. Zenta crawled behind her on hands and knees, somehow dragging herself into the house. Pulling the door closed behind her, she passed out.

By the time Timurs returned from work, it was too late. He found his wife in a pool of blood, an exhausted Aina screaming by her side.

Zenta survived. The baby did not.

After that, things changed.

Timurs started coming home later, reeking of drink, the scent on his breath a sharp reminder of her uncle in his grief.

He stayed up later and later, smoking cigarettes on the porch before joining her in bed demanding sex. On Sundays he slept late, skipping church. He criticised her food. Found fault with her cleaning. Shouted at Aina to be silent. The little light that had sparked in his eyes fading fast.

Zenta held her tongue. Her grief over the loss of the baby was deep. She understood his need for time. The memory of her own father's descent into depression was still vivid in her mind. Timurs didn't have Aina to keep him going, not like she did. So, she carried on. Maintaining the house, cooking the meals, building up her vegetable garden. But less money was making it home for food, more and more being poured down Timurs' throat.

The squeeze was becoming tight. She just had to keep going. He would work through it. She just had to hold it together, a little longer.

FORTY-ONE

ZENTA

He arrived early one morning, standing at her doorstep, pail of fresh milk in his hand. She'd seen him before, in church on Sundays, and in town when she ventured in for supplies. Tall, broad-shouldered, the back of his neck always slightly red from the sun. He was one of the few locals who would acknowledge her, a nod, the dip of his hat in passing.

Smiling, he nodded to Zenta. "Morning, Mrs. My wife Mary and I run the dairy just over the way." He pointed across the landscape. But it was so vast and unfamiliar Zenta had no sense of just how far he meant.

"Times are tough," he continued, his Australian accent nasal and thick. "Thought you and the little one could use some fresh milk."

He held out the bucket. Warm, creamy milk, fresh from the teat sloshed in the bucket. Instantly she was transported back to Germany, to a warm farmhouse, a loving family, a sanctuary.

Tears formed in her eyes at his gesture of kindness, pride did not let them fall. It did not stop her taking the milk, either.

"Paldies," she said, Latvian still first on her tongue. "Thank you. Mr...?"

"Mr Koch, Brian, but call me 'Blue'."

"Blue?" Zenta frowned, wasn't that a colour?

Blue grinned. "A nickname, on account of this." He tapped the bright red hair on his head, as though that made any sense.

She nodded anyway. "Thank you, *Blue*. Tea?" She gestured inside.

He shook his head. "Thank you, no. I need to get back to the cows. But if it will help, there's more where that came from." He pointed at the bucket.

Zenta swallowed. She wanted to scream yes, to thank him, to beg for his generosity to continue, but her throat closed over. His eyes softened. "I'll send my son, Bill. It can be tough out here," he said. "We stick together."

True to his word, exactly one week later another knock sounded on the door. A small face, freckles haphazard over the bridge of his nose, shining hair a match for his father's, an unsure smile. "Dad sent me with this." The boy shoved the pail of milk forward, white liquid spilling over the sides. Zenta smiled and took the bucket.

"You are a good boy," she said. "Hungry?"

Hope lit his eyes, but his feet shuffled, unsure.

"I have cake, fresh from the oven. My daughter and I were about to test it. You would be doing me a favour."

A grin, wide and free, split his face. Zenta's heart burst in her chest. The open joy of children, destroyed by war in her homeland, was still something she marvelled at here on the other side of the world.

She stepped aside, allowing the boy to enter her small cottage. He walked past her, confident now, striding boldly for the kitchen. There at the table Aina sat, pudgy legs swinging freely from the chair. She'd grown tall these past months, her limbs stretching into the world around her as she sought to learn more and more. Zenta wished she could pause time, keep her small and safe at her breast forever. A silly thought.

Bill paused, cocking his head as he observed Aina. Then, with a gentle hand, he reached up and smoothed the soft curls around Aina's head. "You are a sweet one," he cooed. Aina reached up, gripping his nose in a saliva-wet hand. "Cake!" she piped.

A huffed laugh from Bill. "Yum!" He exclaimed, rubbing his belly.

"Yum!" Aina repeated, her baby-puff hands patting her round tummy.

Lips curved into a motherly smile, Zenta moved to the cake. The unfamiliar sultana cake had become a staple. The dried fruit was always available at the store. She cut three slices, a generous one for Bill, a standard for herself and a slither for Aina.

"Thank you, Mrs," Bill said, eyes already glued to the cake. His small hands tore off a chunk but before it reached his mouth Aina piped up again, "Cake!"

He looked over at her, face full of wonder. "Here," he said as he passed his piece to her reaching hand.

"She has her own," Zenta said.

"I know, but I can share. Kids like that."

We all do, Zenta thought.

The door to their cottage banged shut. Zenta, standing at the sink, braced herself. His walk was markedly wobbly, his foot-fall heavy and uneven. Taking a deep breath, she moved to the stove to reheat his soup and butter some bread. She'd added fresh milk to the beetroot. Not the same as soured cream, but a nice touch to make it taste more like home. The metal chair scraped along the floor behind her, followed by the thud of his body as it flopped into his chair. She plated his soup, placed the meal before him. He stared at the bowl, face slack with drink, breath heavy through his nose. Then, curling his fingers under the rim of the bowl picked it up and hurled it across the room. Zenta flinched in shock, crouching down instinctively at the violence of the action. Pale pink beetroot slipped down the wall, dripping like blood, pooling on the floor.

"No more of your swill, woman!" Timurs cried. "I want a real meal. I work all day to feed you. I need meat."

Zenta bristled, anger fast and hot flushing her face.

"If you spent less money on beer and drink there would be more for meat. If it weren't for the milk from Brian I don't know how I would feed us all." Zenta snapped. As soon as the words escaped her lips she realised her mistake and froze.

Slowly, Timurs brought his head up to look at her. There was a pause.

"Who is Brian?"

Her mouth went dry as dust, she swallowed. Slowly Timurs rose to his feet, swaying slightly from alcohol. Picking up the freshly buttered bread still by his arm he hurled the slice across the room, right at her face. She stepped aside, evading the flying heel. He moved like lightning, flashing across the room towards her. She stepped back, hands coming before her in instinctual protection.

"I am sorry," she stammered. "I shouldn't have said that."

He stood before her, shoving his face right up against hers, his breath sour from beer. "I work all day for you. You and that child that is not my own! And you dare thank another man for your food!"

"I'm sorry, I spoke without thinking."

"Don't you know the shame of it? To waste myself on another man's get."

"Aina is my niece."

"She is a useless mouth to feed. A burden hanging round my neck!"

Zenta stood stunned. "She is a child!"

"And you are a whore!" He reached up and grabbed the back of her hair, wrenching her head down at a painful angle.

"Timurs!" Zenta exclaimed. "You are hurting me."

He didn't seem to hear her, just continued ranting. "I bed you, night after night, and you never resist. You let me have you, roam your body. But I am not the first, am I?"

"Timurs, please."

"You think I didn't know that first night? That you had been touched by another man before. Fucking WHORE!"

"Please, please calm down. We can talk about this. It is all right."

"Nothing is all right!" he bellowed. He moved suddenly, dragging her physically across the kitchen, heading for the stove. The metal of the stovetop was still hot, the remaining soup steaming in the pot. He grabbed the pot with his free hand, smashing it against the oven, metal on metal screeching. Then he pressed her. Shoving her face down towards the still glowing top. Panicking, Zenta braced her hands against the stove, fighting with all her might to keep her face from the radiating heat.

He was strong, days of physical work on the railways had built his slight frame. But he was drunk. Zenta twisted and he lost his footing, stumbled, his grip on her hair loosening just enough that she could wriggle away. Enraged he lunged for her; taking her head in two hands he propelled her face-first into the kitchen bench. Her forehead connected with the edge, sharp and hard. Light exploded in her vision as she slumped to the floor. But Timurs wasn't done. Grabbing her hair again he screamed in rage, throwing her across the room. She lay sprawled across the laminate floor, chest heaving. He pulled back his leg and swung, heavy boot connecting with her ribs. She heard a crack. His foot went back again. She screamed in terror and pain as he kicked her again and again, then reached down to throw her bodily against the wall. She screamed again, her cry echoing out into the dark night.

No one came.

She knew they wouldn't.

Later when Timurs had passed out in bed, Zenta crawled to the sink. She ran water, dipping a tea towel into the lukewarm fluid, and dabbed at her face. Everything hurt. She tasted blood on her tongue. One hand gripping her throbbing ribs, she limped to Aina's room.

The bed was empty. Horror sluiced through Zenta's gut. Had he hurt her daughter?

"Aina," she croaked, panic rising.

A small sob sounded from under the bed. Zenta fell to her knees, looking under the loosely sprung mattress. There, pressed back against the wall, was Aina. Curled tight like a hedgehog in the snow, shivering with fear.

Zenta's heart cracked. That fear, so raw, so primal.

"It's all right, my child," she whispered. "Come."

Aina shook her head, shuffling further under the bed. Zenta went to reach for her but her ribcage screamed in protest, bone scraping on bone, stealing the breath from her lungs.

A crushing fatigue settled over her limbs, her eyelids suddenly too heavy to hold open.

"That's all right, my love. You stay there. I will rest here, on your bed. You can join me... when you are ready."

Heaving herself to her feet she collapsed onto the small cot, pulling a sheet up over herself. She lay still, hands on her heart, trying to breathe in shallow puffs to avoid the sharp stabbing pain that shot through her chest if she moved too much. A body, small and warm, crept into the bed beside her. Wordlessly Aina snugged herself against Zenta, her little hand reaching up. Zenta caught it, drawing it to her lips to kiss.

"Sleep now, little one," she whispered.

And so they lay, pressed together, hand in hand, as Aina drifted off to sleep.

But rest would not come for Zenta. The final veil to the truth had been stripped away. Timurs was not the place of safety she had believed. Her need for the familiarity of Latvia that he represented had blinded her to his real nature.

Here, Aina was no longer safe.

FORTY-TWO

ZENTA

1951

The dry wind whipped across the yard. Zenta reached up, unpegging the bedsheet from the line as it billowed out in the breeze. "Mama-Zee!"

Turning, she tented her hand over her eyes, looking down the long, red dirt driveway that led from her home.

Aina was running, light on her feet. Happy to be home from school. She was always happy, before he came home.

Zenta tongued the fresh split in her lip, moistening the cut so she could smile without it starting to bleed, and opened her arms to the sprinting Aina.

Aina leaped into her embrace, arms still soft with childhood, coming tight around her neck.

"Es mīlu tevi," Zenta whispered to her daughter.

"I love you too."

Breaking apart, Zenta folded the final sheet into washing basket. Hooking it on one hip, she walked hand in hand with her daughter back to the small house. These were the precious hours. Between the end of school and closing time at the pub. Here was where she and Aina really lived.

"How was your day?" Zenta asked, as she stacked the washing neatly into the linen cupboard. Timurs liked things to be orderly.

"Good," Aina said.

Her school was small. Just one classroom, one teacher and students of all ages. It serviced the region. Some students travelled up to an hour on a locally run school bus to attend. Aina was lucky to be a short walk away.

"And what did you learn?"

"Mostly counting."

"Mostly?"

"Cheryl likes counting. I don't." Aina fell silent, Zenta paused, eyeing the child. What wasn't she saying?

But before she could press, Aina continued, suddenly enthusiastic. "Mr Wilson read us a story! About a beautiful black horse and a boy who loved him."

"That sounds like a lovely story."

"It was," Aina looked out the window wistfully. "Not as good as your story of the white deer that disappears in the snow..."

Zenta smiled to herself. She made a point of sharing her culture with Aina as much as possible. Fairy tales, food traditions, language. It was her way of keeping a little piece of Latvia alive, even here in the middle of a desert.

"I wish I could see snow."

"It is magical!" Zenta agreed. "White and fluffy, it shines in the light of the sun and the moon."

"Bill thinks it would be scary."

"That's not like Bill, he's usually very brave!"

The one-time milk boy and Aina had formed a solid friendship since she'd begun at school. He'd recognised Aina the very first day as Zenta dropped her at the schoolhouse. Zenta hadn't wanted to send her child to school. It felt too far away from her, dangerous, but her father's values, still strong within her, forced her hand. Aina deserved an education, even if the thought of being separated from her opened a crack in Zenta's heart. Nervously gripping Zenta's skirts, her small chest heaving with the effort of holding in tears, Aina had stood at the school gates. Zenta had pressed her eyes closed, willing herself not to cry. It would not do to upset Aina further.

Then Bill had appeared, all skinny limbs and open smiles.

"Hi, little one," he'd said, "remember me?"

Aina had brightened instantly, stepping from her hiding place at Zenta's leg.

"Morning, Mrs Vanaga. Aina's first day?"

"It is," Zenta had said, voice a loose, unstable thing.

"Don't worry," Bill had said, standing taller. "I'll watch her."

He'd taken Aina's hand in his and led her away. The crack in Zenta's chest wedging open further with each step. Aina hadn't looked back.

Now the two friends walked to and from school together most days, often sneaking off to the river's edge to play, especially in the heat of summer. A mirror of two other children, and the dreams of youth, a long time ago. It warmed something cold and sharp in Zenta's heart.

"Bill says the cold can kill you," Aina explained.

"Well, that's true. But if you dress well, and light a fire, it is nothing to fear."

Aina nodded. "I'll tell him at school. So he knows he doesn't have to be scared."

"A good idea."

They passed the afternoon in the kitchen together, grating vegetables for fritters and, as it was Friday, soaking yesterday's rye bread in milk and sugar for a dessert.

"Collect me some apricots," Zenta said, passing a bucket to Aina.

Timurs had planted her a row of the delicious fruit trees as a wedding present. It had taken years for them to fruit, but this season their produce was strong, fat and round. Zenta liked to top the rye pudding with slices, for extra sweetness. A mix of the traditional Latvian pudding and this new culture they were shaping here in Australia.

Aina took the bucket and skipped happily out to the young trees, taller than her but still spindly with youth. In time they would be mighty fruit producers. Zenta had plans to make jam.

Timurs was home by dinner, unsteady on his feet but mercifully affable. They ate their vegetable cakes in silence then he took a bottle wrapped in a brown paper bag out into the backyard, cigarette dancing from his lips. He liked to stroll through the gathering dusk, enjoying the cooling breezes that sifted through the trees. Zenta was happy for him to go.

She was just putting away the last dish, rubbing it dry with the final edge of a soaking tea towel, when the knock sounded at the door. Frowning, she removed her apron, hanging it neatly on the rack. Aina looked up from the kitchen table where she sat reading in the evening twilight. Ruffling her hair as she passed her child, Zenta made for the door. Pushing the squeaky screen aside she stopped dead, her hand fluttering to her mouth.

"My God!" she breathed, chest heaving.

There on her doorstep stood a ghost.

Shorter than Zenta remembered, her round face hardened into tight lines, the corners of her smiling mouth turned down. She was thinner even than the last time they met, a hardness about her eyes that was all new.

It was her and it was not. Like a misshapen reflection in a window, or a shadow in a nightmare.

"Hello, sister," Estere said. "May I come in?"

.   .   .

Seven years, it had been seven years since Estere had erupted into the bakery and blown their lives apart. Forced to her knees, a gun to her head, their parents beside her.

Shock rattled through Zenta's limbs, coursing through her body. Her stomach was a leaden ball in her gut. She had dreamed of this day. Imagined the joy of finding her sister alive, escaped from Latvia, just like her. She had also dreaded it and what it would mean for the lie she still maintained.

"Mumma?" A soft hand on her skirts, a curious peek out to the stranger on the porch.

Estere sucked in a sharp breath. "Aina?"

She knelt down by her suitcase, bringing herself to Aina's height. Switching to English she said, "Come here, little one."

Step cautious, Aina moved slowly from behind Zenta's skirts. Zenta felt her throat closing over, the pounding of her heart deafening in her ears.

Aina came to stand before Estere, her small frame lit by the final dying rays of the sun. Estere cocked her head to the side, brows knitting, and looked up at Zenta, a question in her eyes.

Zenta wasn't yet ready to answer that question. Rallying, she gripped Aina's tiny shoulders.

"Aina, this is Estere. My sister from Latvia. Be a good girl and fetch the rye pudding from the pantry. We will join you shortly."

Aina nodded, turning to do as she was asked. "Pleased to meet you," she chirped as she went inside.

"She doesn't know me?" Estere asked, reverting to Latvian.

"She knows some things, but no details," Zenta evaded. "She is just a child."

Estere nodded, eyes roaming about the outside of the little house.

"This isn't much," she said. "But compared with where I've come from, it is enough."

Their eyes met.

And everything fell away. Zenta's fear, her hesitation, her worry. Her sister was alive. By some unfathomable miracle her sister had found her. She stepped forward, pulling Estere into a fierce hug, a small cry escaping her lips. She was so thin, skin and bone beneath a worn cotton blouse.

"You must be tired," Zenta rambled. "Come in, we have rye pudding, well, as close as I can make to it here, and tea."

Estere responded by tightening her arms about her sister. "Just a moment," she whispered. "I just need to hold you for another moment."

So Zenta stayed, wrapped in her sister's arms, tears streaming down her face.

Shortly afterwards, Estere ate her pudding slowly, savouring each mouthful. "Just like mother's," she said.

Zenta smiled cautiously. "What happened, Estere? Where are Mother and Father?"

Estere glanced across the table to where Aina sat, still reading. "Her English is exceptional. How is her Latvian?"

Zenta understood. "Aina, dear. Time to get ready for bed. You can take your book with you. I will be there to tuck you in shortly."

Aina popped off her chair and skipped over to kiss Zenta good night.

"Night, Ma-Zee."

"Good night, my darling."

She turned to Estere. "Good night, Aunty." She smiled, then trotted off to her room.

"She will still be fully clothed when I go to her, head firmly in that book," Zenta said, pride flickering across her face. "It's the only one we own, she's read it a hundred times. She'll read it one hundred more, I am sure."

"She is a good girl. You have raised her well."

Silence fell between them, tight like a bow.

Zenta cleared her throat. "Where are you staying?"

"I was hoping..." Estere gestured generally.

"Of course. Of course you must stay here."

"Your husband won't mind?"

Zenta blinked in surprise. "How do you know about Timurs?"

Estere laughed softly. "I didn't. But your hands are too soft to be a working woman's and there are a man's boots at the door. Not Aleks' then?"

The mention of his name sent a spear of pain through her body. Time had not blunted the loss, it was a wound Zenta knew would never heal. "He didn't make it."

Estere reached across the table, taking Zenta's hand, squeezing gently. "I am sorry."

Zenta closed her eyes, taking in a deep breath.

"We have both lost much." She opened her eyes, now limned with tears. Sniffing sharply, she straightened.

"What happened to you?" Zenta asked, pushing their conversation forward. "Where have you been these past five years? How did you find us?"

"A camp, another camp, and Americans."

Zenta frowned, Estere smiled sadly. "The Nazis took us to Salaspils. When the Soviets liberated it, I ran. I made it to a Displaced Persons camp in Germany, run by soldiers from the United States. I was... unwell. They took care of me in a local hospital. When I was strong enough I joined the refugee community. But no one could find record of you, or Aina." She glanced behind her at Aina's closed bedroom door. "Not until three months ago. You would not believe my surprise when I learned you were in Australia! That you were a passenger on the very first ship to sail from Bremerhaven."

"I thought you were dead. All of you."

Estere gave a dismissive wave of her hand. "You misunderstand. You were right to leave Europe, to get as far away as you could. There is nothing there for us, not now." She seemed to slump into herself and Zenta knew. She'd always known.

"How did they die?"

"Father never left the bakery. Otto shot him where he knelt. He used Tomass' gun."

Zenta's hand flew to her mouth to cover her horror. She had stood there, the night after. She had seen the ash, and coals of the bakery fire. And there, in the ruin of her home had lain the body of her father. She hadn't known. She hadn't said goodbye.

"Mother and I were taken to the camp in Salaspils. They worked us hard. Physical labour from sunrise to sunset, on just a small roll of bread or a thin porridge. Mother lasted less than six months."

Estere stopped, closing her eyes. "We weren't meant to survive."

"But you did."

"I did." Estere nodded, mouth drawn down. "The memory of Aina kept me going." She gave a laugh, sad and small. "The hope that I would hold my baby again."

"She kept me going too," Zenta replied. She watched her sister in the cool light of her electric lamp. Estere was hollowed out, barely a shell of the woman she had once been. But the truth about Aina, it couldn't wait.

Glancing down at her hands clasped before her, Zenta took a deep breath, ready to confess.

"Estere, I …"

The back door smacked shut. Zenta tensed instantly, sitting straight, hands smoothing her skirts. Estere looked on in surprise as a short man, the stink of booze and tobacco wafting before him, stumbled into the kitchen.

Blinking with the exaggerated slowness of the drunk, Timurs regarded Estere. "Who are you?" he demanded.

Zenta was on her feet, hands nervously pressing down her skirts. "Timurs, this is my sister. Estere."

Timurs took a deep drag on the cigarette hanging from his lips and blew the smoke out slowly before him.

"Come for the tramp? About bloody time. You owe me," he drawled before shuffling away towards his bedroom.

Zenta was trembling. Avoiding Estere's eyes she paced for the laundry, gathering blankets and sheets. "We have a spare room," she said, face laced with shame. "I will make it up for you."

Estere nodded in silence.

As Zenta made her way to the spare room she could feel her sister's eyes boring into her back. Shame wrapped itself around her heart. Timurs was a bad husband, Zenta knew that. So why did it feel worse now that Estere was there to see the truth? Shaking her head Zenta snapped the sheets out to cover the worn mattress. She didn't know what to expect, now that Estere had returned. And that terrified her.

That night as she lay beside Timurs, a fresh bruise from a casual slap before bed shining on her cheek, Zenta knew. She could never tell Estere what happened to her baby. Not only was the lie of Aina's parentage too entrenched, too welded to Zenta's life, but the truth of her niece, that Zenta didn't know where she was, or if she'd even survived, was too big, too horrible to face.

Another loss?

Estere couldn't bear it.

Timurs snorted, rolling over, his bloated body belching the stink of stale alcohol into the room around them. Zenta shrank away from him. A violent, unpredictable man. Seeking stability, she had married him. Instead, she'd trapped herself and her child in an existence of perpetual fear.

Cowering from her husband as he snored, a new idea began to take shape in Zenta's mind. A plan, a hope to set her daughter free.

FORTY-THREE

ESTERE

They told Aina that Estere was her mother the next morning. The girl sat at the kitchen table, feet swinging freely from the too-high chair. Estere stirred a pot of porridge on the stove, her back to Zenta. She focused on the bubbling oats, the warm, malty scent as they cooked usually so comforting. That morning it churned her stomach.

She'd slept poorly, the room too hot, the air too thick, the sound of Timurs' snoring echoing through the small house. She didn't like this country. Its vast plains, its unbearable heat. But she was here. She'd come for her daughter.

As the gentle warble of the magpies had replaced Timurs' bleating nose, she'd risen, walking softly into the kitchen. Zenta had already been up, arms covered in flour to the elbow. Her little sister hadn't changed. And yet, she had. Her eyes darted quickly, never settling, her shoulders tight, twitching at every unexpected sound. Estere supposed she had changed too.

"We have to tell her," she'd said.

"I know," Zenta replied. She didn't look up from her kneading.

Now Zenta moved to the kitchen table, her step slow, hesitant.

"Darling," Zenta said. A chair scraped as she took a seat by Aina. Estere sucked a breath in through her nose, readying herself. She'd no idea what to expect, how Aina would react to the news they were about to share.

"You know I love you very much..."

Aina was silent as Zenta spoke. She was still silent after Zenta finished. Bracing herself, Estere turned to face them. Zenta was stretched towards the girl, hands on the table, palms up in supplication. Aina had curled back into her chair, arms hugging herself, eyes cast down. Pulling away from the truth, trying to block it through sheer force of will.

Suddenly her head snapped up. Her eyes found Estere's. She froze, wide-eyed with fear. Like a stoat facing a fox in the forest.

She leaped to her feet, chair crashing to the floor behind her. Tears, sudden and immediate, gushed down her cheeks. "No!" She cried, stamping a foot into the floor before rushing from the room and out into the red dawn.

"Aina," Zenta called, moving to follow her. Her face contorted in pain.

"I'll go," Estere offered. Surprisingly, Zenta acquiesced.

She followed the depressions of the girl's flight across the front of the house, Aina's footsteps clearly visible in the sea of deep red sand. They led away from the house, under a line of apricot trees, their leaves, slick with morning dew, glinting in the rising sun. Estere ducked her head, the rich scent of ripening fruit enveloping her senses. Through the trees the footsteps continued, out into a thicket of scrubby bush. Estere followed. Twigs cracked beneath her feet, scratchy, sharp leaves poking at her stockings. The patchy scrub obscured Aina's path. Estere was no tracker. Hands on hips she paused, surveying the bushland around her, low bushes, the ghostly shape of gums, lit scarlet in the brightening morning light. Eventually her eyes spied something that did not belong. Off to her left, a glimpse of Aina's bright blue dress. Estere sighed heavily and continued on, picking her way through the bush.

The child was lying on her belly, fingers in the red dust, fidgeting. Estere walked up in silence, coming to a stop beside her. Aina looked up, pushing herself into a sitting position. Together they watched the galahs pecking at the worms in the soil. The bright pink of their plumage a shock to Estere's eyes. Aina didn't seem impressed.

At length, Estere spoke, "She'll always be your mother; one way or another."

She felt Aina shuffle, and knew she had the child's attention.

"She has raised you since you were born. It is right to love her as a parent." She looked down, eyes soft. "I think it's lucky."

"What is lucky?" Aina looked up at Estere, blue-green eyes, so unfamiliar, staring hopefully.

"You get to have two mothers."

Her lips twisted to the side, her expression unsure. Estere lowered herself into the dirt, curling her legs under herself to sit beside the child. Her child. She watched Aina's profile as she ran her fingers through the sand, drawing circles and wavy lines, and felt nothing. For years she'd dreamed of this. Pictured opening her arms to her daughter, pulling her close, breathing her in. And never again letting her go. She'd imagined her joy, the pulsing beat of her heart as the tear through its centre was finally healed. She'd planned what she'd say, how she would tell her of her father, how she'd find his love again through their child. How she'd find a way to live again. A way to leave the past behind.

None of this was right. None of this was how it was supposed to be.

"Can I read to you?"

Estere blinked, surprised by the sound of Aina's voice. She looked over at her child; a single blonde lock had curled before her nose. She reached across and tucked it behind Aina's ear.

"I'd like that," she said.

A hand, small and gritty, slipped into hers. The girl smiled.

They walked back to the house hand in hand. Zenta was waiting on the front porch, hands gripped tightly before her. Seeing them she rushed forward, taking Aina into a fierce hug, hands smoothing the little girl's cheeks, wiping away the dust that had gathered on her tear-streaked skin.

"I am going to read to Estere," Aina said. Zenta pressed a kiss to her brow.

"What a lovely idea."

The boy arrived that afternoon. He'd let himself in the back door, didn't even knock.

"Afternoon, Mrs Vanaga," he said politely, hands in his pockets.

"Afternoon, Bill," Zenta replied, walking to the pantry and collecting a cob of bread. "You are here to check on Aina?"

The boy paced to the table, noticing Estere.

"Oh," he stammered, momentarily shocked. "Afternoon, Mrs." He nodded as though doffing a cap, a warm smile hovering on his lips. Then he blinked, eyes going wide as he shot a look between Estere and Zenta. Zenta placed the bread on the table, handing the boy a knife. He cut two thick slices.

"Aina," Zenta called, "Bill's here."

She turned her attention to the boy. "She's had a big day, but I think a trip to the river might be just the thing."

Aina appeared, light on her feet, skipping across the kitchen. Hands firmly clasped together, the two children headed for the back door. "Be home for supper," Zenta called.

"I will, Ma-Zee."

Estere watched her sister standing, hands on hips, her eyes on the doorway.

"So, that's Bill," she ventured.

Zenta started, turning back to her, brows furrowed.

Estere shrugged. "Aina told me about him, in between reading. Actually, she talked more about him than the book."

A knowing smile curved her sister's lips. "They have been friends since we first arrived here. He looks out for her."

"A good boy."

"A beautiful boy."

Estere stood slowly, crossing the space between the sisters. Without a word she took Zenta into her arms, holding her close.

"I'm sorry about Aleksandrs."

Zenta stiffened. Then, a sob, low and hoarse, rattled from her chest and she melted into Estere.

Rocking her sister slowly as she'd done so often when they were young, Estere smoothed Zenta's long blonde hair. "I know, I know," she crooned.

It was a pain she understood, hard and cold and deep. Aleksandrs and her Valdis, taken by war. Nothing would ever make it right.

"I've never been able to talk about it," Zenta sobbed. "About him."

Estere closed her eyes, sighing heavily. She understood. She kept Valdis locked in her heart too.

"You can talk to me," she said.

FORTY-FOUR

ESTERE

The warm, sticky juice dribbled down her arm, mingling with the sweat that gathered in the crease of her elbow. Plucking the soft, round peach from the tree, skin fuzzy against her fingers, Estere squeezed, testing, then discarded the overripe fruit onto the ground. Left too long on the tree, or riddled with holes from feasting birds, bruised or runted, those peaches were left behind, to rot and split and join the earth along with the other imperfect fruit. Only the useful fruit made it into her gathering bucket, to be carted to the sheds at the end of the property ready for processing, packed into crates, onto trucks, then trains, destined for the canning factories in the city of Adelaide, hours away.

Pausing to cast her forearm across her brow, drying her skin as best she could, Estere stretched her aching lower back. Above her the midday sun beat down, its heat unrelenting. Summer in this country seemed to go on without end. Heaving a sigh, she reached up again, two hands, two peaches, fat and plump, perfect. Into the bucket they went.

Later, as the slanted light cast long shadows of rustling peach leaves across the dried earth, Estere hauled her bucket to her hip and made her way to the sheds along with the rows of other fruit-pickers, their day of toil over once again.

It was tough work, picking fruit. But it was a job. A way to make money, a way to get out.

These past few months living with Zenta had been the stuff of nightmare. Estere had seen the truth of Timurs immediately. She'd spent enough months in the German labour camp at Salaspils to know the type. Weak, angry, abusive. Zenta passed her days in silent tension. Aina was lively and joyful until his shadow darkened the evening doorway. It seemed escaping Latvia had not been enough to find safety for Zenta.

Estere had to get out. She had survived one prison, she would not stay in a new one, not even for her sister.

So, she'd found work doing the only thing she could find. She toiled under a burning sun sweating through her dress, day, after day, after day. Early to rise, early to rest. A rueful smile twisted her lips. The exact life she'd fought so hard to avoid in Riga. But that was a different place and a different time.

She followed the line of other workers into the shed, poured her fruit into the waiting crate, stacked her bucket and made her way out into the softening dusk. A cool breeze carried the scent of river mud and sun-sweet stone fruit to her nose. Pausing by the wash trough, she pulled her handkerchief from about her brow and plunged the yellow cotton into the water. It was luke-warm from the heat of the day, but better than nothing. Sponging the tacky sugar of fruit pulp from her neck and chest, she leaned against the rough wood of the shed, eyes turned to the vast blue sky above. A star was already showing through the fading light of the sun.

"Gonna be a pretty one." A rough, familiar voice drew her from her musing. Its owner lumbered over to rest an elbow against the shed behind her. Bright, smiling eyes, skin browned by the sun, the scent of sweat and fruit emanating from his faded shirt, Dale ran a hand over his chin, scratching at the stubble that lined his jaw. He was one of her fellow fruit-pickers, more friendly than most of the men, who all seemed to think she'd cheated their brother, son or uncle out of a job.

She'd come to understand how lucky she'd been when Mr Jones hired her for this work.

Estere cocked her head at Dale. "I don't understand?"

Her English had improved immeasurably since her arrival in Australia, but so often she was sure these locals were speaking a different English to that she'd been taught in the arrival centre.

Dale pointed a soil-crusted finger out across the farm. "The sunset. The season's changing, nights are cooling. Brings more pinks and purples as the land cools."

"You think this is cooler?"

Dale huffed a laugh. "Might not seem it yet, but trust me," he tapped a finger to the side of his nose, "she's turned. Autumn winds are on their way, then all this," he gestured to the farm beyond, "dried leaves and twigs and once the frost sets in, months with nothing to do."

Estere blinked. She hadn't considered that. Of course the fruit wouldn't grow all year. But under this burning sun, it was hard to imagine this country ever getting icy.

"What will you do then?" she asked Dale.

He shrugged, tucking his hands under his pits, turning his face to the sky. "Move on, follow the work."

"Where?"

"East, probably."

"East," she repeated, mind whirling. She'd arrived on the East Coast when she travelled from Latvia, hadn't she? But this country went on forever. How far did "East" go exactly?

"What about here?" she asked. "Is there other work?"

"There is, but not much. The Riverland is a summer place, unless you work in town, or on the railways." He paused. "You were lucky to get this work, in truth."

Estere thought of Timurs and his sweat-stained shirts, and oily hands. She sniffed in disapproval.

"You heading home?" Dale asked.

Estere nodded.

"I'll walk you."

They kept an easy pace, puffs of dirt swirling at their feet, coating their shoes, sticking to the dregs of fruit juice that remained on the soles.

"Your English is getting better," Dale said, and Estere regarded him from the corner of her eye. "Must be hard, living somewhere so different."

"Why do you care?" Estere demanded, turning her head to face him directly. No one else seemed to think about it, why should he?

A blush, red and deep, flushed up Dale's neck, mottling his cheeks. "I didn't mean no harm," he said, hands out before him. "I just know it's hard to start again, that's all."

Estere considered him a moment. "You aren't from here?"

A quick grin flashed across his face. "I ain't from nowhere," he said. "I make my home where I lay my head."

"And where is that?"

"Where there's paying work."

They walked on in silence until the rusting old letter box that marked her sister's driveway came into view.

"This is my home," Estere said, coming to a stop.

Dale looked down the drive, expression hopeful.

Estere stepped back. "I will see you tomorrow," she said, her voice firm. There was no way she would be inviting him in, not this close to Timurs' return from his day on the railway.

Dale nodded, rueful smile on his lips. "That you will. Good evening to you, Miss Estere." He turned and sauntered off down the dirt track.

That evening as she and Zenta stood at the kitchen sink, clearing away the day's dishes, the uneven, heavy thump of

Timurs' drunken gait banged through the house behind them. And Estere decided.

She did not know how, but she was certain. When winter cast its first kiss of frost across the fruit fields of the Riverland, she would be gone.

FORTY-FIVE

ESTERE

"I am leaving now. This is your last chance to change your mind."

Estere stood by the little car. Dale waited impatiently behind the wheel. A tearful Aina, snug in a freshly knitted cardigan, sat in the back seat.

Dale honked the horn. He'd waited long enough.

"She is your daughter. She must stay with you," Zenta called, her face crumpling into a ruin of pain.

Estere eyed her sister knowingly, arms crossing over her chest. It had been hell living here these past months, what with Timurs and his moods, Zenta walking on eggshells, and little Aina, so afraid. The war had never left them.

Dale had been her only solace. His ready laugh and happy eyes had eased a burden she was unwilling to face. He was a good man. She liked him. But he was leaving, following the work across the country to Victoria. And Estere was going with him.

A sharp wind whipped across the dirt of the drive, its chill biting through her thin stockings. Time to go.

Estere opened the car door, turning back to Zenta one last

time. She could see the division on her sister's face, torn between choices. But she was out of time. Zenta had to decide, once and for all, who Aina belonged to.

"Last chance, Zee," she called, voice firm. "Am I taking *my* daughter?"

She emphasised the "my", subtly, but clearly, shifting the meaning of the question.

For a moment Estere thought Zenta had changed her mind, that she would step forward and claim back the child. Her feet shuffled, her arms tightened, hands fluttering towards them.

Then Timurs appeared behind her, his bulk a frame of menace at Zenta's back. "Of course you're taking her. I've done your job long enough."

Zenta froze, hands still at her sides.

The sisters' eyes locked across the sandy soil. Understanding passed between them, a truth and a promise. Estere nodded, climbing into the car. Dale fired the engine and pressed down the pedal, the wheels spinning momentarily in the sand before the car jerked for the drive.

"No!" Aina sobbed, pressing her little forehead to the window, face a mess of snot and tears.

"It will be all right, child," Estere said. "You are safer with me."

Aina didn't respond, her eyes locked to the window staring back at Zenta long after her sister had disappeared from view.

They took two days to drive to Melbourne across vast plains of cleared land, crops of yellow and purple and green, impossibly large, stretching to the very edge of the horizon and beyond. The city was large and sprawling and grey. The blue stone of the buildings blended with heavy clouds overhead. Rain drizzled on and off throughout the day, darkening the skies and making the streets perilously slick to tread. Estere gave Aina one of her scarves to tie about her head against the chill. The child knew nothing of real cold, but there was no need to suffer on sentiment.

Dale found work at the docks, the port of Melbourne had no shortage of jobs, and Estere settled Aina at a local school. She filled her days with the tasks of a mother, mending stockings, knitting cardigans, shopping for and preparing food. At night Dale would return, smile wide on his open face, and they would share stories of their days as he stoked the open fire.

For a time Estere was happy.

It didn't last for long.

The splash of the water, the smell of boat oil on Dale's skin, the chill off the currents. It was like she was back in Riga, but wrong. The dock was too large and wide, the water a muddy slice through the city, not crisp like the Daugava in her Riga. And Dale was not Valdis, no matter how much she wished he could be. It was a truth she'd known deep in her gut since the first time he cupped her chin and pressed his whiskered lips to hers. Living with him made that truth impossible to ignore. He laughed too often, ate too fast, made love too little. Everything he did reminded her of what he wasn't, all that she had left behind.

The final straw came one Sunday as they made their way home from church. Dale, loping casually at her side, had suddenly gone stiff. "Wait here," he said, striding away from Estere and Aina.

Estere watched as he approached two men, one walking heavily with a cane. She couldn't hear their words, but their body language, tight, tense, told her something was wrong. Suddenly, the man with the cane reared back and spat down onto Dale's shoe. The two men left, the taller one shoving Dale as he passed.

"What was that about?" Estere asked as Dale returned to them.

"They lost their brother in the war," Dale said. In the moment Estere let it slide, not wanting to upset Aina walking at her side.

That night Estere confronted him. "Who were those men, why did he spit on you?"

Dale sighed, his large fingers raked through his hair. "We were mates at school," he said. "We did compulsory military training together when the war started. I did what I had to, nothing more. They stayed on."

Estere blinked. "I don't understand."

"They felt it was their duty, to go to war, fight for England. They volunteered for battle in Europe. I didn't."

Fury, hot and burning, shot through Estere. She realised she was shaking. "You could have fought? You could have helped?"

Dale looked up at her in surprise. "I thought you, of all people, would understand. War is death. Why would I go and risk my life for people I don't even know?"

"So, you'd fight for Australia then? Just not other people."

"Yes," Dale said. "I'd fight for my home. Estere, what is wrong?"

He stood from the table, crossing the room to take her in his arms.

"Don't touch me!" she screamed, slapping his hands away. "Coward!"

"Estere! Stop this. Be reasonable..."

Estere spun on her heel and stormed from the room and out into the cool Melbourne night. Roaming the rain-slicked streets, her mind whirled, her heart hammered in her chest as she thought of home, of Latvia, of the faces of the men she and Valdis tried to save, of the bang of the gun that took her father, of the hunger and despair, the ever-present stench of death in the camp at Salaspils.

The truth was, she did understand. Having lived through the hell of occupation and war, how could she wish that on anyone? And yet she'd faced it. Stood beside Valdis and risked it all to fight for her people, for what was right.

She'd lost everything. Dale had lost nothing.

It was just another reminder of the differences between them, that Dale was not the man she was trying to replace. She didn't love him.

So as the first buds of spring brought colour to the bare trees of the city parks, she left, packing Aina onto a train and making for another town. Another start. It would become the first of many. New man, new town.

As the train rocked away from Flinders Street Station, Aina twisted her hands in her lap, and asked, "Are we going to visit Ma-Zee?"

"No," Estere barked, feeling tired and harassed and irritable. "We are going on an adventure, just you and me."

"When can we visit Ma-Zee?"

"Another time." Estere sighed, turning from the child to focus on the countryside that whizzed past the carriage window, brown and muddy and damp.

Aina fell silent, her little shoulders slumped.

They landed just north of Mudgee in New South Wales. There was a job going, running the district switchboard. A new set of copper wires were being rolled out across the more remote areas of the country, allowing people to talk through a network that traced between towns. The switchboard was in a small house in the centre of a farming district, so accommodation was included.

Estere loved that job. A large panel of sockets lined the wall, plugs and wires running between them. When a local wanted to make a telephone call a white bulb would light up. Estere, pressing a receiver to her ear, would listen to who they wanted to call, and move the right plug to the right socket, or dial a number, then disconnect her receiver, leaving them to their conversation. Sometimes, she stayed on the line, listening as ladies planned church lunches and farmers ordered crops and machinery. She met her next man, Norman, on the line. The lonely farmer often rang just to flirt with Estere.

The first she knew of the problem was a knock on the door and a frowning policeman.

Aina.

In the quiet of night, as Estere slept in the cot right beside her, the child had crept to the switchboard in the adjacent room, pushing plugs into sockets at random.

"Do you know Ma-Zee? Zenta? What about Bill? He lives in South Australia, by the river."

People across the region had been woken at all hours of the night by the small, desperate voice of a child on the other end of the line.

Estere made tea for the officer and tried to explain. It ended with another suitcase, another town. A sadder Aina.

They moved to Sydney, a shining beacon of a city, its harbour backlit by the brilliant orange of a setting sun, like something from a dream. Estere took a position at a small grocery store, and found a flat in a nearby apartment block. The rooms were small and cramped, the electricity unreliable, the hot water non-existent. A fat black rat scurried across the kitchen floor.

"I don't like it here. It smells funny," Aina announced on the first night.

"And I don't like you, so there," Estere snapped, grabbing up a broom to poke at the fleeing rat. She was lost, adrift. It had been years since Estere had known the feel of home. As her body recovered in the survivors' hospital, her mind stayed trapped in torment. Horrors assailed her; the silence where Tomass' laugh should ring, her father sprawled across the bakery floor, the rattle of her mother's final breath, the bright red burst from Valdis' skull. She was engulfed, suffocating, alone. The thought of Aina was all that had kept her going.

She'd clung to the hope of reunion as she dug her way out of the dark. But she'd found no peace, only the creeping doubt over whether this child before her was indeed her own.

Estere was a shell, the war had taken all she was, all she ever could be. She had nothing left to give.

And nothing could quiet those memories.

At least they had a roof over their heads, the child should be grateful, should understand she was lucky.

Aina shrank back, her face contorted in hurt. Estere sighed but didn't apologise. She'd meant it, after all.

That night as she lay in bed, sweat pooling in the creases of her body, the soft sound of Aina's sobbing drifted to her ears. Irritated, she banged on the wall between their rooms.

"Go to sleep! You've an early start tomorrow."

The sobbing continued.

Estere banged again. "She let me take you, you know. Remember that. Stop crying for someone who let you go. She's gone. I am here."

Aina went silent.

Estere lay still in the deepening silence. The air drifting in from her open window was thick with moisture, holding the heat of the day in a clinging veil across the apartment, offering no relief from the building summer heat. She should feel guilty, she knew. Three new towns in less than six months, a new mother, changing men. Aina's life had been flipped upside down. Estere should feel compassion, should ache to cradle the girl in her arms, to comfort her fears and sorrows.

Yet her heart remained closed. Numb.

The war had never left her either, she supposed.

FORTY-SIX

ZENTA

2018

My family stand before me, faces dropped in open shock.

"Wait," Heather says, brows furrowed in confusion. "Are you saying that my mother was your niece? Estere's child?" She gestures to my sister's plaque.

I nod.

"No," Aina says, head shaking, hands clenching into fists at her side. "Estere was my mother. You brought me here, to safety, because she asked you to." Her eyes are glazed. Estere always said she had her father's eyes.

I lean forward, hands going out to her. "Aina, please listen."

Suddenly her focus sharpens, centring on me. Realisation. Understanding. The lines of her face seem to deepen before me.

"No," she whispers. Turning on her heel, she strides away across the cemetery.

"Mother, wait!" Crissy steps forward.

Aina does not turn back. She reaches the low wire fence

that forms the cemetery boundary and steps over it, heading into the bush.

"Mum! Stop!"

Crissy turns to me. "This is a black lie, Mamina," she hisses. "A terrible, big, black lie." She strides between the headstones, following Aina, a bewildered Peter and Lily on her heels.

I watch them go. I make no move to stop them.

Heather stays with me. Silent as she takes it all in. After a minute, she comes to sit beside me, folding her hands in her lap.

"Are you all right?" It is a ridiculous question, but I nod anyway.

"That was an impossible choice you had to make. To give your niece up..."

I don't reply, I am spent, I have nothing left.

"And then you gave Estere your child. Why?"

I breathe in deeply through my nose, straighten, gathering myself. "I made a promise to protect my daughter. That I would do anything, give up anything. It was my way to honour it."

"Protect her from Timurs?"

"Yes."

A breeze rustles the dry gum leaves overhead and I breathe the scent of eucalyptus deeply into my lungs. "I heard nothing for five years. No phone calls, no letters. Nothing. It was the worst time of my life. Not knowing where they were, if my daughter was safe, happy..."

Estere's silence. I'd never forgiven her that. I pause, watch a finch, small and quick as it dances over a headstone, centring myself.

"Without warning they both appeared on my doorstep. Aina looked just like her father, my Aleks." His name, unspoken for so many decades, rings off my tongue, strong, beautiful.

The memory pierces my heart. The yeasty scent of rising dough in my nose, hands sticky with my work, as I prepared the morning bread. And the girl of eleven, the same age I was when my world turned upside down, standing at my door, the last softness of childhood soon to sharpen from her features. My Aina, returning home to me.

At that moment I knew; in the babe we created in the darkness of war, in the child I'd birthed and given away, now standing before me, somehow, Aleks had come home.

His promise to find me had been made flesh.

And I vowed I would never be parted from my daughter again. Never.

"This time when Estere left, my daughter stayed," I continue to Heather. "Aina struggled. She missed the woman she thought was her mother. They had spent five years together, after all. I thought I could overcome it. But she was tortured by Estere's absence, by the belief that her mother didn't love her..."

"You loved her?"

My heart squeezes at the question. "I've never stopped. My heart struggled to find its way to my daughter. But it did. And then I realised, the love had always been there."

My hand hovers over my heart, the aching emptiness a tunnel to my past.

"Aina never understood my love. Not after I sent her away. And when she came of age, she left too. Her choice this time."

I picture Aina, back rigid, eyes fixed forward as she strode down my drive. I could have stopped her. But I didn't.

"She turned up again later, her own child, Crissy, holding her hand. She came and went over the years. Crissy stayed with me." Warmth has come into my voice, I can hear it. It reflects my heart.

Heather smiles. "Crissy was your second chance."

I'm glad she's understood. "I think so, yes."

"What happened to Timurs?"

"He died in 1954, just three years after my sister left. Crushed while unloading a railway sleeper from a cart. It broke his back. He lived a week in hospital, lots of pain medication, crying for his mother, and someone named Irina. I don't know who she was. I don't think I ever really knew my husband."

"That's a terrible way to go."

"It is."

"You were compensated?"

I look up at her incredulously, "It was the fifties! I don't know about in America, but here that certainly wasn't a thing back then. Well, not like now. I received two months of his pay in a lump sum and was sent on my way. It was all right. I got work in town." I grin sheepishly. "At the local bakery."

Heather's face lightens. "That is nice."

Light dapples through the gums, warming spots on my skin. I turn my face into it, savouring the radiant heat of the sun.

"I didn't hate him. My husband," I say. "He was kind, sometimes. I think he wanted to care for me, but he was just too broken inside, in here." I tap my chest, over my heart. "I was too."

"I am not sure anything excuses him beating you."

"No. But I have forgiven it. It was a long time ago."

"And Estere?" Heather looks over at the small plaque. "My grandmother?"

I blink slowly. "She never came back after dropping Aina off when she was eleven. The police pronounced her officially dead in the eighties. I'd given up long before that. When she left that last time, it was final."

Smiling at Heather I offer what I can. "I can see her in you, your grandmother. You have her smile, you walk with her confidence. I think you have her bravery, coming all the way out here..."

"Thank you."

I look down at the ground beneath my feet, fuss with my skirts before settling my hands on my thighs. The time has arrived for my questions.

"Your mother, the niece I gave away... did she, live well?"

I feel Heather shuffle beside me. I wait, hoping she will speak, afraid of what she'll say. In a lifetime of difficult choices, parting from my niece is one I can never forgive myself for.

"Mum was happy," Heather says.

My heart speeds up, beating firm in my chest.

"Alma and Stefans called her Anne, more American. And she lived well, right to the end. My father, Phil, he loved her truly."

"How did she die?"

"Cancer, last year."

I can hear the sorrow, the rawness. Heather is still grieving the loss of her mother. Perhaps we never stop. "I think that's why I'm here," she continues. "I wanted to know more about her past, about my family. I think it's a way to feel connected to her.

"Grandma and Grandpa often spoke of her aunt left behind in the cold of northern Germany, who gave her up to save her life. Until today, I didn't understand just how true that was."

"She had a good life?"

A small, sad smile curves Heather's lips. "Yes."

My throat seizes tight. How many nights had I wondered? How many prayers had I sent to God? Did my niece live? Or did the cough carry her away? Were Alma and Stefans true friends? Or did they abandon her? I wouldn't have judged them either way, how could I? I abandoned her first, after all...

But I hoped, against reason, against experience. I hoped.

"Thank you," I whisper.

The sound of crunching grass draws our attention and we look up to see Crissy approaching through the trees, Lily and Peter at her side.

She comes to stand before me. Her face blotched red and puffy with tears. "Mother won't come back. You've really upset her, Mamina-Zee."

I have hurt her too, I can see it. Her face is full of pain. The hurt is deep. I weather her hurt. I understand it. I deserve to feel it, at least for a little while.

"Well, come on then, Mamina-Zee," she says, "let's get you home before the evening chill."

Lily offers her hand to help me up. I gratefully accept.

"Will you be all right from here?" Crissy addresses the question to Heather.

"Yes, thank you. I will be on my way."

Crissy nods, places a hand on my elbow and draws me away.

We are nearly to the car before Heather calls, "Wait!"

She is on her feet, bustling over to us.

Stepping before me, her face scrunched and earnest, she says, "Your niece was happy. She died surrounded by family. Me, my brothers. She lived a good life. Because of you."

She turns to Crissy. "Whatever choices were made, that has to be worth it, doesn't it?"

Crissy sniffs, her expression closed. She isn't ready for this, it's too soon.

Heather smiles at me, then, voice firm and powerful, "Your choice saved my mother's life. If you hadn't given her to my grandparents, she would have died in that barn. Your sacrifice meant she lived and my family lived."

I don't know when the tears started or how long they have been coursing down my cheeks, but they are dripping off my chin, soaking the collar of my dress.

"Mamina, come, let's get you home."

I allow Crissy to draw me away, I've no strength left for this day, nothing inside me at all. I am insubstantial, fleeting, blurry. I am nothing but the past.

And I've just set it free.

FORTY-SEVEN

AINA

2018

A gentle breeze carries the scent of tannin and mud to Aina's nose. Sneakers beside her, socks tucked into the centre, neatly rolled, toes buried in the dry earth, she sits. Soft currents shift on the river's surface, catching the fading yellows and oranges of sunset. Above her head, the long fingers of eucalyptus leaves rustle, dark in the back light of gathering dusk.

Running her palms down her faded trousers, Aina cups her knees, chin resting on their pointy tops. Her tears have finished, leaving the sticky tightness of salt on her cheeks.

It is too much, this truth that Zenta confessed. A secret, the size of Aina's whole life. What is she to make of it? What should she think? Pulling her knees in tighter to her chest she hugs herself against the rising chill.

She remembers nothing of her life before Australia. Latvia is a distant country known only through Zenta and Estere's stories, language and food customs. How often had Estere asked her if she remembered her father? The disappointment had burned in her irises as Aina shook her head. Valdis. The mythical perfect man. The memory Estere could never forget. But Aina had never had a chance of remembering him. He wasn't even her father!

A single dragonfly appears, buzzing over the rippling river, the vibration of its wings loud on the silent air of coming night. Zipping and zapping it surveys the waters below then, quick as a flash, shoots up and out of view, its translucent wings and fat insect body lost against the darkening skies.

A small smile surprises her lips. A memory of a happy time, here by the waters. A time when she had a mother, and a father, and a best friend. A time when she knew who she was. A time when things felt stable. Playing in the water of the Munda-gunda Creek, her stockings discarded, her skirts hitched up to free her limbs for the waters, Bill's high-pitched laughter ringing through the skies.

Realisation plunges through her, dropping her stomach down towards the earth. That time was a lie, too. And Zenta. Behind every loving embrace, her gentle presence, a dark truth churned and bubbled.

Some part of her had always known it was a lie, those days spent splashing in the river with her friend, the evenings reading by Zenta's oven fire. Perhaps that's why she chose to leave as soon as she was old enough. After Estere carted her away to cross this vast, red land, movement just made sense. It was a way to escape the truth her heart knew but her mind refused to acknowledge, imagining it would be better some-where else, that if she kept searching, she would find where she belonged.

But no matter where you run, you can't escape yourself.

It was too much.

The vibration of her mobile breaks into her consciousness, drawing her from her memories and pain. Slipping her hand into her slacks she pulls out the offending device. How she hates it, this small rectangle that tethers her to others, no matter where she is or what she is doing.

Crissy's name blinks to life on the screen, then the buzzing stops, the screen going dark.

Nine missed calls.

Guilt twists through her core. Crissy. Her daughter.

Pregnant too young, too messed up to do better. Aina had run from her daughter too. How much of this pain could have been avoided if Zenta had just told the truth?

Huffing out a heavy breath, Aina sets the phone down by her shoes. Coming to her feet she steps to the river's edge. Tea-stained water caresses her flesh, pimpling her skin as she descends into its cool embrace. Mud squelches between her toes. Arms wide, she lies back, floating for a moment on the river's surface, eyes watching as the first stars glint in the deep blue hue that promises night is close.

With a final long release of breath, she slips beneath the surface.

It is time to let go.

Surrender.

FORTY-EIGHT

ZENTA

2018

My eyes open to a new dawn. Pale with the promise of warmth, my limbs feel heavy with fatigue. I slept fitfully, my mind invaded by visions, memory holding me in its grip like a vice. The souls of the lost tormenting my dreams. I need to get the loaves ready, light the oven, but my fingers throb, and my mind skitters away. I can think only of Aina.

I shuffle into the kitchen, my ankles aching, and eye the pantry. But I can't bring myself to bake.

Instead, I head outside. I walk between the canary cages, throwing off their blanket covers, so the birds can watch the sunrise with me. They flit about the cages, light and easy. Their plumage fluffed from sleep, soon sleek against their little bodies. They spread out through the cages, their eyes turned to the light of the horizon, and begin to sing.

In the gum tree beside the house, a noisy miner caws.

"Shoo!" I hiss. It watches me with a beady eye. "Go on, get!" I wave my hands at it until, annoyed, it flaps away through the morning air. Greedy birds, I've caught them trying to steal canary seed from the cages on more than one occasion.

Back in the house Crissy is up. Her hair is unbrushed, her eyes puffy from lack of sleep. She's wrapped in a fluffy pink night robe. I watch as she lights a match for the stove and wonder if that robe is inflammable. I will never stop being a mother, the habit runs too deep. I suspect it is how all mothers feel.

She hears me, turns. "Mum isn't home yet. She's been out all night."

There is concern in her voice, but also despair.

I should reassure her, I know. Remind her that this is something Aina does, that she always comes back. But today, I can't. I am not sure I believe it. Silently I ease myself onto a chair at the table.

Crissy paces before me. "Where would she go? I tried her housemate Sue last night. But she hasn't gone home."

"Of course not, her car is here," I say, rubbing my fingers along my forehead. It's starting to ache.

"I should try the church. Pastor Taylor has always been good to Mum. Maybe she went there."

"Crissy..."

"No, I should call the police. She's a missing person. How long do you have to wait until you report a missing person? Is it twenty-four hours..."

"Crissy, stop!"

Her pacing halts. She's finally heard me.

I stare at her drawn, panicked face. My heart squeezes. I understand. I've been in her shoes. The first time Aina left me, and the second... I find the words I should say, "She always comes back, Crissy. When she's ready."

But this time is different. We both feel it, the dread uncoiling along our limbs. We are both afraid. We are thinking of Estere. She left and never came back. Perhaps this time Aina will do the same.

Crissy collapses into a kitchen chair, elbows on the table, head in her hands. "How?" Her voice is barely a whisper. Shaking her head, she looks up at me. "How, Mamina? How could you lie to Mum?" A pause, tears welling in her bright blue eyes. "How could you lie to me?"

I sigh, heavy, the weight of my life pressing down on my chest. "Letting her go was the only way I could save her from my husband," I say. "When Estere brought Aina back, it was too late. The lie was too big. The truth didn't matter anymore. Stability did. Just as it did when you came to my door."

Crissy regards me through a rictus of hurt, lips trembling, she says, "Then why tell us now?"

My throat constricts, I swallow, opening my mouth, but before I can speak a hideous squawking erupts from the back-yard, high and trill and frenzied. I'm on my feet as quickly as I can be, heading for the door. Crissy beats me outside, of course.

As I step onto the back porch, I hear her gasp of shock. She's standing in front of my birdcages, hand clasped over her mouth, eyes wide with horror.

I make my way to her side, look into the cage.

There on its back, its little legs straight up in the air, lies one of my canaries. It is still, lifeless, its belly pierced through, a mess of blood and feathers strewn about its tiny body.

Dead.

I look up at the branches of the gum and meet the murder-er's beady eye. Black and glassy, the noisy miner stares down at me, a bloody yellow feather stuck to its beak.

"Oh, that poor little bird." Crissy's eyes swim with tears, she's on the verge of breaking down.

"Go inside." I take Crissy's arm and lead her towards the door. "Put the kettle on."

"It's a sign, isn't it? A sign that Mum's not coming home, not this time. This is all your fault! You never should have told us!"

Her words tear my heart in two. I drop her arm, turning away.

"Mamina-Zee? Where are you going? I'm sorry, I didn't mean that... Mamina, stop."

"No," I say, voice firm.

Crissy recoils, her expression hurt. She's desperate, struggling. I should be gentler. But I am hurting too. Overtaken by fear and memory. My baby girl is out there, somewhere, alone, wounded to her very soul.

And it's my fault.

I am barely holding myself together. I have nothing left to offer Crissy, no comfort to spare. Guilt a stone in my belly I shuffle away from her to my chicken coop, my mind a whirl of torment. I pause at the hutch, lean against the cage. Inside, my hens coo and shuffle, oblivious and content.

Crissy's question settles over me: why did I tell them the truth? After so long, so many years? Was it selfish pride? A desire to claim what was mine before death rose up to take me? Or a need to free the guilt, so long held in my heart? The answer doesn't matter. I made a choice. And now I must accept the consequences. I shake my head. The weight of the years of my life pressing down, heavy, long, ending.

The screen door bangs behind me. "Grand-mina, come quick," Peter cries before disappearing back inside.

My heart lurches, but I dare not hope, not this time.

Bracing myself, I return to the kitchen.

FORTY-NINE

ZENTA

2018

Rumpled, shivering, Aina stands in the centre of my tiny kitchen.

My family are gathered in a circle around her, shoulders quaking, tears wetting their cheeks. The sob surprises me, bursting out of my mouth before I can stop it. My family turn, hands wiping wet cheeks, lips cast in trembling smiles.

I meet Aina's eyes, she turns away. I am dismissed, but I don't care. She has come back. Love has called Aina home.

Together they move to the kitchen table and take a seat. Crissy is holding Aina's hand in a white-knuckle grip. Peter and Lily hover close. They are a unit. I stand apart.

Silently I shuffle to the laundry and collect a blanket. Aina accepts it grudgingly and wraps it around her quaking shoulders.

"Where have you been?" Crissy asks, eyes misty with tears.

"By the creek," Aina replies, stiffly.

Crissy sniffs loudly.

"I'll make tea," I say.

My hands are shaking, moving in jerky uneven motions, like they aren't mine at all. I drop the first match, and the second, before I succeed in lighting the stove.

Behind me Aina is talking. "I am sorry I worried you. I just needed some time." Her voice is sincere, repentant.

"You smell like a wet rat," Peter says, voice higher-pitched than normal, anxious.

A huffed laugh. "Yes, I went for a swim with the sunset. It's the best time of the day for a swim."

"Always best to swim with an adult though, Peter," Crissy cautions.

"Weren't you cold?" he asks.

I hear the chatter of her teeth, imagine her curled in a ball, soaking wet and shivering beneath a cloudless night sky.

"A little, but it was a beautiful night."

I squeeze my eyes shut, my heart lurches. She must have been freezing, but she stayed by the river; away from me.

"Well, you are home now," Crissy says. "That's all that matters."

The kettle boils. I set out the mugs, tea leaves, sugar and make a pot. And I realise Crissy is right. Aina is home, that is all that matters.

As I lie in bed, eyes staring at the moonlit gums beyond my window, one fat mosquito worrying near my ear, she comes.

The hinge of my door creaks, the sticky static of bare feet on cheap lino flooring marking her advance. She slips beneath the covers as she always has, one hand taking mine beneath the sheets. Swollen now with age, like mine, but undeniably hers.

My heart calms its stutter. Aina is home.

We lie that way for minutes, hours, I don't know. I don't care. I simply savour the warmth of her, the sound of her breath, the familiar smell, my smell.

At length she sucks in a deeper breath. I wait.

"Mother... I mean, Estere," she pauses, trying out the truth, feeling it on her tongue, "she knew?"

The memory floods back, Estere's face the last time I saw her filling my mind. The accusation on her lips, the hatred in her eyes.

"How could you?"

"I had no choice."

"There is always a choice."

"Perhaps..." I hedge, unsure of where Aina's thoughts are heading.

"I think she knew, on some level at least," Aina says, voice soft.

"I think so, yes." I feel her relax a little, I sense there is comfort for Aina in this possibility. It is enough.

"And she took me anyway, despite her doubt."

"She did."

Aina falls silent, lost in her own thoughts and memories, the shifting sands of herself.

"Why?"

"Estere had lost so much..." I begin.

"No, not that. It wasn't that."

I close my eyes to the darkened room, choosing my words.

"He wasn't a good man. My husband. The war... it broke something in him."

"Yes. I think I remember."

"It was not that I didn't love you. I did. But I had so little left."

"I understand."

She is being honest, I know. I have seen the same emptiness in her eyes. She squeezes my hand. The past rears up before me. Small fingers in my palm, her body, hot with fear, pressed to my side, the smash of glass from the kitchen, the shouts of rage.

I release a shaking breath and open my eyes. That is past. That is done.

Now. I choose now.

Beside me Aina shifts onto her side, facing me in the dark.

"What did you name me? Before you arrived at the camp? What did you call your baby?"

"Aleksa."

"For him?"

"Yes."

"He was a good man."

"Yes."

"I thought she left because of me," Aina says, voice soft. "After she was gone, it just hurt too much. Abandoned by two mothers. I didn't know how to stay. I thought I wasn't enough."

I press my lips together, swallow hard. It hurts to hear this, but I have to listen.

Aina continues. "She had nothing left. She lost her parents, her lover, her child. You still had me..." Her voice drifts to silence.

They cut deep, those words. Aina has forgotten, Estere still had me. It wasn't Aina who wasn't enough. We were sisters. We were all that was left of our family, our home, of Latvia. Her familiarity was a living connection to the bakery, to Riga, my brother, mother, father. To Ava, and Aleks. Someone else to hold the memories, so precious and fragile, someone who could truly understand our past, and share that terrible burden. But Estere couldn't forgive me. She abandoned me to my guilt. After all we had lost, she still chose to leave me. That had been a hurt too much.

She places her free hand on my stomach, its weight both foreign and familiar. We stay like this in silence, the only sound the gentle rustle of gums in the warm breeze that rises up from the heat of the red earth. And I drift into a dreamless sleep.

FIFTY

ZENTA

2018

It is November the 18th, Independence Day. One hundred years of Latvia, broken by occupation and war, but one hundred years nonetheless. The anniversary of our freedom, the freedom my father fought for and later, died for.

The dawn sun shines brightly through my worn curtains. Outside my canaries chirp and flap, greeting the day. The chickens will be hungry, I think as I ease myself up from bed. It has been a heavy few days. Yet, somehow I feel lighter, a weight sluiced from my back I'd not realised I bore. Shaking my head I draw on my nightgown. Enough indulgence. My great-grandchildren are here, I need to bake.

I make my way from the room on aching feet, my legs unstable, my shuffle slow, halting.

Voices drift on the morning-cool air. Bright light illuminates the kitchen.

Around the table they stand: Aina, Crissy, Lily and Peter. Aina is talking, pouring flour into a small mound on the surface before her, fingers working the dough.

"Push hard, put your body into it."

"When do I add these?" Peter says, holding up a small glass jar of dried caraway seeds.

"Later, for now, knead."

I stop just before the fall of the light, obscured in the shadows, and watch. My daughter, her child and her grandchildren. My family. They are making bread. Baking. Mother passing on to daughter the way of our family, just as my mother did with me, my father watching on, pride shining in his eyes. Our tradition in the rye flour.

Peace settles into my bones as my great-grandchildren hold sticky dough-caked fingers before them. Lily pretends to wipe her fingers on her brother's cheek. Their laughter rings out, joyous and high as they continue their task, readying the loaves.

And I know. It will be okay. Despite it all, the fear, the loss, the sorrow and grief; despite my choice. My family is here, in my kitchen, together. It will be okay.

Wiping a tear from my eye I walk into the kitchen. Peter sees me first. "Grand-mina, look!" he says proudly, gesturing to his dough. It is wonky, poorly mixed and lumpy.

It is perfect. Just like him.

"Well done," I say, smiling as I plant a kiss on his crown. His soft blond hair silken against my lips.

He beams and continues to knead.

Aina and Crissy regard me over his head. Aina turns away. She has not forgiven me, not yet. But Crissy smiles, the lines of tension around her eyes have softened.

It is a start.

Careful not to disturb them I shuffle out into the waking day. Slowly I make my way to the scrub that borders the back of my yard, the dusty trees, the spindly brush. Sharp leaves poke my ankles, drawing blood from beneath my stockings. Breathing deeply, I fill my senses with this land, the floral eucalyptus, the acrid soil, the dry breeze. In the distance the tang of muddy river. It mixes with the scent of baking dough and caraway that drifts from the kitchen, overlapping my worlds, integrating.

I close my eyes, picturing a different view. Cobbled streets, pastel-painted buildings rising into a grey sky. The crunch of boots in the snow, the crack of ice melting on roofs. The cry of gulls on a salt-laden wind. The warmth of the bakery ovens, the scent of fresh bread cooling. In my heart the two visions merge and blend, two lands, two peoples. One home.

My home.

That is what I built here, a place for me, for my family.

Where Estere was always a fighter, I had to find my strength, learn it, cultivate it, and I did. I built this place of safety for my family, a sanctuary against the world. I won't let anything happen to it.

I cannot chance it again.

There is one thing left to do.

I wait in the dark of night until the sounds of my family preparing for bed go silent. Peter's cough, Aina's pacing walk. The last bedroom light flicks off, my home now lit only by a sliver of silver moonlight that peeks in through the curtains.

I ease myself up and out of bed, padding slowly to my dresser. I open the middle drawer, hands delving in deep, searching. Pressed against the drawer back, encased in old woollen jumpers, nestles a small biscuit tin. My fingers brush the cool metal of the tin and I pull it from its hiding space.

Back at my bed I sit, the tin in my lap, a bright red picture of a rosella on its front. Slowly I run my hand over the box. I crack the lid.

There in the tin sits an envelope. Old, yellowing at the edges, creased from handling. On its front my name and address in the looping scrawl of Estere's handwriting.

I gather up the envelope gently, lovingly, and press it to my heart. A single tear tracks down my cheek.

It floods back, immediate, real, as though I am living it for the first time. The day the first letter came. The shock, the fear when I saw it sitting in the letter box.

Estere, offering understanding, begging forgiveness and asking to come back to us. But I had found my way to my daughter by then. My beautiful, grieving Aina, so lost, struggling to heal after Estere's abandonment.

What new turmoil would she bring, what new pain? No, Estere couldn't come back. Not again. It was a risk I couldn't survive.

I had to protect my daughter. And myself.

I burned the letter. I burned them all, each new one as it arrived. I stopped opening them, consigning them to the flames of my oven the moment I'd plucked them from my letter box. Never telling Aina of their existence, despite how she missed Estere and longed for her return. I'd let my sister take my daughter from me once before. It had been the ruin of me. I would not make the same mistake twice.

So, I reduced each letter to ash. All except this final one, a stamp in the corner proclaiming Air Mail. It was the last, I knew it would be. On this one there is no return address, only the words: Riga, Latvia.

Estere's choice.

My choice too.

She was always bound to Latvia, to our people and our freedom. I thought I was too. The warmth of the bakery, the memory of fishing at the river's edge. But in the end it was not the place that held me, it was the people. My father, my mother, my brother. Ava. Aleks.

Riga, the bakery, they are meaningless without the people who filled the narrow paths and walls. I belong here with the living: my Aina, Crissy, Lily, Peter. My family. Home will always be where they are.

And I will do anything to keep them safe.

My eyes flick open and I come to my feet. Silently I totter across my lounge and into the kitchen. I know these floors, I know where the creaks lie in wait to wake sleeping guests. Tonight everyone is exhausted from the events of the last few days, my confession, Aina's disappearance. Their bellies are overfull of the food of celebration. They sleep deeply. I will not be heard.

Coals still smoke in the oven, black-bodied, red-tipped, steaming. I swing open the oven door and pause. I gaze down on the envelope one final time, press a kiss to the musty paper, then toss it onto the coals.

For a moment nothing happens, then slowly, slowly smoke starts to rise around the edges of the envelope. Soon the paper erupts from its centre in a bright red plume of fire. It sparks to life, furious and hungry, burning hot and quick until the envelope is reduced to nothing but ash.

I watch on long after the last of the envelope has been devoured, as the coals die back down to black, tiny embers of orange the only remaining evidence of my choice.

I close the oven door, careful not to make a sound, and make my way back to bed.

One secret is enough. Aina cannot face any more. Nor can I.

I will take this truth to the grave.

EPILOGUE
ESTERE

Riga, Latvia 1990

She'd thought the boat was bad. Air travel was far, far worse in her opinion. As she walks along the hallway to customs she aches in her very bones, her throat parched as though she's spent the night in the Australian outback. She's grateful for the loose fit of her dress. She can't understand the young people in jeans she follows from the plane.

Humans were not meant to fly. Luckily, she won't ever have to again.

At Passport Control a man with a kindly face accepts her documents. Her feet shuffle, her hands wring together. She can't help it. She'll never be comfortable showing her papers, not after surviving Soviet and Nazi occupation.

A broad smile blooms across his face as he looks up at her. "Laipni lūdzam! Welcome home!"

She blinks in surprise before nodding. He's right, after all.

But she's exhausted. The trip has taken almost two full days of planes and layovers, of passport checks and documents. She is barely up on her feet.

Outside the airport she finds a taxi, tells the driver the address of her hotel and leans back in her seat. The cheap leather is torn in several places. She doesn't care, it won't be a long trip.

Her eyes are heavy and closing as they pass through streets on the west bank. It feels wrong, unfamiliar. Panic surges in her heart. Has she made the wrong choice?

Then she sees it. Stretching before her, bold and wild and free. The Daugava. The taxi mounts a new bridge, speeding over the coursing currents. She grips the handle and quickly winds down her window, leaning out, pressing her face into the winds that rise up off the river. Salty, cold. The currents rush inland today, streaking through the heart of Latvia. Overhead a gull screams as it hovers on the air currents above the water, searching for prey.

She turns to the driver. "Take me to Brīvības piemineklis, the Freedom Monument."

Their eyes meet in the rear-view mirror; his crease in a smile.

He is forced to stop about a block away; the streets are too full of people. She climbs out, collecting her small bag from the boot and joins the throng of revellers. People, young, old, male, female, dressed in shirts and scarves, or jeans and beanies, are all gathering together on Freedom Boulevard.

She follows, swallowed by the crowd. Her heart beats faster and faster as they approach the monument.

There it stands, grand and tall, reaching for the skies. Her breath catches, tears springing to her eyes. Around the statue people are milling, dancing, singing *"Dievs Sveti Latviju"*, God Bless Latvia, the carmine and white flag hoisted above their heads in celebration. It has not flown here in fifty years.

A young man appears before her, dark eyes shining, smile splitting his face in two, a flare of red pimples across one cheek. She does not know him, he does not know her, but it doesn't matter. His arms come around her in a fierce hug. A sob escapes her throat. As he pulls back, she realises she is laughing.

What began with the Baltic Way, a line of citizens, hand in hand across the three nations of the Baltics, unbroken from Estonia, through Latvia and ending in Lithuania, a statement of independence, of nationality, has ended today.

May the 4th, 1990. Today the Latvian Supreme Court has voted and proclaimed the Restoration of Latvian Independence. The occupation by the Soviet Union has ended. Forty-five years of oppression, finished. More than fifty years of occupation complete.

Latvia is free.

Just as her Valdis always dreamed.

She pushes forward, making her way to the statue's side. Pressing a hand to the cool stone base, she looks up at the three stars the figure is holding to the sky.

"*Brīvā Latvija!*" she cries.

Later, after checking into her small hotel room, she finds a post office, purchases an envelope and stamp, addresses it. She does not include a return address, only Riga, Latvia. It will be enough.

The letter will set her sister free.

She'd known the truth in her heart years before she confronted her sister. That Zenta had lied. That her child was lost. The confirmation had been too much. She'd left. At first she searched for her child, but records are only as good as the details that are shared. With no birth date to match to her child's name, and so many displaced people who'd fled Latvia, there was no hope. Her Aina had vanished. But Estere could not stop, driving herself on, determined in the face of awful reality. Until her hope gave out. In that moment of despair she'd turned back to her sister, but it was too late. Zenta had cut her out.

Finally she is ready to accept Zenta's choice. And honour

her own. There is no other place for her; Latvia is the only home her heart will ever accept. It is time to let go and start again.

She pushes the letter into the postbox.

She walks the streets, takes the long way, winding past Riga Central Market, past the train station, slowly circling towards the centre of the old town. A mix of dread and hope pulses in the pit of her stomach.

The close, cobbled roads open on to Rathausplatz, the town hall square, still empty. Cleared foundations are all that remains of the once grand House of the Blackheads. But there are plans to rebuild, or so she has heard. Around her the people of the city are going about their days, women in jeans, scarves over their heads pulled tight against the chill, modern-style and tradition walking as one. The sun slants coolly down the sky, casting a pale yellow over the buildings.

She walks on, passing the church of St Peter, its formidable spire repaired to its former glory, shining hope across a new city, a free city.

Coming to the corner by the Riga Dome Cathedral she pauses. The narrow street beyond is cast in the shadow of gathering dusk. Her chest squeezes tight, her breath coming in small, short bursts.

Steeling herself, she plunges on.

It has been rebuilt. Painted in a pale shade of yellow. *Established 1870. Rebuilt 1988*, is scrawled across the top of the display windows. Inside rows of cob bread and pastries gleam under bright fluorescent lamps. It's beautiful.

The lump in her throat is a physical thing. This place, reduced by war to a memory of horror and pain, is now reborn, a representation of all she and Valdis fought for. Estere lost everything in that fight: her home, her family, her life with Valdis and their child. And later, her sister.

She left Latvia with nothing, and with nothing she has returned, but found something beautiful.

Latvia is free. Like the bakery before her, the people of this nation are changed, scarred, but at their core they remain the same. They are Latvian. From the ashes of oppression her people will rise and rebuild. And so will she.

Estere closes her eyes, smells the caraway, hears the slow rhythmic kneading of her father working the bread, the faster pace of her little sister.

She opens her eyes.

The sign on the door reads, "Open".

She smiles.

Squaring her shoulders, she steps across the threshold.

The bell above the bakery door chimes...

A LETTER FROM THE AUTHOR

Dear reader,

Thank you for reading *The Baker's Secret*. Zenta's story is one that is close to my heart. I hope you enjoyed discovering her journey as much as I enjoyed revealing it. If you would like to join other readers in hearing all about my Storm Publishing new releases and bonus content, you can sign up for my newsletter!

www.stormpublishing.co/lelita-baldock

Or, you can sign up to my own newsletter.

www.lelitabaldock.com/writing-newsletter

If you enjoyed this book and could spare a few moments to leave a review, I would be truly grateful. Even a short review can make all the difference in encouraging a reader to discover my books for the first time. Thank you so much!

The Baker's Secret is loosely based on my own family history, mirroring my grandfather's journey from Latvia to Australia during the Second World War. The research and writing of this novel has been a deeply personal endeavour, as I learned about the experiences of the Latvian people during their fight for freedom.

Thank you once again for being part of this incredible

journey with me. I hope you'll stay in touch – I have many more stories and characters to share with you all.

Sincerely,

Lelita Baldock

ACKNOWLEDGEMENTS

Writing *The Baker's Secret* has been an incredible journey, sometimes challenging but ultimately deeply rewarding. Fortunately, I did not have to travel it alone.

Thank you to agent Annakarin Klerfalk from Intersaga Literary Agency, for believing in this story, and me, from day one.

To my editor Kate Gilby-Smith, I am eternally grateful for all your hard work and genuine passion. You have taught me so much more about the skill of telling a compelling and emotional narrative.

To my soul-sisters, Bec and Kim, thank you for the hours of time bouncing around plot ideas and for letting me spoil the twist so I can test it will land.

My family: Mum, Dad and Rick, for always reminding me that I "can", when I don't believe it myself. Especially to you, brotherly, for never accepting my self-doubt, even for a second.

To my fluffy writing-buddy Jazzy, you will never understand the peace and comfort your presence (and purrs) bring, so I'll just have to spoil you with more tuna treats.

And to my beloved husband Ryan, you have shown me what true love is. Thank you for creating a life of love and joy with me and for holding my hand every day as I follow my dreams.

And finally, to the Museum of Occupation in Riga and to all the Latvian citizens who have shared their stories of life under occupation. This history is raw and deep and must never be forgotten. Thank you for your bravery.

Printed in Great Britain
by Amazon